Big Summer

BOOKS BY JENNIFER WEINER

FICTION

Good in Bed

In Her Shoes

Little Earthquakes

Goodnight Nobody

The Guy Not Taken

Certain Girls

Best Friends Forever

Fly Away Home

Then Came You

The Next Best Thing

All Fall Down

Who Do You Love

Mrs. Everything

NONFICTION

Hungry Heart

FOR YOUNG READERS

The Littlest Bigfoot

Little Bigfoot, Big City

Big Summer

Jennifer Weiner

A NOVEL

ATRIA BOOKS
New York London Toronto Sydney New Delhi

ATRIA BOOKS
An Imprint of Simon & Schuster, Inc.
1230 Avenue of the Americas
New York, NY 10020

This Atria Books hardcover edition May 2020

Manufactured in the United States of America

1 3 5 7 9 10 8 6 4 2

Library of Congress Cataloging-in-Publication Data has been applied for.

ISBN 978-1-9821-5934-4

To Meghan Burnett

Nobody heard him, the dead man,
But still he lay moaning:
I was much further out than you thought
And not waving but drowning.

Poor chap, he always loved larking
And now he's dead
It must have been too cold for him his heart gave way,
They said.

Oh, no no no, it was too cold always
(Still the dead one lay moaning)
I was much too far out all my life
And not waving but drowning.

—"Not Waving but Drowning" by Stevie Smith

Prologue

1994

By the second week of September, the outer Cape was practically deserted. The tourists had packed up and gone home. The roads were empty; the glorious beaches were abandoned. It was a shame: by September, the ocean was finally warm enough for swimming, especially if it had been a hot August, and the paths that wound through the dunes and cranberry bogs and secret blueberry bushes, the ones that were pickup spots for men in summer's high season, were deserted, and the bushes were full of ripe berries. She and Aidan could fill their pockets and pick beach plums out of their bushes between the cottage and the beach. They would each bring a metal pail, and they'd recite *Plink! Plank! Plunk!*, like the heroine of *Blueberries for Sal*, as each plum rattled to the bottom.

You'll go crazy out there, her father had told her when Christina asked if she could take the summer cottage that perched on the edge of the dune in Truro. It's too empty. Too lonely. No one to see, nothing to do. But he hadn't told her no. As the first weeks and months had passed, Christina had come to cherish the solitude and the silence, the slant of late-afternoon sun that warmed the floorboards where her ginger cat slept.

With the summer people gone, she could have her pick of parking spots on Commercial Street when she and Aidan went to Provincetown. If he'd behaved himself at the grocery store, she'd buy him an ice-cream cone at Lewis Brothers or a malasada at the Portuguese Bakery. She'd learned every quirk of the cottage, the way the doors swelled up when it rained, the creak of the roof as the beams settled at night. When there were thunderstorms, she could go out to the deck and watch lightning crack over the water of Cape Cod Bay, letting the rain wash her face as she imagined that she was standing at the prow of a ship, she and her little boy, alone on the storm-tossed seas.

Sometimes, that was how she'd felt. Her mother was dead; her sisters and brother, the closest in age a decade her senior, were strangers she saw on holidays; and her father had been puzzled when Christina had asked for the cottage, then furious when he learned the reason why. "Daddy, I'm pregnant," she'd told him. His face had turned pale, then an unhealthy, mottled red; his mouth had worked silently as he glared. "And I'm keeping the baby. I'll raise it on my own."

When he'd raged, demanding to know whose baby it was, Christina had simply said, "Mine." He'd yelled at her, spittle flying from his lips, insisting that she tell him the name of the man she'd spread her legs for, demanding to know whose whore she'd been. He called her all the names she'd expected to be called and a few that had surprised her; he'd said "You have broken my heart," but she'd kept quiet, silent and still as he shouted and threatened. Eventually, he'd relented, the way she knew he would.

Fine. Go. Wish you all the joy of it, he'd muttered, and handed her the keys and a list of phone numbers, for the caretaker and the plumber, the trash hauler and the guy who kept the furnace running. She'd stayed in Boston long enough to give birth, and then, as soon as her stitches had healed, she'd taken herself and her baby to Truro, following Route 6 as it snaked and narrowed, over the bridge at Sandwich, up to Hyannis, past Dennis and Brewster, Harwich and Orleans, Eastham and Wellfleet, then into Truro, onto a rutted dirt path that ended at the bluff, where the cabin stood. She'd worried that Aidan would fuss or cry on the ride up, but he'd sat, awake, in his car seat, like a wise old owl, his eyes open as they bounced along the lane and parked on the patch of matted grass in front of the cottage. "We're home," she'd said, lifting him into her arms. He was just three weeks old, but she thought he understood.

The cottage wasn't grand. It was a summer place, with no central heat, ripped screens on the windows, no dishwasher in the kitchen, and just a handheld nozzle in the tub to serve as a shower; a place with threadbare sheets and mismatched napkins and kitchen cabinets filled with chipped hand-me-down mugs and garage-sale glasses, nothing like the grand, sprawling summer palaces that the rich folks who'd discovered Truro had started building, high on the dunes. Christina never cared. She loved every imperfect piece of it. The pared-down quality and the quiet were exactly what she needed after New York. In spite of her father's warning, she'd made some friends, and they had helped her insulate the walls and showed her how to use steel wool to fill the holes that admitted families of mice every winter. She bought space heaters, layered braided cotton rugs over the creaky wood floors, bought heavy wool blankets for the beds. She found ways to acquire the things she needed, trading heirloom tomatoes for jars of honey and firewood; writing wedding vows in exchange for a cashmere blanket, revising a personal ad in exchange for a pale-blue bud vase. She'd made the summer cottage a home, and she'd crafted a life full of routines and rituals for herself and her son. Oatmeal for breakfast, with honey from the honey dripper; a cherry Popsicle from Jams after a day at the beach; three stories before bedtime, two from books and one made up.

That night, after Aidan fell asleep, Christina wrapped herself in a soft fringed cashmere shawl, poured a glass of wine, and stepped through the door and onto the deck, barefoot, to listen to the wind. In the darkness, the breeze was strong off the sea, with an icy edge. It had been almost seventy degrees that afternoon, warm enough for swimming, but she could feel winter in the wind.

She walked back inside, through the cluttered kitchen, past the rows of Mason jars that she'd spent the morning filling while Aidan was in preschool, putting up the tomatoes and green beans and pickles she'd grown herself; through the living room, its crooked bookshelves filled with fading, water-swollen paperbacks, and wicker baskets that held Aidan's Legos and Lincoln Logs. Her writing desk, one of the handful of good antiques that came with the house, stood in the corner, with her laptop closed in its center, abandoned beneath a framed vintage poster of Paris.

In the bedroom, she made sure Aidan was sleeping, then bent close to trace her thumb along the curve of his cheek. He'd just turned four, but already, he had started to lose the sweet babyish plumpness that made squeezing him feel like embracing a warm loaf of bread. Still, the skin on his cheek was as soft as it had been the day she'd first held him. *My treasure*, she thought, as her eyes prickled with tears. When Aidan was first born, and she was half-crazed with loneliness and hormones, when her stitches ached and her breasts dripped when he cried, everything made her weep, including her predicament. Especially her predicament. *You chose this*, Aidan's father would remind her when he'd found time to come around. *You had a choice.* It was true. She'd gone into the situation completely aware, telling herself that the glass was half-full, not half-empty, and that a piece of someone else's husband was better than no man at all. When she'd found out she was pregnant, it had felt like an unexpected gift, like a miracle. Who was she to say no to the possibility of this life, or the way it would remake her own?

Once, when she was still with Aidan's father, he'd told her he would leave his wife for her. She had let herself picture every part of the life they would have together, a grand, bold-faced life in New York City, but by Aidan's fourth year she was long past that fantasy. She'd never believed him; not really. Deep down, in the place where she could be honest with herself, she always knew the score. He'd wanted escape, fun, a fling: nothing permanent. He would never leave his wife, and her money.

But she had Aidan. Her prince, her pearl, her heart's delight. Even if the two of them had been starving on the streets, she would have been happy. Aidan brought her daisies and Queen Anne's lace clutched in his grubby fist, and pails with glittering lady slipper shells, still gritty with sand rattling at the bottom. Aidan smacked soft, honey-smeared kisses on her cheeks after breakfast and called her his beautiful mama.

Someday, she'd go back to the city, and gather up the threads of the life she'd left behind. She'd hunt down her old editors and pitch them stories; she'd reconnect with her old friends, and send Aidan to school there. Maybe she'd fall in love again, maybe not. But if, in the end, she never lived the glittering, rich-lady life of her youthful imaginings, she'd have a life that made her happy.

Christina bent down and started to sing. "Blackbird, singing in the dead of night; take these broken wings and learn to fly; all your life, you were only waiting for this moment to arise." Her story was almost at its end, but, that night, she had no idea. That night, as she sat in her son's darkened bedroom, with her shawl wrapped around her shoulders, listening to the wind whine at the corners of the cottage, she thought, *I never knew that I could be so happy.* She thought, *This is the way it was always meant to be.*

Part One

Chapter One

2018

"OhmyGod, I am *so sorry*. Am I late?" Leela Thakoon hurried into the coffee shop with a cross-body bag hanging high on one hip, a zippered garment bag draped over her right arm, and an apologetic look on her face. With her silvery-lavender hair in a high ponytail, her round face and petite figure, and her emphatic red lipstick, she looked exactly the way she did on her Instagram, only a little bit older and a little bit more tired, which was true of every mortal, I supposed, who had to move through the world without the benefit of filters.

"You weren't late. I was early," I said, and shook her hand. For me, there was nothing worse than showing up for a meeting feeling flustered and hot and out of breath. In addition to the physical discomfort, there was the knowledge that I was confirming everyone's worst suspicions about fat ladies—*lazy, couch potatoes, can't climb a flight of stairs without getting winded.*

Today I had wanted to look my best, so I'd worked out at six in the morning and cooled down for an hour, unhappy experience having taught me that, for every hour I exercised, I'd need thirty minutes to stop sweating. I'd arrived at the coffee shop Leela had chosen twenty minutes ahead of time, so that I could scope out the venue, choose an advantageous seat, and attempt to best project an aura of cool, collected competence—*#freelancehustle*, I thought. But if I landed this collaboration, it would mean that the money I earned as an influencer would be more than the money I made doing my regular twenty-hour-a-week babysitting gig, and possibly even more than my dog's account was bringing in. I wouldn't be supporting myself with my online work, but I'd be closer to that goal. In yoga that morning, when we'd set our intention, I'd thought, *Please*. Please let this happen. Please let this work out.

"Want something to drink?" I asked. I already had my preferred summer beverage, cold brew with a splash of cream and extra ice, sitting in front of me.

"No, I'm fine," said Leela, pulling the metal water bottle of the environmentally aware out of her bag, uncapping it, and taking a swig. *Oh, well*, I thought. At least my coffee had come in a glass and not plastic. "I'm *so glad* to meet you." Leela draped the garment bag over a chair, smoothed her already smooth hair, and took a seat, crossing her legs and smiling at me brightly. She was wearing a pair of loose-fitting khaki shorts, pulled up high and belted tight around her tiny waist, and a blousy white top with dolman sleeves that left her slender arms bare. Her golden skin, a deeper gold than I got even at my most tan, glowed from the sunshine she'd probably enjoyed on a getaway to Tahiti or Oahu. There was a jaunty red scarf around her neck, pinned with a large jeweled brooch. She looked like a tiny androgynous elf, or as if someone had waved a wand and said, *Boy Scout, but make it tiny and cute and fashion*. I was sure that some piece of her outfit had been purchased at a thrift shop I'd never find, and that another had been sourced from a website I'd never discover, or made by some designer I'd never heard of, in sizes that would never fit me, and that it had cost more than one month of my rent. The entire rent, not just the half I paid.

Leela uncapped her bottle and looked me over, taking her time. I sipped my coffee and tried not to squirm, breathing through the insecurity I could feel whenever I was confronted by someone as stylish and cute as Leela Thakoon. I'd worn one of my favorite summer outfits, a hip-length pale yellow linen tunic over a plain white short-sleeved T-shirt, cropped olive-green leggings with buttons at the cuffs, and tan platform sandals, accessorized with a long plastic tortoiseshell necklace, big gold hoop earrings, and oversized sunglasses. My hair—regular brown—was piled on top of my head in a bun that I hoped looked effortless and had actually required twenty minutes and three different styling products to achieve. I'd kept my makeup simple, just tinted moisturizer to smooth out my olive complexion, mascara, and shimmery pink lip gloss, a look that said *I care, but not too much*. In my previous life, I'd dressed to hide, in a palette limited to black, with the occasional daring venture into navy blue. These days, I wore colors and clothes that weren't bulky or boxy, that showed off my shape and made me feel good. Every morning, I photographed and posted my outfit of the day (OOTD), tagging the designers or the places I'd shopped for my Instagram page and my blog, which I'd named *Big Time*. I kept my hair and makeup on point for the pictures, especially if I was wearing clothes I'd been gifted or, better yet, paid to wear. That had entailed a certain outlay of cash, on cuts and color and blowouts, in addition to a lot of trips to Sephora and many hours watching YouTube makeup tutorials before I'd found a routine that I could execute on my own. It had been an investment; one that I hoped would pay off.

So far, the signs were good. "Oh my God, *look* at you," Leela said, clapping her hands together in delight. Her nails were unpainted, clipped into short ovals. A few of them were ragged and looked bitten at the tips. "You're *adorbs*!"

I smiled back—it would have been impossible not to—and wondered if she meant it. In my experience, which was limited but growing, fashion people tended to be dramatic and effusive, full of hyperbolic praise that was not always entirely sincere.

"So what can I tell you about the line?" she asked, removing a Moleskine notebook, a fountain pen, and a small glass bottle of ink from her bag and setting them down beside her water bottle. I tried not to stare. I did have questions about the clothes, and the collaboration, but what I really wanted to know was more about Leela. I knew she was about my age, and that she'd done a little modeling, a little acting, and that she'd made a few idle-rich-kid friends and started styling their looks. The friends had introduced her to celebrities, and Leela had started to style them. In a few years' time, she had amassed over a hundred thousand social-media friends and fans who followed her feed to see pictures of beautiful people wearing beautiful clothes in beautiful spots all over the world. By the time she'd announced her clothing line, Leela had a built-in audience of potential customers, people who'd seen her clients lounging on the prow of a yacht in the crocheted bikini Leela had sourced from a beach vendor she'd discovered in Brazil, or walking the red carpet in a one-of-a-kind custom hand-beaded gown, or dressed down in breathable linen, handing out picture books to smiling children in poor villages all over the world.

When Leela had launched the brand she was calling Leef, she'd made a point of saying that her collection would be "size-inclusive." She didn't just want to sell clothes to straight-size women, then toss big girls a bone in the form of a belated capsule collection or, worse, ignore us completely. Even better, in the videos I'd watched and the press release I'd read on her website, Leela had sounded sincere when she'd said, "It's not fair for designers to relegate an entire group of women to shoes, handbags, and scarves because the powers that be decided they were too big or too small to wear the clothes." *Amen, sister*, I'd thought. "My clothes are for every woman. For all of us." Which sounded good, but was also, I knew, a bit of a cliché. These days, designers who'd rather die than gain ten pounds, designers who'd rather make clothes for purse dogs than fat people, could mouth the right platitudes and make the right gestures. I would have to see for myself if Leela was sincere.

"Tell me what got you interested in fashion," I asked.

"Well, it took a minute," Leela said, smiling her charming smile. "I've always been drawn to . . . I guess you'd call it self-expression. If I were a better writer, I'd write. If I were a better artist, I'd paint or sculpt. And, of course, my parents are still devastated that I'm not in med school." I saw a fleeting expression of sorrow, or anger, or something besides arch amusement flit across her pretty features, but it was gone before I could name it, erased by another smile. "High school was kind of a shit show. You know, the mean girls. It took me a while to pull it together, but I made it out alive. And I figured out that I know how to put clothes together. I know how to take a ten-dollar T-shirt and wear it with a two-thousand-dollar skirt and have it look like an intentional whole." I nodded along, like I, too, had a closet full of two-thousand-dollar skirts and other components of intentional wholes. "So I found my way to working as a stylist. And what I found," she said, lifting her shoulders and straightening in her seat, "is that women still don't have the options that we should." She raised one finger, covered from knuckle to knuckle with gold rings that were as fine as pieces of thread. "If you're not in the straight-size range, there's nothing that fits." Additional fingers went up. "If you've got limited mobility, you can't always find clothes without hooks and buttons and zippers. If you're young, or on a budget, if you want clothes that are ethically produced, and are made by people who are paid a living wage, I don't want women to ever have to compromise," she said, eyes wide, her expression earnest. "You shouldn't have to decide between looking cute and buying your clothes from a sweatshop."

I found myself nodding along, feeling a pang of regret for every fast-fashion item I'd ever picked up at Old Navy or H&M.

"Once I started looking at what was available, it was obvious to me—I wanted to design my own clothes," Leela said. "I know how great it feels—and I'll bet you do, too—when you put a look together, and it just . . ." She paused, bringing her fingertips to her lips and kissing them, a clichéd gesture that she somehow made endearing. "It just works, you know?"

I nodded. I did know. Once I'd started searching out clothes that fit and looked good on the body I had instead of the one that I wanted, I had discovered exactly the feeling Leela Thakoon was talking about.

"I think everyone deserves to feel that way. Even if you don't fit the skinny, white, long-straight-blond-hair mold. Even if you've got freckles, or wrinkles, or wide feet, or you're one size on the bottom and a totally different size on top." She put her hand just above her breast, like she was pledging allegiance to inclusive fashion. "All of us deserve to feel beautiful." She looked at me, her eyes meeting mine, and I nodded and found myself unexpectedly blinking back tears. Normally, I would have had a hard time mustering much sympathy for a woman whose worst problem with clothes was that they were too big. You could always get your pants cuffed and your shirts and dresses taken in. You could even pick up things in the children's section, where everything was cheaper, but if you were plus-size, there wasn't much you could do if the size of a designer's offerings stopped before you started. Still, I respected Leela's attempt to offer kinship, to point out that even tiny, exquisitely pretty world travelers with famous friends didn't always fit into the box of "beautiful."

"So that's why!" She smiled at me brightly, asking, "What else can I tell you?"

I smiled back and asked the open-ended question I used at the end of all of these conversations. "Is there anything else you think I need to know?"

There was. "For starters, I don't work with sweatshops," Leela began. "Every single item I sell is made in the USA, by union workers who are paid a living wage."

"That's wonderful," I said.

"We use fabrics made from natural, sustainable materials—mostly cotton, cotton-linen blends, and bamboo—that's been engineered to wick sweat and moisture and withstand five hundred trips through the washing machine." She paused, waiting for my nod. "We recycle as much as we can. We'll have a trade-in program, where you can exchange a worn garment toward credit for something new. We've designed our manufacturing and our shipping with an eye toward keeping our carbon footprint as small as possible, and with annual goals for reducing it as well."

"Also great," I said, and found, again, that I was impressed in spite of myself.

"We are, of course, a woman-led company with a non-hierarchical management structure." She gave a small, pleased smile. "True, right now it's just me and my assistant, so it's pretty easy, but as we grow I'm going to keep it that way. We're small at the moment," she said with that beguiling smile, "but when we expand—not if, but when—we're going to be as inclusive as possible. That means race, gender, age, ethnicity, and size. I want to make clothes for everybody."

"That's terrific," I said, and meant it.

"Best of all," she said, reaching across the table and giving my forearm an uninvited squeeze, "the pieces are *luscious*." She popped to her feet, picked up the garment bag, and held it in both hands, offering it to me. "Go on. Try them on."

"What, right now?"

"Please. It would be such an honor," she said, her smile widening.

Thankfully this coffee shop had a spacious bathroom that was covered in William Morris–style wallpaper, with fancy soap and hand lotion and a verbena-scented candle flickering on the reclaimed-wood table beside the sink. I hung the bag from a hook on the inside of the door. *Luscious*, I thought, bemused. It sounded like a brand-new code word for fat, like *Rubenesque*. But I'd take it. I'd always take a well-intentioned gesture toward kindness and inclusion over the rudeness that had underscored too many of my days.

I unzipped the bag. According to the promotional materials, each piece of the capsule collection had been named after a woman in Leela's life. They were all designed to work together, each could be dressed up or dressed down, and the collection could "keep a working woman covered, from office to evening, seven days a week." It was the impossible dream. In my limited experience, clothes didn't work this way. Yoga pants still looked like yoga pants, even if you wore them to the office with a blazer on top; a bridesmaid's dress was still a bridesmaid's dress, even if you hemmed it or dyed it or threw a cardigan over it and put it on for a trip to the grocery store.

I told myself to keep an open mind as I removed the first hanger from the bag and gave the dress a shake. It had an A-line silhouette, three-quarter-length sleeves, and a waistline that gathered under the bust. The fabric was a silky blend of cotton and something stretchy and synthetic, light and breathable, but with enough weight to drape well. Best of all, it was navy blue, with white polka dots. I adored polka dots.

I shucked off my leggings and top, pulled the dress off, shut my eyes, and let the fabric fall over my head and shoulders, past my breasts and hips, unspooling with a silky swish. I turned toward the mirror and held my breath.

For all women—or maybe just all plus-size women, or maybe just me—there's a moment right after you put on a new piece of clothing, after you've buttoned the buttons or zipped the zipper, but before you've seen how it looks—or, rather, how you look in it. A moment of just sensation, of feeling the fabric on your skin, the garment against your body, knowing here the waistband pinches or if the cuffs are the right length, an instant of perfect faith, of pure, untarnished hope that *this* dress, *this* blouse, *this* skirt, will be the one that transforms you, that makes you look shapely and pretty, and worthy of love, or respect, or whatever you most desire. It's almost religious, that belief, that faith that a piece of silk or denim or cotton jersey could disguise your flaws and amplify your assets and make you both invisible and seen, just another normal woman in the world; a woman who deserves to get what she wants.

I opened my eyes, gave the skirt a shake, and looked at myself in the mirror.

I saw how my skin glowed, rosy, against the navy blue, and how the bustline draped gracefully and didn't tug. The V-neck exposed the tiniest hint of cleavage; the wide, sewn-in waistband gripped the narrowest part of my body; and the skirt, hemmed with a cute little flounce of a ruffle that I hadn't noticed at first, flared out and hit right beneath my knees. The sleeves were fitted, snug without being uncomfortable—I could lift and lower my arms and stretch them out for a hug, and the cuffs sat between my elbows and my wrists, another visual trick, one that made my arms look as long as the skirt made my legs appear.

I turned from side to side, taking in the dress, and me in the dress, from every angle the mirror would give me. I could already imagine it working with my big fake-pearl statement necklace, or with my dainty amethyst choker, with my hair in a bun, or blown out straight. I could wear this with flats, I thought. I could wear it with espadrilles or wedges or stilettos. I could wear it to work, with sneakers and a cardigan . . . or out on a date with heels and a necklace . . . or just to go to the park, sit on a bench, and drink my coffee. As Leela had promised, the fabric breathed. The dress moved with me, it didn't pinch or bind or squeeze. It flattered, which, in my mind, meant that it didn't make me look thin, or different, but instead like the best version of myself. It made me feel good, made me stand a little straighter. And . . . I slipped my hands down my sides. Pockets. It even had pockets. "A unicorn," I breathed.

"Knock knock!" called Leela, her voice merry. "Come out, come out wherever you are!"

I gave myself one last look and stepped out of the restroom. In the coffee shop's light, the dress looked even better, and I could notice little details, the subtle ruching on the sides of the bodice, the tiny bow at the base of the neckline, the embroidered rickrack along the cuffs.

"So what do you think?"

I thought about trying to be coy. I thought about trying to be as effusive as fashion folk typically were. In the end, I gave her honesty. "It's amazing. My new favorite dress."

She clapped, her pretty face delighted. "I'm so glad! The dress—we call her Jane—is the backbone of the collection. And there's pants . . . and a blouse . . ." She clasped her hands together and pressed them against her heart. "Will you try them on for me? Pretty please? I've only ever seen them on our fit model. This is my first chance to see them, you know, out in the real world."

I agreed. And, to my delight, every piece was just as comfortable, just as flattering, and just as thoughtfully made as the Jane. The high-waisted, wide-legged Pamela pants were chic, not frumpy, a world away from the palazzo pants that grandmothers wore on cruises; the white blouse, named Kesha, had princess seams and a clever hook-and-eye construction to guarantee that it wouldn't gape. I normally hated blazers, which always made me look boxy and approximately the size of a refrigerator, but the Nidia blazer was cut extra-long in the back and made of a stretchy brushed-cotton blend, with cute zipper detailing on the sleeves in a perfect shade of plum.

The last piece in the garment bag was a swimsuit called the Darcy. I lifted the hanger, swallowing hard. Swimsuits would probably always be hard for me. Even after all this time, all the work I'd done to love my body—to at least accept the parts I couldn't love—I still cringed at the cellulite that riddled my thighs, the batwings of loose flesh under my upper arms, and the curve of my belly.

The swimsuit had a kind of vintage style. There was a skirt, but it wasn't the heavy, knee-length kind I'd remembered from my own mother's infrequently worn bathing suits, but a sweet flounce of ruffles that would brush the widest part of my thighs. *You can do this*, I coached myself, and pulled the suit on, over my underpants, and adjusted the straps.

Another deep breath, and I looked in the mirror. There were my thighs, so white they seemed to glare in the gloom. There were my stretch marks; there were the folds of fat on my back; there was the bulge of my stomach. I shut my eyes, shook my head, and told myself, *A body is a body*.

"Daphne?" Leela called. "Is everything okay?"

I didn't answer. *Deep breath*, I told myself. *Head up.* I slicked on red lipstick and slid my feet into my wedges. I made myself smile. Finally, I looked again, and this time, instead of seeing cellulite or rolls, or arms or thighs, I saw a woman with shiny hair and bright red lips; a woman who'd dive into the deep end and smile for the camera and live her life out in the open, as if she had just as much right to the world as anyone else.

Holding that thought in my head, I opened the door. Leela, who'd been bouncing on the tips of her toes for each previous reveal, went very still. Her hands, which she'd had clasped against her chest, fell to her sides.

"Oh," she said very softly. "Oh."

"It's perfect," I said, and sniffled.

"Perfect," she repeated, also sniffling, and I knew that not only had I found the swimsuit and the clothes of my dreams, but I'd landed a job, too.

Once I'd changed back into my own clothes, I returned to the table. Leela, beaming, extended her hand.

"I'd love to hire you as the exclusive face, and figure, of Leef Fashion." Her hand was warm, her grip firm, her gaze direct, her smile bright.

"And I'd love to accept. It's just . . ."

Leela looked at me, her face open and expectant.

"Why me?" I asked. "I mean, why not someone, you know, bigger?" *No pun intended*, I thought, and felt myself flush.

Leela tilted her head for a moment in silence, her silvery hair falling against her cheek. "I like to think that building a campaign is like putting together a great outfit," she finally said. "You pull a piece from here, a part from there. And everything has to fit. When I thought about who would fit my brand, I knew I wanted someone like you, who's just starting out. I want to make magic with someone I like; someone who is just at the beginning of her story. I want someone real," she concluded. "Well, as real as anyone ever is on social. And you're real, Daphne," Leela said. "That's what people love about you, that's why they follow you. From that very first video you posted to the review you did of that workout plan . . . BodyBest?"

"BestBody," I murmured. That had been a doozy. The company had sent me its workout plan, a sixty-dollar booklet full of exhortations about "Get your best beach body now," and "Be a hot ass," and "Nothing tastes as good as strong feels," and shots of slim, extraordinarily fit models with washboard abs and endless legs demonstrating the moves. I'd done the entire workout plan, all twelve weeks of it. I'd filmed myself doing jump squats and burpees, even though I'd been red-faced and sweaty, with parts of me flopping and wobbling when I did mountain climbers or star jumps (none of the models had enough excess flesh for anything to flop or wobble). My carefully worded review had alluded both to the challenging workouts and the punitive language, which I'd found distracting and knew to be ineffective. *Research shows that shaming fat folks into thinness doesn't work. And come on—if it did, most of the fat women in the world would have probably disappeared by now*, I'd written.

"You have an authenticity that people like. You're just . . ." She tilted her head again. "Unapologetically yourself. People feel like you're their friend," Leela said, looking straight into my eyes. "You're going places, Daphne, and I want us to go together." She extended her cool hand. "So, what do you say?"

I made myself smile. I was delighted with her praise, with her confidence that I was going places. I was also still thinking about the BestBody review and how the truth was that the workout had left me in tears, so disgusted with myself that I'd wanted to take a knife to my thighs and my belly. I hadn't written that, of course. No one wanted to see anything that raw. The trick of the Internet, I had learned, was not being unapologetically yourself or completely unfiltered; it was mastering the trick of appearing that way. It was spiking your posts with just the right amount of real . . . which meant, of course, that you were never being real at all. The more followers I got, the more I thought about that contradiction; the more my followers praised me for being fearless and authentic, the less fearless and authentic I believed myself to be in real life.

Leela was still looking at me, all silvery hair and expectant eyes, so I took her hand. "I'm in."

She smiled and bounced on the balls of her feet, a happy little elf who'd just gotten a raise from Santa. We shook and started talking terms—how much she'd pay for how many pictures and videos posted over what period of time and on what platforms.

We discussed what time of day was best to post, which settings her viewers preferred. “Still shots are great. Colorful backdrops. Walls with texture, or murals. And fashion people love video,” Leela said with the solemnity of a priest explaining the workings of a crucially important ritual. “They like to see the clothes move.”

“Got it,” I said, practically squirming with impatience. I couldn't wait to finish my day, get back to my apartment, and model the clothes for my roommate, to see how they worked with my shoes and my necklaces, to think about where I could wear them and how I could make them look their best.

“Oh, and outdoor is better than indoor, of course. Do you have any plans for the summer?” Leela asked. “Any travel?”

I breathed in deeply and tried to keep my face still. “I'm going to a wedding on the Cape. Do you know Drue Cavanaugh?”

Leela nibbled her lip with her perfect white teeth. “She's the daughter, right? Robert Cavanaugh's daughter. The one who's marrying the *Single Ladies* guy?”

“That's her. She and I went to high school together, and I'm going to be in her wedding.”

Leela clapped her hands, beaming. “Perfect. That's absolutely perfect.”

Chapter Two

I had a few hours to kill before my workday began, so I walked uptown on Park Avenue, through the crush of commuters and tourists, past the pricey apartments and boutiques before turning into Central Park. I was excited—*I'd have so many new fans and followers!* Then I was terrified—I'd have so many new fans and followers! Increased attention meant more scrutiny and scorn. That was true for any woman on the Internet, and maybe extra-true for me. Fat women attracted a special kind of trolling. There were people who were revolted by your body and took every opportunity to tell you so, and the people whose disgust came disguised as concern: *Don't you worry about your health? Don't you care?*

When I looked up, I wasn't surprised to find that my feet had taken me back to where it had all began. In the daytime, the windows at Dive 75 were dark, the door shut tight. It didn't look special, but it was, in a way, the place where I'd been born. The site of my greatest shame and my greatest triumph.

I stared at the door for a long moment. Then I pulled out my phone, opened my Instagram app, went into my stories, flipped the screen so I was looking at my own face, and hit the "Go Live" button.

"Hey, ladies!" I tilted my face to give the camera my good side and tensed my bicep so that my arm wouldn't wobble when I waved. "And guys! I know both of you are out there!" I did have male followers. Just not many. And I suspected that the ones who did like and comment on my posts were less fans than perverts, although maybe that was just me being paranoid. "Let me know if you recognize this spot." I raised the phone to show the bar's sign. Already, I could see the hearts and thumbs-up and applause emojis racing across my screen, the comments—OMG and YOU WENT BACK and QUEEN! as fans reacted in real time.

"Yes, this is the bar where it all went down." I saw more clapping hands, more sparklers and streamers and animated confetti. "And good things are happening," I announced. "I just got some amazing news. I can't tell you what, quite yet, but I can tell you that, for me, getting honest, not hiding, being real, and figuring out how to love myself, or at least, you know, tolerate myself, in the body that I had, has been the best decision of my life." I smiled at the red hearts and party hats, the comments of I LOVE YOU and YOU'RE MY HERO. "If you don't know the story, go to my bio, click the link for my YouTube channel, and go to the very first video I ever posted. You can't miss it." I kept the smile on my face as I let myself remember the night that everything had changed; the night at this bar when I'd decided to stop being a girl on a diet and just start being a girl.

It began when I'd agreed to go dancing with my friends. That would have been a normal night for most nineteen-year-olds in New York City, home on spring break of their sophomore year of college, with free time and a decent fake ID, but for me, each of those things—*bar, friends, dancing*—was an achievement, a little victory over the voice that had lived in my head since I was six years old, telling me I was fat, disgusting, unworthy of love, unworthy of friendship, unworthy of existing in public, even of walking outside; that a girl who looked like me did not deserve to have fun.

Most of the time, I listened to that voice. I wore clothes designed to disguise my body; I'd mastered every trick of making myself small. I'd gotten used to the rolled eyes and indignant sighs that I saw and heard—or thought that I could see and hear—when I sat beside someone on a bus or, worse, walked down the aisle of a plane. I'd learned every trick for taking up as little space as possible and not asking for much. For the last two years, my freshman and sophomore years in college, I'd been dating the same guy, Ronald Himmelfarb. Ronald or, as I secretly called him, Wan Ron, was perfectly pleasant, tall and thin with skin the bluish-white of skim milk. Ron had a beaky face and a fragile, narrow-shouldered build. He was majoring in computer science, a subject about which I knew nothing and couldn't make myself care, no matter how hard I tried to pay attention when he talked about it. I wasn't attracted to Ron, but he was the only guy who'd been interested in me. I didn't have options, and beggars couldn't be choosers.

Mostly, my life was in a holding pattern. I spent most of my spare time exercising, counting calories or points, weighing food, desperate to transform myself, to find the thin woman I just knew had to be living somewhere inside me. My only non-dieting activity was crafting. My mother was an artist and an art teacher and, over the years, with her tutelage and on my own, I'd mastered knitting, crocheting, embroidery, and decoupage, anything I could learn to make something beautiful with my hands. Needle felting was my favorite: I would stab my needle into the clump of wool, over and over and over, each thrust a perfectly directed excision of my anger (plus, the motion burned calories). When I was sixteen, I'd set up an online shop on Etsy where I sold my scarves and purses, embellished birdhouses and stuffed felted pigeons and giraffes, and a blog and an Instagram page and a YouTube channel where I'd showcase my work to the few dozen people who wanted to see it. I never showed myself, not my face or my body. I told myself, *As soon as I lose twenty pounds. Twenty-five pounds. Forty pounds. Fifty.* As soon as I can shop in normal stores and not have to buy plus sizes; as soon as I'm not ashamed to be seen in shorts or a tank top or a swimsuit. Then I will go dancing. Swimming. To the beach. Then I'll take a yoga class, take a plane, take a trip around the world. Then I'll download those dating apps and start meeting new people. But that one night, I felt so tired of waiting, so tired of hiding, that I let the girl I thought was my best friend talk me into meeting her for drinks and dancing.

I'd dressed with special care, in my best-fitting pair of black jeans and a black top, slightly low-cut, to show off my cleavage, hoping that the black would be slimming and that the boobs would distract any man who looked my way from the rest of me. Years of practice had given me the ability to blow-dry and straighten my medium-brown hair and apply my makeup without ever actually looking at myself in the mirror. My minimizing bra had underwires; my shoes had a little bit of a heel; I wore Spanx underneath my jeans; and I'd contoured believable shadows beneath my cheekbones. I felt okay—not good, but okay—as I met my best friend, Drue, and her friends Ainsley and Avery on the sidewalk. The three of them had squealed their approval. "Daphne, you look hot!" Drue said. Of course, Drue looked stunning, like an Amazon at Fashion Week, with red-soled stilettos adding three inches to her height, leather leggings clinging to her toned thighs, and a cropped gray sweater showing just a flash of her midriff.

There was a line out the door at Dive 75. Drue ignored it, sauntering up to the bouncer and whispering in his ear. I had my fake ID clutched in my sweaty hand, but the bouncer didn't even ask to see it as he waved us inside.

We found a high-top table with four tippy barstools in the corner of the bar. Drue ordered a round of lemon drops. "The first—and last—drinks we'll be paying for tonight," she said with a wink. Lemon drops weren't on the list of low-calorie cocktails that I'd memorized that afternoon, but I sipped mine gratefully. The vodka was icy-cold, tart and sweet, the grains of sugar around the rim crunched between my teeth. The bar was dark and cozy, with booths and couches in the back, where people were eating nachos and playing Monopoly and Connect 4. One drink became two, and two became three. With my friends by my side and the music all around me, I was happy and relaxed, as comfortable as a girl with wire digging into her breasts and heavy-duty elastic cutting into her midsection could be, when Drue whispered, "Daphne, don't look, but I think you have an admirer."

Immediately, I turned around, peering into the dark. "Don't look!" Drue said, fake-punching me and giggling. Right behind us was a table of four guys, and one of them, a young man in a dark-blue pullover with red hair and freckles, was, indeed, looking right at me. Behind me, Drue waved. "Lake! Lake Spencer! Oh my God!"

"You know him?" I asked as the guys crowded around us, dragging their chairs and pushing their table up against ours.

Drue took the guy's hand. "Lake is one of my brother Trip's friends. Lake, this is Daphne. Daphne's one of my best friends."

"Hi," I said.

"Hi," said Lake, nodding at my empty glass. "Get you another one of those?"

I thought of the poem attributed to Dorothy Parker: "I like to have a martini / Two at the very most / Three and I'm under the table / Four and I'm under the host." "Sure," I said, feeling reckless, as Drue nodded her approval. The guy disappeared, and Drue wrapped her arms around my shoulders. "He likes you," she whisper-shouted in my ear.

"He just met me," I protested.

"But he was checking you out," Drue said, and hiccupped. "He's into you. I can tell. When he comes back, ask him to dance!"

I cringed. Across the table, Ainsley and Avery were chatting with two young men, while two more were staring at Drue, clearly impatient for her to finish up with me and pay attention to them. Then Lake was back, with my drink in his hand. I took a gulp and slid off my stool, hoping I looked graceful, or at least not like a blubbery trained seal sliding off its box after its trainer had tossed it a herring. The music was so loud I could feel my bones vibrate. "Want to dance?" I hollered at him, and he gave me a thumbs-up and a smile.

On the dance floor, I quickly discovered that Lake's version of dancing was hopping up and down at a pace that had no relation to the beat. *Oh, well*, I thought as we started to shout our biographies into each other's faces. I learned that he was a senior at Williams, studying philosophy, that he and his family spent their summers in the Hamptons, near Drue and her family, and that not only was he friends with Trip, his sister and Drue had been debutantes together. Lake's skin was milky-white under splotches of dark freckles; his nose was a sharp blade with flaring nostrils. His reddish hair was thick and wiry, full of cowlicks, the kind of hair that wouldn't stay in place, no matter how carefully it had been cut, and when his face relaxed it assumed an expression just short of a smirk. Not cute. But who was I to judge? He seemed interested in what I had to say, or at least he was acting interested, and I hadn't noticed his attention straying to any of the prettier girls on the dance floor. We danced, and talked—or, mostly, Lake talked and I listened—and I wondered what would happen as the clock ticked down toward closing time, and the moment when the bartender would inevitably holler, "You don't have to go home, but you can't stay here!"

"'Scuse me," said Lake, giving me a smile. "I'm going to use the little boys' room."

I wasn't especially fond of the phrase "little boys' room," but I could let it slide. Lake departed, but the smell of his cologne lingered, a warm, spicy scent that reminded me of the one day I'd been a Girl Scout. My mom had signed me up with the local troop after she'd noticed, a little belatedly, that I was spending lots of time painting and knitting and reading, and not a lot of time with kids my own age. *Just try it, Daphne, maybe you'll make friends!* she'd said. The troop met in an apartment building on the Upper West Side. Twelve girls sat in a circle on the living room floor and stabbed cloves into oranges to make pomanders for Mother's Day. I'd liked that fine, especially when the troop leader had praised the spiral pattern I'd made. I'd tried to ignore the other Scouts sneaking looks at me, whispering and giggling. When the meeting was over, the leader opened her apartment door and the members of the troop went spilling into the hallway, laughing as they raced toward the elevator. "Free Willie!" one of them called. I couldn't bring myself to turn to see if the leader was still there, and if she'd heard. At home, I told my mother that I didn't want to go back. "It was boring," I'd said. Before I'd gone to bed that night, I'd washed my hands over and over, in water as hot as I could stand it, so I'd stop smelling cloves on my fingers and remembering that horrible ache inside, the plummeting sensation, like I'd swallowed stones, that went along with not being liked.

I went back to the table, where Drue grabbed my arm, "OMG, he likes you!" she squealed as she did a little dance. It stung that she seemed so surprised that a boy was interested, but I was pleased nonetheless, and amused by her antics, as always.

"He's a hottie!" Ainsley crowed.

"And an older man!" Drue shouted. "C'mon, let's go powder our noses."

The four of us linked arms and were on our way. I was flushed, pleasantly tipsy, feeling almost pretty in my jeans and with my cleavage. I did my business, washed my hands, checked my lipstick, and left Ainsley and Avery fussing in front of the mirror.

I stepped into the hallway. To my right was the bar, and the dance floor, by now a knot of writhing bodies, gyrating in time to the percussive thump of the bass. To my left was a door marked EMERGENCY EXIT . . . and Drue and Lake. My body had just registered the sight of them together when I heard the word "grenade" and saw Drue shake her head.

"Dude, do you even own a mirror?" she hissed at him. "Do you think one of the Kardashians is saving herself for you?"

Lake's shoulders were hunched as he muttered something that I couldn't make out. Drue shook her head again, looking annoyed. "I sent you her picture. I told you. Stop being such a pussy." She thumped his shoulder, not a play-punch, but one that looked like it hurt.

"Grenade." I knew what that meant in this context. Not an explosive device, but an ugly girl, upon whom a volunteer agrees to throw his own body, sacrificing himself to give his fellow soldiers a clear path to their objective: the hot chicks.

I could feel myself starting to tremble, my body vibrating with shame. I could hear Ainsley and Avery talking, but it sounded like they were underwater, their voices echoey and indistinct. *But I lost ten pounds!* a tiny, mournful voice in my head was whispering. But of course it wasn't enough, would never be enough. I could have lost twenty pounds, forty pounds, a hundred pounds. It would never be enough to transform me into the kind of girl who belonged with Drue Cavanaugh.

I closed my eyes. I thought about walking home, how the cool night air would feel on my hot face. I'd leave the lights off, go right to the kitchen, and pull a pint of ice cream out of the freezer and a bag of pretzels out of the breadbox, and I'd sit in the dark, eating. I'd let the creamy sweetness and crunchy saltiness fill me, pushing down the pain and shame, stuffing me so full that there wouldn't be room for anything else; not anger, not embarrassment, not anything. *Ben and Jerry, the two men who have never let me down*, I thought.

And then I stopped.

I stopped and asked myself, *What did I do wrong?* Who am I hurting? Is this what I deserve just for having the nerve to leave my home, to dance and try to have fun? I'm fat. That's true. But I'm a good person. I'm kind and funny; I'm generous; I try to treat people the way I'd want them to treat me. I'm a hard worker. A good daughter. A good friend.

I was listing my other fine qualities when Lake and Drue saw me. I saw the surprise cross Lake's face and moved my mouth into a reassuring smile. He smiled back and took my hand, leading me to the dance floor. By the time we'd arrived, the DJ had switched to a slow song, with lyrics about angels and fire and true love forever. Lake put a tentative hand on my shoulder. I thought that I could sense him steel himself before settling the other one between my waist and my bra. I imagined his internal monologue. *Okay. Just a little. It won't be that bad. Probably just squishy. Warm and jiggly, like a waterbed.* He looked at me with his big brown eyes and smiled a warm smile, a smile I would have believed was full of real affection and promise. And maybe it was the booze, on top of the shame, and the knowledge that Drue was somehow involved with this mess, but I decided that for once—just once—I was not going to smile and take it.

I looked down at my legs, my big, strong legs, the legs that carried me along miles of New York City sidewalks every day, legs that had propelled me over hundreds of miles on treadmills and elliptical climbers and stationary bikes and had performed hours of squats and lunges and kicks in various aerobic and boxing and barre classes over the years. *Leg, meet Lake*, I thought, as I picked up my right foot and brought it down—hard—on Lake's toes.

Lake's eyes went wide, and his mouth fell open. He let loose with a shriek, a high-pitched, girlish squeal. "You fat bitch!" he screamed. "You *stepped* on me!"

The music stopped. Or, at least, it did in my imagination. In my imagination, I heard the sound of a record scratch, and then absolute silence. Every eye on the place was on him as he hopped on his left foot and clutched at his right, glaring at me . . . and all those eyes turned to me as I started to talk.

"You know what?" I said. "I am fat. But that doesn't mean you get to treat me like garbage." My voice was shaking. My hands felt icy and my mouth was dry, my heart thumping triple-time as every cell in my body screamed, *Run away, run far away from here, people are looking, people can see.* But for once, I didn't listen. I stayed put. I settled my hands on my hips and gave my hair a toss. Feeling like a character in a movie—the sassy, fat best friend, finally having her brief star turn—I swept one hand down from my neck, past my breasts and my hips to my thighs. "You don't deserve any of this," I said. "You don't deserve me."

Someone said, "Ooh." Someone else yelled, "Tell him, girl!" And someone, possibly the bartender, started to clap. First it was just one person, then another one, then another, until it seemed like everyone in the bar was applauding, clapping for me, laughing at him. That was when I noticed that one of the girls at the edge of the dance floor was holding her phone, filming me. My heart gave another dizzying lurch, like I'd just come over the crest of a roller coaster and realized I wasn't in a car. *What's done is done*, I thought, and, with as much dignity as I could muster, I walked across the dance floor, through the door, and out into the dark.

I was halfway down the block when Drue caught up with me. "Hey," she shouted. I didn't turn. She put her hand on my shoulder and jerked me around to face her. "Hey! What the hell was that?"

"Why don't you tell me," I said, and pulled myself away.

"Look, I'm sorry. I was trying to do you a favor."

I widened my eyes. "Am I supposed to be grateful?"

Drue looked shocked. Probably because I'd never confronted her, or complained about the way she'd treated me, any more than I'd ever stomped on some random guy's foot.

"I didn't ask for your help," I said, and turned away.

She grabbed my shoulder, glaring at me with her pretty face contorted under the streetlight. "Well, you need it. You're dating this guy who you don't even like, and that's after not even kissing a guy the entire time we were in high school."

"So?"

"So either you're gay, which I've considered, or you're in love with me . . ."

I made a rude noise.

"Or," Drue continued, "you needed someone to set you up."

"If you wanted to set me up," I said between clenched teeth, "you could have asked me first."

"Why bother?" Drue said. "You would have just said no."

"And if you decided to go ahead with it anyhow," I continued, "you could have made sure that the guy wasn't an asshole."

"Well, it's not like I've got some huge pool to choose from!" Drue shouted. "You think guys are lining up to date . . ." She shut her mouth. Too late.

"What?" I asked her. "Fat girls? Girls who don't have trust funds? Girls whose fathers aren't on the cover of *Forbes*?"

She kept her lips pressed together, saying nothing. "I don't want your sympathy," I said. The adrenaline was still whipping through my bloodstream, but I could feel exhaustion and my old friend shame not far behind. "I'm done with you. Just leave me alone." I turned around and started plodding in the direction of home.

I'd gotten maybe ten yards away when Drue yelled, "We all just felt sorry for you!"

The words hit me like a spear between my shoulder blades. There it was, the truth I'd always suspected, finally out in the open. I felt myself cringe, shoulders hunched, but I didn't let myself turn around.

"You're a fat little nobody, and the only reason you were even at Lathrop is because families like mine give the school money so people like you can go there."

My cheeks prickled with shame, and my fingers curled into fists, but I couldn't argue. Not with any of it. I was fat. I had gone to Lathrop on a scholarship. Her family was rich, mine was not, and compared with her, I was a nobody.

"You're lucky I ever even talked to you!" Drue screeched.

Oh, I believe it was a mutually beneficial relationship, I thought. She'd given me her attention—at least some of the time. In return, I'd written her papers, retyped her homework, kept her secrets. I'd listened to her endless discussions of boys and clothes and which boys might prefer her wearing which clothes; I'd covered for her when she'd cut class or shown up too hungover to function.

I didn't say any of that. I didn't answer, or let myself look back. I kept walking. For a few blocks, I thought that she'd try to catch up with me, to tell me that she was sorry, to say that I was her best friend, that she hadn't meant what she'd said. I kept my ears pricked for the sound of high heels on the sidewalk. But Drue never came.

I was a few blocks from home when I felt my phone start to buzz in my pocket. I ignored it, feeling sick, imagining the video of me shouting at that guy making its way from text message to text message, from Facebook post to tweet. My face got hot, and the sugar and alcohol lurched in my belly. I felt like my blood was on fire, my body burning with shame and anger, and something else, something different, something it took me almost the entire thirty-minute walk to recognize as pride, maybe even a kind of righteousness. I'd stood up for myself, for once, for better or worse.

I crept into my parents' apartment. Instead of going to the

kitchen, I went to my bedroom without turning on the lights, moving unerringly through the darkness. When I arrived, I turned on the light and looked at the room, trying to see it like I was looking at it for the first time.

My craft table, the one I'd trash-picked from the curb, carried upstairs with my father's help, and stripped and sanded and painted a creamy ivory, stood against one wall. A cobalt-blue pottery vase filled with bright-orange gerbera daisies sat on its center; a wooden chair that I'd painted, with a cushion I'd sewn using a scrap of hot-pink and orange Marimekko print fabric, was pulled up beneath it. I took in the vase, the flowers, the seagrass rug spread over the hardwood floor, the polished brass lamp glowing in the corner, imagining a stranger looking it over and wondering which girl was lucky enough to inhabit such a pretty spot. I'd always hoped that someday I would meet a man who would appreciate that skill; a man who would praise me, telling me how creative I was, what a good eye I had, how comfortable and colorful and cozy I'd made our home, how I made everything beautiful.

I took off my Spanx, wriggling myself out of the punishing spandex and dropping the shaper in the trash. My underwire bra was the next thing to go. I put on a camisole top, cotton granny panties, and my comfiest pajama bottoms. In the bathroom, I pulled my hair back in a scrunchie, and scrubbed the makeup off my face. Back in my bedroom, I sat myself down in front of my laptop and typed the words "body acceptance" into the search engine.

A hundred different links came cascading across my screen: articles. Blogs. Twitter feeds with handles like @YourFatFriend and @fatnutritionist and @PlusSizeFeminist. Health at Every Size websites. Body positive Instagram accounts. Outfit-of-the-day Snapchats that featured girls with their wobbly thighs and belly rolls on display. All the parts I'd tried to hide, out there in the open. Big girls, some my size, some smaller, some larger, in bathing suits and lingerie, in yoga poses, on cruise ships and beaches and in *Sports Illustrated*'s Swimsuit Issue.

My finger hovered over the keyboard as my heart thumped in my chest. I thought, *This is a door. You can close it and stay here, outside, by yourself, or you can walk through it and join them.*

I shut my eyes and stilled my hands. If you had asked me that morning who I was, I might have talked about being a college student, an aspiring artist, a daughter or a friend; a lover of romance novels and needle felting, French bulldogs and Lynda Barry comics. But if I'd been honest, I would have said, *I'm a dieter.* I woke up in the morning planning what I'd eat and how much I'd exercise to burn it off; I went to bed at night feeling guilty about having done too much of the first and too little of the second and promising that the next day would be different. Right then, at my desk, I decided that I was done with it. I was going to eat to nourish myself, I was going to exercise to feel strong and healthy, I was going to let go of the idea of ever being thin, once and for all, and live my life in the body that I had. And I was going to drop a hundred and seventeen useless pounds right that minute, by vowing to never see Drue Lathrop Cavanaugh ever again.

Things had not been easy in my early days as a Baby Fat.

Lying in bed the morning after my night at the bar, I remembered a line from one of the Health at Every Size websites I'd read the night before. *Ask your body what it wants.* Except how was my body supposed to know? It had been so long since I'd eaten something just because it was what I'd wanted.

"Okay," I said to myself. I could hear my parents in the kitchen, keeping their voices low. I could smell the coffee that my dad would drink with cream and my mom would take black, and the Ezekiel bread in the toaster. I felt extremely foolish, until I thought about my dad. Sometimes, at night, when we were watching TV, he would speak to his belly as if it were a pet, giving it a little pat and asking, "A little popcorn? Another beer?" That helped. "Okay, body. What do I want for breakfast?"

For a long moment, there was nothing. I could feel myself start to panic, and I took deep, slow breaths until a thought emerged: *banana bread.* I wanted a slice of warm banana bread, studded with walnuts and chocolate chips, and a big glass of milk on the side. Right on the heels of that idea came the words "absolutely not." Banana bread was made with eggs and butter and chocolate chips and walnuts, full-fat yogurt, processed white flour, and a cup and a half of white sugar. Banana bread was dessert. I hadn't let myself eat banana bread in years . . . and if I started eating it, I wasn't sure that I'd be able to stop.

I went back to my laptop and the article I'd skimmed. *You might worry about feeling out of control . . . like, as soon as you start eating a formerly "forbidden" food, you won't be able to stop. That might even be true, the first few times you introduce a "bad" food back into your diet. We encourage you to eat slowly and mindfully, savoring each bite, listening to your body, eating when that food is what you want, stopping when you're full.*

I found a recipe. I got myself dressed. In the kitchen, my father was trying to solve the crossword puzzle, and my mom was helping him. As I pulled a shopping bag out of the cupboard, I heard him ask, "What's a six-letter word for Noah's resting place?"

"I'm going to Whole Foods," I told them.

"Too many letters," said my dad.

"Ha ha ha." I thought I sounded normal, but I saw him look at me before exchanging a glance with my mom.

"Everything okay?" he asked.

"Everything is fine," I said.

"We need cumin," he said, and raised a hand in farewell. My mom said "Be careful," the way she did when either one of us left the house.

I walked to the Whole Foods on Ninety-Second and Columbus. I bought my dad his cumin and got eggs, butter, Greek yogurt, chocolate chips, and the ripest bananas I could find. Back in the kitchen, with my parents watching without comment, I melted butter, cracked the eggs, and spooned yogurt into a measuring cup. I smushed bananas in a plastic bag. I browned the walnuts in the toaster oven. I mixed everything together and scraped it into a greased loaf tin.

When the banana bread was in the oven, I got comfortable on the couch, then opened my texts. Darshini, one of my other high school friends, was first. *Saw this last night*, she'd written. *You okay?* I felt unease settle into the pit of my belly. My chest felt tight, my knees felt quivery, and my heart was thumping so hard I could feel my chest shake. The link was to YouTube. I clicked, and there I was, in all my black-clad, wobbly, triple-chinned, furious glory. "Fat Girl Goes OFF" read the headline.

I wanted to scream and to drop the phone like it had stung me, and I must have made some kind of noise, because when I looked up, both of my parents were staring at me.

"Sorry," I said. "Everything's fine." I saw them exchange another glance, communicating in their private marital Morse code. My mother pressed her lips together as my father reached for his phone. I held my breath and turned my attention back to my own screen, to my own face. There were already thirteen thousand views. And—I stared, feeling my jaw drop, feeling terrified—eight thousand green thumbs-ups.

Don't do it, I thought, but I couldn't help myself. With my heart in my throat, I scrolled down to see the comments.

Landwhale, read the first one. Well, I'd been expecting it. And I liked whales! They were graceful and majestic!

I'd do her, the next commenter had written.

Roll her in flour and look for the wet spot, a wit beneath that comment had advised. I winced, feeling sick as I kept scrolling.

You GO girl, another commenter had written. *Wish I was brave enough to tell off a guy like that.*

Me too, the woman underneath her had written.

Me three.

The oven timer dinged. I looked up and saw that my father was still working at the crossword; my mom had moved on to the real estate section. "One point two million dollars for a studio!" she said, shaking her head. So the world hadn't spun off its axis; the house hadn't fallen down around me. The sun had come up in the morning, and it would still set that night.

I put on a pair of silicone oven mitts, bent down, and grasped the sheet pan that I'd put underneath the banana bread, in case of drips. The sheet pan had mostly been used to oven-roast zucchinis and onions, peppers and tomatoes, and, as a treat, the occasional thinly sliced potato. I wondered what it made of its new circumstances as I set the banana bread on top of the stove. My phone dinged. I looked to see if it was Darshi again, or if it was Ron, or Drue, who, so far, had not reached out. The screen said DAD, and the text said *Proud of you.* I felt my eyes prickle as I lifted my head long enough to give him a thumbs-up.

I thought about googling for articles about how to survive online humiliation and public shaming—it had happened to enough people by now; surely someone had written a guide for getting through it. Instead, I made myself do one of the relaxation exercises a long-ago yoga teacher had taught me. *Name five things you can see.* My mother. My father. The dining room table. The newspaper. The banana bread. *Name four things you can touch.* The skin of my arm. The fabric of the dining room chair cover. The wood of the kitchen table, the floor beneath my feet. The three things I could hear were the sound of cars on Riverside Drive, the scratch of my father's pen on the page, and my own heartbeat, still thundering in my ears. I could smell banana bread and my own acrid, anxious sweat.

I'd been on the Internet long enough to know that these things never lasted, that the outrage being poured onto, say, a *New York Times* columnist who'd overreacted to a mild insult could instantly be redirected toward a makeup company whose "skin tone" foundations only came in white-lady shades, before turning on a professional athlete who'd sent a tweet using the *n*-word when he was fifteen. The swarm was eternally in search of the next problematic artist or actor or fast-food brand, and nobody stayed notorious, or canceled, forever.

It won't last, I told myself. It isn't real. Real was what I could see, and touch, and smell. This was just pixels, moving invisibly through space, mostly bots and strangers who'd never know me in real life.

I went back to YouTube, where another eighty-three comments had been posted during my absence. Ignoring them, I copied the video and moved it to my own channel. I'd been using the same image as my social-media avatar for the last three years, a picture of two knitting needles stuck in a skein of magenta yarn. I deleted that shot and replaced it with a screen grab from the video that showed me with my mouth open, one hand extended, finger pointing at the cringing bro, the universal pose of Angry Lady. My first thought was *You can see my chins.* My next thought, hard on its heels, was *But I look brave. And at least my hair looked nice.*

I went to my biography. Underneath *Daphne Berg, Vanderbilt U, NYC native, happy crafter*, I added *fierce fat girl*, along with the hashtags #sorrynotsorry and #justasIam. I changed the name of my blog from *Daphne's Crafty Corner* to *Big Time*.

The banana bread was cool when I touched it. I cut a thick slice and put it on my favorite plate, which was white with a pattern of blue flowers. I pulled a fork out of the silverware drawer, folded a cloth napkin, and set it on the table. I took a seat. Unfolded the napkin and spread it over my lap. Used the fork to remove a generous wedge from the slice. Popped it in my mouth and closed my eyes, humming with pleasure as I chewed, tasting the richness, feeling the textures, the hot, slippery melted chocolate, the crunch of the nuts, the yielding softness of bananas and butter. I ate every morsel and used the side of the fork to scrape the plate clean.

Chapter Three

After I'd finished my video, I slung the garment bag securely over my arm and walked away from the bar without looking back. At Eighty-Sixth Street I caught the crosstown bus to Madison Avenue. Five minutes later, I arrived at the sidewalk in front of Saint David's School just as the crowd of nannies and mommies (with the very occasional daddy) was reaching its peak. With five minutes to kill, I opened Instagram. Already, my video had thousands of views, hundreds of likes, and dozens of comments. *So pretty*, typed curvyconfident. I double-tapped to like what she'd said. *Where's your shirt from?* asked Joelle1983. I typed in *Macys but it's like four years old. I think Old Navy has something similar—will check later!* "Feeding the beast" was how I thought of it. Not that my followers were animals, but it could get exhausting, the way I had to be extremely online all the time, clicking and liking and answering back, engaging so that the algorithms would notice my engagement and make my feed one of the first things people saw when they opened the app, so that I'd get more followers, so that I'd be able to charge more for my posts.

Like, like, comment; comment, comment, like. I worked my way through the replies, until one of them stopped me: *I am a teenage girl. How can I be brave like you?*

I paused, with the phone in my hand and my eyes on the sky, reminding myself that this so-called teenage girl could be a sixty-eight-year-old man living in his mom's basement, trolling me. I told myself that, no matter who'd asked the question, my reply wouldn't really be for her (or him)—it would be for everyone else who'd read it. And one of those people could very well be a fat teenager, a girl like the one I'd once been, wondering how she could be brave, the way she thought I was.

I resisted the impulse to type out a fast, glib *Fake it 'til you make it!*, which was more or less the truth. I wasn't brave every minute or every day, or even most minutes of most days . . . but I could act as if I were, almost all the time. Which meant that most of the world believed it. But did this theoretical girl need to hear that someone she respected was only pretending?

I cut and pasted the message and put it in my drafts file for later consideration, just as the final bell rang and dozens of boys in khaki pants and blue blazers came racing toward their caregivers. I put my side hustle in my pocket, and my real job began.

Three years ago, the Snitzers—Dr. Elise and Dr. Mark—had hired me to take care of their kids, Isabel and Ian, for four hours after school let out. I would pick the kids up, feed them snacks, supervise homework, and ferry them to their various engagements. Izzie had ice-hockey practice, playdates, and birthday parties; Ian had his therapist. Izzie was part of a running club and sang in a choir. Ian had his allergist. Izzie was a sweet, outgoing girl, but Ian was my favorite. He reminded me of me.

That afternoon, as usual, Ian was one of the last boys out the door. Ian, his mother had told me, had been born two weeks early, barely weighing five pounds, and he'd been a tiny, colicky scrap of a thing. He'd grown up to be a boy with a narrow, pale face, a reddened nose thanks to constant dripping, wiping, and blowing, and pale-blue eyes that were frequently watery and red-rimmed. When he was a baby, his mother had doctored his mashed peas and carrots and sweet potatoes with olive oil and butter, cramming calories into him to help him grow. He'd gotten shots and exposure therapy; he even had a mantra to recite before eating wheat or dairy. All of it had helped, but Ian was still wheezy and rashy and small for his age. Today, like most days, he was stooped under the weight of a backpack that probably weighed more than he did.

"Do we have time for a snack?" he asked as he used his forefinger to loosen the knot of his tie, an incongruously adult gesture that never failed to amuse me when eight-year-old Ian performed it.

I consulted my phone. We had fifteen minutes to traverse the two blocks that would get us to East Ninety-First Street in time to collect Izzy at Spence. "If we eat fast."

Ian nodded. "That's fair."

"How was your day?"

Ian sighed. "We had PE, and I got picked last again."

"Aw, man." Ian rolled his eyes at my sad attempt to sound hip, but I could see a smile playing around the corners of his mouth. "Seriously, though. I can't believe schools are still doing it this way. Letting kids pick teams."

He looked up at me. "Did you get picked last ever?"

"Um, did I get picked last always?" I asked lightly. *Keep it moving*, I told myself. If I got mired in memories of gym class horror, I'd be crying by the first intersection. "What will we be enjoying this afternoon?"

"Chocolate croissant at Sarabeth's," he said promptly. "Are you trying to change the subject?"

Ian didn't miss much. "I one hundred percent am."

"Were kids mean to you when you were in third grade?"

"On occasion. But you know what? I survived. And you will,

too. And those jerks who were mean to you will probably peak in middle school, whereas you have many, many years to excel." Ian smiled at that. I wondered when he'd realize that some bullies just stayed that way, that some of the little jerks just grew up to become bigger, rich, successful jerks, and that the scales didn't always balance in the end.

We walked into Sarabeth's. The woman behind the counter smiled when she saw Ian. "The usual?" she asked.

Ian nodded. "Yes, please."

"You're a regular!" I said. He rolled his eyes, but he was glowing with the pleasure of being recognized, standing a little taller as he looked around to see who might have heard. *Everyone likes being seen*, I thought, and stowed that observation away for later use in an Instagram post.

"Who was mean to you?" Ian asked, once we'd found a table. "Was it that girl? The one who came to our house?"

I pulled an allergen-free, lavender-scented wipe out of my bag. "Hands."

Ian wiped his hands and started to eat. "It was, wasn't it?" His voice sounded dolorous, even with a mouthful of chocolate and pastry. "I'll bet she got picked first."

"That, my friend, is a bet you would win."

I wished that Ian and Izzy had never met Drue, that my former best friend had never dragged my employers and their kids into our drama. But, as Drue had pointed out, I hadn't given her any other option. I'd ignored her emails and the texts she sent after she'd gotten my phone number from our alumni association. I hadn't opened the direct messages she'd sent on Instagram and Facebook and Twitter, and I'd thrown the letter she'd mailed me into the trash, unopened. When she'd left word with my parents that she was trying to reach me, all I'd said was "Thanks for letting me know." And even though I was sure that they were both desperate to hear the story about what had gone wrong between us. they hadn't pushed, or pried, or asked questions.

Finally, Drue had done an end run and had gone to the Snitzers. Dr. Elise, it emerged, sat on the board of one of the museums where Drue was a member of the Young Friends, and she had been delighted to facilitate the reunion of two old friends. She'd even enlisted Ian and Izzy. "We've got a big surprise for you!" Izzy had said one afternoon, making me sit while Ian solemnly wrapped a blindfold around my head. Each kid had taken a hand, and they'd led me into the kitchen. I'd smelled chocolate as they'd helped me take a seat. "Surprise!" they'd shouted. I'd pulled off the blindfold to see a frosted cake on the table, with candles blazing.

Confused, I'd said, "It's not my birthday."

"That's not the surprise!" Izzy crowed. She and Ian went into the foyer. A minute later, larger than life and twice as beautiful, in high pale-beige heels and a navy-blue blazer that probably cost more than I would earn all week, was Drue Cavanaugh. My old best friend.

"Hey, Daphne!" she'd said, as if we'd seen each other fifteen minutes ago at our lockers at the Lathrop School after a day of classes instead of six years ago, on a sidewalk outside of a bar, after a fight.

I stared at her. "Blow out your candles," she said quietly. "Make a wish." As if I'd been hypnotized, I bent and did as she'd told me. I blew out the candles, but I didn't make a wish. My mind had gone completely, distressingly blank.

"It's your friend!" Ian crowed. "Your friend from school! She wanted to surprise you!"

"Are you surprised?" Izzy had asked, dancing around me in her tulle tutu.

I could barely breathe, could barely speak. "I am. Yes. Hey, can you two monsters give us a minute?"

The kids, placated by slices of cake and glasses of milk, had gone to the den for a bonus half-hour of screen time. Drue had helped herself to the slimmest sliver of cake. "Thanks, Josie," she'd said, dismissing the Snitzers' cook in the impersonally friendly tone of a woman who'd spent her whole life telling the help what to do. Josie had nodded and bowed her way out the door.

And then it had been just the two of us.

I imagined that I could feel the air changing, some kind of shift in the atmosphere signaling the gravity of this moment. *Name five things you can see.* The refrigerator. My hand on the table. My black shirt. The stainless-steel refrigerator. Drue's highlighted hair. I could still smell the cake that Josie had made, the good scents of chocolate and butter and vanilla, and I could hear Izzy and Ian squabbling about what to watch, but all of that felt very far away. I imagined that we were in a bubble, my old friend and me, floating, alone together, apart from the world. Just the two of us.

"What are you doing here?" I asked.

Drue removed her jacket. Underneath, she wore a long-sleeved ivory silk blouse, with mother-of-pearl buttons at the cuffs and a bow at the collar, and a pair of beautifully cut, high-waisted, wide-legged navy-blue pants. Her earrings were pearls, each one set in a circle of tiny, brilliant diamonds, and her hair was pulled into a loose bun at the nape of her neck. *Work look*, she'd probably tag it, if she'd posted it on what she called Fashion Fridays on her Instagram page. I did my best to avoid Drue's online presence, the same way I'd tried to avoid her IRL, but it wasn't easy. Especially not after the *New York Times* had included her in a round-up of rising businesswomen who were using social media effectively. *With her breezy yet down-to-earth tone and balanced blend of philanthropy, Boss Girl–style tips and fashion, Drue Cavanaugh of the Cavanaugh Corporation has become a must-read for the rising generation of young women who want to have it all, and look good while they're getting it*, the piece had read, quoting an advertising executive's praise of Drue for putting a fresh, young, relatable female face on the staid old family brand.

Drue pulled out one of the chairs at the kitchen table and sat down. "I need to talk to you."

Instead of sitting, I looked across the table at her as I said, "I don't think we have anything to say to each other."

"Please, Daphne," she said. "I know you're still mad, but can you just give me a minute? Please?"

I stared at her for what felt like a long time. Her features were still perfect, hair still shiny; she was still chic and gorgeous and flawless. I could feel the old, familiar longing, and could remember how easily she'd pulled me into her orbit with the unspoken promise that, if I got close to her, if I did what she wanted me to do, I'd end up elevated by proximity; looking like her, being like her, having that beauty and the power and confidence it conferred.

"Please," she said again, her voice cracking. *Or maybe not so much confidence.* I sat down and pushed my empty plate away. I wouldn't have been able to eat, even if I'd wanted to. Whatever appetite I'd had had fled.

"Five minutes," I said curtly. "I have things to do."

Drue crossed her legs and toyed with her fork. "Could I have some water?"

Here we go, I thought, and went to get a glass. I could have used a drink myself, but I couldn't permit myself even a sip of water with Drue, any more than Persephone should have allowed herself a single pomegranate seed down in hell. Water would turn into coffee, which would turn into a glass of wine, which would turn into a bottle, and then I'd invite her back to my place. She'd keep my glass full, and I'd be spilling whatever secrets I had to spill, agreeing to anything she wanted. I could feel her allure, as insistent as the tide, the way the water tugged you when you stood at the edge of the ocean with your feet in the sand.

I set the glass in front of her so hard that some of the water splashed out. "Why are you here?"

Drue sighed. In the late-afternoon sunlight, she was even more beautiful than she'd been in high school, like a pearl polished to its highest gloss, but she kept fidgeting, smoothing her hands against her thighs, tapping the floor with one toe. *She's nervous*, I thought. Then I thought, *Good.*

"Well?"

Instead of answering, Drue extended her arm, angling her hand so that there was no way I could miss the enormous diamond ring on her finger.

"I'm getting married," she said. "To Stuart Lowe."

I stared at her mutely. I knew, of course. I didn't follow Drue, but I did live in the world, where there were newspapers and gossip blogs and *People* magazine, and all of those had made Drue's impending nuptials impossible to avoid. I knew Drue was engaged, and I knew her intended had been last season's star on *All the Single Ladies*, a dating show where, over twelve weeks, one eligible bachelor worked his way through a pool of eighteen women, taking them on dates in different locales (most of which had been chosen because of their willingness to pay promotional fees to the network), finally narrowing his choices down to two lucky ladies, and proposing to one during the finale. Eight months ago, Stuart Lowe had put a ring on the finger of his "winner," a blond, breathy, baby-voiced nanny from Minnesota named Corina Bailey. Two months after that he'd dumped her, telling the world that he was still in love with his college girlfriend: Drue Lathrop Cavanaugh.

So I knew. But what did Drue want from me? Did she expect me to start celebrating with her? Shriek with happiness, jump for joy, act like this was the best news I'd ever heard? Like she was still my friend, and I still cared?

"Congratulations," I said, keeping my voice expressionless.

"Hey," said Drue. She stretched out her fingers to brush my forearm. I jerked it away. "It's been great to see how well you're doing. Truly."

I shrugged.

"I can't believe that Jessamyn Stanley follows my high school BFF," Drue burbled. Jessamyn Stanley was a plus-size yoga instructor, a black woman with close-cropped hair who posed in sports bras and yoga pants and occasionally smoked weed on camera and was pretty much the opposite of all of the yoga instructors I'd encountered during my dieting years. I'd been delighted to find her, and Mina Valerio, another plus-size black athlete who ran ultramarathons in a body that looked like mine, and even more thrilled when they'd followed me back.

"And Tess Holliday!" Drue continued. "And Lola Dalton!" Tess Holliday was a top plus-size model; Lola Dalton was a comedian who'd actually retweeted a video I'd made about how, for plus-size women, getting a sports bra on was the workout before the workout.

"How's Darshi?" she asked, her voice bright and upbeat, as if the three of us had been besties. As if Darshi hadn't been one of her favorite targets back in the day.

"She's doing very well. Finishing up her dissertation at Columbia, actually. We're roommates."

"Wow. That's really great."

"What do you want, Drue?" I was glad to hear that my voice was pleasant but businesslike.

She rubbed her hands against her thighs again, and smoothed her hair, giving me another look at her ring. "I need people," she said softly. "People to be in my wedding."

I schooled my face into blankness and fixed my eyes on a point just above her head as Drue kept talking.

"My fiancé . . . he's got all these friends . . . he's got, like, eight groomsmen, and I don't have that many. I don't have anyone, really." Her voice cracked. Her chest hitched. Her eyes gleamed with the sheen of tears.

I turned away. "What about the gruesome twosome?"

Drue made a small, familiar gesture, one I'd seen her employ a dozen times, always in relation to some guy she'd been seeing, a flick of her hand that meant *I'm done with him.* When I kept staring, she sighed. "Ainsley's in Tokyo for some job thing," she said. "And Avery isn't interested."

There was a story there, I thought as Drue pulled in a deep breath and sighed it out. "I haven't been perfect," she said. "I know that. And I've missed you." Her eyes shone with what looked like sincerity. "I've never again had a friend like you." She tried to smile. When she saw my stony expression, the smile slid off her face. Looking down, she said, "The wedding is going to be covered everywhere. We'll be in *Vogue*, and *Town & Country*, and we're hoping for the *Times'* Vows column. And it's going to look ridiculous if I'm up there all by myself." Her eyes welled with tears.

"You don't have anyone?" I heard myself ask.

"I've got two cousins, and one of them is pregnant." She used her hands to sketch an enormous belly in the air. "She might not be able to make it to the wedding. And my assistant said she'd do it. Stuart's got a sister. And I asked one girl from college, and one girl from grad school. They said yes. Probably because I said I'd pay their airfare."

Am I supposed to feel sorry for you? I thought. As if she'd heard me, Drue started to cry for real. "I haven't been a good person. Maybe I don't even know how to be a good person. And I know I don't deserve your forgiveness. I was awful to you, but I don't have anyone else, and you were the only one . . ." She gulped, then wiped her cheeks, and looked at me with her reddened eyes. "You were the only one who ever just liked me for me." In a tiny, un-Drue-like voice, she asked, "Will you be in my wedding? Please?"

I curled my hands into fists, digging my fingernails into the meat of my palms, and stared at her in a way I hoped managed to communicate my utter incredulity at the very thought that I'd ever participate in her wedding. Drue bowed her head and swayed forward, close enough for me to smell her shampoo and perfume, both of them familiar, both immediately taking me back to the cafeteria at Lathrop, and her bedroom, where I'd spent dozens of nights sleeping on the trundle bed on the floor next to her. There was a guest room, of course, but on the nights I spent there we always ended up in her room, together.

"Daphne, I know I was awful. I've been in therapy." Her lips quirked. "I'm probably the first one on either side of my family to do that." Her laugh sounded rueful, the kind I'd never heard from her before. "WASPs don't get therapists, they get drunk and have affairs." Another sigh. "High school was not a good time for me, and I took it out on other people."

Part of me was dying to ask for details, to try to make some sense of what she was telling me. I had so many questions, but I forced myself to keep quiet and warned myself not to trust her, not to open the door and let her hurt me again.

"My parents haven't been happy for a long time. I don't know if they ever were happy, but when we were in high school, it was . . ." She shook her head. "It was bad. My father would go on business trips for months at a time, and when he'd come home, they'd have these knock-down, drag-out, screaming fights." She picked up her fork, broke off a tiny bit of cake, and mashed it flat with the tines. "My father had affairs. Lots of affairs. Remember how we used to go to Cape Cod in the summers, and then we stopped?"

"I figured it had something to do with that mansion your dad bought in the Hamptons."

Drue managed half of a smile. "Do you know why we bought that house? My mother's parents told us—told him—that we couldn't come back to the Cape." She waited until, finally, I asked, "Why?"

"Because every summer, my father would sleep with some family's au pair or babysitter, so my grandmother finally put her foot down." She touched her hair, toyed with her fork, recrossed her legs under the table. "My parents didn't have a prenup. So if they'd split up, my dad would've fought my mom over the money she had when they got married. It would have been ugly and expensive for both of them, so I guess they just decided to, you know, tough it out." Drue wrapped her arms around her shoulders. "It was awful."

"So why didn't you tell me?"

Drue made a face. "Remember Todd Larson?"

I nodded. Todd had been one of our Lathrop classmates. Todd's dad had been a city council member until his name was found among the boldfaced entries in a Washington madam's little black book.

"And Libby Ross?"

I nodded again. Libby's mom had found out that Libby's dad was cheating after she'd snooped on his Fitbit readout and noticed his heart rate spiking suspiciously at two in the morning for three nights in a row when he was allegedly at a great-aunt's funeral in Des Moines. When that fact had come out in open court in the middle of their lengthy and contentious divorce hearings, the gossip websites had feasted on the scandal for days.

"I couldn't talk about it. Not even with you."

"You think I would have told people?" My voice was incredulous.

"My whole life, my parents told me not to trust anyone who wasn't family."

I rolled my eyes. "It wasn't like you were in the mafia." When Drue didn't answer, I said, "Okay, so you were going through some stuff. Your parents were fighting. Lots of kids' parents were fighting, or getting divorced. Do you think that excuses the way you treated me?"

"No," she said. Her shoulders slumped. "You know what they say. Hurt people hurt people."

"Who is they?"

"I don't know." Drue's voice was small and sad. "My therapist? Oprah?"

I snorted. "Since we're sharing quotations, how about 'Fool me once, shame on you, fool me twice, shame on me'?" I wanted her to leave; to get out of this house, to stop calling, stop texting, stop writing, stop trying. I wanted her to leave me alone. But then, unbidden, my mind served up a picture: the two of us, in seventh grade, in pajamas, on a Monday morning in December. I'd slept over on Sunday night, and around midnight it had started to snow, an early-winter blizzard that had canceled all the city's schools. We woke up to find the city covered in a blanket of pristine white. The streets were empty. Everything was quiet and still.

"I wish we had hot chocolate," Drue had said. Abigay, the family's cook, had left early the day before, trying to get home to her own children while the trains were still running. When I asked Drue where Abigay lived, Drue had shrugged, saying, "Queens. The Bronx. One of those places."

"We can make hot chocolate," I said. Drue had gone looking and reported back, "There's no mix," and when I'd found cocoa powder, sugar, and milk and made us a pot from scratch, she'd been as amazed as if I'd shown her actual magic. We carried our mugs over to the sofa by the window and sat there, looking down at the empty street, watching the snow fall. Her parents must have been somewhere in the house, but neither one of them made an appearance or disrupted the silence. There'd been a Christmas tree, a real Scotch pine, in the Cavanaugh living room, perfuming the air with the smell of the forest. I remembered its tiny white lights twinkling against the green branches, the richness of the hot chocolate on my tongue; and how happy I was, how thrilled to be in Drue's company on that beautiful wintry day. We'd cut out snowflakes from gold and silver foil wrapping paper, and watched six episodes of *Buffy the Vampire Slayer*. By the end of the afternoon I'd confided my crush on Ryan Donegan, one of the best-looking boys in ninth grade. By the second period of the day on Tuesday, Ryan had walked up to me in the hall and said, in front of at least six of our classmates, "Sorry, Daphne, but I don't like you that way." When I'd confronted Drue she'd shrugged and said, "You were never going to be brave enough to tell him on your own. So I did it for you. What's the big deal?" Then she'd stopped talking to me, as if my anger was unreasonable, as if it had been my fault.

No, I thought. Absolutely not. No way was I letting her get close to me again. But then, right on top of that thought came a memory of a different sleepover. I'd been older, maybe fourteen, and I had woken up in the middle of the night, needing to use the bathroom. Rather than going to the one attached to Drue's bedroom and possibly waking her, I slipped out into the hallway and was tiptoeing down the hall when I heard a loud, male voice ask, "Who're you?"

I stopped, frozen and terrified, and turned toward the opened door. In the shadows, I could see a desk with a man-shaped bulk behind it. A glass and a bottle sat on the desk in front of him. Even from a distance, I could smell the liquor.

"I'm Daphne Berg. Drue's friend."

"What? Speak up!"

In a quavering voice, I said my name again. The man repeated it, in a vicious falsetto singsong: "I'm Daphne Berg. Drue's friend." His slurred voice turned the last two words into *Drue'sh fren*. "Well, I'm Drue's father. Or so they tell me." He made a barking noise, a version of a laugh. "What do you think about that?"

I wasn't sure what to say, or even if I was supposed to answer. I knew that Robert Cavanaugh was a big deal—rich, powerful, a man who had the ear of presidents and the chairman of the Federal Reserve, according to Drue, who salted her conversation with references to him. *My father says, my father thinks. My father says a guaranteed minimum wage is a terrible idea*, she'd announce in our Contemporary America class, or she'd casually drop *My father thinks the Israeli prime minister's kind of a jerk.* She'd told me about her plans to work with him at the Cavanaugh Corporation after she graduated from Harvard, which he, too, had attended. But, as large as he loomed in my friend's life, I'd never set eyes on Drue's father until that moment, three years into our friendship.

He squinted at me through the whiskey-scented gloom. Finally, after a pause that felt endless, he waved a hand at me, a clear dismissal. I scurried back down the hall, all thoughts of the bathroom forgotten.

The next morning, I'd woken up to find Drue standing in front of the mirror over her dresser, lining her eyes, and the memory had assumed the quality of a bad dream. "I think I saw your father last night," I said. From my bed on the floor, I could see the way her body seemed to go on high alert at the words "your father," the way her shoulders tensed. Without turning, Drue slid her gaze away from mine. Her voice was even as she answered, "He must have come home late. He was in Japan," but I saw one toe start tapping at the carpet. I thought about my own father, a high school English teacher who had a beard and a potbelly and who was invariably kind. If he'd startled Drue in the middle of the night he would have apologized, probably even warmed up a mug of milk for her and asked if she wanted a snack.

All of that history was unfurling, fast-forwarding in my brain in the Snitzers' kitchen with Drue in front of me, waiting for an answer. I could feel the old anger, the wounds as fresh as if they'd been inflicted the day before. I could hear her voice, jeering at me—*We all just felt sorry for you!*—and remember how that had hurt, even worse than that guy calling me a fat bitch. I thought, *So help me, if she tries to take credit for it, if she tells me that if it wasn't for her then that night would have never happened and that video would have never gone viral, and I wouldn't be an influencer, I will throw a mixing bowl at her head.* My stomach was twisting, and my mouth tasted sour. The words were there, just waiting for me to say them: *You ruined my life.* I was just starting to speak when a thought occurred to me: *Had she?*

Had she really?

Here I was, a young woman with a good job, an education and family and a community of friends, in the real world and online. A young woman who shared a nice two-bedroom apartment with a good friend, a real friend, and had enough money to pay her bills and buy more or less what she wanted (within reason); a girl with a sweet dog and a supportive family, a little bit of fame, and exciting prospects for a future. Sure, high school had sucked, but didn't high school suck for most people? Maybe I could be the bigger person (*ha ha ha*, I thought, then winced, and wondered if I'd ever be able to unlearn the habit of self-deprecation). Maybe I could forgive her. Maybe that would be the best thing, a gift I could give myself. I could stop hating Drue Cavanaugh. I could lay that burden down.

"I really did miss you," Drue said. Her voice was small. "And no matter what you decide, whether you forgive me or not, I wanted to tell you that I was sorry in person. I treated you horribly, and I'm sorry."

I turned toward our reflection in the stainless-steel refrigerator, Drue all confidence and couture, me all anxiety and Ross Dress for Less. Over the years, I'd played out endless iterations of our reunion in my head. Never once had it gone like this.

"So look." Drue smoothed her trousers over her knees and stood up, giving me another tremulous smile. "Will you please at least think about it? I can't imagine getting married without you."

I closed my eyes, just for a second. "I don't think I can act like everything that happened is just . . ." I made a sweeping gesture with one hand. "Just pfft, gone, because you apologized. It's going to take me some time."

"The wedding's not until June." Her eagerness almost undid me, the desperation just beneath the gloss. I'd been that desperate, once, so eager to be included, and to have Drue and her friends acknowledge me as their equal. To be one of them, part of their pack, and to move through the world with the knowledge that I belonged, that I mattered, too.

"I need some time," I began.

"I'd pay you," Drue blurted.

I stared at her, feeling my mouth fall open. Drue was trying to smile, but her lips were trembling, and her hands were twisting as she clasped them at her waist.

"I mean, I can see that you're doing well. Really well. But everyone could use a little extra, right?"

I took a deep breath. Here was something else that none of the versions of an encounter with Drue I'd imagined had featured—feeling sorry for her. And I was—I could admit it—thinking about Instagram, and how I could profit from what she was offering. I knew from experience that pictures on beaches, or in any exotic setting, especially one that came with a whiff of exclusivity, spelled clicks, and likes, and traffic. A cute picture of a swimsuit? Good. Cute picture of the same swimsuit on a beautiful beach? Better. And if the beach was at Portofino or St. Barth's, some walled-off or members-only province of the ultra-rich and famous, where the air was rare and mere mortals weren't allowed? Best of all.

It was tempting. I also knew that Drue wouldn't stop. If her assault on my employers didn't work, she would go back to my parents next. Or she'd take out a billboard in Times Square. I sighed, and Drue must have heard capitulation, or seen it on my face. She smiled at me, opening her arms, then dropping them and reaching for her phone. "Picture!" she cried. "We need a picture!"

Of course we did. I'd just gotten through telling her that everything was not fine between us, that there was still work to be done, but I knew she'd post a shot that would make it look like there'd never been a rupture, like she'd never betrayed me or hurt me, like we'd been in each other's lives all along. In space, nobody could hear you scream; on the Internet, nobody could tell if you were lying.

Sixty seconds later, Drue had taken, edited, cropped, filtered, and posted a picture of the two of us. She had her arm around my shoulder, her cheek leaning against the top of my head, and both of us were smiling. *Me and my BFF and bridesmaid!* she had written. I felt unsettled, angry, and increasingly certain that I was being used, but with her arm around me, with the familiar smell of her shampoo and hairspray and perfume in the air, I could also feel that old familiar pride, like I'd aced a test for which I hadn't studied, or pulled a guy way out of my league. Drue's regard had always felt like that. Like I'd won something valuable, against all odds. Like I'd taken something that was never meant to be mine.

By the time I made it home that night, my follower count had climbed by two thousand. Maybe this will be a good thing, I told myself, feeling the strangest combination of nausea and hope, excitement and despair. I was excited about the wedding, and Drue's return. I was disappointed in myself for letting her back into my life so quickly, for putting up so little resistance. I was frustrated that I'd let her promulgate the lie of it all online and post a smiling picture, and the version of the truth most useful to Drue. I was already dreading having to tell my friends and family that I'd let Drue back into my life. And I'd been glad, more than anything else; glad that Drue still wanted me around, glad that my friend and I were together again.

When every crumb of the chocolate croissant had been devoured, Ian and I collected Izzy, a round-limbed, pink-cheeked, cheerful ten-year-old, and ferried her to hockey practice. At Gristedes, I picked up everything on the Snitzers' list: black beans, garlic, shallots, a half-gallon of almond milk, honeycrisp apples, and four salmon fillets. At the dry cleaner, I collected Dr. Elise's dresses and Dr. Mark's shirts. At the pharmacy, I paid for Ian's asthma inhaler refill. He took the inhaler and one of the bags of groceries; I carried the other and the clothes, and together, we walked to the Snitzers' apartment building on East Eighty-Ninth Street.

"Can I ask you something?" Ian inquired as we entered the lobby. It was dinnertime. I could tell by the cluster of delivery guys waiting by the service elevator, each carrying plastic bags fragrant with curry or ginger and garlic or hot grease and grilled meat. Ian had told me that the building's board had voted not to let delivery people ride the residents' elevator—lest, I suppose, the smell of ethnic food or the sight of ethnic deliverymen and -women offend the residents.

"Ask away."

Ian's body seemed to slump. "Remember how I told you about Brody Holcomb?"

I nodded. Brody Holcomb was the class asshole, who'd already gotten in trouble for claiming he'd misheard the teacher's explanation of Ian's allergy to peanuts and tree nuts, after telling everyone that Ian had a penis allergy. That kind of wit.

"His parents had to come to school after that thing that happened. And the dad looked just like Brody! All big, and . . ." Ian waved his free hand around his face and body, in a way I thought was meant to communicate *handsome and powerful*. "At school, they tell us 'it gets better.' But what if Brody never changes? What if he just grows up to be like his dad?"

I considered my options as Ian trudged into the elevator, which zipped us to the Snitzers' floor. Eight felt very young to understand the world as it was. Then again, Ian was smart. Not just smart, but wise. *An old soul*, his mother liked to say.

“Sometimes things do change,” I said carefully. “Sometimes things do get better.” I was thinking about myself, my years at the Lathrop School, and how I’d longed for transformation. I was thinking about Drue, and wondering if she’d actually changed at all. “And here’s the good news,” I said, putting my hand on Ian’s bony shoulder and giving it a squeeze. “Even if things don’t get better, you can always make them look good on the Internet.”

Chapter Four

"Class, we have a new student joining us today!" It was the first day of sixth grade at the Lathrop School, which was allegedly one of the best private schools in the city and, not coincidentally, the school my father had attended and where he currently taught English to juniors and seniors. My parents had tried to get me into Lathrop for kindergarten. I'd gone for the playdate and the interview, and I'd been admitted, but the financial-aid package the school had offered to the children of Lathrop teachers wasn't quite generous enough. They'd tried again when I was in fourth grade, with the same results. The third time had proved the charm.

The night before, I'd made sure my favorite denim short-alls were clean and my light-blue T-shirt spotless. I had a new pair of Nike sneakers, white with a blue swoosh, bought at the Foot Locker, on sale. I'd straightened my hair and pulled it back in a ponytail, and my mom had lent me a pair of earrings, gold and dangly, with turquoise beads. She'd taken a picture of me in my carefully chosen clothes and a tremulous smile, holding a sign she'd painted in watercolors: *First Day at the Lathrop School!* The shot was probably already on her Facebook page, getting oohs and ahhs and likes from my aunts and uncles and grandmother, and all of my mom's friends.

My knees felt wobbly as I stood up so Ms. Reyes, my homeroom teacher, could introduce me. "I'd like you all to meet a new student, Daphne Berg." I smiled, like I'd practiced at home, thinking, *I hope they like me. I hope someone will be my friend.* I hadn't had many friends at my old public school. Most of my free time was spent with books, or with scissors and paper and a hot glue gun, not other kids. Most of the time, that was okay with me, but sometimes I was lonely, and I knew my parents worried about my friendlessness. It was one of the reasons they'd pushed so hard for Lathrop to take me.

"Welcome, Daphne," said Ms. Reyes.

All the kids paused in their chatter and looked me over, but Drue Cavanaugh was the first one that I really saw. She was sitting in the center of the front row, dressed in tight dark-blue jeans with artful rips on the thigh and at the knee. Her loose gray T-shirt had the kind of silkiness that cotton could only attain after a hundred trips through the washing machine. On top of the T-shirt she wore a black-and-white-plaid shirt. Her face was a perfect oval, her skin a creamy white with golden undertones and a sprinkling of freckles. Her nose was narrow and chiseled; her lips were full and pink; her shiny, streaky blond hair was gathered into a casually messy topknot. She wore silver hoops in her ears and a velvet choker around her neck, and I could see, instantly, that my clothes and my hair and my earrings were all wrong; that she looked the way I was supposed to look, effortlessly beautiful and stylish and cool. I felt my face flush with shame, but, unbelievably, the beautiful girl was smiling at me, patting the empty seat next to her. "Daphne can sit here," she said. Ms. Reyes nodded, and I slipped into the seat.

"Thank you," I whispered.

"I'm Drue," she said, and spelled it. "It's an old family name. Short for Drummond, if you can believe that. If I was a boy I think my parents were going to call me Drum." She wrinkled her nose charmingly, and I smiled at her, charmed. Then she smoothed her hair and turned back to the conversation she'd been having with the girl on the other side. When the bell rang, she gathered up her books and flounced away without another word to me, leaving only the scent of expensive shampoo in her wake.

Weird, I thought. I didn't see her again until lunchtime, and she came gliding toward me in the cafeteria where I stood, frozen, trying to figure out if I should buy a slice of pizza or eat the lunch my dad had packed.

"Hey, Daphne? It's Daphne, right?" When I nodded, she asked, "Do you have any money?" She made a face and said, "I'm completely broke." Flushed with pleasure, thrilled that she'd remembered my name, I mentally committed to my packed lunch and reached into my pocket for the five dollars my mother had given me, just in case none of the other sixth-graders had brought lunch from home.

"Thank you!" she caroled, before bouncing away. As I watched her go, a girl with round glasses and a mop of shiny dark curls approached. "Did she ditch you?"

"Oh, no," I said, even as I realized that was exactly what had happened: "No, she just needed money."

The other girl gave a not-unfriendly snort. "Ha. That's a good one." She had medium-brown skin and wide brown eyes beneath thick, curved eyebrows, and she wore jeans and sneakers with a silky-looking light-blue kurta on top. Her mouth glittered with the metal of her braces; her glasses caught the light. I was tall for my age, and she was short, with skinny hips and a flat chest. The top of her head barely reached my shoulders.

"What do you mean?" I asked.

The girl blinked at me. "Drue Cavanaugh? Drue *Lathrop* Cavanaugh?" I stared. My new companion shook her head in pity at my ignorance.

"If Drue actually forgot her money, which, PS, doubt it, the lunch ladies would just give her whatever she wanted," she said. "Her mother's family founded the whole school."

"Thank you for telling me," I made myself say. I didn't feel grateful. I felt angry. Maybe she hadn't meant to, but the new girl had made me feel dumb.

"Don't worry. She's a bitch. I'm Darshini Shah, but my friends call me Darshi. You can sit with me if you want to."

She pointed to a table in the corner. Other kids were already sitting there. One of the girls had pale white skin and a frizzy ponytail and a constellation of pimples covering most of her forehead. Two boys, one black and one Asian, had taken out a chess set and started a game. My people, I thought, feeling resigned.

I followed Darshi across the room. We were almost at the table when I heard Drue call my name from a table in the center of the cafeteria, where she was sitting with two girls dressed the way she was.

"Daphne? Hey, Daphne! Aren't you going to sit with us?"

I stopped and turned. Behind me, I could feel Darshi waiting.

"I'm sitting here," I said. "But maybe I can sit with you tomorrow."

A strange expression, surprise and anger mixed with amusement, moved across Drue's face. The two girls at her table were easier to read. They both just looked shocked.

For a moment, it felt like everyone in the cafeteria was staring at us. Then Drue stood up, unfolding herself gracefully from the bench. "Then I will sit with you!" She nodded at the other girls, and, after exchanging an irritated look, they, too, picked up their plates and followed Drue over to Darshi's table. I ended up with Drue on one side of me, Darshi on the other, and the two girls from Drue's table sitting across from us.

Darshi introduced me to the curly-haired girl, whose name was Frankie, and to the chess players, David and Joon Woo Pak. Drue introduced me to her friends, Ainsley and Avery. The two of them looked like imperfect copies of Drue. One had blond hair, and one had brown, but they both sported versions of the same high, haphazard buns. They wore variations of Drue's outfit: dark-rinse jeans, vintage tees, and Doc Martens boots. Ainsley's face was long and rectangular as a coffin, and Avery had thin hair and squinty eyes. They made Drue look even prettier, like a stunning solitaire set off by a pair of smaller, flawed diamonds. I wondered, uneasily, if that was the point of the two of them, and if it was, what that might make me.

Darshi's friends were eating actual food, but all Drue and Ainsley and Avery had were Diet Cokes and plates of salad: iceberg lettuce, a sprinkling of fake bacon bits, a few chickpeas, and no visible dressing. I flashed back to the dry tuna on lettuce that my nana had tormented me with during the summer she'd stayed with me, when I'd been six and my parents had been working at a summer camp in Maine. *Is this what girls here eat?* I wondered. Clearly, not all of the girls: Frankie was eating a cheeseburger from the hot-food line, and Darshi had opened up a Thermos full of pale-brown pureed chickpeas over rice.

I unzipped my backpack. It was a plain dark-purple nylon backpack, and I had spent a week before school started embroidering patterns on the back, starbursts and paisley swirls in threads that were orange and turquoise and indigo blue.

"Ooh, whatcha got?" Drue asked, leaning over to look. Shyly, I unzipped my lunchbag and showed her what my father had prepared. There was a Tupperware container of poppy seed flatbread crackers, spread with cream cheese and topped with slivers of lox and circles of cucumber. There was a small bag of homemade trail mix with fat golden raisins, dried cranberries, walnuts, and coconut flakes, and a container of cut-up carrots with a cup of yogurt-dill dip, a hard-boiled egg with just the right amount of salt and pepper in a twist of wax paper, a pair of clementines, and a half-dozen Hershey's Kisses.

"Chocolate!" said Drue, helping herself to a Kiss. It should have been aggravating, but the funny, sneaky way she plucked just one foil-wrapped chocolate was instead endearing. "Nice lunch."

I felt like I owed her an explanation. "When I was little, I loved *Bread and Jam for Frances*," I said. "Do you guys know that book?"

Ainsley blinked. Avery shrugged. Darshi said, "That's the one about the badger, right?"

"Oh, I remember!" said Drue. "And she wants to just eat bread and jam for lunch, and so her mother makes her eat it for every single meal?"

"Yes," I said, delighted that there was something Drue and I had in common. "My favorite part of the book was the description of all the foods the other badgers brought to school. So my dad made me this. He calls it a badger lunch."

Ainsley bent her head and whispered something in Avery's ear. Avery giggled. Ainsley smirked. Drue ignored them both.

"You're so lucky," Drue said. "God. I don't think my father even knows where the kitchen is in our house. He'll just hand me a few hundred bucks whenever he's home and we're both awake at the same time."

"Does your father work nights?" I asked. It was the only explanation I could imagine for a dad who wasn't awake at the same time as his daughter. Ainsley tittered. Avery rolled her eyes.

"Ha," said Drue. She smiled, looking amused, the way I imagined I would look at an insignificant creature who had managed something surprising—a mouse that did magic tricks, a golden retriever who'd stood on his hind legs and burst into song. "No. He travels. For business."

"The Cavanaugh Corporation?" said Ainsley. "You know? That's her family."

Drue swatted Ainsley's shoulder. "It's fine."

Except it wasn't, I realized. I should have known that a girl with the last name Cavanaugh was one of those Cavanaughs, the same way I should have realized, somehow, that Drue's mother's family had founded the school.

Drue picked up one of my clementines without asking permission. Darshi gave me a look from the side of her eyes: *You see?* I watched as Drue removed the peel in a single, unbroken curl, before turning to Ainsley and saying, "So, did you end up going to the thing?" Ainsley giggled. Avery twirled a piece of her hair, folding it over so she could examine it for split ends. The three of them launched into a discussion of a Labor Day party at someone's house, laughing and picking at their salads, ignoring me and everyone else at the table.

While Drue and her friends chattered and giggled and moved their food around, I answered Darshi's questions about my previous school and doggedly ate my way through everything my dad had packed, without tasting any of it. At the bottom of my lunch bag was a note. I turned away, meaning to slip the note into my pocket, but somehow Drue, who'd been talking to Avery, was suddenly looking at me again.

"What's that?"

"Nothing," I said, and crumpled the note, which read *Mom and I are proud of you and love you very much*, into my hand until it was a tiny, hard ball. I pushed it into the very bottom of my pocket as the bell rang. Drue, Avery, and Ainsley rose in unison, lifted their trays, and marched toward the trash cans. I trailed behind them to toss my own trash and walked to my next class alone.

On my way to phys ed, my last class of the day, Darshi Shah grabbed me. "I need to tell you something."

"What?"

Darshi pulled me into an empty classroom. A Spanish classroom, I guessed, judging from the posters of Seville and Barcelona on the walls and the conjugation of the verb that meant "to go" on the Smart Board. With a toss of her curls, Darshi said, "Drue Cavanaugh is bad news."

"What do you mean?"

"She uses people. She'll make you think that you're her friend, but you're not." Darshi pulled off her glasses, then put them on again. "She did it to Vera Babson in fourth grade, and she did it to Vandana Goyal in fifth grade, and then she did it to me."

I looked Darshi over, her glasses and braces, her name-brand-less sneakers and her wild tumble of hair. I pictured Drue and her friends, their effortless updos, their beautiful clothes. I remembered something my father had told me over the summer, when we'd been talking about my new school. *The friends you make at Lathrop will be your friends for the rest of your life.* "Okay," I said. "Thank you for telling me."

"You think I'm lying." Darshi's voice was resigned, her expression forlorn.

"No!" I said, trying to sound like I meant it.

"Just watch out," she said as the late bell trilled. At my old school, the class changes had been signaled by harsh buzzers that gave the school the feeling of a prison. Lathrop had actual bells.

"Okay," I said, in a loud, hearty voice. "Okay, well, thanks again." I hurried away from her down the hall, toward the sounds of a coach's whistle and sneakers squeaking on hardwood floors . . . and there was Drue, in her Lathrop School T-shirt and blue and white cotton shorts, waiting for me at the entrance to the girls' locker room, which had floors tiled in the school colors of blue and white, and skylights, and wooden lockers, and shower stalls with curtains.

"Hey!" she cheered, and did a bouncy little dance. Her legs, I saw, were smooth and tan, unmarred by a single scab or scar or swath of unshaved hair. My own legs had pink, squiggly stretch marks around the knees and on my upper thighs, and I knew, without looking, that there was at least one patch of leg hair I'd missed in the shower that morning. "Will you be my partner? Please? I'm terrible at volleyball." She gave me a dazzling smile, and I found that I was helpless not to smile back.

"Ladies!" yelled Ms. Abbott, as I scrambled into my gym clothes. "On the court now, please!"

Drue grabbed my hand and led me out to the gym.

"Daphne's with me," she announced, and pulled me against her, into the zone of her protection and approval and everything that it conveyed.

Chapter Five

At seven o'clock, after both Dr. Snitzers had come home and the kids were washing up for dinner, I took the subway to the apartment that Darshi and I shared on the edge of Morningside Heights, not far from where I'd grown up. Darshi and I had kept in touch all through college and especially after the bar fight, so after I'd been back home for two years, and Darshini had returned to go to graduate school, we'd agreed to find a place to share. My mother's starving-artist grapevine meant that we'd known about the listing a day before the rest of the world, and we'd scooped up a decently sized two-bedroom in a not-very-fashionable neighborhood. The apartment, a third-floor walk-up, had tiny, oddly shaped bedrooms, but also a good-size kitchen and a wood-burning fireplace, which I liked, and was quiet, which Darshi appreciated, and over the past few years, we'd made it our own.

I looped the garment bag over my arm and started the climb. It was Tuesday, one of the weeknights that Darshi didn't have class or office hours. Normally, I would be looking forward to our weekly ritual of takeout and bad reality TV, but that night, all I felt was dread. For more than a week, I'd been keeping my secret.

Tonight I was going to tell Darshi that Drue Cavanaugh was back in my life—and, by extension, her life, too.

As soon as I was through the door, my dog Bingo was scampering around my knees, her stocky body whirling in circles of delight: *You're back! You're back! You're back!*

I'd acquired Bingo a few days after the bar-fight video. I'd been plodding along Broadway, going nowhere in particular, mostly because moving through the real world reminded me that the online one was mostly an illusion—or at least not as real as it felt. Most of the people currently discussing my looks and my body were strangers, I would tell myself as I walked. Some of them weren't even people at all.

My father was at work—Lathrop's spring break hadn't lined up with mine. My mother was home for most of the day, teaching art classes in the afternoon and at night. I'd told her about the video by then, although not about Drue's role in the whole affair, and she'd been fussing over me like I was an invalid, giving me teary, pitying looks, asking if I wanted tea or some chicken broth, or offering to let me use the gift certificate I'd bought her for Mother's Day to get a massage. ("Do you think having a stranger touch me is going to help?" I'd almost snapped.)

It was better to be out of the house. So I'd gone for long, rambling walks, sometimes spending an hour or two in a bookstore or a museum before returning home. That afternoon, I'd been on my way home when I had walked past a pet store on Broadway and noticed the sign in its window: *Take Home a Friend.*

I considered the sign. I'd lost a friend, that night at the bar. Clearly, I could use a new one. Our building permitted pets, although we'd never had one. Mrs. Adelson at the end of the hall had owned a succession of Highland terriers, while the Johnsons on the fifth floor had a small, high-strung Chihuahua.

The dog in the window had the stumpy body with the broad chest and corkscrew tail of a pug or a French bulldog, but instead of being flat and wrinkly, her face had a short snout, and ears that stood straight up in the air and swiveled at my approach. Her coat was brindle, russet brown with dark-brown bands, and her eyes were big and brown. Per her sign, she had just been spayed, and she wore a red knitted sweater and a plastic cone around her neck to keep her from licking her stitches. As I peered through the window, she was halfheartedly gnawing a cloth toy that she clutched between her front paws. The poster in her window identified her as "pug/terrier/?" and read "Hello, my name is BINGO. I was a stray in Georgia and was found wandering the streets. I'm a sweet, shy girl who has come up north looking for a furever home. I am a little anxious, but I'll be a loyal friend once I get to know you! Please come in and say hello!"

When I opened the clear plastic door to her cage, Bingo stood, gave my fingers a grave sniff, and allowed me to pet her. When I stopped, she nudged at my hand with her snout: *Did I say you could stop?* When I began to scratch behind her ears, she sighed, wriggling with pleasure. Her dark eyes were sad—*I've seen some things*, they seemed to say—but she seemed happy enough in my company. And the article I'd read that morning had said that one of the fastest ways to get over pain was to volunteer, to donate money or time, to do a good deed, or to help someone who needed helping. Maybe I couldn't help someone at the moment, but maybe something would do.

Thirty minutes and one large check later, I had a pet bed, pet vitamins, chew toys, poop bags, eight pounds of nutritious organic kibble in my backpack, and Bingo, on a leash, trotting politely beside me. She cringed at loud noises and large men, and, when a trash truck came rumbling toward us, she planted herself against my ankles and refused to move, so I was forced to scoop her up and carry her the length of the block, tucked underneath my arm like a football. "Don't get used to this," I told her, setting her down once the trash truck was gone. At 101st Street, I told her we were almost home. "So take care of business here." Bingo seemed to have heard me, dropping into an obliging crouch, then vigorously kicking dirt over her leavings. I cleaned up the mess and brought her upstairs.

"You got a dog?" said my mother. After one look at my face, she bent down to fuss over Bingo. "Hello there, cutie!" she said. Bingo toured the apartment, gravely sniffing at the rug and the legs of the furniture, peering underneath the couch. She allowed my mother to scratch behind her ears, then she hopped onto the couch, turned three times in a circle, and fell asleep with a contented sigh.

It worked out well. Back at school, when my classmates asked "How was your break?" I could answer "I got a dog" instead of saying "I was in a viral video because some guy called me fat and I stomped on his foot." Bingo proved to be an excellent companion, mellow and pleasant, easygoing, and extremely photogenic. My parents doted on her as if she were a grandchild. My mother knitted and crocheted her sweaters; my father used his air fryer to make her dehydrated meat snacks.

"I just walked her," Darshi called from the living room as Bingo raced from one end of the apartment to the other, then back again. Workout completed, she stood at my feet, panting, tongue lolling as she gave me her best beseeching look. I rummaged in the box of Alpine Yum-Yums as Bingo's tail revolved frantically and her eyes seemed to sparkle in anticipatory delight.

"What do you think? Thai or Burmese?" Darshi asked. "Or are we going to keep scaling Mount Mahima?"

The month before, Darshi's older brother Charag had gotten married in a three-day-long, six-event celebration that had culminated in a hotel ballroom in New Jersey. The party had featured hours of dancing—first Garba and then, after midnight, the DJ had started playing Beyoncé and Demi Lovato. The lavish vegetarian buffet had been replenished all night long. At the end of the night, Darshi's mother had stood by the door, piling each departing guest's arms with food, neatly packed and labeled by the caterers. For weeks after the wedding, we'd gorged on dhokla and shrikhand and three different kinds of dal, and we'd still barely made a dent in the stash that Darshi had started to call Mount Mahima, in honor of her brother's bride.

We decided to heat up some of the khadi and order spring rolls and peanut pancakes.

I tossed Bingo the treat and went to my bedroom, clipping my camera into the tripod that I'd affixed to the doorframe. I fired off six shots of myself holding the garment bag, chose the best one, cropped it, threw on my favorite filter, and added the caption that I'd typed up on the trip home: *Wondering what's in the bag? I can't tell you lovelies what's in store yet, but it's going to be (pun intended) HUGE. Big things are happening, and I'm so grateful to each and every one of you for following along on this journey. I know you've heard it before, but I never thought I'd be in this place, where I'd be posting pictures of myself for the whole world to see. I thought my body was unacceptable, and that I had to hide. That's what the world tells us, right? But now, maybe, if enough of us stand up and show ourselves, just as we are, if we post about our thriving, busy, messy, beautiful lives, our daughters won't have to swallow the same lies.*

I added the appropriate hashtags—#showus and #plussizebeauty and #celebratemysize, #plussizestyle and #effyourbeautystandards and—my favorite—#mybodyisnotanapology. I tagged the brands that had made the foundation on my face, the liner on my eyelids, and the berry stain on my lips, as well as my tunic, my leggings, and my shoes, and tried not to feel guilty, knowing that I was leaning into the "thriving" and "beautiful" more than the "messy" and "busy." Tomorrow, I promised myself. Tomorrow I'd post something a little more honest—a workout picture with my makeup-less face, or an unfiltered shot of my legs in yoga pants. I grabbed a picture of Bingo jumping for another Yum-Yum and posted it on her Instagram page, and padded into the living room that Darshi and I had furnished with Craigslist finds and parental cast-offs—an old couch that my parents were getting rid of; a glass coffee table from the Shahs. Together, my mother and I had papered one of the living room walls with squares of scrapbooking paper, putting together a pattern of glittery golds and pale greens, and I'd decoupaged inexpensive trays from Ikea with scraps of old wallpaper and wrapping paper. The wooden *jharoka* that Darshi's grandmother had given to her as a housewarming gift had pride of place on the south-facing wall—"A wedding gift! From Rajasthan!" Darshi's Nani ma said, nodding proudly as Darshi's brother and father had wrestled the heavy carved piece into place. In the kitchen, the pressure cooker Darshi's mother had bought for us sat next to the toaster oven. "You'll make *idli*," Dr. Shah had said, nodding as if this was a given, and Darshi had nodded back, smiling, waiting for her mother to turn around before mouthing the words "I won't." My craft table stood against the far living room wall, piled with plywood boxes in various stage of completion, the ones I called memory boxes. I customized them with photographs, old postcards, wallpaper or wrapping paper or pictures from vintage children's books, and sent them to customers on Etsy, who would pay up to a hundred dollars for a unique and personal gift.

"How's the littlest Snitzer?" Darshi asked as I sat down on the couch with Bingo beside me. Darshi's braces had come off in eighth grade, and she'd swapped her glasses for contacts the following year. She still had her curls, but now they were an orderly tumble, glossed with argan oil and falling halfway down her back. She was still petite, but her narrow hips were now curvy and her chest was no longer flat. In college, Darshi had come out as bisexual, but only to her closest friends and her older brother. For the past six months, she'd been dating a woman named Carmen, whom she'd met at a dance sponsored by Columbia's gay-straight alliance, but she hadn't yet told her parents about Carmen, or about her sexual identity. Her plan was to finish her dissertation first. "That way, it'll balance," she'd said, using her hands to mime a scale. "Girlfriend on one side, doctor on the other."

I'd told her that I thought her parents would be fine, that they loved her and would be happy that she'd found someone with whom she could build a life. Darshi had just snorted. "It's cute that you think that," she'd said.

In the living room, I gave Bingo's ears a scratch. "Ian's fine. And guess what? I got the job with Leef!"

"Congratulations!" she said. "Now show me the clothes!"

I went back to my bedroom and put on the Jane dress, then the Pamela pants, then the Kesha blouse with the Nidia blazer, and, finally, the swimsuit, the Darcy. I twirled and posed as Darshi clapped and cheered, and took a few pictures for use once the campaign began. Most of the influencers I knew had partners—husbands or guys who referred to themselves, unironically, as Instagram boyfriends, and who'd obligingly interrupt date night or a picnic in the park to snap shots of six different outfits. I had my tripod, my mom, and Darshi.

Once I'd rehung everything and zipped it all back into the garment bag, I put on my favorite pajamas, wine-colored silk in a paisley pattern. I'd found them in a secondhand store on the Upper East Side and imagined they'd once belonged to some elderly male Wall Street potentate, who'd worn them to sip whiskey and puff a cigar, after a long day of exploiting the proletariat. In the living room, Darshi, in blue sweatpants and a Lathrop School sweatshirt, poured us both glasses of wine. "To Daphne. May this be the first of many wonderful things." We drank, and when the food arrived, we filled our plates, and we watched *All the Single Ladies*. Or, rather, Darshi watched, hooting and scoffing, and I kept my eyes on the screen, half of my attention on the machinations of the women as they attempted to win the favor of a handsome bachelor named Kyle; the other half on how I was going to tell Darshi my news.

By the third week of sixth grade, Darshi and I had settled into a comfortable friendship. Most days, I sat with her and her friends at lunch, and we'd spend time together outside of school, browsing for clothes at the Housing Works thrift shop or hanging out in the Barnes & Noble on Eighty-Sixth Street. We both liked to read, although I loved mysteries and romance, and Darshi adored horror and true crime. Darshi lived with her parents and two brothers in a two-story, four-bedroom brick house in the Whitestone neighborhood of Queens that had a yard and a two-car garage. I'd spent the night there, and she'd slept over my house, too. Darshi and I got along, but Darshi knew that she would always be Drue Cavanaugh's runner-up, that once or twice a week Drue would call out "Daphne! Come sit with me!" and I would go without a backward glance. I knew that Drue wasn't a good friend and that I should have let go of the idea of being part of Drue's crowd, but I couldn't make myself do it.

All through sixth grade and into middle school and beyond, I was Darshi's friend, but I was Drue's creature. I became a regular guest at the Cavanaughs' apartment on the Upper East Side, which had floor-to-ceiling windows that gave panoramic views of the city, the Hudson River, and Central Park. I met Abigay, the Cavanaughs' cook, who had freckled cheeks and a gap between her front teeth that you could see when she spoke or when she smiled, and could make any dish you could think of. "What's your pleasure, my ladies?" she would ask, in her singsong Jamaican accent, when Drue and I came into the kitchen (Drue would dump her bags by the door, a move that would have gotten me a lecture had I attempted it at my house). The first time I'd heard that request, I'd asked for apples and peanut butter. Drue had taken her hair out of its bun, then gathered it up again. "How about *gougères*?" she'd asked. Abigay had pursed her full lips and given a nod. Soon, the house smelled of buttery, cheesy baking dough. "What are *gougères*?" I'd asked Drue, and she'd shrugged and said, "I don't know. I just read about them in a book."

In return for this largesse, for the invitations and the snacks and the chance to sit with Drue at lunch, I would pass messages to Drue's crushes and break up with them when she was through; I kept watch when Drue shoplifted at Saks and Barneys, and I wrote English papers after Drue would narrate for me a general idea about what she wanted to say, usually lying sprawled on her bed, staring up at her ceiling. And every time, after a few days' worth of attention, Drue would ignore me, looking right through me, as if I had ceased to exist.

I hadn't yet heard the word "gaslighting," but I knew that Drue made me feel like I was crazy, like I couldn't trust my own ears or eyes. I also knew that, by every available metric, I belonged with Darshi, and Frankie Fogelson, David Johnson, and Joon Woo Pak. The smart kids, the dreamy, artsy ones, the misfits, the geeks. They were generous, loyal, and kind. But none of them was as alluring, as interesting, or as much fun as Drue. She made me angry and resentful, and she made me doubt myself and even, sometimes, hate myself, but she also made every day that I was with her an adventure. For every time that Drue cold-shouldered me, ignoring me in class or in the lunchroom, there'd be a day when she'd grab me as I walked into homeroom, voice urgent as she whispered the details of her night or her weekend into my ear, asking for help, for advice, needing to know how she should deal with the two boys who both liked her, needing me to read over her history homework. Needing me.

One Saturday night she surprised me. "Hey, can I do one of these eating adventure things with you and your dad?"

I squirmed. I'd felt silly, telling Drue about our adventures:

how my father and I would read the papers and the food blogs and the magazines, looking for something we'd never tried. Our roamings had taken us to all five boroughs, where we had sampled tamales, sticky rice in lotus leaves, Burmese tofu, Filipino fried chicken, Russian *draniki*, Polish pierogis, Georgian *khinkali*, and tonton dumplings filled with chopped and seasoned pigs' feet. I'd eaten roast goat, chicken feet, suckling pig, soup dumplings and dan dan noodles, fermented duck eggs, alligator and grilled kangaroo, durian, purple yams and jackfruit.

The rule was, we'd try a new place every Sunday. My father would choose the restaurant. It was my job to plan our transportation, to read up on the country or region we'd be sampling, and to locate a bookstore or library or coffee shop near the restaurant, where we could sit and read after our meal, and maybe have dessert.

Darshi had joined us a few times, and had even steered us toward her family's favorite spots in Jackson Heights, but I'd felt silly telling Drue about our Sundays, knowing how childish it probably sounded—an afternoon with Daddy!—to a girl who'd smoked pot in eighth grade and lost her virginity in ninth. But Drue had listened, her expression thoughtful and sincere. She'd asked me questions—*What's the weirdest thing you've ever eaten? What did you like the best? And it's just you and your father, all day long?*

I'd told her that she was welcome to join us, with no hope that she ever would. But that chilly, sunny October morning, she buzzed our door bright and early. Her face was shining between her pink cashmere scarf and her pink pom-pom hat. "So what's the plan?"

Instead of trying a new place, my dad and I had agreed to break our own rules and take Drue to an old favorite, a place with an exotic cuisine that wasn't so challenging or unfamiliar that she'd leave hungry. We took the E train out to Jackson Heights and walked along streets filled with signs in Spanish and Punjabi, advertising DVDs and phone cards, eyebrow threading and spirit baths, until we reached the Himalayan Yak on Roosevelt Avenue. The walls were draped with prayer flags and carved wooden panels, and every table was full. I knew that Drue wasn't used to waiting, or to restaurants that didn't take reservations, but she was patient and quiet, standing beside me until we were seated, and a waitress with a glossy dark ponytail came to fill our water glasses. My dad gave her a brief bow and a murmured "Namaste."

"He does that everywhere," I whispered to Drue, feeling a combination of embarrassment and pride. I thought that she would think it was corny, how my father tried to learn how to give a polite greeting in the language of whatever nation or region had supplied the day's cuisine. "It's respectful," he'd told me.

"My father says everyone in America should speak English," Drue said, a little sheepishly. Of all the many times I'd heard Drue invoke her father, this was the first where she'd ever sounded anything but proud.

"He's certainly not the only one who feels that way," my father said mildly. "Personally, I think it's respectful." I saw Drue's eyes get wide as she noticed the entry for goat bhutan, which was a dish of stir-fried goat intestines, liver, heart, and kidneys, served with green chilies, onions, tomatoes, and herbs.

My dad ordered pork dumplings called momo, deep-fried red snapper, sautéed bok choy, yak sausage, goat thali, garlic naan, and for dessert, a kind of thick rice pudding called kheer. Drue looked around, wide-eyed, first at the diners, then at the food. I was worried she wouldn't eat anything—by then, I'd heard her and Ainsley and Avery whispering and giggling about the lentils Darshi sometimes brought for lunch, saying that Indian food all looked like baby poop, but Drue surprised me, gamely tasting everything, even the yak, while my father regaled us with stories of students from years gone by—the girl who'd printed a final paper right from the web and hadn't even bothered to erase the Internet Professor logo, the boy who believed that one should dress in inverse proportion to how much one had studied, and arrived for his final in a rented tuxedo and tails.

After we'd stuffed ourselves, we packed up the leftovers and took the G train to Brooklyn. I knew, but maybe Drue didn't, that the G was the only train that didn't go to Manhattan. That afternoon, it was filled with mostly nonwhite passengers, with a smattering of hipsters and the occasional elderly Polish woman. I noticed her staring, but if she had thoughts, she didn't share them with me.

We went to Sahadi's, my father's favorite Middle Eastern shop on Atlantic Avenue. Drue and I wandered along the rows of knee-high glass jars containing every variety of nuts—pistachios and peanuts and almonds and cashews, roasted and salted or unsalted, shelled or unshelled. At the counter, the customers took numbers, and a preternaturally calm Middle Eastern man with a neat mustache took their orders, while a pair of women scooped hummus and baba ghanoush and kibbe balls into plastic containers. Drue even ordered a half pound of pumpkin seeds and murmured her thanks when my father said, "My treat." After we'd paid, we carried out bags to a restaurant called Tripoli, where we sat, drinking tea and eating slices of sticky, honey-drenched baklava. My father did the Sunday crossword puzzle, I read an Agatha Christie mystery, and Drue, who'd come prepared, paged through the current issue of *Vogue*. When it was time to go, Drue politely declined another subway trip, using her cell phone to call her father's car service instead.

"Want to take anything home?" I asked, swinging the bags of Tibetan leftovers at her.

She gave me a rueful smile. "I can't even imagine what my mom would do if she found something deep-fried in our refrigerator. My parents . . ." She looked like she was going to say more, but just then a Town Car came around the corner and pulled up at the curb.

Drue opened the door, then surprised me by hugging me hard. "This was the best day of my life," she said. Before I could respond, or confirm that she was kidding, she closed the door, and the car drove off, leaving me holding bags of Tibetan leftovers, feeling unsettled and sad.

At home, my father unpacked in the kitchen, rearranging the leftover Swedish meatballs and the braised short ribs he'd made during the week to make room for the dips and the kibbe balls.

"I'm glad Drue got to come." My father's head was buried in the refrigerator. I couldn't see his expression as he said, "I think she was hungry."

As if, I thought. "They have a chef who makes them anything they want."

"So you've mentioned." My father closed the refrigerator, wiped his hands on a dish towel, and began straightening the sections of the *New York Times* on the kitchen table. I went to my bedroom to work on the watercolor I'd been painting for my mother's birthday and to think about my friend and how there were things you could be hungry for besides food.

I knew that on Monday there was every chance she would ignore me. It wouldn't matter. I would still want to be her friend, because she was everything I wanted to be. She was beautiful, and funny, and glamorous; a long, unfurled ribbon of cool, where I was a sweaty pretzeled knot of striving. I wanted her to be my friend, I wanted her to tell me her secrets; I wanted to be pretty by association, if not in real life. I wanted her intermittent kindness, and as much of her company as she'd give me. I wanted to be just like her, and, if I couldn't, I at least wanted to be by her side. Whatever she needed from me, I would give her. Whatever she needed done, I would do.

• • •

When our show was over, Darshi packed up the leftovers. I washed the dishes and took Bingo out for her last walk of the night, opening Instagram and tapping *like like like like* on dozens of comments while she peed. The *how can I be brave like you* question was still waiting, and I still wasn't any closer to an answer. *It's easier for white women*, I thought, trudging back upstairs, thinking that, no matter what people believed my body told them, at least it wasn't compounded by preconceptions about what the color of my skin might suggest.

I found Darshi in the kitchen, a mug of chai in her hands. She'd taken out her contacts and put on her glasses, big, round-framed ones that I thought were relics from middle school. The longer I procrastinated, the harder it would be to tell the truth, and the more grounds Darshi would have to accuse me of trying to hide it from her. And so I said, "Hey, so listen."

Darshi tilted her head. I breathed deeply and, on a single exhalation, said, "Drue Cavanaugh came to the Snitzers' place last week. She apologized to me. She's getting married in June, and she asked me to be one of her bridesmaids. And I told her that I'd do it."

For a long moment, Darshi just stared. "I can't believe you," she finally said.

My heart sank. Clearly, this wasn't going to be easy. "She's desperate," I said.

"I can imagine."

"She doesn't have any friends."

Darshi snorted. "You're telling me there aren't college versions of us? Some other girls she used up and threw away?"

I said, "There probably are. Although Drue says she's been in therapy."

That earned another snort, with a side of eye roll.

"She's really desperate. She offered to pay me."

Darshi set down her mug and crossed her arms over her chest. "Now I actually am surprised."

"What do you mean?"

"I mean, the Cavanaugh Corporation's in trouble." She stalked, stiff-legged, to her shoulder bag, yanked out her phone, and pulled up an article from Bloomberg News. *Cavanaugh Corp Looks to Offload Troubled Fifth Avenue Flagship*. I skimmed the story, reading out loud.

"The Cavanaugh Corporation purchased the skyscraper at the corner of Fifty-Third Street and Fifth Avenue two years ago, the crown jewel of its real-estate portfolio . . . blah blah blah . . . two major tenants have departed, one more on its way out . . . What's an LTV ratio?"

"Loan to value," Darshi said crisply. "You want your rents covering as large a percentage of the building's price as possible. Theirs are not."

"And distressed debt? That doesn't sound good."

"It's not. Basically, the company paid way too much money for the property, and now they can't sell it or rent it." She gave me a pointed look. "I've heard banks won't lend to them any longer. If Drue's offering to compensate her bridesmaids, I hope she got a good rate."

I inhaled, curling my toes into the soles of my shoes, mustering the arguments I'd rehearsed in my head. "Do you believe that people can change?"

"People? Yes. Drue? No. Drue Lathrop Cavanaugh isn't 'people.' She's always been exactly what she was. Exactly what she is." Darshi went to the door to pick up her laptop and her bag, trailing the scent of coconut conditioner behind her. Her sweatpants swished as she walked. I followed after her, and Bingo trailed after me.

"You don't even want to give her a chance? You don't want to be the bigger person?" The stiff line of Darshi's shoulders, plus her silence, gave me her answer. "Look, I'm not denying that she's been awful. But if you'd seen her . . ."

Darshi turned, arm extended, one small hand held out, palm flat; a traffic cop insisting on *stop*. "I know Drue," she said. "I've known her longer than you have. She was my friend first." Her voice was quiet. She sounded calm and eminently reasonable as she sat down on the couch, tugging the cuffs of her sweatshirt down over her wrists. "I know her, and I know you. You are susceptible to Drue Cavanaugh. She's your Kryptonite." Darshi's voice was dangerously soft. "And you might be hashtag-strong-woman on the Internet. Even in real life, sometimes. But mark my words. She's going to hurt you. And I'm done with being her first runner-up. If she fucks you over again, I won't hang around to pick up the pieces."

That was when I knew how seriously she was taking this. I could curse casually, could let out a loud "Motherfucker" if my hot glue gun burned my fingers or a hearty "Goddamnit" when I found my freshly dry-cleaned cashmere wrap in Bingo's dog bed. Not Darshi.

"She won't." I was promising myself as much as Darshi. "I won't let her."

Darshi took off her glasses, breathed on one lens, and began rubbing it clean with her sleeve.

"I mean, maybe Drue hasn't changed, but I have. I'm not the same as I was in high school. Right?"

Darshi exhaled onto the other lens.

"Right?" I asked again. Before she could answer, or say that I was wrong, I began to make the case. "I'm more confident. I'm more secure. I'm more comfortable in my own skin. And that's not all just faked for Instagram." *Just considerably amplified.* "I know who I am, and I know what I want. I'm not going to be—"

"Ensorcelled?" Darshi said without looking up. "Beguiled?"

"Used," I said.

Darshi gave me a long, level look before putting her glasses on, hooking each earpiece precisely over its corresponding ear. I wondered what she was worried about: if it was Drue hurting me again, or if it was Drue taking me away from her.

"Hey," I said, keeping my own voice gentle. "Look. I didn't listen to you the first time you tried to warn me. I'm listening to you now."

Darshi didn't respond.

"Just because I'm doing this, it doesn't mean I'm going to forget what she did. And, really, if I can forgive her, that's kind of a gift I'm giving to myself, right? Isn't that what people say?"

Darshi frowned. "Which people are these?"

I shrugged, hearing Drue's voice in my head. *I don't know? My therapist? Oprah?* "Just people. And look," I said, "there are worse things than spending a weekend around a bunch of hot groomsmen. You realize that of all the sex I've had, most of it was with Wan Ron?"

Darshi smiled a little at my ex-boyfriend's name, the way I hoped she would, before her face closed up. She tugged at her sleeves again and picked up her mug. Without looking at me, she said, "You do whatever you want. On your head be it."

"On my head be it," I repeated. Darshi got to her feet, walked to her bedroom, and closed the door almost noiselessly behind her. Bingo, who'd seated herself at my feet, looked up hopefully, perhaps sensing that the conversation had come to its end and that, to signal its conclusion, I might be willing to part with a rawhide Busy Stick, or an Alpine Yum-Yum. Her stump of a tail made a shushing noise on the floor as it wagged.

"Come on," I said. I was reaching for the treat box when Darshi's door swung open.

"And keep her away from me," she said, speaking each word distinctly, her voice hard. "You can do whatever you want. But I can't make any guarantees for my own behavior if I ever have to see Drue Cavanaugh's face again."

"That's fine," I said. "You won't. I promise."

For a moment, she stayed silent. "Can I ask you something?" she finally said.

"Sure."

She went quiet again, silent for so long I wasn't sure she was going to ask anything. "Was it worth it?" she finally said.

Was it worth it? In the years we'd lived together, Darshi had asked very little about Drue, and I hadn't offered any information, figuring that she didn't want to know. Obviously, I'd been wrong. A part of her did want to know the details, to hear what I'd had that she'd missed. The obvious answer would have been a hearty "No, it wasn't worth it," a firm headshake, an apologetic smile, a loud and inclusive lament about how badly Drue had treated me and how foolish and shallow I'd been and how Darshi was my true best friend.

But that wouldn't have been honest. And if Darshi wanted to know the truth, I had to give it to her.

"Not always," I said. "Not even most of the time. Not when she was ignoring me, or when I knew she was making me do her dirty work. Or, you know, humiliating me online." I winced, remembering how I'd worn an unfortunate sweater, fluffy and white, and how Drue had posted a picture of me next to a picture of a llama. *What are you so mad about?* she'd asked when I'd called her up and demanded she take it down. *It's funny! Can't you take a joke?*

"But sometimes . . ." I remembered the day senior year that Drue had decreed Ferris Bueller Memorial Day. We'd watched the movie the night before, and when it was over, Drue had looked at me, smiling the smile that promised adventure and trouble. "We are going to do that," she'd said.

"Do what? Cut school?"

"Cut school and do whatever we want."

"I'm not getting on a parade float." *No need*, my poisoned mind whispered. *You're practically the size of one already.*

"Maybe we can just go to a parade. If I can find one." Drue was already working her phone.

"So which one of us is Sloane?" Drue was between boyfriends, which meant that there were two or three boys, at Lathrop and elsewhere, who were in contention for the job. I, of course, had never even been kissed. Wan Ron was still years away.

"No Sloane," said Drue. She rested her phone on her chest and smiled at me. "No boys. Just the two of us."

I'd called my parents to ask permission to spend the night at Drue's, and in the morning, after Drue had headed off to Lathrop, I called them again to say that I'd caught a cold and that I was going to stay in the guest room and drink Abigay's chicken soup.

"Feel better," said my mom. I felt a pinch of guilt for deceiving her, overshadowed by my excitement at the prospect of an adventure with my friend.

An hour later, I used the Cavanaugh landline to call the front office, pretending to be Mrs. Cavanaugh, whose Upper East Side lockjaw Drue and I had both long since mastered.

"Drue's great-aunt Eleanor has passed," I informed the receptionist. "Our driver will collect Drue at ten o'clock in front of the school."

Instead of questions, I'd gotten a gulped "Yes, ma'am." I was sure that the entire staff knew about Drue's family's history with, and generosity to, the Lathrop School. Luckily, none of them seemed to know anything about the health of her great-aunts. At nine-forty-five, I'd hopped in a car—I'd called for an SUV in case anyone was watching—and collected Drue on the sidewalk. "Why couldn't we both have just pretended to be sick?" I asked.

"Oh, we could have," she said, "but that wouldn't have been in the spirit of the movie."

We went to the Guggenheim and had lunch at the fancy restaurant, where we'd planned on peeking at the reservation book and impersonating another guest, as Ferris had done, but it turned out that the reservation book was an iPad, impossible to see. Drue's parents had a Jacuzzi-style tub big enough to host a bridge foursome, but instead of going back to her place, Drue had decreed we'd end our day at Elizabeth Arden, where I'd had my first massage and my first facial. We'd put on robes and spent an hour in the Relaxation Room, gossiping and laughing, sipping cups of peppermint tea while our feet soaked in bowls of warm, rose-petal-dotted water. Drue told me the story of her great-aunt Letitia, whose beloved toy poodle had expired during a visit to the Cavanaughs' home over Christmas. "Aunt Letitia was completely beside herself. We told her we'd take care of it, but none of the vets in the city were answering their phones. My dad wanted to wrap Jasper up in a trash bag and throw him down the trash chute, but my mother wouldn't let him."

"So what did you do?"

"Trip was home from college, so we borrowed his cooler, and we filled it with ice, so that Jasper wouldn't, you know, start to decompose." Her nose had wrinkled cutely at the thought. "We were just going to keep him there until the vets opened up. Which would have been fine, except my stupid brother's buddies came to take Trip to some party, and they didn't notice that the cooler was full of dead toy poodle and not beer. They were halfway to the Hamptons before they figured it out."

I smiled, remembering that story. I was still smiling when I looked into Darshi's suspicious face. "Sometimes it was amazing."

Darshi's eyes seemed to soften. "Yes," she said quietly. "I always thought it would be."

Chapter Six

"Daphne!"

I plastered a smile on my face and turned in the direction of the broad-shouldered fellow with the surfer's tan and the petite brunette by his side. Drue and Stuart's engagement party had started twenty minutes previously. The guest of honor had collected me at the Snitzers' at the end of my workday, and so far, the two of us hadn't made it more than five feet past the front door. I gave my hands a quick wipe on my skirt as the couple came barreling toward me. I was wearing my Jane dress and a pair of black suede sandals that had added inches to my height and were already making my feet ache. Drue, in a dress of glittering silver paillettes that made her look like a moonbeam with limbs and a face, was behind me, delivering a stream of whispered, champagne-scented commentary into my ear.

"Okay, so that's my brother, the practice pancake, and his wife, Caitlin, who's too good for him." Drue stopped talking the instant her brother made it into earshot and hugged her sister-in-law. I vaguely remembered meeting Trip, whom I'd seen just in passing at the Cavanaughs' apartment, but he seemed to remember me.

"Great to see you," he said, hugging me, as his wife said, "I can't wait to get out to the Cape!"

"I've never been, but I'm excited to see it," I said. It had been less than a month since Drue's reappearance, but she hadn't wasted any time reintegrating me into her life, featuring me on her social media, or pressing me into maid-of-honor duties. So far, there'd been a bridal brunch, a dinner at Indochine with the groom and his parents, and three separate celebratory cocktail parties, culminating with this one, which Drue and Stuart were hosting in their brand-new penthouse apartment in the neighborhood that had once been Spanish Harlem and had just started to be called Carnegie Hill.

I'd barely had time to take a breath and smooth my dress before a tiny elderly man with a bald head and teeth too white and too regular to be anything but dentures tottered toward us.

"Uncle Mel," Trip whispered, taking over Drue's duties. "He's . . . ah, Drue, how would you describe Mel?"

"A pervert," said Drue, then turned her dazzling smile at Uncle Mel, who said, "Now, who is this beautiful young lady?" before wrapping his arms around my waist and burying his face between my breasts.

Drue giggled. Trip snickered. I shot them both a dirty look, then looked down helplessly at the tanned, age-spotted dome of Mel's head.

"This is Daphne," Drue said, putting her hand on his shoulder and gently but firmly extracting him from my person. "My best friend from Lathrop and my maid of honor."

"Daphne. A pleasure," said Mel, giving my breasts another longing look and extending his hand.

When he was gone I managed a breath, and a sip of my seltzer, before the next wave of friends and relations crashed over me. I met, in short order, an aunt and an uncle and their children, two Harvard friends, and a colleague from the Cavanaugh Corporation.

"You okay?" Drue asked when they'd gone. She wore a wide gold cuff bracelet on her right wrist; pearl and diamond earrings hung from her ears. Her hair hung in a sheet of shimmering bronze and gold that fell halfway down her back, and her makeup was dramatic, with shimmery gold eye shadow and highlighter glinting at her cheek and brow.

"I'm fine," I said, smoothing my hair and looking around. Mr. Cavanaugh was at the bar, talking to some other middle-aged men in dark suits, and Mrs. Cavanaugh had drifted to the windows that looked out at the northernmost end of Central Park. All night, I had watched the two of them make their way through the apartment, artfully crisscrossing the space without ever coming near each other. "How are things between them?" I'd asked Drue in the Uber on our way home from the Indochine dinner. She'd pursed her lips, then immediately unpursed them before she could damage her lipstick, but I saw her leg bob up and down as her toe tapped on the car's floor. "I think they've just kind of decided to live separate lives and make appearances together when they have to."

Delightful, I'd thought, picturing my parents, the way my mother would pull a cold beer out of the refrigerator when she heard the elevator doors slide open, so that she could hand it to my father the instant he walked through the door; and the way my dad would settle my mom's feet in his lap when they watched the British police procedurals they both liked. I pictured them dancing together in the kitchen, swaying to old R&B, my father's arms around my mom's waist, her cheek resting on his shoulder. The two of them hadn't spent a night apart, they liked to say, since the night I was born, when my mom sent my father home from the hospital to get his last good night's sleep.

"So, do you think I'll get a chance to actually talk to the man of the hour?" I asked Drue, who stood on her tiptoes to look at the crowd. It hadn't happened so far. Even with all of the cocktail parties, the most Stuart and I had done was exchange pleasantries.

"I don't see him right now," Drue said. "Oh, but there's Corina Bailey! Let's go say hi."

"Wait, what?" Corina, as I and the viewing public well knew, was Stuart's former fiancée, the one to whom he'd proposed on TV, in a season finale that five million viewers had watched. Corina was the one he'd dumped to be with Drue. The last I'd heard, via *US Weekly*'s website, a heartbroken Corina was trying to make a go of it as a celebrity DJ in LA (of course, on *US Weekly*'s website, every newly single person was heartbroken). "You invited Stuart's ex to the party?"

"And to the wedding." At my shocked expression, Drue looked even more pleased with herself than she usually did. "We're all adults, Daphne. Stuart and Corina went through a very intense experience together. They're still friends."

"Wow." I pressed my fingertips to my temples, then spread them wide, miming an explosion. "Mind, blown. So is Corina the same as she was on TV?"

Drue made a scoffing sound. "Not even close. For one thing, I think she actually can talk like a grown-up, if she wants to. For another . . ." She paused, considering. "Well. She isn't what people think. And she's definitely not my friend. But if she shows up, it's a story. *People* magazine will probably write something. They might use a picture, too."

"Got it." I put my glass down on a table by the door, next to a Chinese bowl with a blue-and-white pattern that was probably a costly and pedigreed antique. A caterer immediately materialized to whisk the glass away. I could hear music from the jazz trio in the next room, the clink of cutlery, the slosh of ice and booze in shakers, the cries of "Gordy! Great to see you, man!" and "Marcus! How long has it been!" I heard backs being slapped and lips forming air kisses; I could smell cremini arancini and stuffed figs wrapped in bacon and the butternut squash soup being served in shot glasses, with a dollop of crème fraîche and a sprinkling of chives. The smells should have been delicious, but I was so nervous that they made my stomach turn.

Just then, a pair of male hands covered Drue's eyes. She squealed "Stuart!" and turned around. There was Stuart Lowe, even more handsome (if slightly shorter) in person than he was on TV. Drue gave him a long kiss, to cheers, and the clinking of glasses and whoops, and a few guys yelling "Get a room!" When he let her go, he gave me a much more perfunctory hug and a dazzling smile. "Daphne. Great to see you again."

Stuart Lowe wore a dark-gray suit with a subtle chalk stripe, a white shirt, and a blue and orange tie. His cuffs were monogrammed, his cuff links were gold, and his teeth were the same color as the teeth of every reality TV show contestant I'd ever seen, a shade I'd come to think of as Television White. He had one arm draped over Drue's shoulder, and she was gazing up at him with a look of melting adoration that struck me as showy, a suspicion that was strengthened when she pulled out her phone, stretched out her arm, and snapped a selfie of the two of them.

Stuart pretend-wrestled the phone away from her and turned toward me, smiling.

"So Drue's been telling me about your artwork."

"Oh," I said, surreptitiously wiping my sweaty hands on my skirt again. "That's generous. It's just crafts, really."

"Daphne's an influencer," Drue said, her voice full of pride. She put her arm around me and gave me a squeeze.

Stuart introduced me to his sister, Arden, whom I also recognized from the show, where she'd briefly appeared during the hometown visit episode. Arden had her brother's coloring, the same dark hair and dark eyes, but where he was matinee-idol handsome, she had a kind of rabbit-y look, with thin lips, big front teeth, a gummy smile, and a pointy chin. Clearly, Stuart had scooped up the best the Lowe gene pool had to offer, and Arden had yet to succumb to the injectables many New York women used to rearranged their faces.

"So how does being an influencer work?" Arden asked.

I couldn't tell if she was truly interested, or if she was just being polite, but I answered anyhow. "Well, you start off with some kind of online platform, like a YouTube channel or a blog," I began. Arden nodded along as I explained how I'd started my blog, how I'd found my sponsors, and how I'd started to make money, with companies sending me pieces of clothing, or sometimes just links to their websites so that I could pick something out, along with a code for my followers to use when they clicked through to make a purchase. "How much would you get from each sale?" Arden asked. "Not a lot," I told her. "Especially not when you factor in the time it takes to style and photograph the clothes, and write about them, and promote them, and send the brand your analytics when the campaign is done."

As I talked, the Lowe parents wandered over. Mrs. Lowe had brown shoulder-length hair and Arden's thin-lipped smile; Mr. Lowe had Stuart's compact build and a line of Frankenstein-y stitches circling his bald spot. "Hair transplant surgery," he said cheerfully, patting the bristly new growth. "The doctor promised it would all be filled in by the big day."

That, I decided, was my cue. "Excuse me," I said, and headed off to take a stroll through the place where Drue and Stu would be building their life together. The apartment was lovely, full of custom millwork and gleaming floors, decorated in tasteful shades of beige and greige and cream, with gold and navy-blue accents. I saw granite and white marble countertops, textured wallpaper and glass-paned cupboards and the framed black-and-white photographs that Drue told me she and Stuart had started to collect. The centerpiece of the dining room was a modern lighting fixture with eight frosted-glass bulbs at the ends of undulating stainless-steel tubes. It looked like an electrified octopus, and I knew that it had cost more than five thousand dollars, because Drue had told me.

As for the guests themselves, I thought, sourly, that they

looked like the results of a successful eugenics experiment, filled with members of what Darshi called the Lucky Sperm Club. The women were all slender; the men were all fit; everyone had perfect teeth and gleaming hair and beautiful, expensive clothes. A handful of the men, like Uncle Mel, looked their age, but most of the men and all of the women seemed to have hit the pause button at fifty and spent the next years with their faces getting tauter and rounder instead of sagging and wrinkled. I tugged at the hem of my dress as inferiority and shame settled over me like a familiar cloak. I forced myself to stand up straight as I edged toward the wall to people-watch.

I spotted Drue's father holding court in the living room with a glass of some amber-colored liquor in his hand. He was still dark-haired and handsome, the picture of the successful executive in a suit that had probably been made to measure, but when he excused himself from the group of people he'd been talking to and made his way to the bar, the droop of his shoulders and the way he seemed to plod across the Brazilian mahogany floors suggested weary resignation instead of father-of-the-bride joy. He looked like a man at a business function that he wasn't enjoying instead of a man celebrating his daughter's big day. More than once I saw him glance at the heavy gold watch on his wrist as he waited for his drink, or rock back and forth, from his heels to his toes and back again, as if he couldn't wait to make a break for the door. And I saw the way Drue's eyes would follow him, even when she was in a conversation with someone else; the way she seemed to be waiting for him to notice her, praise her, congratulate her, even just acknowledge her.

Lily Cavanaugh was perched on a couch on the opposite side of the room, in a gleaming teal taffeta skirt with a black jersey boat-neck top that put the ridges of her collarbones on display. While Mr. Cavanaugh seemed impatient, she just looked bored, her gaze moving from bookcase to fireplace, from antique bar cart to abstract artwork with an expression that said *I've seen all of this before.* When she caught sight of me, her eyes stopped moving. She trilled my name—"Daphne!"—in her husky voice, crossing the room to take both of my hands in hers. Her hair was pulled back in a sleek twist; her lips were so plump and shiny that they looked like two tiny glossy sausages parked on the lower half of her face. She smelled the same way I remembered from high school, like heavy, musky perfume with undertones of cigarettes, and she had the same aristocratic voice, the same sharp jawline and imperious tilt to her head. Drue told me that in college, Lily Cavanaugh had ridden horses competitively, and Drue's father, to her sorrow. "Should've stuck with horses," Drue would say.

"You look lovely," she said.

"Oh, thank you, Mrs. Cavanaugh," I said. "It's so good to see you again." I tried not to think too hard about what this terrifyingly thin, terrifyingly chic woman's real opinion of my looks might have been. "You must be so happy for Drue."

She gave me a brittle smile and said, "Well." I wasn't sure if that was the beginning of a longer reply or her answer in its entirety, but I didn't have a chance to find out, because the next minute, Drue was grabbing my arm.

"*Mére*, I'm going to steal Daphne for a minute. She needs to meet the rest of the bridesmaids!" Drue pulled me into another living room—this one with a flat-screen TV, disguised as a painting, hanging over a fireplace—and introduced me to Minerva, a petite woman with dark hair pulled severely back from her face. Minerva spoke with a faint, unplaceable accent. Her skin was blemish-free and creamy, her eyes were big and brown, subtly tilted at the corners, and her makeup was so extreme, with contoured cheekbones and thick, black brows that extended above and beyond her own eyebrows, that I thought if I ever saw her makeup-free, I wouldn't recognize her. "Minerva is the pore whisperer. Her salon was just named one of the best in the city in *New York* magazine!"

"And Drue's my very best client," said Minerva. A bridesmaid/facialist, I thought, feeling a little giddy. Because of course!

I met Natalie, Drue's assistant, a striking young woman with dark, glossy skin, full red lips, and a corona of curls that framed her face and added four inches to her height. Natalie wore gold cuffs on each wrist and gold bars through her ears. "You have got to check out Natalie's Instagram," Drue said. "She does this steampunk Afro-futuristic thing. It's amazing!" I met Cousin Pat, who was expecting, and Cousin Clair, who'd just had a baby. They reminded me of Ainsley and Avery back in high school; both pale, imperfect copies of Drue, with versions of her features and her hair. Cousin Pat looked ready to pop—"eight weeks to go," she said, with a tense smile and an expression suggesting that I wasn't the first guest to ask about her due date. Cousin Clair had the haunted, sleepless look I'd seen before on the faces of mothers with newborns. They gave Drue tired smiles and me limp handshakes.

"And come meet Corina!" Drue led me to a flaxen-haired woman in a dress made of floaty panels of beige and cream-colored lace. Corina was tiny, maybe five feet tall, with rosebud lips and wide pale-blue eyes. Some of her hair had been plaited into a narrow braid that followed the curve of her head. The rest hung loose, halfway down her back. She looked otherworldly, like a fairy princess, with her dreamy gaze and her hair, which was such a pale blond that it looked almost silver under the light.

"Hi, honey," Drue said, bending to embrace Corina.

"Hi, sweetie," Corina said back, in the breathy whisper I remembered from the show. "Thank you so much for having me." She looked around, wide-eyed and pleased-looking. "New York City is amazing. The Big Apple. I can't believe I'm here!"

"Is it your first time in the city?" I asked.

"My first time since the show."

"Oh, right," I said, remembering. The cast of *All the Single Ladies* had spent a long weekend in New York. One of them—not Corina—had been chosen for a Dream Date: a ride through Central Park in a horse and carriage, followed by dinner at a restaurant that had paid for the privilege of being featured on the show. The rest of the women had stayed in their hotel suite, forming and re-forming alliances and gossiping to the camera. "You didn't get out much, though, right?"

She shook her head, silvery hair swishing. "I'm just so glad to be here. And so excited! I want to see the Statue of Liberty . . . and the Empire State Building . . . and Times Square . . ." Drue and I exchanged a knowing, native New Yorker glance over her head.

"And I'm meeting an agent!" Corina said. Her voice was high and breathy, like a parody of a little girl's.

"For DJing?" I asked.

"For Instagram!" she said. She widened her eyes. "There's already a diet tea that wants to collaborate. And a waist trainer!"

"Lucky you," said Drue, giving me another eye roll over Corina's head. I forced myself to smile. Of course all of the participants in reality shows were hot commodities on social media. Of course Corina had brands lining up to hire her. Of course I had to suffer humiliation and shame to get my tiny toehold on the Internet, while petite, pretty blondes had fame and fortune handed to them, with a pot of diet tea and a waist trainer. Of course.

Shame and envy and impotent rage washed over me. I made myself breathe, made myself focus. Name five things you can see. *Rich person, rich person, rich person, rich person, and me*, I thought, and smiled.

After Corina had drifted off toward the bar, Drue pulled me into a corner, where we sat down on a blue velvet chaise longue. "So what do you think of Stuart?"

What could I say? "He seems great. Very friendly and smart."

Drue gave me a look of fond exasperation. "That's all?"

"Well, we haven't really talked."

She rolled her eyes. "What's to talk about? He's hot, he's famous, and he went to Harvard. And he's launching the most amazing business." She straightened her back, raised her chin, and folded her hands at her waist. "Two words," she said, with a smile lifting the corner of her mouth. "Brain smoothies."

I blinked.

"He's going to make brain-food smoothies! Smoothies with organic ingredients designed to boost mental performance."

"So, not smoothies made out of brains?"

Drue shook her head. "No brains. Just oat milk and CBD oil. Folic acid. Manganese. All that good stuff!"

Stuart hurried over. He was smiling, but his expression was vaguely alarmed. "Are you making my smoothies sound silly?"

"I'm not making them sound anything!" Drue said, snaking her arm around his waist and resting her head on his shoulder. "I'm describing them in a full and factual manner."

"She's making them sound silly," Stuart said, half to me, half to himself. His smile seemed to have lost a few degrees of wattage. "They're not. We've got researchers on our board. These ingredients have been scientifically proven to boost performance."

"Mental performance," said Drue. "Not sexual." She nudged him. "Maybe in a year or so, we'll roll those out."

Stuart's smile showed his teeth. He gave her a squeeze that looked like it might have hurt.

"Sex smoothies!" I said. My voice was too loud, too hearty, too big. "My goodness. The future is now!"

"You know it." Stuart looked past me, over toward the door, his face lighting up as he saw someone. "Brett!" he hollered. "Hey, man, over here!"

Brett came barreling toward Stuart, arms open for a hug. As the two of them thumped chests and slapped backs, I felt my heart fall, as if someone had opened a trapdoor in my solar plexus and my insides were preparing to plummet onto the floor. I shrank backward, shot Drue a desperate look, then stood up, fast, and said, "I think I'm going to get another drink." I hurried over to the bar, head down, with Drue right behind me.

"What?" Drue asked. "What is it? Do you know Brett?"

Did I know Brett. The previous fall, I'd finally worked up the courage to download a dating app, the one that introduced you to friends of your friends. I had not been hopeful, but the weather had turned cool, and the holidays were coming. I pictured myself walking through Central Park underneath a canopy of bright leaves, holding hands with a faceless man, or bringing someone home for Chanukah for my parents to meet. So I'd tried. I'd posted a shot of my face and had taken care to also include not just a full-body shot, but a picture where I'd posed with other women, in case potential matches wanted to compare and contrast. After rejecting "full-figured," "plus-size," "curvy," and "Rubenesque," I'd used the word "fat" as part of my description. Brett and I had exchanged phone numbers, texted for three days, and talked on the phone for two more, conversations that started off superficial—*Where do you live? What do you do?*—moved through personal, and tiptoed right up to the edge of racy. By the time we were ready to meet in person, he was calling me *Daph*, and I knew the names of his parents, his childhood dog, and his favorite book and sports team, and the story of his last relationship. He already sounded a lot more impressive, a lot more lively, than my previous beau, whose finest quality, according to Darshi, was that you barely knew he was around.

By the night we were going to meet for drinks, I was sure he was The One, the pot of gold at the end of my rainbow, the man I would marry or, at least, have fulfilling sex with. I used a Groupon to have my hair blown out and styled, and gave the girl who'd shampooed me an extra ten bucks to stick a pair of false eyelashes on my lids, a feat I could only manage about fifty percent of the time. I wore one of my favorite dresses, a form-fitting knee-length tank-style in a flattering shade of fuchsia. I got to the bar early and arranged myself at a high-top table for two, sitting very straight, with my knees pointed one way and my neck angled in the opposite direction, because, once, I'd read a model saying that the less comfortable you felt, the more natural you looked. My lipstick was perfect, and my curls were still curling. When Brett walked in, in navy-blue suit pants and a light-blue shirt, with his suit jacket hooked on two fingers and hanging over his shoulder, my heartbeat sped up. Our eyes met. I waved. He smiled.

"You must be Daphne," he said.

"I must be." In person, he was a little older-looking than he was in his pictures, his hair a little thinner and his teeth less bright, but who was I to complain? He was the guy whose voice I'd fallen asleep to the night before, lying in bed with the phone pressed to my ear.

He looked me over—or, at least, he looked over the parts of me that he could see. "I'm going to get a beer. What would you like?"

It was the year that everyone was drinking Aperol spritz, so that's what I requested. I watched his back as he went toward the bar, the bald spot that had not been part of my fantasies gleaming under the bar's pin lights. I watched as he walked past the bartender, past the people sitting at the bar, all the way to the hostess stand. I watched as he walked past the hostess. I watched as he walked out the door.

For a minute, I just sat there, stunned, numb, sad, ashamed. Angry, too. I imagined getting up and giving chase, running him down on the sidewalk, demanding to know what the fuck his problem was. Big I might be, but I was also in good shape. I didn't think I'd have trouble catching up. Only I knew what had happened. He thought he'd known what I looked like, and that he'd be okay with it, but I'd been worse in person, worse than he'd even imagined. Besides, I couldn't make a habit of telling guys off in bars, in a world where any random stranger could record it and put it online. Once was a novelty. Twice was a pattern. I wouldn't be able to write about this for my blog or my Instagram stories. Not anytime soon, at least. Not while it was still so raw. It hurt. And nobody wanted unvarnished pain on their feed, unless it was served up with a side dish of uplift, or some kind of lesson—*and that's when I learned that superficial, small-minded men don't matter*, or *and that's when I realized that, if I loved myself, it didn't matter if some jerk from Tinder didn't want me*. Maybe I'd get there in a few days, I thought, as I peeled off my fake eyelashes and began the slow trudge home.

In Drue's living room, I looked over my shoulder to make sure Brett was still occupied and that he hadn't seen me. Drue was staring at me. I realized I'd never answered her question. "No," I said. "I thought I knew that guy, but he just reminded me of someone else. Bad first date."

She made sympathetic noises and patted my arm, until her mother called for her imperiously. I carried my water to the window, where I stood, breathing slowly, trying to collect myself, wondering what it was about this apartment, this party, these people, that had me so on edge. Even before Brett's arrival, I'd felt unhappy and off-balance. Was it Drue, and being back in her presence after all these years? Was it that she was getting married and I was still single? Or that she was so beautiful, and I . . . was beautiful in a different way, I made myself say in my head. I took another sip of water, another deep breath. I looked out the window, down at the street, and finally, it clicked. I could forgive myself for not seeing it immediately. The block had changed. Once, there'd been a Catholic church, a gloomy pile of foreboding brownstone. There'd been a bodega on the corner, with a wig shop and a nail salon next door. The church hosted Weight Watchers meetings in its basement, and I'd been here before, almost twenty years ago, the summer of Nana.

The Lathrop School paid well, but not so well that my parents didn't need to look for summer jobs. The year that I was six, they'd both gotten hired at an overnight camp in Maine. My dad would be the aquatics director, teaching kids how to kayak and canoe. ("Do you know how to kayak and canoe?" I'd asked, and my father, who'd grown up in Brooklyn, had smiled and said, "I'll learn.") While he was on the water, Mom would run the arts and crafts program. They'd get room and board, a private cabin, and generous salaries. The only problem was, I wasn't old enough to attend as a camper, or to be left in their cabin by myself. So they invited my mother's mother to come down from Connecticut and stay with me in New York.

"Daphne and I will have a wonderful time!" Nana had said. I didn't say anything. I couldn't tell my parents that Nana scared me. Where my mom and my Bubbe, my father's mother, were soft and warm and smelled good, Nana was sharp-edged and skinny, and had stale coffee breath and none of my mother's gentle ways or affinity for baked goods. Her gray hair was clipped short, and her eyes, magnified by her reading glasses, looked like a pair of poached eggs. My mom wore brightly colored, loose-fitting clothes: blousy tops, long skirts with hems that draped the floor, or smocks with pockets full of tape and buttons, bits of trim, a pair of earrings and her house keys, pennies and butterscotch candies. Bubbe carried a giant *New Yorker* tote bag, with a rattling keychain and her phone and its charger and whatever library book she was reading, a backup library book in case she finished that one, and a squashed peanut-butter-and-apricot-jam sandwich, in case she or I got hungry. Nana wore spotless white blouses and crisply pressed black pants with no pockets. She carried a small, immaculate purse.

Before Nana arrived, my mother sat down with me on my bed. "Nana loves you," she began. "You know that, right?"

I nodded, thinking that if someone really loved you, you didn't need to be told. Nana sent me presents for Chanukah and my birthday, and kissed my cheek and hugged me hello when she saw me and goodbye when she left, but the hugs and the gifts felt like acts of obligation. I didn't think I was the kind of granddaughter Nana had hoped for, a small, neat, pretty girl to take to *The Nutcracker* or for tea at the Plaza. That summer, my hair hung halfway to my waist and was frequently tangled. I had scabby elbows and skinned knees, and I was tall for my age, and round, like my parents. Nana didn't seem to actually enjoy having me around, the way Bubbe did, when we'd visit her in Arizona or she'd come for the holidays. Bubbe kept a special stepstool in her kitchen just for me to use when I was there, and she let me sleep in her big bed at night.

My mother had pulled me against her. "If you miss us . . . or if Nana does something that makes you feel bad . . ."

I kept quiet, watching as my mom pulled a pink square of paper out of her pocket and used a thumbtack to affix it to the center of the corkboard over my desk, a board normally filled with my paintings and drawings. "This is our number," she said. Her voice had softened, and she sounded more like herself. "We'll call you every night. But you can call us if you need us. Anytime. No matter what."

The next morning, Nana arrived, pulling a black suitcase and wearing a pair of gold knot-shaped earrings and a bracelet of gold links around her wrist. Her fingernails were freshly manicured, salmon-pink ovals that were pointy at the top. "Daphne!" she said, forming a smile shape with her mouth. Nana hugged me and kept one arm tight around me as, with the other, she waved my parents out the door. "Don't worry about a thing. Daphne and I are going to have a wonderful time!" I stood at the window, watching as my parents piled their duffel bags and a tote bag filled with all of the *New Yorker*s my dad planned to read into the trunk of the car. My father slammed the trunk. My mother blew one last kiss. Then they pulled away from the curb and made their way up Riverside Drive toward the Henry Hudson Parkway. I could see my mom's hand sticking out of the window, waving at me, until they turned a corner and were out of sight. And then Nana and I were alone.

Nana looked me over. Her voice was bright, but her body was stiff. "We're going to make some changes here," she said, and bent down to the cupboard beneath the sink, pulling out a trash bag. As I watched, she opened the refrigerator and tossed into the bag a loaf of white bread, a container of sour cream, three sticks of butter, and the Tupperware container half-full of chocolate-chip cookie dough (sometimes, my mother would bake two cookies for each of us after dinner, and other times she'd allow me to have a spoonful of dough for dessert). The remainder of a half-gallon of orange juice went down the drain, followed by the half-and-half.

"Juice is nothing but sugar. And white food is bad food," Nana said. "It's basically poison." *Poison?* I thought. My parents wouldn't give me poison! But I kept quiet as Nana ransacked the pantry, dumping out the canisters of sugar and flour, the box of shortbread cookies, the cereal I liked to eat in the morning and the wheat crackers I had with cheese and an apple in the afternoon. "Processed carbohydrates," she explained, waving the box in an accusatory way.

"Those are bad?"

Nana confirmed that they were, and said more things about hydrogenated fats and added sugar. Finally, she rummaged around in my mother's desk until, with a muttered "A-ha!," she found the stashed Toblerone and Cadbury bars that my mom would share with me sometimes at night while we watched TV. Into the trash they went.

For the next half hour, Nana bustled through the apartment, opening every drawer and cupboard, humming tunelessly as she threw things away. I thought about trying to rescue one of the chocolate bars, but even as I thought it, Nana was twirling the ends of the bag and tying them into a knot.

"You and I are going to eat healthy while your parents are gone," she said. "Just wait until they see you when they get back! They'll be so happy." That was the first time I'd heard that there was something wrong with how I looked; the first inkling that my body was disappointing or somehow problematic. I knew that I was bigger than other kids, but until then I'd never realized that "big" was a bad thing to be.

For dinner that night, Nana prepared broiled salmon with lemon juice squeezed on top, with broccoli on the side. When my father made salmon he marinated it in soy sauce and garlic and a little maple syrup, and when my parents gave me broccoli they served it with a saucer of ranch dressing, but the ranch dressing, I knew, had been dumped down the sink, along with the maple syrup, and this salmon was unpleasantly fishy, dry on top and slimy inside. I poked at my food and moved it around my plate, hoping that Nana would take the hint that I was still hungry. Instead, she looked at me with approval. "Only eat until you're full, and then stop eating!" she said. "The most important exercise for weight loss is the push-away. Want to see it?"

I didn't. I wanted to cry and then have a dish full of ice cream. But Nana was looking at me expectantly, so I nodded. Nana set her hands on the edge of the table, pushed herself back, and stood up. "Get it? You push *away* from the table!"

My heart sank.

"And now, let's have dessert!" Nana said. For a minute, I felt hopeful. Maybe we'd walk downstairs and sit on the stoop and wait for the ice-cream truck's jingle. Maybe Nana had thrown away the packaged shortbread cookies because she didn't like store-bought things. Maybe Nana was going to bake, like Bubbe did!

Instead, Nana reached into her purse and pulled out a tiny foil square of chocolate. "Let it melt on your tongue. Savor it," she instructed, but I gobbled my square in one bite and looked at the clock. It was just after seven. My stomach growled. Nana narrowed her eyes, like I'd made the noise on purpose.

"Let's go for a walk," she said. And so out we went. We walked over to Broadway and followed it uptown, past the Chinese grocery store and the Korean chicken-wing place, past the ramen restaurant and the ice-cream parlor. Nana didn't stop, or even glance at these places. She set a brisk pace, arms pumping, moving so quickly that there was barely time to look around. Every block or so she'd glance down at her watch, until finally she said, "There! That's forty-five minutes!"

Back in the apartment, while Nana took a shower, I scoured the pantry and every shelf of the refrigerator, but I couldn't find a single thing that would taste good. There was whole-wheat bread that I could toast, but I only liked toast with sugar and cinnamon sprinkled on top, or with apricot jam and butter, and Nana had gotten rid of all those things except cinnamon, which was no good on its own.

When my parents called, I told them that I loved them and that everything was fine.

I went to bed with my belly aching from hunger and loneliness. When I woke up the next morning, I could smell coffee coming from the kitchen, a good, familiar smell. Maybe it was a bad dream, I thought, and when I heard Nana call "Breakfast time!" I jumped out of bed, used the bathroom, washed up, and raced to the table, where I found a poached egg, a single slice of dry toast, an orange, and a large glass of water. I inhaled the egg, the orange, and most of the toast while Nana took her time, sipping and nibbling, setting her slice of toast down between bites and giving me meaningful looks until, with my remaining crust, I did the same, before going to my room to paint.

For lunch, we ate tuna fish, mixed with lemon juice instead of mayonnaise, and celery chopped fine, served with lettuce and another slice of toast. After lunch, Nana hustled me to the bus stop, and we rode uptown and walked to the pool at Riverbank Park. Nana's spine seemed to stiffen at the sight of the kids playing in the sprinklers. We could hear English and Spanish and languages I didn't recognize. I saw her elbow clamp down tight against her purse and tote bag. But maybe that was just to keep me from even thinking about asking for money when we walked by the snack bar near the roller-skating rink, and I could smell French fries. When we reached the pool, Nana stood by the chain-link fence as I pulled off my shirt and shorts. "Swim laps," she suggested. I couldn't find the nerve to tell her that what I normally did at the pool was play Marco Polo with other kids, or swoop down toward the bottom of the deep end and then back up, pretending I was a mermaid. On the way back to the bus, she said, "I brought you a snack!" This time, I didn't even let myself get hopeful, so I wasn't disappointed when she gave me twelve almonds in a plastic bag and a plum. Dinner was the same as the night before, only with a chicken breast instead of salmon and, instead of the chocolate square, two dusty brown oval-shaped SnackWell's cookies for dessert. They had a chalky texture and were so sweet that I could feel my face pucker. "See? Zero grams of fat," said Nana, tapping the box with her fingernail. I'd left a bite of chicken and two broccoli trees on my plate, at Nana's instructions. "Always leave food on your plate," Nana said.

"Why?"

"To show that the food doesn't have power over you. That you're in charge, not your appetite."

I'd never thought of my appetite as something separate from me, something that needed to be tamed. "How do I be in charge?" I asked.

Nana led me through a push-away and smiled the way she did everything else: thinly. Her lips pressed into an almost invisible line. "Get used to being hungry," she said. "It won't kill you, I promise." She smoothed her pants against her narrow hips. "If you feel hungry, that means you're winning."

That night, when I went to bed with my belly a small, aching ball, I told myself, *That means I'm winning*. It wasn't much comfort. On the nights that followed, I would lie under the quilt my mother had made me, imagining the foods I'd once enjoyed: My father's pancakes, fresh out of the pan, dolloped with butter and crisscrossed with syrup. A hot dog from Sabrett's that would snap when I bit it and fill my mouth with savory, garlicky juice. Carrot cake studded with walnuts and raisins, topped with dense cream-cheese frosting, or the apple crisp my mom would bake after she and my dad took me apple-picking in October at an orchard in New Jersey.

For five days, I endured spartan meals, doll-size portions, the swimming and the walking and the push-aways. On Saturday morning, Nana and I took the bus uptown, to what turned out to be a Weight Watchers meeting being held in a church basement. "I'm a lifetime member," Nana told me proudly, handing a white envelope-size folder to a woman behind a desk and holding her head high as she stepped into a curtained cubicle and onto the scale. We found seats on folding metal chairs, and I looked around. The room was full of women, maybe fifty or sixty of them, with three men. Some of the women were white, some were black, and some were brown. Some were just a little heavy, and some were so big that they had to perch awkwardly on the chairs, which creaked and teetered underneath them, and some didn't look heavy at all, which gave me the worst feeling, as I wondered if even thin women still struggled with their appetites, and had to come to a place like this to get help.

The woman next to me gave me a whispered "Sorry," as she readjusted herself on her seat. I wondered why whoever was in charge hadn't gotten larger, more comfortable chairs, or at least spaced them out a little instead of cramming them up against one another. Then I thought that maybe the discomfort and the shame were the point, and that the women were meant to be embarrassed, and that their embarrassment would keep them from eating. The woman next to me was black, with medium-brown skin and shoulder-length braids, and the two women behind us were murmuring quietly in Spanish. Even though Nana didn't seem comfortable around people who weren't white when she encountered them at the pool or in our neighborhood, she seemed perfectly at ease here

The meeting leader was an older black woman named Valerie, with freckled, reddish skin and short, curly hair that was longer on one side of her head than the other (after a few weeks of regular attendance, I heard Nana whispering to another member about Valerie's wig, which was when I realized that those curls weren't her own). Valerie's eyebrows were skinny, plucked arches, her body was tall and lean and long-waisted. She had a long, scrawny neck with a soft wobble of a chin underneath it, the only part of her that was still fleshy and soft. Valerie's voice was a marvel. It could go from a soft whisper to a confiding murmur to an exhorting shout, and hold the crowd spellbound, bringing them to silence with just a whisper. She reminded me of the Reverend C. L. Franklin, whom I'd heard on my parents' Aretha Franklin CDs. She spoke in the same kind of preacherly cadences, encouraging the weak, congratulating the strong, welcoming backsliders back into the fold, and celebrating with the women who'd hit their goal weights.

Valerie would begin each meeting by showing a poster-size

picture of herself. In a blue satin dress with her hair in a short, black bob and bright red lipstick on her lips, she didn't even look like the same person. Her breasts and belly bulged, her hips were so wide they seemed to strain the seams of her dress. She had a wide smile on her face, a paper plate of food in her hands. There was only Valerie in the picture, but, if you looked closely, you could see a man's arm at the edge of the frame. Sometimes, I would let my mind wander while Valerie talked, and wonder if the hand belonged to a father or a brother or a husband or a boyfriend, someone who'd loved Valerie when she'd been that big.

"That was me," she would begin, her voice serious and quiet. "Oh yes! Oh yes it was!" she'd say, as if someone had voiced their doubt out loud. "I was twenty-six years old." Her voice would get louder and louder as she went through her litany. "I weighed *three hundred pounds*. I was *morbidly obese*. Borderline *diabetic*. I had *sleep apnea*. I couldn't walk up a flight of stairs without needing to catch my breath." By then, women would be nodding along with her, all of them listening raptly, even the ones who'd heard the very same litany the week before and the week before that. Valerie would lower her voice. "I'd tried it all. Grapefruit. Cabbage soup. Slim-Fast. Did I call 1-800-Jenny? You know that I did. And then . . ." She would pause, hand uplifted, looking over the room, making eye contact with different members. "Then I found this program. And this program . . ." Another pause. Valerie would put her hand on her heart and say, "This program gave me back my life."

I'd never been to church, but I imagined that church was probably something like Weight Watchers, with rituals and repetition, confessions and forgiveness and exhortations to stay the course in the upcoming week. I thought it was nice, how the women all seemed to want to help each other. When Valerie would open the floor, saying "Ladies, let me hear about your triumphs and temptations," someone would start talking about an upcoming party, or a business trip, or how there'd been birthday cake at the office, and everyone would want to help.

"They know I'm on a diet!" the birthday-cake woman had wailed. "And I couldn't not eat it! I had to be polite!" I listened as the other Weight Watchers proposed solutions—*Tell them you're allergic! Take a slice and say it's for later and throw it away!* I wondered if this was what being an adult was: endless denial, requiring limitless willpower. Then I would think about what kind of job I could find where birthday cake was served in the office.

After a week and a half of deprivation, I had the bright idea to tell Nana I was going upstairs to visit the DiNardos' cats. "Be back by bedtime," she said, stirring Sweet'N Low into her coffee. "And take the stairs, not the elevator." I took the stairs two at a time, galloping up to the fifth floor and presenting myself, red-faced and panting, to Mrs. DiNardo, who seemed surprised to see me. I'd helped my mother take care of Muffin and Mittens before, when the DiNardos went away. Mom would pour dry food into the cats' bowl, change their water, and clean their litter box, and I would pet them, to the extent that the stand-offish Persians wanted petting, but I'd never stopped in to see the cats while the DiNardos were home.

"How are you holding up? You miss your mom and dad?" Mrs. DiNardo asked.

I nodded, scratching Muffin (or possibly Mittens) behind its ears. I waited until Mrs. DiNardo had gone back to *Dancing with the Stars* before easing open her pantry door. I found a half-full bag of marshmallows and a bar of unsweetened baking chocolate and shoved them both into the pouch of the sweatshirt I'd worn with theft in mind. In the refrigerator, I found a few hot-dog buns and added them to my stash. I played with the cat for another few minutes, then got to my feet.

"Good night, Mrs. DiNardo!" I called. I felt bad about stealing food, but I was sure the DiNardos could afford to replace what I'd taken. On the fourth-floor landing, I crammed four marshmallows into my mouth and chased them with a hot-dog bun. I hid the rest of the treats under my mattress, and supplemented my one-egg breakfasts and dry-tuna lunches with a few marshmallows or a square of the unsweetened chocolate, which was so bitter it made my face ache.

Every Saturday morning before we left for Weight Watchers, Nana would weigh me. "The trick to staying healthy is never gaining weight in the first place," she said. I would stand on the bathroom scale in just my underwear and nightgown. "I've never weighed more than five pounds more than I did the day I was married," she told me, sucking in her cheeks and turning from side to side, inspecting herself in the bathroom mirror, moving her body and face through the same series of poses that I'd seen my mother perform a thousand times. "I weigh myself every morning, and if I see that needle creeping up, I cut back." *Cut back where?* I wondered. Would she eliminate the single square of chocolate she permitted herself every other night? Would she reduce her afternoon snack from twelve almonds to six? What was left for her to deny herself?

"So many women my age let themselves go," Nana lamented one Saturday after the meeting. I was instantly struck by the phrase. While she kept talking, I thought about how it would look: women unbuttoning their jeans and unzipping their dresses, running toward tables full of carrot cake and apple crisp. Their breasts would bounce; the extra flesh of their upper arms would jiggle; their thighs would ripple and shake as they raced toward rivers of butter, plains of prime rib, mountains of mashed potatoes and ice cream and birthday cake.

I will never forget the look on my mother's face on that hot August afternoon when my parents came home: first shock, then sorrow, and what looked like a flash of envy that quickly turned into sympathy, and from sympathy to anger. "Oh," she said, and opened her arms. She felt warm and soft against me, her scent mixed with the unfamiliar tang of bug spray and sunscreen.

"How about a hug for Dad?" said my father. He tried to smile as I embraced him, but his forehead was furrowed, and his lips were a little white around the edges. I helped them carry their luggage inside and upstairs to where Nana was sitting in the kitchen.

"Jerry!" Nana said, smiling as she stood, smoothing the fabric of her slacks over her hips. "How was Maine?"

"Maine was good," he said. "But, Denise—"

As if she hadn't heard him, Nana said, "And doesn't Daphne look wonderful?" Lowering her voice, she said, "I thought about sending you a picture, but we wanted it to be a surprise."

By then my mom had made it upstairs. Holding her duffel bag in her hand, in a voice that was frighteningly quiet, she said, "Mom. We talked about this."

"What?" Nana asked. She raised her hands, fingers spread, in the air, an exaggerated look of innocence on her face. "What did I do? Is it a crime to want my granddaughter to be healthy?"

"Daphne," said my father, "go to your room, please."

I hurried down the hall and closed my bedroom door. Part of me didn't want to hear them, but a larger part was powerless to resist. I pressed my ear against the seam where the door met the wall and listened to a three-way fight conducted mostly in whispers, with the occasional shout. I heard Nana hissing at my mother, saying, "You of all people know how hard it is to lose weight once you've put it on," and my father growling, "You had no business doing this to Daphne."

"Oh, that's fine for you to say," Nana said. "You have no idea what it's like to go through life as a fat woman. No idea at all."

I closed my eyes. Had Nana been a fat woman? Was she talking about my mom? Was I destined to be fat, just like my mother? And was it really that bad?

I pressed the pillow over my ears when the shouting began,

my nana yelling at my dad, "You're not doing her any favors with those food trips of yours," my father yelling back, "I don't want her hating her own body! Isn't it enough that you've made your own daughter miserable? Do you have to do the same thing to her daughter?" I was lying on my bed when I heard the door slam, then my father's tread in the hallway. His face was red, and his hair stood up in tufts, but his voice was gentle, and his hand was warm around mine.

"How about you and I go for a walk?" he asked. We went to Ben & Jerry's on 104th Street, where I got the hot-fudge sundae with mint chip ice cream I'd been dreaming about since Nana's arrival. My father told me stories about their time in Maine: the camper who'd finally learned how to swim after being too scared to even put his face in the water, the canoers who'd gotten lost in a thunderstorm. Finally, he said, "How'd it go with Nana?"

"I was so hungry," I said. By then my spoon was clinking against the glass as I scraped up every bit of hot fudge, gobbling it down, even as I heard Nana's voice saying that sugar was poison, and Valerie, the Weight Watchers leader, talking about how she'd weighed three hundred pounds and how awful that had been. "She only let me have, like, one tiny bite of chocolate for dessert. She threw out all the sugar and all the butter!"

"She shouldn't have done that," my father said. "There's absolutely no reason to restrict what a growing girl is eating." He put his hand on my shoulder and squeezed. "You are fine, just the way you are," he said. "Bodies come in all shapes and sizes. Don't ever let anyone make you feel any differently."

I wanted to believe him, but by then, of course, the damage had been done.

At Drue and Stuart's apartment, with the party continuing behind me, and with Brett lurking somewhere nearby, I finished my water, went back to the bar, asked for a shot of tequila, and slugged it down, feeling my throat burn, along with my eyes. *I am going to die alone*, I thought. I wanted to go home, back to my safe little nest, to sit with Bingo in my lap and Darshi on the couch beside me, or maybe even back to my parents' place, away from all these beautiful people who, just by living, made me feel inadequate, at once enormous and small.

I'd stepped into the hallway and summoned the elevator when I heard a man's voice, coming from the shadowed corner at the end of the hallway.

I held my breath and listened. The man was Stuart. His face was toward the wall, his body bent in a protective curve as he spoke intently to someone I couldn't see. "It'll be fine," I heard him say. "I promise."

The elevator dinged. Stuart turned around. Quickly, before he could see me, I stepped inside, punching the down button until the doors slid shut. As the elevator descended, I thought about Mr. Cavanaugh's fidgety impatience, about Mrs. Cavanaugh's enlarged lips and Mr. Lowe's transplanted hair. I wondered how many of the guests were faking something—confidence, friendship, maybe even love. I wondered how many had ulterior motives—fame or fortune or just proximity to someone who had both. I thought about the cousins, wondering if Drue had paid for their tickets and hotel rooms, or made generous contribution to their kids' college funds. I recalled her gorgeous assistant, wondering if she'd been offered a raise right around the time the save-the-date cards had gone out and Drue had recruited her as a bridesmaid. I walked out into the darkness, feeling unsettled, unhappy, a little envious, a little nauseated. And all of those emotions felt familiar, as comfortable and customary as drawing breath. It was the way Drue Cavanaugh had always made me feel.

I was almost out the door when I heard Drue calling me. "Hey, Daphne! Wait up!"

I turned around and there she was, hurrying through the

lobby in her moonbeam dress with her high-heeled shoes in her hand. When she saw that she'd gotten my attention, she dropped her shoes by her feet, stood up very straight, and declaimed,

My wife and I have asked a crowd of craps
To come and waste their time and ours . . .

In spite of myself, I smiled. Back at Lathrop, the English teacher who'd gotten us started on Philip Larkin with the poem about how your parents fuck you up had also taught the poem called "Vers de Société," about the pain of loneliness versus the discomfort of social interaction.

"I had to get out of there," Drue announced. "Couldn't stand it. Come on, let's go get some French fries! With gravy!"

"I don't think you can bail on your own engagement party," I murmured as my stomach growled.

"Who's going to stop me?" Daphne giggled, and I thought, *Who ever does?* "Besides," she said, leaning her head briefly on top of mine and exhaling tequila vapors, "I can't stand any of those people."

"Drue," I said, "you're marrying one of those people in a few weeks."

She wrinkled her nose. If I'd made the gesture, I would have looked like a constipated rabbit. On Drue it was charming. "Meh," she said.

"Meh?"

"Well, not a permanent meh." She waved her hand. "Stuart's fine. Just, you know, right now, I'd rather be eating disco fries with you." As always, I felt my stupid heart lift and swell at the thought of being noticed, being seen, being chosen; the joy of having this gorgeous, wealthy, important person bestowing her attention on me. "So can we?"

I turned, looking over my shoulder, thinking that maybe

Stuart would come looking for his fiancée, or that maybe Drue's parents would have hunted her down. I saw no one but a drowsy-looking doorman, half-asleep behind half a dozen screens showing security-camera feeds, and an older couple, the man in a tuxedo, the woman in an evening gown, coming home from a night out. And Drue, in her shimmering dress, hair and cheekbones glittering gold, was waiting for my answer, smiling in a way that promised mischief and adventure.

"Dear Warlock-Williams: Why, of course," I recited. Drue grinned. She smacked a noisy, possibly drunken kiss on my cheek and grabbed my hand. "Wait, wait!" I handed her the pair of flip-flops I'd stuffed in my purse, for my own feet, and she said, gratefully, "You're the best." Together, we went out into the darkness, Drue chattering about some cousin's awful boyfriend whose Instagram account had nothing but posts of right-wing political screeds, along with pictures of their elderly Pekingese dressed in holiday-themed hats and sweaters. "It's like, Trump, Trump, dog, Trump, Trump, some country singer he hates, some football player he hates, and then more Trump, and then the dog again, and you know I *like* dogs, I do, but honestly . . ." I was half-listening to her chatter, half-remembering the line of poetry that had preceded the bit I had quoted, about how "sitting by a lamp more often brings / Not peace, but other things. / Beyond the light stand failure and remorse / Whispering *Dear Warlock-Williams: Why, of course*—"

Chapter Seven

On the third Friday in June, I stepped off the ferry in Provincetown, Massachusetts, at the very tip of Cape Cod. The air was fresh and sweetly salty; the sky was a deep, scoured blue, ornamented by a few puffy white clouds. A dock extended into the water; motorboats and sailboats bobbed at anchor or crisscrossed on the water, bright sails snapping in the breeze. Waves were lapping gently at the golden, sandy shore, and the forecast called for more of the same: a week of clear, sunny days and crisp, starry nights. Perfect. Because Drue Lathrop Cavanaugh never got anything less than perfection.

We lingered on the dock, with a member of Drue's team of wedding photographers crouched down on the wooden boards, taking pictures with her camera and then, at Drue's insistence, with both of our phones. I'd worn another Leef dress for the trip, a prototype of a garment that hadn't even been put into production yet, a navy silk dress with a halter-style top and a knee-length skirt that swirled fetchingly in the wind. I'd accessorized with a navy-blue straw sunhat and a red lip, and I'd felt extremely nautical, if not a little overdressed next to Drue, who'd made the trip in cutoff shorts, a faded Lathrop T-shirt, and flip-flops. "I'll be spending the rest of the weekend in corsets and heels," she'd explained. "I'm going to dress down while I can."

A Town Car collected us and our luggage at the end of the dock and drove us twenty minutes west to the town of Truro, Provincetown's next-door neighbor, where Edward Hopper had lived and painted, and where Drue's maternal family had summered for generations.

"Stuart and I thought about doing it in the Hamptons, but that's so predictable," Drue said. "And here, there's a lot more leeway with what you can do on the beaches. Wait 'til you see the party tonight." She shimmied in the back seat, smiling.

Fifteen minutes later, the car rolled up a long driveway lined with crushed white shells and parked in front of a modern, low-slung home clad in silvery cedar shingles. There was a swimming pool and a hot tub in front, surrounded by a deck, rose and hydrangea bushes, pots of pink and red and purple impatiens in bloom, rows of lounge chairs with dark-blue cushions, and blue-and-white-striped umbrellas. Drue led me through the door and up a flight of stairs. "Your suite, madam," she said, swinging the door open with a flourish.

I stepped inside. "For real?" I asked, looking around. "For real, for real?"

"Yep!" She leaned close and squeezed my shoulders. "All yours."

The room was enormous, airy and high-ceilinged, with floors of some light-colored wood polished to a high gloss. The king-size bed was dressed in crisp white and blue linens, piled with more pillows than two people (or, really, even four or five people) could reasonably need. To the left of the bed, the bathroom stood behind a wall of smoked glass tinted shades of blue, ornamented with wood carvings meant to evoke waves. Beyond the bed, a wall of floor-to-ceiling windows overlooked a private deck with a round, white-cushioned daybed, and square planters overflowing with lavender and more hydrangeas and, on one side, a wall of boxwood hedges. Even with the sliding glass door shut, I could hear the hiss and rumble of the ocean.

"Do you love it?" Drue clapped her hands. "Tell me you love it."

I spun around slowly. "It's amazing."

"And look!" Drue led me out to the deck, through a wooden door, painted red, set in the middle of the hedge. Drue opened it. Hidden inside was a hot tub surrounded by lounge chairs, a cocktail table, and a stack of fluffy white towels. "Your bedroom and mine share it." She gave me a broad wink. "Just put a sock on the doorknob if you're entertaining."

"As if."

"Hey, weddings make people romantic! You never know."

I spun around slowly, looking from the bay to the hot tub to the mansion where I'd be staying. "It's incredible."

"I want you to be happy." Drue put her arm around my chest, pulling me back until she could rest her cheek on the top of my head. "I'm so glad that you're here. That you agreed to do this."

I let myself lean back against her, smelling her hair and her perfume. *She's your Kryptonite*, I heard Darshi saying . . . but when Drue said "Thank you," I felt myself smile. Maybe she really had changed. Maybe I was doing the right thing.

Below us, the beach was swarming with crews of workers, in the process of erecting a series of tents. The wedding ceremony would be held at a winery a few miles down the road, but the rehearsal dinner tonight, and the pre-wedding photographs tomorrow, would be on the beach. Because there were no fancy hotels in Truro, in addition to taking over the nicest hotel in Provincetown, the Cavanaughs had rented half a dozen homes on the bluff near the Lathrop family seat, where the wedding party and immediate family would stay. Each house had been given a name for the occasion. Drue and I were in Sea Star, a three-story, four-bedroom house. Our bedrooms were on the second floor, and two more bedrooms were on the ground floor, the larger of which had been turned into a spa/salon/dressing room, complete with massage tables, mirrors, and a reclining chair with a steam machine beside it for Drue's facialist/bridesmaid Minerva to use. The top floor was one large room, a combined kitchen/dining/living room with floor-to-ceiling windows that overlooked the bay. The caterers had set it up as a hospitality suite, with a rotating buffet of breakfast, lunch, and dinner, and snacks in between, not to mention a round-the-clock open bar.

Stuart and his folks were next door, in a place called Sea Breeze. Drue's parents and maternal grandparents were in the Lathrop family home, Sea Glass. Other, lesser participants and guests had been assigned to Driftwood, Starfish, and Clearwater (that last, Drue whispered, was on the other side of Route 6 and didn't even have a water view).

Back in my bedroom, a wooden bench with a woven seagrass seat stood at the foot of the king-size bed, with a giant, beribboned "Welcome to Our Wedding" basket at its center, with #DRUEANDSTU underneath it. The basket was crammed with goodies, all carefully selected by Drue after endless consultation with me. There were bottles of wine and prosecco, bags of smoked and candied nuts, biscuits and crackers, an assortment of dried fruit, salmon jerky and bluefish pâté, chocolate truffles, each wrapped in gold foil, a hangover-helper kit, which included Advil, Alka-Seltzer, some kind of herbal headache cure, and condoms ("In case any of Stuart's friends get frisky," Drue said with a wink). In the bathroom, I knew there would be soaps and scrubs and monogrammed bath bombs, along with razors, toothbrush and toothpaste and mouthwash, hairspray and mousse and bobby pins, and pretty much anything else that a guest might have forgotten to pack. "The nearest drugstore's back in P-town," Drue had explained. My gifts were in there, too—I'd made sachets, scented with lavender verbena, tied with curls of silver ribbon, with Drue and Stuart's monogram embroidered on the front. A heavy-stock card with a schedule of the weekend's events, with the word WELCOME in gold at the top, was tucked into the basket, between the cheese twists and the bag of dried apricots. I picked it up and read through it. "There's an app for the wedding?"

"It's got the schedule and maps and all the hashtags for stuff. Now come on," she said, plucking the bottle of prosecco out of the basket and pulling me to my feet. "The party starts in three hours! We have to get ready! We have to pregame!"

"Hold on! I'm downloading the app," I protested as Drue pretended to tow me to the door. Being near the ocean always improved my mood, and between Drue's enthusiasm, the beautiful setting, and a suitcase full of gorgeous clothes that I was being paid to wear, it was almost impossible not to feel happy.

"Please. You probably know the schedule better than I do," Drue said. I wasn't sure that was true, but I at least knew the weekend's contours. Tonight, there would be a rehearsal dinner featuring a clambake on the beach. Tomorrow morning, there'd be optional paddleboard yoga, followed by a brunch for the female wedding guests in our house, Sea Star, with a companion brunch for the men next door at Sea Breeze. After brunch, we'd all get our hair and makeup done and get into our dresses. The photographer wanted us on the beach at five o'clock sharp, just as the setting sun would tint the air peach and tangerine and gold ("Sunsets on the outer Cape are magical!" Drue had told me, and I hadn't wanted to mention the story I'd read in *Scientific American* that had explained that the lovely sunsets were the result of all the pollution that had drifted up the East Coast). At six-thirty, a bus would come to drive us to the winery. At seven o'clock, a string quartet would start to play the wedding march, and the ceremony would begin. When it was over, there'd be a cocktail hour and dinner at the winery, and dancing all night long, first to the music of a band, then to a DJ, flown in from Holland for the occasion. Every single detail had been covered, up to and including the installation of a funicular for guests who were too incapacitated or too inebriated to manage the four flights of stairs from the beach back to the houses.

Don't count other people's money, my nana liked to say. In general, I tried to follow her advice, but as the wedding had gotten closer I'd found it almost impossible not to keep a running estimate of how much the entire affair would cost. The home where we were staying rented for $18,000 a week. I knew because I'd looked it up online. The other places had to come with similar price tags. Then there was the cost of the food, and the musicians (string quartet for the ceremony, twelve-piece band for the party, big-deal DJs flown in from Los Angeles and overseas). There were the florists from New York, and makeup artists, also from the city. Drue's dress alone had cost more than any car my parents had ever driven, and it was one of three that she'd be wearing on her wedding night. The whole affair could end up costing more than a million dollars. A lot of money under any circumstances; maybe a crazy amount if Darshi was right and the Cavanaugh Corporation was in trouble.

"Just let me hang up my dress," I said, detaching my arm from the bride's. I wanted to unpack, to explore my room, and to answer the emails that had hit my inbox as soon as I'd logged on to Sea Star's Wi-Fi (the password was "DrueandStu2020," because of course it was). I also wanted to check in with Darshi, who was spending the weekend at an economics seminar in Boston, one that she swore she'd signed up for prior to Drue's reappearance in our lives. I hadn't pressed her, but I had wondered if Darshi had wanted an excuse to be nearby, if she thought that I'd need to be rescued at some point before the weekend was over.

After confirming that the bathroom, with its freestanding bathtub and its open-air shower, was just as luxe-y as the rest of the room, I hung up the clothes that I'd packed. *I hear yr going 2 B in VOGUE*, Leela Thakoon had texted me, followed by a string of exclamation points and heart-eye emojis. I, too, had heard those whispers, and that Drue and Stuart were in the running to be featured in this week's Vows column in the *Times*. "Which is huge, because some big-deal agent is getting gay-married in Aspen tomorrow night," Drue confided.

"I think you're just supposed to say 'married.'"

Drue had patted my arm and poured me a glass of prosecco. "You're cute," she said. "Meet me downstairs. We'll get our hair done."

Once the rest of my clothes were unpacked, I gave my bridesmaid's dress a shake. Drue, thank goodness, had not decreed that her bridesmaids had to all wear the same dress. Instead, she'd picked out a fabric—chiffon—and a range of shades, from sand to taupe to pale gold to saffron, and let us choose our own designs. When I'd learned that most of the bridesmaids were having their dresses made, I'd asked Leela if she'd be willing to design something. Leela had eagerly agreed, and she'd outdone herself. The silhouette was simple: a sweetheart neckline; wide shoulder straps that would leave my arms and the top of my chest bare and keep my bra covered; a boned bodice that would hug my torso from breasts to hips, where the skirt flared out full. Somehow, Leela had managed to fold the shimmery gold fabric into dozens of tiny pleats that gave the fabric the illusion of motion, so that even when I was standing still the dress looked like a pond ruffled by a breeze.

"You'll look like Venus, rising from the sea," Leela had said, hands pressed against her heart.

I'll look like Venus, rising from the all-you-can-eat buffet, I thought before I could stop myself. I didn't want to dwell on the pain that Drue had caused me. I wanted to believe that she was truly sorry and that we could move past it. I wanted to enjoy this beautiful place with my best friend.

From the beach, I could hear someone performing a microphone check on the newly constructed stage and the lulling sound of the waves. A familiar excitement was humming in my chest, an anticipatory buzz. When I was a little girl and my parents took me on trips to the beach, I could remember feeling this way, when the traffic slowed down and I could sense but not see the ocean; when I knew that fun was close. *Maybe it will be wonderful*, I thought. *Maybe I'll meet the man of my dreams.* With the breeze against my face and half a glass of prosecco fizzing inside me, it felt like a night made for miracles; a night made for falling in love.

Chapter Eight

I gave my bridesmaid's dress a final shake, hung it up, and pulled on another one of Leela's creations, a spaghetti-strapped, down-to-the-ground maxi dress in a bold hot-pink floral print, called the Daisy. Downstairs in the beauty suite, Drue was already in a chair, eyes closed, with Minerva tending to her face while another woman worked on her hair. "Is that you?" Drue called, and patted the seat beside her. "Come on," she said, "let's get pretty!" At five o'clock, with my complexion smoothed out, my hair pinned up, and my new dress swaying in the breeze, I stood next to Drue at the top of the staircase leading down to the beach and the party.

"Isn't it amazing?" Drue asked. I nodded, truly at a loss for words. The beach had been transformed. The sand was covered in layers of Persian rugs in vivid shades of scarlet and indigo, gold and copper and cream. In between the arrangements of carpets were bonfires—I counted four of them, three already burning and the fourth being lit by a uniformed server. Piles of blankets and embroidered pillows in hot pink and turquoise and gold, some fringed, others stitched with bits of mirrors, were stacked by the fires, and there were long tables set up, buffet-style, underneath tents behind them. Waiters circulated with trays of drinks. It looked like a seraglio had tumbled out onto the sand.

"The bar's over there," said Drue. She pointed toward the center of the beach, where a freshly assembled bar stood, fully stocked and bustling, with tiki torches flaring in a half-circle around it. She pointed again. "Over there is where they're cooking the lobsters and the clams." I could see white-uniformed caterers bustling around behind a screen, carrying platters of food to one of the buffet tables. "Oh, and wait 'til you see what else!"

"What else," I saw as we made our descent to the beach, was a bed. A king-size bed, set on the rug-covered sand, with a curved brass headboard, surrounded on all four sides with gracefully draped mosquito netting that swayed in the breeze. The bed was dressed all in white, from the crisp pillowcases to the down-filled duvet. A placard on the coverlet read "Reserved for the Bride and Groom." Selfie sticks protruded from both sides of the bed, as well as from its base, all positioned to snap the perfect shot. A sign affixed to one of them reminded the guests of the nuptial hashtag, #DRUEANDSTU. There was also, I noted, a hashtag for the mattress company and one for the linen supplier. When I pointed them out, Drue gave a modest shrug. "It was no big deal. Just a couple of brands came to us, and we figured, why not?"

Of course they did, I thought, feeling jealousy twist in my gut.

We left our shoes in the pile at the base of the staircase, where dozens of pairs of Docksiders and Havaianas, Prada flats and Tory Burch flip-flops had already been discarded. I unbuckled my sandals and did a quick scan of the female guests, noting that—no surprise—I was the largest woman there. Possibly even the largest person there. All of Drue's people—and, from the looks of it, lots of Stuart Lowe's, too—were fine-boned folks who looked like they subsisted on salted almonds and alcohol. There were cameras everywhere—one professional photographer gathering guests for posed shots, another snapping candids, and the majority of the guests with their phones out, taking advantage of the gorgeous setting to snap shots of themselves and their friends on the sand or by the water. A three-person video crew, with a fancy camera and a boom microphone, filmed the people photographing themselves.

"Let's get a drink."

"Sounds like a plan," said Drue. I was edging away from the cameras when I heard a dreamy voice behind me.

"Isn't it so so incredible?"

Corina Bailey, the groom's former fiancée, had padded up beside us and was looking rapturously out over the scene. Her flaxen hair was down. She wore an airy white eyelet cotton sundress, suspended from her shoulders on skinny lengths of satin ribbon. "It's the most beautiful thing I've ever seen," she breathed in her babyish voice. As I watched, she gave a dreamy sigh, pressing her hands against her chest in a prayerful pose.

Drue and I looked at each other and, in a moment of perfect BFF telepathy, we both rolled our eyes. Corina gave one more deep sigh and went drifting across the sand, heading toward the water's edge.

"Is she even leaving footprints?" I asked, half to myself.

"Nope. Jesus is carrying her." Drue folded her hands in imitation of Corina's, bowed, and squeaked, "Namaste."

I elbowed her. "You're going to hell."

"Oh, no doubt." Drue winked. "And if you're wondering why Stuart went from a dim-bulb like her to someone as wonderful as me, the answer is, I don't have an answer."

Before I could respond, a woman with a silvery chignon yodeled a "Yoo-hoo!" in Drue's direction.

"Gotta go," Drue said, and went bouncing off in the chignon's direction. I was heading for the bar, planning on finding an out-of-the-way place from which to drink and people-watch, when I heard a male voice, close behind me.

"Signature cocktail?"

I turned to see a guy smiling at me. He was about my age, with curly light-brown hair; emphatic, dark brows; a prominent nose; and a friendly expression. He had broad shoulders and slightly bowed legs. His shorts had once been red and had faded to a pinkish-salmon color; his frayed white button-down shirt was unbuttoned enough to reveal curling chest hair. His skin was olive-tinted and tanned in a way that suggested a lot of time spent outdoors, in the wind and the sunshine. He wasn't movie-star handsome, but he had a friendly, open face. Plus, I noticed, biceps that pressed at the seams of his shirt. He was just a little bit taller than me. In one big hand he held two flutes full of pinkish-orange liquid.

"What's in it?" I asked, as if I didn't know. As if Drue and I hadn't spent an hour in deep discussion on the question of whether she should go with a classic or have their mixologist come up with a bespoke cocktail for the rehearsal dinner, and if it should complement the one served after the wedding, or go in a completely different direction.

"I think they're Bellinis," said the guy. "Champagne and fresh peach juice."

I knew that they were actually called the Drue Gets Lowe, and that they were made with champagne and apricot nectar with a squeeze of lime, but decided not to say so. "Are they any good?" I asked.

"They're very sweet." He handed me a glass. "But I like sweet," he said, smiling as his gaze met mine. My cheeks felt hot as my fingers brushed against his. *Oh, God*, I thought. Did he think I was flirting with him? Then I felt my cheeks get even hotter, as I thought, *Was I?*

"Cheers," he said. "I'm Nick Andros." He clinked his glass against mine.

"Daphne Berg."

"Friend of the bride?"

"You got it."

"Are you staying in the big house?" He nodded in the direction of the stairs that led to the mansion.

"That's right. It's really something. It is big. The biggest big house I've ever been in!" *Oh, God*, I thought, cringing. This was the problem with a life where the male person I spent the most time with was eight-year-old Ian Snitzer. Get me around an actual man my age and I started babbling like a dolt.

"It's the Weinbergs' house." A strange look crossed his face and was gone so fast that I doubted I'd even seen it. He drained his glass, considered it, and said, "That was an experience." He looked at my glass, from which I'd taken a single sip. "But I think I'm going to get a beer. Can I get you something else, or are you going to finish it?"

"I'd love a glass of water."

He held out his hand for my glass. "Still or sparkling?"

"Still, please." He trotted across the sand, and I watched him go, appreciating the view, feeling flattered and confused. Was this guy actually interested in me? Maybe he was using the bar the same way old Brett had done and that would be the last I'd see of him. But a minute later, Nick was on his way back, holding a glass of water and a bottle of beer.

"That raw bar is insane. They've got crab legs. They flew them in from Florida." He shook his head. "Clams and mussels and oysters right here in the bay. I could wade into the water and come out with a bucket of littlenecks."

"Well, you know Drue! Only the best." That was my sneaky way of attempting to learn whether he did, in fact, know Drue; whether he was on the bride's side of the guest list or the groom's. My guess was that he was one of Stuart's buddies, maybe even a groomsman. He had the look: the broad-shouldered body of a rugby player, the worn but high-quality clothes, the easy, almost negligent manner that said *My family has been rich forever.*

But I was wrong. "Drue's an old family friend," Nick said. "But I haven't seen her in years. We were summer neighbors. My family used to have a place in Truro. Drue and I went to sailing camp together in Provincetown."

"Fancy," I said, imagining kids in Izod shirts, khaki shorts, belts embroidered with tiny whales, and Topsiders standing on the sleek wooden decks.

Nick smiled again, shaking his head. "It's the opposite of fancy. The fancy place is the Cape Cod Sea Camp in Brewster." His accent rendered the town's name as *Brewstah*. I smiled, charmed, as he kept talking. "The place we went is called the Provincetown Yacht Club. It's this hole-in-the-wall on Commercial Street, with a bunch of beat-up Beetle Cats and Sunfishes. They charge fifty bucks for the summer, and they teach you how to sail. The camp's mostly for townies. Or the rich families that have been here for a million years and know about it. They send their kids there."

Nobody loves a bargain like rich people, I thought. "Fifty bucks for the whole summer?" I asked, certain that I'd misheard.

He nodded. "You show up at nine in the morning, and you spend the day learning to sail. You get a free hour for lunch, and if it's high tide you ride your bike to the center of town and spend the hour jumping off the dock into the water, or you get a slice from Spiritus Pizza." His expression became dreamy. "It was great. I remember riding my bike around P-town, feeling like I was the king of the world."

"And that's where you met Drue?"

"Yup." He raised his beer to his mouth and tipped his head back as he drank. I watched the column of his throat shift under his smooth, tanned skin as he swallowed. When he finished, he wiped his lips and said, "She locked me in the supply closet."

"She what?"

Looking shamefaced, Nick said, "Drue had this gang of girls, and every few weeks they'd pick someone new to razz. When it was my turn, they'd send me to the store to get a half-dozen snipes, or they'd put hermit crabs in my shoes, or they'd make up names for points of sail so I'd fail my skipper's test." He smiled, remembering. "Beam reach, broad reach, beachward, landward, Squidward . . ."

I nodded, trying to look like I had any idea what points of sail might be.

"And one day, they sent me to get a life jacket, and they locked me in the supply closet." He shook his head, remembering. "Lots of spiders."

"Ugh. Sounds par for the course with Drue."

"So you're a friend?" He settled his arm on top of the cocktail table and leaned toward me.

"From sixth grade."

"Are you in the wedding party?"

"I'm a bridesmaid," I said. "I'll be right up front tomorrow. You won't be able to miss me." *Especially since I'm twice the size of the rest of the bridesmaids*, my traitorous mind whispered. I told my traitorous mind to shut up and concentrate on the cute guy across the table, on his arm, covered in curling brown hair, resting just inches from my own.

"Are you hungry?" he asked. "The oysters look good."

I had no idea what made an oyster look good, but I'd already decided to follow this guy wherever he wanted to take me. "Lead on, Macduff," I said.

He smiled at me as we strolled toward the raw bar. His smile was a little crooked, lifting the right side of his mouth higher than the left, and he was graceful as he walked across the sand. When we got to the buffet, he handed me a plate and picked up a pair of tongs. "Oysters?"

"Yes, please." I heard Nana's voice in my head, telling me that oysters were pure protein, low in calories and practically fat-free. I shooed that voice away, too, as Nick put a few oysters on the plate, shells clinking against the porcelain. He picked up a small silver cup of cocktail sauce and raised his eyebrows. I nodded and added clams, shrimp, a wedge of lemon, and a scoop of horseradish to my plate. Nick filled a plate for himself and led me to an empty cocktail table by the farthest bonfire. I squeezed lemon onto my first oyster, added a dollop of cocktail sauce, tipped it into my mouth, and gulped it down, humming in pleasure at its sweet, briny taste. Nick looked at me with approval.

"That's probably the freshest oyster you'll ever taste."

"It's amazing," I said, and ate another one. I wondered, briefly, if he was one of those guys whose fetish was feeding fat women, or watching them eat, but he hadn't seemed to be staring inappropriately, and he had turned his attention to his own plate instead of mine. He took his oysters with just a squeeze of lemon, I saw.

"So you're from New York?" he asked. "First time on the Cape?"

"That's right." We spent the next few minutes eating seafood and discussing our jobs and education. Nick, I learned, was a Massachusetts native who'd grown up in a suburb of Boston. He'd gone to the University of Vermont—"I was a big skier, but not much of a student in high school," he said—and was now back in Boston, working at a program that taught yoga to at-risk elementary school students.

"I know that sounds a little crunchy-granola," he said, which was exactly what I'd been thinking. "But there's science that shows that yoga breathing really works, and if you teach kids how to regulate their emotions while they're young, it helps them achieve as they get older."

"That's so interesting!" I said, thinking that it also explained his grace, his ease in his body. He didn't move like a man with a desk job. "So, do you have your summers off?" My mind supplied me with a picture of Nick, lounging on the sand, tanned and shirtless in his swim trunks, or cross-legged on a paddleboard, hands in prayer pose at his chest.

"I do. Which is why I'm here, on the Cape. The schools can't pay us a lot, and the businesses up here always need seasonal workers. Plus, it's where I spent my summers growing up. I'm basically a salmon, swimming back to my natal bed."

I smiled, appreciating the word "natal," wondering if he did crossword puzzles.

"I've been a lifeguard at the National Seashore beaches in Chatham, and worked at a bicycle shop in Orleans. This summer I'm the mate on a charter fishing boat."

I resisted the urge to make a dad joke about mates, as my brain adjusted the picture. Instead of Nick lolling on the beach, I was imagining him, still tanned and shirtless, only instead of paddling a paddleboard, he was holding a fishing pole, legs braced and chest muscles bulging as he worked the reel. "I know how that goes. My parents are teachers, too." I told him how my father worked at the school that Drue and I had attended, and that my mom taught art at any place that would have her, and how we'd all spent summers at a camp in Maine. I waited for him to reciprocate with information about his parents—their jobs, their hobbies, his life growing up. Instead, he swung the conversation back to the bride.

"So did Drue ever grow out of being awful?"

I spooned more horseradish on my last two oysters, stalling. "I'd say that it's an ongoing effort. You know. Progress, not perfection. One step forward, two steps back."

Nick nodded toward the groom, currently engaged in a game of touch football with his fraternity brothers. "It seems like she landed a decent guy."

"I haven't spent much time with Stuart." Because the parties

I'd attended hadn't filled in many blanks, my knowledge of the groom was still largely based on what I'd gleaned from TV and from Google. I knew that he was a good-looking guy with a Harvard degree; I knew that the critics had ranked him as among the best of *All the Single Ladies'* bachelors, the one most likely to treat the women he was courting like people and not bodies, which was impressive insofar as the producers would put the ladies in bikinis and hot tubs as frequently as the plot could be bent to accommodate swimsuits and bubbling water.

"Ah. You a big *Single Ladies* fan?" Nick inquired.

"I am," I said. "I can't even lie. That and *Real Housewives*."

He made a face. "You and my aunt. She swears she doesn't watch, but when that Countess Whoever came to Provincetown to do her cabaret act, she wanted tickets for both shows."

This led to a discussion of the *Real Housewives*, and his aunt, who also watched *RuPaul's Drag Race*, and all the drag performers who came to Provincetown in the summer. Nick asked how I liked the big house. When I told him how beautiful it was, and how my room came with a semiprivate hot tub and a private deck, he leaned close. Under the soap and fabric softener, he smelled like beer and sweat, warm skin and sunscreen, the very essence of summer.

"I heard," he said, his voice low, "that Drue's folks paid the Weinbergs thirty grand to rent their house for a week."

I felt my breath catch. "How do you know that?"

He looked down at his beer. "I shouldn't be gossiping."

"Oh, please," I said, "gossip away."

"How about we get a refill on the oysters first?"

I nodded, squeezing my last lemon wedge onto the flesh of the last oyster on my plate and tipping it down my throat. It was firm and sweet, like eating a mouthful of the ocean. I sighed with pleasure, and Nick smiled. The sun was starting to set, tinting the sky gold and apricot and flamingo pink.

Nick led me back to the raw bar, where I refilled my plate, then we strolled over to one of the bonfires. The sand underneath it had been flattened, then piled up at the rug's edges to form a kind of couch, and the seaweed had been raked against the dune. I wondered whose job that had been, and again how much this affair was costing the Cavanaughs.

"So tell me how you met Drue. You guys were school friends?" he asked.

I leaned back against the carpeted backrest, spreading the skirt of my dress over my legs, and gave him the abbreviated version of the story—that we'd been friends through high school, then hadn't seen each other for a while, and had recently reconnected. I wanted to get back to the wedding gossip or, better yet, to learn more about him, but Nick seemed interested in my history, and in life in the city, asking about my job and my life as a babysitter/Instagram influencer.

"I've done some babysitting myself. But I've never met an influencer before."

"Oh, I'll bet you have." I'd had only one glass of wine, an icy Riesling that was perfect with the oysters, plus a few sips of the signature cocktail. It shouldn't have been enough for me to feel buzzed, but I did, warm and expansive, with my joints and my tongue loosened. I leaned closer and whispered, in a mock-ominous voice, "We're everywhere."

"Can I see your page?"

"Of course." As I pulled out my phone, I examined his face for scorn or skepticism, any gesture or expression that would have implied doubt or disbelief that a reputable manufacturer would pay someone like me to model their clothes. But all I saw was curiosity.

"Here we go." The first picture on my Instagram feed was a shot that Drue had taken, of me on the ferry, wearing my navy-blue sunhat, red lipstick, and red-framed heart-shaped sunglasses.

Against the white-painted backdrop of the boat's railings, with the blue sky and the dark water behind me, the colors all popped, although I'd played around with the contrast and the saturation to get it just right.

"Very nice," Nick said.

"So you'll be following me?"

"I have a confession." Nick dropped his voice and leaned in close to me, so close I could almost brush the top of his head with my lips. "I'm not on Instagram."

I widened my eyes in an expression of shock. He grinned.

"I'm not actually online at all."

Now I actually was horrified. "What?" I sat back, staring at him. "No Facebook? No Twitter? No nothing?"

"No nothing," Nick confirmed.

"You mean you won't be posting shots of the wedding bed, with the approved wedding hashtag?" I shook my head. "I'm not sure they're going to let you stay."

"Oh, it gets worse. I didn't even have a smartphone until two years ago."

"Who even are you?" I asked him.

He shrugged. "I just never got around to it," he said. "At first, I thought Facebook was for, you know. Um. Older people. And I didn't need to sign up somewhere to keep in touch with my high school and college buddies when I saw them in real life. So, by the time I made up my mind to do it, everyone had moved on to the next thing." He smiled, wiggling his bare feet in the sand. "Guess I just missed my moment. But what about you? How does the influencer thing work? You use your account to advertise clothes?"

"Clothes, shoes, makeup," I said. "Exercise gear. Heart-rate monitors. My dog endorses organic pet treats. It's a whole hustle."

"How long have you been doing it?"

"Oh, a few years." I cleared my throat, figuring I should tell him my history before he borrowed someone's smartphone and looked it up himself. "I had a clip go slightly viral a while back. After that, a few brands approached me. I'd say it's been a slow build since then."

"And did you always want to be, you know, famous?"

I looked at him to see if he was teasing, but his expression was sincere. "I'm not famous," I said.

He gestured at my phone. "People are giving you money to wear their clothes and feed your dog their treats. That's kind of famous, right?"

I cringed, thinking of a term that I hated: "Insta-famous." I said, "If I'm famous at all, it's only in a very specific circle, to a very small number of people. And it's not about fame. It's about having a community. Connecting with people who care about the same things that you do." I sipped my drink.

"So what's the goal?" Nick's voice was still pleasant, but his expression had become a little guarded, somehow wary. Or maybe he was just genuinely clueless. Maybe influencers hadn't yet colonized Cape Cod, and this was all new to him. "Do you want to hit a certain number of followers? Make a certain amount of money? Or is it just about having a community?"

"You sound like my dad," I said, half to myself. My father had asked me all of these questions and more, usually after I'd pulled out my phone in the middle of a meal, to see how a post was doing, or respond to comments. "The goal," I repeated, using one fingertip to draw circles in the sand. "Okay. Ideally, if I could wave a magic wand and have everything I want, Instagram would be just for community and connection. And I'd make as much money as the big names, without having to deal with . . . you know, everything they deal with." I was thinking of the genuinely famous plus-size influencers and the hard-core hate-followers they attracted. So far, I'd only gotten a smattering of disparaging or cruel remarks, but I knew that the more followers I got, the more of them I could expect.

"I don't know," I said. "Maybe I'll give it all up and just do my crafts and run Bingo's account. Let her be the breadwinner."

This led, naturally, to a discussion of my crafts, which led to me showing him my Etsy storefront and then Bingo's account. Nick told me about the dog he'd grown up with, a flatulent beagle named Larry, who would howl every time he heard the refrigerator opening, and that he hoped to have a dog of his own someday, but that he wasn't home enough to give a pet the attention it would need.

For the next half hour, Nick and I sipped icy wine and ate oysters as the sun descended toward the waterline and the party got louder around us. I learned that the boat he worked on was called the *Lady Lu*, that a mate's jobs included gathering the bait—most of the charters used herring—setting the lines, baiting the hooks, helping clients reel in bluefish and striped bass, extracting hooks from fishes' mouths, and filleting the fish for the passengers to bring home. "It's expensive," he said. "We charge passengers seven hundred and fifty dollars for half a day, which covers our fuel, the equipment, maintenance and upkeep on the boat, all of that. Captain Steve's got regulars. People who go out every year. Fathers and sons, grandfathers or grandmothers and grandkids. For some of them, especially when the little kids catch their first fish, it's the best day of their summer."

"It sounds wonderful." I could picture it—a sunny day, a little girl squealing in excitement as her line bent, Nick standing behind her, coaching her as she pulled in her fish. I could also picture myself with Nick standing behind me, his chest against my back and his arms holding mine.

"It's great," he said, nodding. "I love being outdoors, working with my hands. I'm always sad when summer's over."

For a moment, I let myself imagine relocating to some quaint

Cape Cod town and working with Nick. Getting the boat ready, spraying off its decks or coiling ropes or whatever else one did. Spending days out on the water, in the sunshine, listening to whoops of excitement as people felt the tug of a fish on the line. Heading back to the dock as the sun went down, with the wind in my hair and Nick behind me, his hands warm on my shoulders. Taking pictures that would never be posted or shared, shots of the day that would just be for us.

Nick twirled an oyster shell around his plate with one blunt fingertip. He looked a little sad.

"Everything okay?"

"Oh, sure. Just lots of memories here," he said, his voice low.

"Did you go fishing when you were a kid?"

He jerked his head up, looking almost startled. Then he smiled. "Nah. It wasn't my family's thing."

I wanted to ask him more about his family and what their things had been. I wanted to hear all about the *Lady Lu*, and where his favorite beaches were, and how he liked to cook his bluefish, but that was when the dinner bell began to clang.

"Hope you like lobstah," Nick said cheerfully. He extended his hand, and I gripped it, careful not to let him take too much of my weight as I rose. His palm felt warm and callused, and it felt like the most natural thing in the world when he kept holding my hand as we made our way to the buffet line. The sky was streaked in a hundred shades of orange and gold, and the wind had picked up, sending a fine layer of sand skimming across the beach and churning the tops of the waves into lacy white foam.

"Magic hour," I murmured, looking at the light. Then I remembered that I wasn't just here for fun.

"Hey," I said, pulling out my phone. "Would you mind taking a few pictures?"

"For the 'gram?" he asked with a sly smile.

"Hey, I'm a working girl." I opened up the camera app, handed Nick my phone, and waded into the water, gathering my skirt as the water swirled, warm and foaming, around my knees. I could feel the tide's pull, the suck of the sand beneath my feet. I could smell lobsters and grilled corn on the cob and a whiff of corruption; crabs and fish decaying in the seaweed under the water.

"Turn that way," Nick said, pointing with his chin.

"Oh, are you my art director now?" I asked, turning as he'd directed and smiling as the wind lifted my hair.

"Very nice," he said as the bride strolled by. I called, "Hey, Drue!"

"There you are!" she said, and came trotting past Nick and splashing into the water, where she stood beside me and linked her arm with mine.

"One, two, three," Nick called. I smiled, tilting my head against Drue's. I could feel her trembling, like there was an electrical current running through her, and her eyes were very wide.

"Are you okay?" I asked.

"Sure!" she said. She must have gotten her teeth freshly bleached, or had new veneers put on. Her smile had always been bright, but now it was practically radioactive. "I'm better than okay! I'm getting married tomorrow!"

"I know! I know you are!"

She hugged herself. Ankle-deep in the water, she danced a funny, skipping jig, waving her arms, kicking to splash me as Nick said "Smile!" Maybe she wasn't anxious, I told myself. Maybe she was just exhilarated, euphoric at the prospect of her big day and her life with Stuart.

A minute later, Drue smacked a kiss on my cheek. "Post these!" she instructed, and went trotting away. When Nick gave me my phone, I scrolled through the pictures, holding my breath as I looked. Darshi, who'd become my unofficial Instagram photographer, knew that if she didn't shoot me from above, I risked looking like a collection of chins on top of boobs, but even without that warning, Nick had done a decent job. Better than decent, I thought, looking at one of the last shots he'd taken. Drue and I had both been laughing, facing each other, with droplets of spray that she'd kicked up arcing in front of us. Our mouths were open, eyes closed as we'd laughed, with our hair and skin glowing in that lovely, peachy light.

"Hey, these are great!" I said.

"Glad to be of service."

I threw a quick filter on the best shot and posted it alongside the words "Beautiful dress, beautiful night, beautiful bride," taking care to use Drue's wedding hashtag and to tag all the pertinent accounts, including Leef. As soon as I was done, Nick took my arm and led me to the buffet. People were lining up, the men resplendent in their linen shirts and madras shorts, the women in brightly colored sundresses. I could smell seafood and woodsmoke, perfume and aftershave, wine and beer and champagne, and, underneath it all, the briny scent of the ocean.

Nick and I filled our plates with lobster and clams and corn on the cob, and returned to our spot on the silky rugs in front of the fire at the farthest reaches of the party, in a nook that seemed custom-made for two. We ate, and finally he started to talk about himself: the time he and his cousins had taken their grandmother to play bingo in Provincetown, only, unbeknownst to them, it was drag bingo, and they hadn't had the heart to tell their grandmother that the woman in emerald sequins and matching eye shadow cracking jokes and calling numbers at the front of the room wasn't a peer from her assisted living and was not, in fact, a woman at all. "You'd think her name might've been a giveaway."

"What was her name?"

"Lotta Cox."

I laughed, and he smiled. I was enjoying his company, the

sound of his voice, the sight of his big hands deftly working his lobster cracker, his fingers neatly removing every shred of meat from the claws. A dab of butter gleamed on his chin, and I felt a warm glow, low in my belly, as I imagined how it would feel to lick it away.

"Save room for dessert," Nick said. "They've got an ice-cream sundae bar. It's homemade ice cream from Sweet Escape right up the road." He told me how the place had thirty flavors, and how, the previous summer, he and his friends had tried to eat their way down the board. "We were fine until we got to the fig sorbet. Stopped us all in our tracks. We went right back to Ryder Beach Rumble."

He helped me up again, handed our empty plates to a waiter, and led me to the tables, draped in white cloths, with uniformed servers armed with ice-cream scoops at the ready. It was dark by then, the bonfires piled high with logs, flames snapping and sending swirls of embers into the star-shot sky. The wind had picked up, and the air had gotten almost chilly. The waiters were piling blankets near the fires, along with sweatpants and hoodies, both embroidered with "DrueandStu" in a heart.

"Sweatshirt?" Nick asked, offering me one from the stack.

"No, I'm fine," I said, and added another thousand dollars to the wedding's price tag.

"How about we grab a blanket?" he asked.

Oh my God. I wanted to pinch myself to make sure I wasn't dreaming; that this cute, attentive, adorable guy wanted to sit under a blanket with me. Maybe the universe was trying to make up for high school.

I'd just picked up a bowl and a spoon when I heard raised voices: a man yelling, and a woman trying to calm him. When the wind shifted, the noise became words. ". . . fucking had it with you! I've fucking had it with all of this!"

I turned, craning my neck. There, away from the firepits and near the darkened dunes, was Drue's father, gesticulating with his arms spread wide. Drue was standing in front of him, wringing her hands, looking like she was trying to melt into the sand.

"Daddy," she said in an imploring tone I'd never heard from her before.

"Don't you 'Daddy' me. You and your mother. Peas in a pod." Spit flew from his lips with each explosive *p*. He stabbed one finger up at the dune and the house on top of it. "A hundred thousand dollars for rental houses? Ten thousand dollars for a Bentley to drive you three miles?" He jabbed a finger down toward the sand. "Hand-knotted antique silk rugs on the goddamn sand?!"

Drue sounded like she was crying. "You told me that you wanted it to be nice."

"*Nice* would have been fine. *This* is ridiculous." He kicked at one of the rugs in a fury.

"But I promise . . ." Drue turned her head and put her hand on her father's forearm. I couldn't hear what she was saying, but I could tell that she was offering something, trying to placate him . . . and that it wasn't working.

"Enough!" Mr. Cavanaugh sounded furious. He also sounded drunk. I recognized the slur of his words from the one time I'd encountered him back at Drue's home, in the middle of the night, in the dark. "It's enough!" he shouted again.

"Robert, keep your voice down." If Drue sounded desperate and her father sounded enraged, Drue's mother sounded as cool as the vapors off a chilled martini. She put her hand on her husband's forearm. He shook it off, so hard that she stumbled and almost fell before she recovered her balance. Drue flinched, but her mother's face didn't change.

"You're making a scene," she said.

Robert Cavanaugh shook his head. "You know what? I thought this would work. I trusted you. My mistake." He jammed his hands in his pockets, turned, and went up the wooden stairs, taking them two at a time.

Drue stood, frozen for a minute, her face shocked and unhappy. Her mother said something, and Drue said something back, but the wind had shifted again, and I couldn't make out any words. When Lily put her hand on her daughter's arm, Drue shook her head, turned, and went racing up the stairs after her father.

"Oh wow," Nick murmured. His arm had crept around me, and even though I was worried for my friend, I found that I didn't mind that at all.

Lily stepped back into the firelight and turned back to the crowd. She raised her arms and gave a big, hostess-y smile.

"I apologize for the disturbance," she said, and gave two brisk claps of her hands. "Now, who's ready for sundaes and Irish coffee?"

A few of the younger, drunker partygoers whooped their approval. With an effort so palpable you could hear it, the guests picked up their silverware and resumed their conversations, studiously keeping their eyes away from the hostess and the staircase. When I hazarded a glance in that direction, a woman who I thought was Drue's grandmother had pulled Drue's mom aside and was speaking to her urgently. I also noticed a number of guests on their phones, and wondered how many texts or tweets that little moment might have inspired.

My own phone pinged in my pocket. It was Darshi. SEND UPDATES, she'd written. NEED PIX. My heart sank. I wondered what I'd tell her; if she'd gloat at the details of her nemesis in misery, or if she'd feel sorry for Drue. And I knew that it was time to attend to my maid-of-honor duties, even if it meant sacrificing my chance with Nick.

"I'm going to go check on Drue," I said. "If I don't see you again tonight, I hope I'll see you tomorrow at the wedding."

He smiled again. For a minute, I thought he'd kiss me. Instead, he squeezed my bare forearm, pressing his fingers against the skin. "Go take care of your friend," he said, and nodded at my phone. "If you need any more pictures tomorrow, I'm your guy."

Chapter Nine

I swung by the bar for a glass of ice water and two shots of tequila, and swiped a bottle of white wine from an ice bucket at the side of the bar. With the water in one hand, the shot glasses in the other, the wine under my arm, and two wineglasses tucked against my chest, I hurried up the stairs, the hem of my dress trailing behind me. In the big house, Drue's bedroom door was locked. "Drue?" I called. I knocked and heard the creak of a bed, feet padding across the hardwood floors. "Here comes the bride," called Drue, in a tear-clogged voice. When the door swung open, I saw that Drue had cried or scrubbed off all her makeup. Her hair had been pulled into a ponytail, and she'd swapped her party dress for a Harvard T-shirt and a pair of sweatpants. Her feet were bare, and she'd taken off all her jewelry except for her enormous engagement ring. The man who'd given it to her was nowhere to be seen.

"Okay. Maid of honor here, with the world's best ice water," I said, showing her the glass. "I've got tequila. I've got wine," I said. "And I can go back to the bar and get anything else you want. I'm so sorry about . . ." I paused, considering, and finally went with ". . . all of that. Are you okay?"

Drue stared down at the beverages. Then her face crumpled, and she started to cry, sobbing so hard that she could barely breathe. I set the beverage assortment down on her dresser beside a half-empty glass of champagne that Drue must have acquired at some point, and reached out to draw her into my arms. I patted her back, murmuring "It's going to be okay" and "Don't worry, everything's fine." It sounded as if she was trying to say something, but all I could make out was the word "dad."

"Hey. Deep breaths. Come sit down." I got her settled on the bed and let her cry against me. When her sobs slowed down, she lay on the bed and curled on her side with her back to me, clutching her pillow. I settled a light blanket over her and rubbed her back in circles. When her breathing calmed, I went to the bathroom, wet a washcloth, and pressed it against her forehead and her cheeks.

"That feels good." Her voice was thick and froggy.

"My mom used to do it when I had a fever."

Drue started crying again. "I wish . . . my mom . . ." she choked out between sobs. I kept patting her back, wondering exactly where Drue's mother was, and why she'd decided it was more important to keep her guests comfortable than to check on her daughter. Drue's father, I assumed, had left the premises. I wondered if he'd show his face at the wedding tomorrow. Then I wondered if there was even going to be a wedding tomorrow.

Drue pulled in a shuddering breath and pushed herself upright. She wiped her face dry with the hem of her T-shirt, grabbed one of the shot glasses, and nodded at the other one. I picked it up. "To better days," I said. She clinked her glass against mine. We downed the booze, then I handed her the water. "Hydrate," I instructed, and watched as she swallowed every drop.

She set the glass down and wiped her mouth with her hand. "It's true," she said. "It's all true, what he said." Her voice was raspy, and her face was splotched and flushed.

"What do you mean?"

"About the money." She took another deep breath. "My mom was trying to spend as much on this wedding as she could. Not for me. But to get back at him. That was the entire point of this wedding. She wanted to stick it to him, one last time. They're getting divorced."

"Oh, Drue. I'm sorry."

"Yeah." She bent her head. "I just found out a few days ago. The whole time we were planning this, picking things out, my mom just kept saying that I should have everything I wanted. That it would be, you know, my big day, and how it was what my father wanted for me." Her lower lip was quivering, and her eyes were welling again. She turned away, blinking, tossing the bright spill of her hair over her shoulder. "Things haven't been great for my dad's business the past few years, but I knew that I could pay him back, for whatever the wedding cost. There's a trust fund from the other side of the family. I get it after I turn thirty, or when I get married." She shook her head, trying to smile. "Gotta love the patriarchy. 'You can't have the money until you're old enough to make good decisions, or until you marry some man and let him decide for you.' I mean, what if I got married when I was sixteen, and my husband was seventeen?" She cleared her throat. "Anyhow. My mom was the one who wanted all this. She and my father eloped. Did I ever tell you that?"

I shook my head.

"Yep. Lily got knocked up, junior year of Sweet Briar. She and my dad got married at City Hall. When we were planning, I thought that was why she kept pushing. That it was sort of a makeup for the wedding she didn't have. All of this—the party on the beach, the décor, the bed, the food, the car . . . she chose every single thing. She kept telling me to go for it, to make it fabulous, the party of the year, that he'd want that for me, and I thought . . ." Her voice cracked. "I thought he did. I thought he cared. I thought he was finally going to just show up for me. That he'd see how amazing it was, and he'd think that I was amazing, too. And he'd be proud of me. For the first time ever."

"Drue. I'm sure your dad is proud of you." I thought of the picture in the *Times*; the two of them, up on the roof, with the city spread out underneath them. "How could he not be?"

Drue gave a humorless snort. "He was so hungover at our high school graduation that he left halfway through the ceremony. He didn't even bother showing up when I graduated from . . ." She stopped herself, shaking her head. "It doesn't matter. Water under the bridge. I just thought, you know, he'd try to behave himself at my wedding. Or at least not make a scene." Her lower lip trembled. "Except this isn't about me and Stuart at all. It's about him. Him and her. And I'm just the stick that they hit each other with."

She started crying again. I patted her back, and when she sat up and settled her head on my shoulder, I put my arm around her and held her tight. "You know, you don't have to go through with this," I said. "Or you don't have to go through with it here, like this, if this doesn't feel right. Just take a rain check, and do it in six months, somewhere else. Destination weddings are so hot right now!"

She gave a sad smile. "It's all paid for. Nonrefundable. Everyone's here. Done is done. Might as well." She waved her hand toward the party and sighed again, letting her head droop. "I have three dresses. Did I tell you?" She had, of course, but I didn't interrupt. "One for the ceremony and one for the party and one for the after-party. Three dresses that probably cost more than . . ." Another head shake. "God, I don't want to think about it. And my mother just kept saying, 'Go for it. Get whatever you want. That's what your father wants for you.'"

"You're going to be gorgeous. Stunning. The most beautiful bride anyone's ever seen." I looked her in the eye. "But seriously, Drue, if it doesn't feel right, if it feels like it's about anything besides you and Stuart, you're allowed to call it off. Or postpone it.

I'll call Darshi. She's in Boston. She can be here in less than two hours. We can whisk you off to Bora-Bora."

Drue gave a hiccuppy, sobbing laugh. "Darshi hates me."

"Well," I said, "you did film her picking a wedgie and post it on our class Facebook page."

Drue's next laugh was significantly less sobbing. "That was bad. I should probably apologize."

"You should definitely apologize. I'm sure Darshi would appreciate it. But not tonight. Tonight, just take care of yourself."

Drue wrapped her sinewy arms around me and hugged me hard. "I can't thank you enough for being here."

"My pleasure. It's going to be great. I checked the weather, and it's perfection. High seventies, partly cloudy, slight breeze. Your chiffon overskirt will be blowing, your tendrils will be curling, you'll look like an angel. Now, what can I get for you? More water? Advil? Your fiancé?"

It looked like she was on the cusp of saying something. Her mouth was open, her eyes fixed on mine. *Stay with me*, I thought she'd ask. *Don't go.* And I wouldn't, of course. Because she was the bride. Because she was my friend. Because she was in a state you wouldn't wish on your worst enemy. Then her lips closed. She smoothed her hair and lifted her head and I watched as the veil of wealth and privilege dropped down around her; as she became, once again, beautiful, untouchable Drue Lathrop Cavanaugh: the luckiest girl I knew.

"I'll be okay. I'll just, you know, get my beauty sleep. It'll all look better in the morning." She tried to smile as she gave me a teasing shove. "You should go find that guy."

"What guy?" I asked.

"Oh, c'mon," she said, nudging me harder. "The cutie with the curly hair. The one who took our picture. He likes you. I can tell."

For a minute, I was right back in high school. *He likes you. I can tell.*

"What's his name?" Drue asked.

I made myself smile. "Nick Andros. He said you were in sailing school together."

"PYC!" she said, her face brightening briefly.

"You don't remember him? He says you locked him in the supply closet and put hermit crabs in his shoes."

She laughed and shook her head. "I wish that narrowed it down, but sadly, it does not. I don't know if you're aware of this, but I was kind of a mean girl growing up."

"You don't say."

"I'll bet Grandma Lathrop knows him. Dad said she'd invited half the Cape. That was, like, complaint number thirty-seven. Ask her if you need the dirt on the guy, or his family. She's probably holding up the bar."

Nick hadn't said anything about his family being in attendance. Then again, I hadn't asked. Either way, I wasn't about to start grilling Drue. Not if there was even a tiny chance that they'd hooked up at some point. If they had, I did not want to know.

"Whoever he is, he's adorable. Go on," she said, and gave me an encouraging push. "I'll see you in the morning."

"Are you sure?"

"Positive." At the door, she hugged me—a real hug, not the hands-on-the-shoulder, bodies-apart maneuver I'd seen her perform with other guests on the beach. "Thanks, Daphne," Drue whispered in my ear. "Thank you for being my friend."

I left Drue's bedroom via the deck, thinking that I could use the fresh air. The bonfires and the party lights were vivid against the dark sky and the dark sea. I could smell seaweed and woodsmoke, and could hear the waves and the opening bars of a Beyoncé song, signaling the DJ's arrival.

I was halfway across the deck when a voice came from the dark corner.

"Is she all right?"

I gave a little scream and jumped, whirling around, trying to make out the face and the body that belonged to the voice. "Who's there?"

"I'm sorry." A figure detached itself from the shadows and moved toward me, into the light. "I didn't mean to startle you."

I bit my lip as I looked the stranger over. If Nick and the groom's friends had displayed the gloss and the ease of old money, at home in their own skin, convinced of their own worth, of their own place in the world, this guy was neither shiny nor comfortable. His hair was thick and dark, cut so that it covered his forehead. He had dark skin, thick brows, a narrow face, and big brown eyes behind heavy, plastic-framed glasses.

From the neck down, things only got worse. His chest was narrow, his belly was soft, his hips were wide, and his legs were as skinny as twigs. He wore the same kind of shorts that Nick had been wearing, but while Nick's were faded to a pinkish-maroon and looked soft and worn and comfortable, this guy's shorts were fire-engine red, the waist pulled up high and tight around his midsection, the leg holes so loose that they made his thin legs look scrawny. He was beltless, which was wrong, and his white polo shirt was tucked in, which was also wrong. A plume of chest hair protruded from the V-neck. Instead of bare feet or flip-flops or deck shoes, he was wearing—I blinked to confirm it—sandals. Tevas. With white athletic socks pulled halfway up his hairy shins.

"Is Drue all right?" he asked again, a little more urgently.

"She's fine," I said. "Are—are you a friend?" It seemed highly unlikely that he was Drue's friend; unlikely, too, that he was one of Stuart's buddies.

"A friend," he repeated. "Yes." He cleared his throat. "I work with Mr. Cavanaugh."

"Ah." That, at least, made a species of sense. I imagined he was some kind of tech wizard, socially awkward but brilliant.

"I saw what happened—" He gestured down toward the beach. "I was worried. About the bride."

"Do you know Drue?"

He opened his mouth and then closed it, and shook his head. "Not well," he said. "But still." He touched his chest. His Adam's apple bobbed as he swallowed. "Is her fiancé with her?"

"He wasn't when I left."

The stranger sighed, looking troubled. "I was going to bring her this." He reached behind him and showed me a glass of ice water. "But I saw that you thought of it first. You're her friend from high school, right?"

"Right," I said, and wondered why a business associate of Mr. Cavanaugh's knew so much about the boss's daughter. Then again, he hadn't mentioned anything that couldn't be learned from a quick peek at Drue's Instagram. "Well. I guess I'll see you at the wedding tomorrow!"

He nodded. "Yes. See you there."

Weird, I thought. I crossed the deck and opened the door on Drue's side of the hot tub. Maybe he'd seen Drue at work and become infatuated with her. Maybe he was some lovestruck Romeo, come to torture himself as the girl he loved married another man. Or maybe, I told myself as I opened the door out to my own deck, he's just a normal, decent person who was trying to do something kind.

When I stepped out onto my deck, my heart leapt. There was Nick Andros, sitting on the edge of the round, cushioned daybed with two shot glasses in his hand.

"I thought you could use a drink," he said, handing me a glass.

"You have no idea." I sat down beside him on the daybed, clinked my glass against his, and swallowed it down. The whiskey made my eyes water, and lit up my throat and my chest with a welcome glow.

"This place is insane," he said, tilting his head to look up at the house. "I bet I could move into one of the guest rooms and no one would know I was here."

"You and a family of four," I said.

"So what's going on?" he asked, his face full of concern. "Are you okay? Is she okay?"

I nodded. "I'm fine. Drue, not so much."

He shook his head. "Weddings bring out the worst in people. Two of my cousins got in a fight because Ellie wanted an adults-only wedding and Anne showed up with her baby. In a tiny little baby tuxedo that she'd obviously bought for the occasion."

"Oof," I murmured. I decided not to bring up the fact that Drue hadn't remembered him. She was upset, and maybe she'd been drinking, and then there'd been that fight. Surely the combination of emotion, alcohol, and a four-hundred-person guest list could explain the confusion.

"Do you think there's going to be a wedding in the morning?" he asked.

"Oh, I'm sure the Lathrop Cavanaughs can find a way to sweep it all under the carpet. WASPs, you know," I said, hoping, belatedly, he wasn't one. He must have guessed what I was thinking, because he smiled and shook his head.

"Portuguese Irish Italian," he said. "Lapsed Catholic. We sweep nothing under the carpet. At every family gathering, you're guaranteed two things: a big fight and lasagna. Lasagna at Thanksgiving, in case you don't feel like turkey. Lasagna at Christmas, in case you don't want turkey or ham."

"My kind of people," I said, sighing happily.

"You were nice to go check on Drue." He put one hand on my shoulder and squeezed, just a brief touch, but I felt it over every bit of my skin. "So. What was all that about?"

"I think the bride's parents are having some issues around the wedding," I said, congratulating myself. If they gave out medals for best use of euphemisms, I'd probably qualify.

"Was Stuart in there with Drue?"

"He was not." I decided not to tell him about the weird guy who'd been lying in wait on the deck. I was being paranoid. He was probably just a nice guy, and the world needed more nice guys, more trust and less suspicion.

Nick pursed his lips, seeming to think, before he gave me a meaningful chin-down, eyebrows lifted, I've-got-a-secret look.

"What?" I asked.

He dropped his head. "I shouldn't say."

"Oh, come on," I said, bumping my hip against his side in a playful manner. It felt like nudging a warm stone wall. He was solid. Big and solid. "Now you have to."

"Tell you what," he said. "Is there really a hot tub back there?"

I smiled, looking at him coyly from underneath my lashes. Unless I was way off, he was angling for an invitation, and, while the prospect of sharing a hot tub with Nick was far from unwelcome, I also wanted to hear the dirt on the groom.

He stood, took my hand, and led me back the way I'd come, through the door in the hedges, which he shut and locked behind us. He hit the button that started the hot tub's jets, pulled off his shirt, and dropped it onto one of the lounge chairs. The skin of his shoulders looked enticingly smooth. I could see the muscles in his shoulders, the way his waist narrowed into a V. His chest was obscured with a tangle of dark-brown hair, and a trail of hair led down past his navel and disappeared into the waistband of his shorts.

A braver girl—Drue, for example—might have shucked off her dress and jumped into the water in her bra and panties. I wasn't that girl yet. "Be right back," I said, and hurried inside. I'd packed my trusty black SlimSuit, a garment made of such restrictive material that it took me a good ten minutes to wriggle it on. I'd also brought my Leef swimsuit, the Darcy, so I could get pictures wearing it at the beach. And I'd packed a bikini, one I'd worn only in the privacy of my bedroom. It was navy blue with purple polka dots, a halter top, and retro-style, high-waisted bottoms, making it as modest as a bikini could be. Still, it was, in fact, a bikini, and it did leave a portion of my pale, soft stomach visible to the entire world.

Now or never, I thought, pulling on the bikini, with my white lace-trimmed cover-up on top. I put my hair up in a clip, swiped gloss on my lips, and grabbed my phone. *So much to tell you*, I texted to Darshi. *Huge fight hot guy mysterious stranger more soon.* I could see the bubbles indicating that Darshi was writing back, but instead of waiting for her reply I tossed my phone on the bed and padded, barefoot, back to the hot tub before I could lose my nerve.

Nick was in the water, smiling at me through the steam. I saw his shirt and—I swallowed hard—his shorts on the chair next to the hot tub. Was he there naked?

"Boxer shorts," he called, like he was reading my mind. "C'mon, the water's fine."

In one swift and, I prayed, not ungraceful motion, I pulled off the cover-up, threw it over the back of a chair that I'd judged to be close enough to let me grab it from the water, and got myself into the hot tub. The water was deliciously warm, and there was enough booze in my system to have me feeling happy and expansive, at ease in my skin and at peace with the world. Part of me wondered why Nick was trying so hard to charm me. Part of me scolded myself for doubting that he'd be interested in me. The biggest part of all wanted to put my hand on his shoulder and see if his skin felt as warm and as smooth as it looked. "So tell me," I said.

"What's that?" he called, cupping one hand behind his ear. I scooched myself closer, locating the grooves of a seat beneath the bubbling water. Nick put his arm around my shoulder, pulling me gently against him, and moved my mouth close to his ear. I could feel the warmth of his hand on my shoulder, and his beer-scented breath on my cheek. "Stuart was engaged before Drue, right?"

I nodded. "To Corina. From the TV show."

For a long moment, Nick was silent. I could hear the hot tub's motor, the water splashing on its sides, and the noise drifting up from the beach, the sound of music, along with the smoky scent of the bonfires. "I got here early, so I had some time to kill. I took a stroll down toward Corn Hill, where the public beach is." He jerked his thumb to the left, indicating what I supposed was the beach in question. "I saw Stuart with a girl."

"And the girl wasn't Drue." Nick shook his head. My heart sank on Drue's behalf.

"Do you know who it was?"

"I didn't get a good look. She had very light hair."

Corina, I thought. "Yikes," I murmured. *Corina and Stuart are friends!* I remembered Drue telling me. And besides, if she shows up, it's a story. *People* magazine will probably write something. They might use a picture, too. "What were they doing?"

"Just talking, mostly," said Nick. "But they were close. Like, kissing close."

I found that I could barely breathe. I was shocked. I felt sorry for Drue. But, along with the shock and the sympathy, I felt a wicked, guilty thrill of satisfaction. There was, it seemed, a part of me that was delighted by the idea that Stuart didn't love Drue, a part of me that still wanted to see my old friend get hurt. "I don't get it. If Stuart is still in love with Corina, why didn't he just marry Corina? The network was going to pay for it. They had a broadcast date and everything."

"Who knows?" The muscles of Nick's shoulders rippled as he shrugged. "Maybe Drue had something he wanted. Something Corina didn't."

"Oh my God," I said, and tried to make myself breathe and

think calmly. "I should tell her." I looked at him, waiting for confirmation. "I should tell her, right?"

Nick was quiet again. "Do you think that maybe she knows?"

I felt my mouth drop open. He lifted his hands. "I'm not saying she does. But if she doesn't, isn't she going to be inclined to shoot the messenger?"

"I can't let her marry a guy who's already cheating on her." I slumped against the hot tub's edge. I could imagine the scene: Drue, still teary-eyed, opening her door. Me, wet-haired and wrapped in a towel, saying that her fiancé had been seen canoodling with his ex. Drue telling me that I was lying; that this was payback for that night at the bar, that I was making things up just to hurt her. That I was fat and dumb and ugly and she'd never really liked me, she'd only felt sorry for me; that they'd all just felt sorry for me.

"I don't get it," I said. "I mean, you know Drue." When Nick nodded, I said, "She has everything. She's beautiful, she's rich, she's going to inherit the family business. Why would she marry a guy who wasn't in love with her?"

"I don't know. Maybe she wanted the right kind of guy. Maybe she had a deadline in her head. Maybe nothing else was working out." Nick let water fill his cupped hands and splashed it on his face. He scooped another handful and let it trickle over the top of his head, plastering his curls to his cheeks and forehead. I could see his nails, clipped short, and the scattering of hair on his fingers. My breath caught again, and my heartbeat sped up.

"Or maybe she thinks Stuart does love her," he said. "Maybe he's been lying to her. Stringing her along."

"Oh, God," I said, slumping back into the bubbling water. "What should I do?" I asked. My voice was mournful and small. "Poor Drue."

Nick stretched one arm behind me, groping for the shorts

he'd abandoned on the chair. He pulled a silver flask out of the pocket, unscrewed it, and offered it to me. I took a sip, feeling the whiskey burn a hot trail down my chest. He took a swallow, then tossed the flask back onto the chair and draped his arm around me again, pulling me close.

"I think you just be her friend," he said. "You support her in whatever she decides to do. And you're there for her if it falls apart."

I nodded bleakly.

"Here's to happily ever after." He put his arms around my waist, turned me until I faced him, lifted me up, and settled me into his lap, so close that our noses almost touched. I could see that his eyes weren't brown; they were hazel, flecked with green. Droplets of water gleamed in the stubble on his lip and chin.

"Hey," he said, very softly.

"Hey," I whispered back. I felt my breath catch as Nick's hand cupped the base of my head, and I had a moment to be grateful that the water made me weightless as he pulled me closer. His lips were gentle, tentative at first, barely brushing against mine. He tasted like whiskey and salt. I touched his hair, sinking my hand into his curls, feeling the bones of his head against my palm as the kiss deepened. The bubbling water swirled around us. Steam was rising in the air, shutting out the world, making me feel like we were in our own private grotto, and Nick's lips were hot, and his tongue was moving in my mouth in lazy strokes. It felt so good that I was dizzy, as Nick maneuvered me toward the center of the hot tub, where the water was deeper. He knelt down, still holding me, and it was the most natural thing in the world for me to wrap my legs around his waist. I could feel his chest, firm and strong against mine, and I could feel something else, substantial and wonderfully solid, nudging against me.

Daphne Berg, my mind whispered, *are you really going to hook up with a stranger the night before your best friend's wedding? You absolute cliché.* Meanwhile, Nick's hands were at the clasp of my bikini top. "Okay?" he whispered.

"Okay." He unhooked the strap and gave a happy sigh as my breasts tumbled into his hands. I arched my back as he pressed them together, holding them gently, before bending his head, circling one nipple with the tip of his tongue, then covering it with rough, lapping strokes that made me quiver and press myself even more tightly against him. He held me still, his hands pinning me in place as he gave my other nipple the same treatment, first licking, then biting gently. When I sighed, he bit down harder, and I shuddered with a sensation that was right on the edge of pleasure and pain.

I leaned forward to press openmouthed kisses on the salty skin where his neck met his shoulder. He cupped my jaw, raising my lips to his, and we were kissing fiercely, with my bare breasts pressed tight against the skin of his chest, my hands clutching his shoulders.

"Oh," I sighed, when we finally broke apart. "Oh, wow." Nick's eyes were wide, cheeks flushed, lips swollen, pupils dark in the steamy air. He gave me a crooked smile. "I thought this wedding was going to be boring."

"Same," he said. He took my hand and guided it under the water, letting go just as I made contact with his erection, so that what happened next would be my choice. I exhaled, appreciating his thoughtfulness. Then I gripped him, rubbing with the heel of my hand, moving the cloth gently against his skin. Nick settled his free hand against the small of my back before letting it drift down to cup my bottom. I stretched my hand lower, cupping his balls, letting my fingertips graze the crease behind them. Nick groaned against my neck. He worked his hand underneath the elastic waistband of my bathing-suit bottom, and I was too turned on to think about my jiggly belly, or whether he'd be able to see my stretch marks. He pressed his hand between my legs, moving his mouth back to my breasts, pressing the tip of his index finger against my most sensitive spot. I could feel his stubble scrape my skin, and his teeth closing gently around my nipple, and his tongue flicking at it, as he held his hand perfectly still. I rocked against him, hoping to give him a hint. He pulled back to smile at me, and I growled in frustration. That was when his fingers finally started to move.

"Oh, God." I wriggled, rocking against him as he stroked me, breathing hard, feeling his fingers curving inside of me, with my mouth pressed against the juncture of his neck and shoulder.

"Daphne," he breathed in my ear, "you feel so good."

I pressed my lips to the curve of his ear. "I want you inside me," I whispered. He pulled back to look at me.

"Are you . . . is it safe? I don't have any condoms. I wasn't expecting to make new friends tonight."

"There's some in the gift basket by the bed."

"Thoughtful." Nick vaulted over the hot tub's edge, reaching for a towel. Water sheeted down his back and off his shoulders, and in the steam-thick air, I thought he looked like a statue come to life, all silky skin and muscles, his legs lean and muscled, his bottom high and firm. I could see the ridges of his ribs, the articulation of his abs as he crossed the deck and went to the bedroom. When he came back, facing me, I could see his erection bobbing cheerfully in the night air and had a moment's worth of panic. It had been more than two years since I'd been with a guy, and that had been a forgettable hookup with a colleague of Darshi's, and Nick's erection was sizable. He must have seen me looking, because he gave it a few lazy strokes before rolling the condom into place. "Hurry," I whispered, and he gave the condom one last tug, with a look of intense concentration, like he was getting ready to take a test.

I decided that I wanted to make him smile, that I wanted to make him gasp and sigh, the way he'd made me gasp and sigh.

"Come here," I said. Nick hopped into the water. I glided

over to him, settled myself against him. He touched me, stroking with just the very tip of his finger. "God," he murmured, "you're so slippery."

"Come on," I said, and took hold of his sheathed erection. He waited, looking up, his eyes on mine. I took a deep breath, closed my eyes, and lowered myself down, inch by slow inch, until he was all the way inside of me. *I'll bet you make love like a fat girl*, Alec Baldwin's character had once said to Tina Fey's neurotic, self-conscious character on *30 Rock*, and after I'd heard it, whenever I had sex I would hear it echo in my head; the idea that fat girls tried harder in bed, that guys expected exotic tricks or above-average willingness to make up for our extra pounds. I didn't know tricks. All I had was desire and enthusiasm. But Nick seemed satisfied as he gazed up at me, gripping my breasts with just the right amount of pressure. I waited until I couldn't possibly hold still for another second. Just when I was getting ready to move, he groaned and grabbed my hips, thrusting, first gently, then harder. I tossed my head to get my wet hair off my face, taking him in more deeply, and as the water churned around us, Nick kissed me, and I forgot to be ashamed, or worry about how things sounded, or how fat girls made love. I could feel the warm water lapping at my back. I could hear the splashes, the tiny clicking noises of wet flesh on lubricated rubber, our breath coming faster and louder, Nick's soft gasps. His hands slid from my breasts to my hips, but he was letting me set the pace, letting me take my pleasure, letting me use him, and that thought alone, along with the expression on his face as he watched me, was almost enough to push me over the edge.

Almost, but not quite. I took his hand off my hip and guided it down to where our bodies were joined. Nick made a strangling noise, and his hips jerked as he pushed deep inside me, and as I put his fingers where I needed to feel them.

"Oh!" I cried, as I felt it begin. He held me tight, angling his hips and thrusting hard and fast, and I threw my head back, feeling my climax ripple through me, crying my pleasure into the wide, dark sky.

I woke up at just after five in the morning, as the early-morning light was starting to spill through the floor-to-ceiling window. I'd forgotten to pull the shades down. I'd forgotten to text Darshi. My phone, which I'd forgotten to charge, was on the bedside table, flashing urgently.

I yawned, smoothing the tangled, stiff nest of my hair, smiling at how good I felt. Round One had been in the hot tub, and Round Three had been on the bed, and in between, we'd been kissing by the windows, and Nick had pushed me until my back was flattened against the cool panes.

"Nick, we can't," I'd whispered, because there were people out on the deck. I could hear them and could smell their cigars.

"Shh," he'd whispered, nuzzling the nape of my neck, then kissing his way down my body. "We can if you're quiet." I'd set my teeth into the inside of my lip to keep from moaning as he'd licked me, his tongue teasing and flickering, so gently and gradually that I'd wanted to scream. I'd never thought I'd had an exhibitionist streak, but the idea that there were people, right there, with only a few inches of glass between the wedding guests and our naked bodies, had made me wild, and more than happy to return the favor as soon as I trusted my legs to hold me again.

I stretched my arms above my head and gave a happy sigh. God, I'd missed sex! Not just the way it made you feel completely connected to another person, but the way it made you feel completely at home in your own body. And, as good as the sex had been, the best part of the night was the moment when we'd both woken up together, after the second time, before the third. Nick had pressed his forehead to mine, looking right into my eyes.

"Hi," he whispered, in his low, sleep-scratchy voice.

"Hi," I whispered back. He'd stroked my cheek with his thumb, looking at me. It hadn't lasted long, just long enough for me to construct our entire life together in my head, from our marriage (a much-smaller wedding in Cape Cod) to our lives running a charter fishing business/Etsy store. I'd make memory boxes and birdhouses; he'd take families fishing, we'd spend every night together. "You're such a sweetheart," Nick had whispered. I'd tilted my head for a kiss, and he'd eased his fingers inside of me. "Is it okay?" he'd asked, seeing my tiny wince.

"I'm fine," I'd told him. It had hurt, but in a wonderful, sweet way. "Don't stop."

I rolled over. The other side of the bed was empty. The pillowcase was smooth, the sheets and comforter pulled tight, as if no one had been there at all.

"Nick?" I called, keeping my voice low. No answer. I got up, wrapping the soft, fringed blanket from the foot of the bed around myself, and peeked into the bathroom. It was empty. There was literally no sign of him—no clothes, no shoes, no wet towels or man-size footprints, not even a condom wrapper by the side of the bed. Maybe last night didn't happen. Maybe I'd made the whole thing up. Except I could see a purplish-red mark on the top of my breast, and between my legs, and in my lower belly and the insides of my thighs, I felt deliciously sore.

I slid open the glass door and stepped onto the deck, feeling the breeze against my bare shoulders. It was going to be a beautiful day. The sky was already streaked orange and rust, and I realized, with a guilty pang, that we hadn't turned the hot tub off. Wisps of steam were rising in the air, and I could hear the motor chugging above the sound of the waves.

I looked through the door in the hedge. Something was in the water. *A bird*, was my first thought as I crossed the deck and got close enough to see.

It wasn't a bird. It was Drue. She was facedown, in a bikini, with her blond hair tangled around her head, swaying in the water as the jets pumped. I screamed her name and grabbed at her body, and the stiff wrongness of it was immediate, gutting. It felt like I was moving a doll and not a person as I tried to yank her out of the water. "Help!" I screamed, and got her up and out and down to the deck, where I knelt, pressing my ear to her wet chest. No heartbeat. I touched my fingers to her neck. No pulse.

"Drue!"

I pounded her chest, then tilted her head back, opening her mouth, trying to remember the CPR class I'd taken a million years ago. "Help!" I shouted. "Someone help me!" But even as I heard doors open and people pounding across the deck, even as I pressed my lips to hers and started to breathe, I knew that Drue was dead. Everything that had ever been inside her, everything, good and bad, that had made my beautiful, terrible friend who she was, all of it was gone.

Part Two

The Summer Friend

Chapter Ten

"One more time," he said. The man's name was Ryan McMichaels, and he was a detective with the Truro Police Department. He was in his fifties, a white man with blue-gray eyes and a jowly face above a blocky body. His hair was iron gray, thick, almost bristly as it stood in spikes over his head. A fat and neatly clipped caterpillar of a mustache sat above his thin lips. His eyebrows were also thick, but unruly, full of wiry hairs poking out in every direction. His reddish skin looked angry at being exposed to the sun, or maybe he'd just given himself an especially aggressive shave before coming to the murder scene. He wore a red tie, knotted tight under his throat, a gold wedding band on his left hand that kept catching the light as he moved his arm around, asking me about this morning, asking me to tell him everything, from start to finish, the whole way through.

It was not quite eight in the morning, not quite three hours after I'd discovered Drue, and I was still shaky and terrified and heartbroken. What had happened? Where was Nick? And why hadn't I heard anything when my best friend was presumably drowning just outside my door?

The hours after Drue's death had been a jumbled blur. I'd

remembered screaming, and people coming—Minerva, looking ghostly under a glistening layer of face cream, and a guy from the catering crew, with his apron flapping around his waist as he ran. Someone had pulled me away from the hot tub and led me back to my room. At some point, someone else had brought me a cup of hot coffee. I remembered sitting on the bed, my hands wrapped around the mug, shaking like I'd been thrown into a tub of ice. Through the window that faced the water, I saw Drue's body being loaded onto a stretcher as cops photographed the scene; through the windows that faced the front of the house, I saw the woman with the silvery chignon from the night before help load Mrs. Cavanaugh into the back of an enormous Escalade, then climb in behind her.

I'd gotten dressed, washed my face, brushed my teeth, and finally noticed my phone, still lying on my unmade half of the bed. Dully, I picked it up and saw texts from last night scroll across the screen. *Where are you*, Darshi had written at eleven p.m. *I need details*. A line of question marks at midnight about an event that seemed like it had happened in another lifetime. And, at one o'clock in the morning, *If Drue messed this up for you I will kill her.* Followed by the emojis for a bride, a knife, and a skull.

I must have gasped. Then, quickly, I deleted the texts, knowing that it wouldn't matter. Text messages existed in the cloud, in the ether, in perpetuity, like every single other thing on the Internet. My friend was dead, and my roommate had just unknowingly turned us both into suspects.

Eventually, Minerva had returned to my room. "The police want to talk to you."

I stood up. "Hey," I said, my voice steady, my tone casual, "did you happen to see a guy named Nick anywhere around?"

She looked at me, unblinking. Without answering, she'd gestured toward the stairs, where Detective McMichaels had been waiting. He'd led me through the empty living and dining room and into a small pantry just off the kitchen, with a built-in desk and shelves full of canned food, boxes of pasta, and canisters of sugar and flour. A lobster pot, high as my knees, sat on the floor, next to a package of paper cocktail napkins printed with the announcement that at the beach, it was always Wine O'Clock. I'd sat and told him my story, then I'd gone through it all again, and now he was looking at me, eyebrows raised in expectation. Instead of starting my story for the third time, I asked, "Do they know what happened? How she . . ." I swallowed hard. "How she died?"

"It's too early to tell," McMichaels said. True, but I'd heard the whispers, before the cops had come and cordoned off the crime scene, when people were still out on the deck and I'd been able to hear them through my bedroom's sliding doors. *Maybe she was drunk, and she passed out and drowned. Maybe she hit her head.* Someone had remembered the story of an NFL player's toddler who had drowned after her hair had somehow gotten stuck in a hot tub's drain, and someone else had mentioned the bride who'd been paralyzed the night before her wedding, after a bridesmaid pushed her into a pool.

"If you don't mind, I need you to walk me through the events one more time."

My lips felt frozen when I said, "This wasn't a . . . a suspicious death, was it?" I'd thought about saying *unnatural*, but wasn't it unnatural anytime a healthy young person died?

"Please, miss. If you could just answer my question."

"Of course," I said. I told him how Drue and I had taken the ferry over from Boston the day before, how we had gotten ready for the rehearsal in the afternoon, and descended the stairs together as the party on the beach began. "Drue spent most of the night circulating. I had dinner with one of the other guests, an old friend of Drue's, a guy named Nick Andros."

"So you didn't spend much time with Drue last night?"

I shook my head. "I only saw Drue for a few minutes, here and there. We took pictures." I reached for my phone.

The detective said, "I can take a look later. Why don't you keep going?"

Deep breath. "We'd just gotten up to get dessert when the fight started."

"What fight was this?" he asked, his tone neutral.

"Drue's parents were fighting," I said. "Lily and Robert Cavanaugh. This was down on the beach, right by the stairs."

"And the fight was about . . . ?"

"The cost of the wedding. I mean, I think. That's based on what I heard. Drue's dad was yelling about how much the rugs cost—the rugs they'd put on the sand—and the houses they'd rented. Drue was trying to talk to her dad, and he started yelling at her. He said that she and her mother were like peas in a pod. He went up the stairs, and Drue went after him, and then I got some drinks and went after her."

"What drinks?"

"Two shots of tequila. A glass of ice water. A bottle of wine."

He raised his eyebrow. "I didn't know what she'd want," I said, hoping that I didn't sound defensive.

"You went to Miss Cavanaugh's bedroom?"

"That's right."

"Did you see Mr. Cavanaugh? Speak to him?"

"No," I said, remembering how relieved I'd felt when I'd found Drue alone, how reluctant I'd been to confront her father. "Just Drue. She was very upset. She told me that she'd learned that her parents were getting divorced. They were fighting because her father thought the wedding was just a way for her mother to stick her dad with a huge bill."

"Did Drue indicate when she'd learned that her parents were divorcing?"

"She just said that she'd found out recently," I said. "She said she'd just found out. I'm not sure if she meant just then, down on the beach, or at some other point, but it had been recent."

"So you came up from the beach to see her?"

I nodded.

"With the drinks?"

I nodded again.

"There was bottled water in all of the rooms, right?" When I nodded, he asked, "Why did you carry a glass of ice water all the way up the stairs when there was bottled water waiting?"

"I don't know." My voice was a whisper. "I thought, water with ice and lemon was nicer, you know? It was fancier. And I wanted her to have something nice. So she'd know I cared."

For what felt like a long time, he looked at me, unspeaking, as if he was waiting for me to blurt out, *I did it!* "Go on," he finally said. "What happened next?"

"I tried to get her to calm down. I sat with her for a while, on her bed. We talked."

"About?"

"About the fight. Her parents. The wedding. I asked if she wanted to go through with it, and she said she did. I asked if she wanted me to stay with her. She said she didn't. That I should go, that she'd be fine." A lump swelled in my throat. "She told me I was a good friend."

"This was about what time?"

"Right as they were serving dessert. So maybe nine o'clock, nine-thirty? It had finally gotten dark."

"Was Miss Cavanaugh drinking?"

"At the party? I don't really know. Like I said, she was circulating. Talking to her guests. I wasn't with her much."

"How about in her room, after the fight? Did she drink any of what you brought her?" Maybe I was being paranoid, but I thought I could hear accusation in his tone.

"We both did the shots, and I made her drink the water. I

don't know about anything else." I thought I remembered seeing a bottle of champagne on the dresser, along with a glass, but I hadn't actually seen Drue drinking, so I decided not to mention it.

"What happened next?" The detective's face was expressionless, but I could feel judgment, rolling off him in noxious waves as we returned to the post-Drue part of my night.

"I went outside, to go back to my room, and there was a guy there."

"That would be our nameless stranger."

I nodded, too weary and heartsick to protest at what sounded a lot like mockery. "He said he was a business associate of Mr. Cavanaugh's, and that he was concerned about Drue. He'd brought her a glass of water, but then he said I'd beaten him to it."

McMichaels's forehead wrinkled. "Did he say how he knew Drue?"

"No. From work, I guess. I mean, Drue works—worked—with her father. So if this guy knew Mr. Cavanaugh, he might have known Drue, too. From work."

Another nod. More tapping. "What then?"

"I went back to my room and found Nick waiting on my deck."

"This would be Nick Andros?"

"Yes. Him. He and I were in the hot tub, talking for a while."

"About?"

I opened my mouth to say that Nick had told me he'd seen the groom and his ex-girlfriend in a clinch on the beach, then stopped myself. It was a piece of information that I'd overheard, possibly not even true. Nick could tell them himself, provide them with an eyewitness account instead of secondhand information. Assuming someone could find him. "Oh, nothing much. Just, you know, the wedding. The dinner. How amazing everything was."

"Amazing," McMichaels repeated.

"That's right."

"And then what?"

"I'm sorry?"

"What happened after you concluded your conversation?"

Sex! I wanted to shout, feeling a blush creep up my chest. We did the sex! Three times! *Oh, sure,* my inner Nana whispered. *Tell the nice detective that you had sex three times with a man you'd known for less than three hours and who was gone when you woke up. Then just stretch your arms out for the cuffs. Hopefully they'll fit.*

I cleared my throat. In a very small voice, I said, "We, um, spent the night together. In my room. We fell asleep at some point, and when I woke up, he was gone."

I wanted to keep talking, to explain, to tell Detective McMichaels that I'd never done anything like this before, not even close, that I'd only slept with four men in my entire life, and most of it hadn't even been good, but I pressed my lips together and made myself wait for follow-up questions.

"Tell me about your relationship with the deceased," Detective McMichaels said.

The deceased. I'd had my arm around her waist less then twelve hours ago; I could still feel her last hug, could still smell hairspray and prosecco and feel her tremble against me, and now she was *the deceased.* She couldn't be gone. It couldn't be real.

I gripped my coffee cup, hard, with a hand that still felt shaky. "Drue is . . ." I cleared my throat and swallowed hard. "Drue was one of my oldest friends. We met back in sixth grade."

He nodded. "What can you tell me about Miss Cavanaugh's life in New York City?"

"I'm probably not the best source on that. Drue and I hadn't been close for a while. Over the last few months, we'd been getting to know each other again, as adults." I decided to give him the truth, figuring that if I didn't, he'd hear it from someone else, and he'd think I'd been trying to mislead him. "I was surprised when Drue asked me to be part of her wedding. Surprised, but happy."

"Why were you surprised?"

I felt my limbs go numb and my face grow cold. The detective knew—or would know soon—that Drue and I had been reunited for less than three months. He knew that her corpse had been found floating in a hot tub outside my bedroom. He knew that the guy who could have provided my alibi was gone. Maybe he even knew that there'd been texts on my phone about killing Drue.

"Listen," I said, my voice quiet, but, thank God, steady. "I was very happy Drue asked me to be in her wedding. I was happy she still cared enough about me to want me to be part of her big day. I was happy to be here. I had no reason to want to hurt her."

McMichaels gave me a look that seemed to last a week. I held my breath, waiting for him to tell me to start the story again, the way he'd done twice before. Instead, he stood up, turned, and reached onto the shelf behind him, the one that held the Cuisinart and extra stacks of plates. He pulled down a sheaf of papers and handed them to me.

"What's this?" he asked.

I stared at the first page, at a mock-up in the style of a wedding invitation. *You are cordially invited to (sponsor) the wedding of Drue Cavanaugh and Stuart Lowe*, it read, in an ornate, scrolling font. There was a photograph of Drue and Stuart, one that I recognized from Drue's Instagram. The happy couple stood in front of the Eiffel Tower. Drue's hand was extended to show off her engagement ring, and Stuart's arms were wrapped around her as he held her against his chest. Only the picture had been edited, so that, extending from her back and his back were blank price tags, reading YOUR BRAND HERE. At the bottom, the invitation said, *Say yes to the dress (or the flight, or the hotel, or the wedding favors, or the wine). Please RSVP for this once-in-a-lifetime brand synergy opportunity.*

I turned the page and saw a mock-up of the bed that had been set up on the beach the previous night, and a picture of a generic bride and a groom on a bluff over the ocean, exchanging vows at sunset. YOUR HASHTAG HERE, the text invited, with more blank price tags and arrows pointing to the bed, the rugs, her dress, his watch.

"It's a pitch deck," I told the detective.

"A what now?"

"A pitch deck." I adjusted my posture, pressing my legs together, trying to think. "A solicitation for businesses to advertise on Drue and Stuart's social media." I paged through the document. It was four pages long, and it made its case clearly: two hot young influencers, each with hundreds of thousands of fans and followers, were getting married; and brands, from airlines to hotels to fashion retailers to home goods purveyors, were invited to get a piece of the action. Pony up, the copy said, and you will see your brand featured and mentioned in conjunction with THE SOCIETY WEDDING OF THE YEAR. *On a beautiful private beach in exclusive Cape Cod, Massachusetts, Drue Lathrop Cavanaugh of the Cavanaugh Corporation will say "I Do" to Stuart Edward Lowe of* All the Single Ladies *fame*, I read. *Millions of desirable millennials will follow their feeds to see photographs and videos of the ceremony, the party, the afterparty, featuring Holland-based DJ 7en, and the happy couple enjoying the honeymoon of a lifetime. There will be guaranteed glamour, celebrity sightings, and maybe a surprise or two! Make sure those consumers see* your brand *when they watch!*

"So what does this mean?" the detective asked.

I felt breathless, like I'd fallen from a great height and landed hard. "Drue and Stuart were trying to get sponsors for their wedding."

Detective McMichaels frowned. "Sponsors?"

"Right. Businesses that would pay to be featured on Drue and Stuart's social media."

I flipped to the third page, where there was a schedule of events, with Twitter handles and hashtags for the winery, the caterer, and the disc jockey, some of whom, I assumed, had swapped their goods and services for the exposure the wedding guaranteed. The last page had Drue's and Stuart's biographies, along with the number of Twitter and Facebook and Instagram and Snapchat followers they'd amassed. Other wedding guests were listed beneath them, with more pictures and statistics. *This inclusive celebration will feature celebrity facialist Minerva de los Santos,* I read, *and rising influencer/Afrofuturist Natalie Jonnson.* My breath caught when, right below a picture of Natalie in metallic wraparound sunglasses and a flower crown, I saw my own face. *Plus-size influencer Daphne Berg will be a featured wedding participant*, read the copy. In the shot they'd chosen, from my own Instagram page, I was dressed in one of Leela's outfits, posing in front of the brick wall that it seemed every influencer in the five boroughs had, at one point or another, used as a backdrop.

I stared at the document, mouth dry, eyes hot. *She was using me*, I thought, and felt something inside of me crumple. *Of course she was. Of course she didn't want me to be her friend again.* Of course she had ulterior motives. She wanted to get the fat girls on board, to make us feel included without actually doing the work of including us. And I was the bait; I was the beard, the flag she could wave in front of my plus-size sisters to convince them that she was on their side.

I cringed, remembering bits and pieces of the party, or things Drue had said, realizing that I should have put this together much, much sooner. I remembered the video crew prowling the beach, Drue holding a signature cocktail and giving an interview that must have been live-streamed to her feed. I remembered noticing the mattress company's hashtag, on a card next to the bed on the sand, and how Drue had brushed it off. *A couple of brands came to us, so we figured, why not?*

I must have looked as shocked as I'd felt, because McMichaels's voice was almost gentle when he asked, "You didn't know about this?" I shook my head and waited for him to say, *Sounds like you didn't know much*, or *I'm surprised she could do this without you*, or *Wow, you were really in the dark, dummy!* Instead, he asked, "How much money could Miss Cavanaugh and Mr. Lowe expect to make from something like this?"

I did some fast math, considering my own rates, and what I'd heard about what real celebrities could pull in. "It depends. For someone like me, it's a hundred dollars for every ten thousand followers. So if I've got thirty thousand followers, some company will pay me three hundred dollars to feature a photo of its yoga mat, or pet treats, or whatever. But it's different for celebrities. The big ones get millions of dollars for a post. Sometimes more."

The bushy eyebrows went up. "For just one picture?"

I nodded. Drue and Stuart combined had somewhere around a million followers. If they got all of the sponsorships they'd been seeking—from the airline that would take them to their honeymoon and the hotel where they would stay, from the caterer and the bakery providing the wedding cake and the company that had made the tablecloths and napkins for the wedding dinner, for all three of Drue's wedding dress designers . . . I worked my mental calculator, and finally said, "If this worked the way they hoped, it could have paid for the whole wedding. Going forward . . ." I imagined the possibilities, the maternity and baby-specific brands Drue could work with if she got pregnant, the barre and boxing and spinning brands when it was time to lose the baby weight. "I couldn't even guess."

"But a lot."

When I nodded, McMichaels pointed one thick finger at the word near my name on the pitch deck. "You're an influencer." He said it as a statement, but I heard it as a question. Which made sense. How could I be operating in the same world as gorgeous, glamorous Drue?

"Well, not a very influential one."

Ignoring my poor attempt at humor, he asked, "Were you advising Drue on how to make money from her social media?"

I shook my head. "There are companies you can hire to do stuff like this for you. Professionals." I pointed at the pitch deck. "This was made by a professional."

"So you had no idea that this was going on?"

I thought about the party the night before, all of the photographers, the video crew. She was probably streaming it on her stories, I thought, and kicked myself for not noticing. I thought about Drue in her bedroom, telling me that she'd promised her father that she could pay him back for whatever the wedding cost. "No," I said in a small voice. "I had no idea."

The detective stood up. In the bright summer light, he didn't look even slightly grandfatherly. He looked stern, and angry, and determined. "There has not been a suspicious death on the Outer Cape since 1994," he said. "And that went unsolved for years. It was an embarrassment." He pronounced the word precisely, giving each syllable equal weight, and he gave me another hard look. "We don't know how your friend died. But I promise you this: we aren't going to end up with egg on our face again."

"Good," I whispered. My mouth felt very dry. "That's good."

"One more thing," he said. His voice didn't rise and his expression stayed mild as he looked down at his notebook. "The wedding planner gave me a list of all the guests for last night's event." He looked up. "There's no Nick Andros on there."

I blinked. "What?"

"That man you said you met last night. His name isn't on the guest list."

"But . . ." I closed my eyes and clasped my trembling hands together. "He told me that he was an old friend of Drue's. They both spent summers on Cape Cod. They went to sailing school together. Maybe he forgot to RSVP?" Even while I was stumbling for an answer, I was remembering that Drue hadn't recognized Nick. Not when I'd asked him to take our picture; not in her bedroom when I'd said his name.

McMichaels was staring at me with absolutely no sympathy on his face. He tap, tap, tapped at his pad, and turned it around so that I could see what he'd just googled: *Nick Andros is one of the heroes in Stephen King's apocalyptic thriller* The Stand.

I tried to keep calm, or to at least look calm, even as I felt my heart and belly wobble and lurch like they'd come unmoored inside me. The insides of my thighs still felt sore and bruised from what Nick and I had done the night before.

"He told me that he worked for the school district in Boston, and that he grew up spending summers on the Cape. He said he's working on a charter fishing boat." The detective continued to stare at me blandly. "Maybe Nick is his middle name!" I knew how desperate that sounded, but it was all I could think of, and maybe it was true.

"Would anyone at the party remember seeing you with this gentleman?" There was a hairbreadth pause before McMichaels said "gentleman," but I heard it.

I shook my head. My mouth was dry. Snatches of the previous night were replaying themselves in my memory; things he'd done that had seemed romantic at the time and now seemed sinister in retrospect: Nick asking if I was a friend of the bride's, asking if I was staying in the big house. Nick with his hand at the small of my back, saying *Let's go sit over here, where it's quiet.* Nick steering me away from the rest of the guests, toward far-off tables, or into secluded nooks, and me, stupidly flattered, thinking he wanted me all to himself. Nick pushing me against the glass, saying *Don't make a sound. No one can know we're here.*

McMichael was looking at me hard. "Is there anything else you can remember?"

I screwed my eyes shut, trying to remember. "He said he worked on a boat named the *Lady Lu.* He said he knew about people behaving badly at weddings, because two of his cousins got in a big fight. He told me he wasn't online, at all." My face felt like it had been flash-frozen, my tongue felt clumsy and thick.

"Can you think of anyone who would want to hurt Drue Cavanaugh?" McMichaels asked.

It's a long list, I thought. And, I realized with a sinking feeling, if someone had asked me for that list six months ago, I probably would have put myself at the very top.

Chapter Eleven

I staggered down to my bedroom on legs that felt like frozen logs. I wanted to call my parents, and Darshi, and I'd have to call the Snitzers, too, but before I could do that, my phone started to ring.

"Daphne?" Leela Thakoon's emphasis-on-every-third-word was warm in my ear. "How are *things*? OhmyGod, I can't believe how *gorgeous* it looks there, you lucky duck! And did you see, your picture last night got more than two thousand—"

"Leela," I said. My voice was thick. It was all still starting to register, and it still didn't feel real. "Drue is dead."

There was a pause. Then a gasp. "Dead?" Leela breathed.

"I woke up this morning, and she was in our hot tub . . ." I swallowed hard. I could still feel the peculiar stiffness of Drue's body against mine, the wrongness of it. She would never smile again, never drink another cocktail or kiss another boy. She'd never get married, never go on the honeymoon she'd planned, never have children. Tears spilled down my cheeks.

"Oh my God," Leela said. "That's *unreal*. I can't believe it!"

"I know," I said. "I can't believe it either."

"What happened? Is there anything I can do?"

"They don't know. I found her this morning, just a few hours ago. She's gone now. An ambulance came, and they took her."

"You *found* her? Oh, God. You poor *thing*." Leela's voice was sympathetic. "Had you guys been drinking a lot?"

"No. Not me. I don't know about Drue." But even as I was speaking, I was shaking my head. Drugs and drinking made you lose control, and Drue was all about keeping a tight grip.

"Daphne, I am so, so sorry. I can't even imagine what you must be going through. Please, if there's *anything* I can do for you . . ." Leela lowered her voice. "Do you need me to send you something to wear for the funeral?"

I felt tears prickling my eyes, and my throat felt tight. *The funeral.* The day before, all I'd been thinking about was Drue's wedding, and now her parents would be planning her funeral instead. It felt heartbreaking, incredibly unfair. "Thanks, Leela. I think I'll be okay."

"Take care of yourself. And, seriously, Daphne, if there's anything I can do for you—anything at all—I'll have my phone on."

I thanked her for her consideration. As soon as she'd hung up, I called home. My mother snatched up the phone almost before it got through a single ring.

"Daphne? Oh my God!"

"Hi, Mom." There was no need for me to ask whether she'd heard the news. The sorrow in her voice told me that she was more than up to speed.

"I just saw a push alert this minute. My God, poor Drue," she said, sniffling. "And her poor parents. To lose their daughter on her wedding day." There was a brief, muffled interlude, then my father's voice was in my ear.

"Daffy, you all right?"

"I'm fine," I said, wiping my cheeks as more tears spilled out of my eyes at the sound of my childhood nickname, which my dad hadn't used since I was seven or eight. "Except I don't think I can come home. The police . . . I was the one who found her, and the police don't want anyone leaving."

"You *found* her?" I heard my mother wail.

"Judy, calm down," my dad said. To me, he said, "Why won't they let you leave?"

"I don't know. I guess they might have more questions for me, is all." No way was I getting into the details of how the guy I'd been with while my best friend had been murdered had disappeared. My mother would never stop crying, and my dad would be on the next plane up, with every lawyer he could find in tow.

"Do they have any idea what happened?" he asked.

"Not yet. I don't even think they know how she died."

"It's been all over the news in the last half hour," said my father. "You know. 'Heiress Found Dead on Wedding Day.'" He lowered his voice. "You're in some of the stories."

My heart gave an anxious lurch. "What? Why?"

"Nothing bad. It's just your name. Some of the places are using the picture of the two of you from your Instagram. The one where you're in the water, laughing." *The one that Nick took*, I thought, feeling my throat get tight. I remembered how I'd felt Drue trembling when I'd touched her. How she'd laughed, splashing me, doing her little dance in the shallows. How she'd hugged me at her bedroom door and said, *You're the best friend I ever had.* I wondered how many strangers had seen the picture and, at this very moment, how many of them were crawling through my Instagram, scrutinizing everything I'd ever posted for clues about Drue.

"Are you sure you're okay?"

"I'm fine," I said, hearing my voice crack. I wanted to ask him to come get me, I realized, like I was a little kid waiting to be picked up after school. Except he couldn't come, because I couldn't leave.

"Hang on." I heard footsteps followed by the sound of a door, opening and closing. I imagined my father was leaving the living room, getting out of my mom's earshot, probably heading to their bedroom. I could picture him, in his weekend clothes, a plaid shirt with a frayed collar that disqualified it from the workweek rotation, and a pair of the baggy pale-blue jeans that only middle-aged men ever seemed to wear.

"I didn't want to ask this in front of your mother," he said, "but are the police treating this like a suspicious death?"

"I don't know," I whispered. "The detective talked to me for a long time. He had all kinds of questions about Drue, and her parents, and her fiancé, and . . . and everything," I concluded. "But I don't even know how she died."

There was a pause. "I saw Drue's father once. So this would have been twelve or thirteen years ago."

"Where was he?"

"In Midtown, near Central Park South. I was up early, by that place on Fifty-Seventh, you know, where they have the bialys."

I knew the place he meant, and that it was different from the place that had the bagels, and the place with the whitefish salad.

"It must've been six o'clock in the morning. And I saw Robert Cavanaugh in an overcoat and a suit. All dressed up, with a woman in a fur coat." My father paused. "It wasn't Mrs. Cavanaugh."

"Oh, boy," I breathed. *A summer friend*, I thought. One of his extracurricular sweethearts, one who'd left Cape Cod or the Hamptons and made her way to the city. "Did he see you?"

"I don't think so. And even if he had, I'm not sure he would have recognized me. Drue's mother might have known me, but I think I maybe met her dad twice, the whole time the two of you were close." My father's voice was dry when he said, "Robert Cavanaugh wasn't a parent-teacher conference, back-to-school night kind of parent. Not the kind of parent who was going to show up to put the books in boxes at the end of the book fair. I mostly knew him from the papers."

"Drue said her parents hadn't been happy for a long time.

She told me that she knew in high school that her dad had been unfaithful, and that her parents couldn't get divorced, because everyone would talk. And they didn't have a prenup. They had a huge fight last night, at the party. Before . . ." I swallowed. "Before Drue died."

"Be careful," said my father. "And come home as soon as you can."

"Thanks. I will. I love you, Dad."

"I love you, too."

Tears were rolling down my cheeks, dripping off my chin. I was thinking of Drue's father, on the beach the night before, screaming in his daughter's face, then turning his back. I pictured him walking around at six in the morning with another woman, bold as brass, as Nana might have said. I thought of my own parents, dancing in the kitchen, and it occurred to me for the first time ever that Drue might have believed that of the two of us, I was the lucky one. "I should go."

"Go ahead," said my father. "And please give our sympathies to the Cavanaughs."

I promised that I would, and placed my next call. Darshi picked up her phone even faster than my mother had picked up hers.

"Daphne!" I could hear voices in the background. I imagined my friend at her conference, enjoying a cup of coffee and a croissant in some pleasant midlevel hotel where no one had died tragically the night before. "What happened? I saw the news alerts. Are you okay?"

"I'm fine. But . . ." I gulped. "Drue's dead."

"I know. It's on all the news sites."

"I was the one who found her." I made myself breathe. "And, Darshi, I was with a guy last night, the one I texted you about, and he's not here. I woke up this morning, and he wasn't in the bathroom, or anywhere, he was gone, and he gave me a fake name, and I . . ."

"Daphne. Slow down. I can barely understand you! Just breathe. I'm going to go to my room. I'll call you right back."

I ended the call and sat, trying to get it together, waiting for my phone to buzz in my hand, trying not to remember Darshi's warning: *If she fucks you over again, I won't hang around to pick up the pieces.* Maybe my friend would make an exception if it was Drue's death, and not Drue herself, that had done the fucking over. *Name five things you can see*, I told myself, and looked around my room. But all I could see was Drue's body, stiff and lifeless, her hair swirling around her as she lay facedown in the water. When the phone rang, I shrieked, and jumped a foot off the bed. My heart thundered as I answered the call.

"Hello?"

"Okay, I'm ready. Start from the beginning," Darshi said.

"Drue is dead. No one knows how it happened, and I can't find my alibi. The guy I was with—whoever he was—he gave me a fake name. And do you remember our texts from last night?" I whispered, and paused in a manner that I hoped communicated *You sent me texts with knife emojis.* There was a beat of silence, then Darshi inhaled sharply.

"She probably just got drunk and passed out and drowned in the hot tub. Or choked on her own vomit."

I gave a horrified whimper. Darshi's voice was dispassionate. "It happens," she said.

"Yeah. Except what if that didn't happen this time?" I dropped my voice to a whisper. "I deleted everything, but I don't know if they can find texts."

"I've got people who can tell the cops where I was last night," Darshi said.

"Good for you! I don't!" I hissed. "Not unless I can find this guy!"

"Okay," she said. "Let's think. In the unlikely event that this wasn't just an accident, who would have wanted Drue dead?"

I shook my head, hearing the word "Everyone" as clearly as if one of us had spoken it.

"Here's what you need to do." Darshi's voice was steady. "Chances are she died accidentally. If that isn't what happened, you need to make a list. Write down anyone you can think of who'd want to hurt her. Her exes. Stuart's exes. Are the police looking at Corina?"

"If they watch Lifetime, I'm sure they are."

"I'd check. And, Daphne, you've got to find the guy you were with last night."

"I know that," I moaned. "Don't you think I know that?"

"Where could he have gone?"

"I have no idea. Darshi, I don't even know his real name."

"What do you know?"

"I know that he's a local. At least, he said he was a local. He could be anywhere."

"What did he tell you his name was?"

"Nick Andros. I knew that sounded familiar."

"The deaf-mute guy from *The Stand*," said Darshi. "Hmm. Do you think there's a clue there somewhere?"

My head was starting to throb, right between my eyebrows, and my stomach felt like I'd swallowed a ball of lead. "I have no idea."

"What else did he tell you?"

"He said he knew Drue from sailing camp, and that he worked on a boat called the *Lady Lu*."

"Let me do my Internet magic," Darshi said. "Meanwhile, try to keep calm. Write down every single thing you remember about the guy. And when you're done, start asking people questions." When I started to splutter my objections, Darshi said, "If this was suspicious, the cops are probably looking at everyone who had any kind of beef with Drue. You need to get off their list, and the best way to do it is to start making one of your own."

Chapter Twelve

I found a notebook in my gift basket, made of soft hand-tooled leather, with the wedding date embossed on the cover in the same font as the invitations, the programs, and the "Welcome to Cape Cod" letter in the basket. I'd helped Drue find an artist on Etsy to make them. The girl had been so excited to be part of Drue's high-profile wedding that she'd knocked twenty percent off her price without either of us asking. I wrote DRUE'S ENEMIES on the front page. Then, instead of listing them, I turned the page and began to write everything I could remember about Nick.

Curly, medium-brown hair. Hazel eyes. A little taller than me—five nine? Five ten? Tan. Callused hands. Six-pack abs. No tattoos. At least, none that I'd noticed, and I thought I'd gotten glimpses of every inch of him. He did have a scar on his ankle and a birthmark high on his left hip. I wrote that down and blushed, remembering exactly what we'd been doing when I'd seen them. I wrote down *teaches breathing/yoga/emotional regulation in Boston*. I wrote *University of Vermont* and *Provincetown Yacht Club*. I wrote down *Lady Lu*. I struggled to remember the names of the cousins who'd fought about a wedding. Annie and Emma? Something like that. I realized that he'd never mentioned his parents. He'd talked about an aunt and uncle and a grandmother; he'd referred to a family home on the Cape . . . and he'd asked me questions, kept me talking, while saying very little about himself.

I wrote it all down. Then I googled the Provincetown Yacht Club, which had a primitive-looking website fronted by a beautiful picture of a sailboat on the water. The phone number was listed under Contacts. I pressed the button that would make the call.

The phone rang and rang. Just as I was about to give up, a gruff, deep female voice said, "Yuh?"

"Hi! Hello. Is this the Provincetown Yacht Club?"

"Yuh."

"My name is Daphne Berg. I'm hoping you can help me." This was a strategy I'd read about and used when dealing with customer service people on the phone. Starting off asking for help makes people feel like they are on the same team as you. "I am trying to figure out the name of one of your former campers."

"Yuh?"

"I'm having a surprise party for my best friend, and she spent her summers in Truro, so I'm trying to round up her old gang. I know she was friends with this guy, but if she ever told me his name, I've forgotten it."

"When would this have been?"

"About thirteen or fourteen years ago."

"Huh."

"Were you there?" I asked. "At the club?"

"I'm the founder." I thought I could detect the thinnest thread of amusement in the women's voice. "Dora Fitzsimmons. I've been here every year since we started." *Stah-ted.* "If your friend went here, she'd know me. I guess I remember just about every one of my sailors."

"Okay. That's great."

"Who'd you say your friend was?"

"I didn't. But her name is Drue Cavanaugh, and—"

Click. The line went dead in my ear.

I looked down at the phone and called back, only this time it just rang and rang. Fuck. The woman probably thought I was a reporter or something. Fuck, fuck, fuck. I moved on and discovered that the *Lady Lu* actually existed, and had not just a phone number but a website. *Fishing tours by the half day or full! Bass and bluefish! You catch a "keeper," or your money back!* And—thank you, God—a click-through gallery full of beaming men, women, and children displaying their catch. But, after ten minutes of scrolling through pictures, I'd hit the end of the gallery and all I'd gotten was a headache. No Nick. When I called the number, I got an answering machine. "If we're not picking up, it's because we're busy reeling in those big 'uns, but if you leave your name and number, along with the dates and times you're interested in, we'll get back to you as soon as we're on land," said a voice that was not Nick's. Typing "yoga" and "breathing" and "Boston elementary schools" and "Nick" into Google got me a yoga instructor named Nick with a degree from BU. He was cute, but he was not my guy.

What now?

I put the notebook down and decided to go next door, to Sea Breeze, and eavesdrop on the other guests. Maybe I'd overhear something that might jog my memory, or help me find my vanished paramour, or give me some names to add to my list.

Five minutes later, I stood at the entrance of the house next door, taking a moment to gather myself. When I knocked, I found the door unlocked. I walked inside, into a living room that felt like a meat locker. The air-conditioning had been cranked up high, making the room glacially chilly. It made sense. By now, the house should have been filled by a dozen people getting dressed, jostling for space at the mirrors, touching up their dresses with steamers, and blow-drying their hair. Now, the living room was half-empty, with some guests slumped on the white linen couches, others sitting at the dining room table, toying with plates of miniature muffins and fruit, looking woebegone, or grief-stricken, or hungover, or just bored. To make things worse, I realized belatedly that the outfit I'd chosen—Leef's crisp white blouse, the Jill, and a high-waisted black skirt, the Tasha—made me look like a member of the waitstaff.

But maybe I could make that work, I thought, as I spotted the woman in the chignon who'd grabbed Drue the night before and had piled Lily Cavanaugh into the SUV that morning. Given her resemblance to Lily Lathrop Cavanaugh, I guessed that she was Drue's grandmother. Spying an empty tray, I put a plate on it and carried the tray toward the corner where Grandma Lathrop was having an intense, whispered conversation with a woman who looked so much like her that she had to be her sister—maybe even the great-aunt whose dead dog had ended up in a beer cooler. The two of them had identical silvery hair, the same fine-boned frames and heart-shaped faces, but Grandma Lathrop was taking genteel sips from a porcelain cup of coffee, while Great-Aunt Lathrop had both hands wrapped around a tall Bloody Mary, like she was worried the glass would fly away if she loosened her grip.

"Will you go?" I heard Aunt ask as I came over with my tray.

Grandma shook her head. "There's no point. You know that Lily is given to hysterics. They'll sedate her and send her right back."

"And I suppose Robert's with her," Aunt said, her voice rising slightly as she spoke, turning the statement into a question.

That guess earned an audible snort from Grandma. "I imagine he at least headed in that direction. He's off to see one of his friends by now, I assume."

"It's a disgrace," murmured Aunt.

Grandma waved an imperious, veiny hand. A heavy gold signet ring hung loose on one knobby finger; a large, square-cut emerald sat on the finger beside it. "That man has been a disgrace for years. And I, for one, am glad we can finally stop pretending."

I edged away from them, bending over a coffee table and pretending to be busy gathering cups and crumpled napkins.

"Thank God we made Drue get her will notarized," Grandma said. "Thank God she has a will at all. At least now that . . ." Her lips curled. ". . . television star won't get all of it."

Aunt murmured something that I couldn't hear.

"Oh, yes," Grandma blared. "Our lawyer insisted. Drue had all of these ridiculous bequests. She wanted to leave Robert half of it"—a noisy sniff let me know what Grandma thought of that, and of him—"and a million dollars to some charity for schoolchildren in Boston."

"That was kind of her," Aunt ventured. Grandma sniffed.

"Half a million dollars to some high school chum. And to each one of Robert's by-blows."

At this, Aunt looked shocked. "Did Drue know?" she asked.

Grandma shook her head. Her expression was grim. "I don't know how she found out. I wouldn't put it past that fool to have told her himself. Miss?" She raised her voice. I straightened up and froze when I felt her gaze on me.

"More coffee?" I squeaked.

"And less eavesdropping," she said tartly, handing me her empty, lipstick-stained cup.

"I'm sorry," I whispered. My heart was thundering in my chest, and I felt light-headed. *Money to some high school chum.* Could that have been me? Under normal circumstances, an unexpected windfall might have been a good thing, but if it turned out that Drue hadn't died of natural causes, it meant that I had a theoretical windfall, and an all-too-real motive.

"And I'll have another one of these," Great-Aunt Lathrop

said, gulping down the last of her drink and passing her glass, empty except for a red-tinged stalk of celery, over to me. My heart was beating even harder; my thoughts racing frantically, careening around my head. I needed to find out what the will said, and if I was the high school chum who'd gotten lucky. I needed to find out who Mr. Cavanaugh's by-blows were, and if Drue had known any of them.

"Right away," I said.

"And here's a tip," Aunt replied. She hiccupped and said, "Make sure you get paid in cash."

I nodded and hurried away, knees wobbly and heart pounding, to drop off the dirty dishes and score a Bloody Mary. *Say the Cavanaughs were broke*, I thought. Say Drue was marrying Stuart for money or, more likely, the money they could earn together by treating their wedding and their honeymoon and possibly even their entire lives as a branding opportunity. Who would want her dead? Stuart? Corina Bailey? Some other big-name bridal influencer, angry at being edged out of the action?

In the kitchen, I found a giant coffee urn. I filled the coffee cup, found a fresh pitcher of cream, and carried them to the bar.

"I need a Bloody Mary," I told the bartender.

"Popular choice this morning," he said as he stirred and poured.

I carried the drinks back to the Lathrop ladies and took a look around. Drue's grad-school friend Lainey had donned her "Drue & Stuart"–monogrammed hoodie, which struck me as in not very good taste. She was sitting at the dining room table, typing on her laptop. Natalie, Drue's assistant, was curled on her side underneath a blanket, seemingly asleep on the love seat. Pregnant Cousin Pat had pulled a chair into the corner and was hunched over her phone. "No," I heard her say as I drifted close enough to listen. "None of us can leave until the police talk to everyone."

I opened one of the sliding doors and stepped onto the deck.

It was windier than it looked from inside. The air was fresh and cool, scented with salt and pine. A stiff breeze churned the waves to lacy froth. I breathed in and turned, preparing to head back and resume my eavesdropping when a familiar voice called my name.

"Hey, Daphne?" I turned and saw Arden Lowe, the not-groom's sister, in yoga pants and a tank top that revealed wiry arms and jutting clavicles. "Can I speak to you for a moment?"

Arden led me through the living room, down a flight of stairs, and out to the pool on the other side of the house, where there was barely even a whisper of breeze. The water's surface was pristine, without so much as a leaf or a pine needle to mar its surface. The attached hot tub—I swallowed hard at the sight of it—was bubbling away pointlessly, wisps of steam swirling around its surface. The air smelled like chlorine and chemicals. I took a seat at a chair that was one of four set up around an umbrella-covered table. Arden perched on the table's edge.

"How are you doing?" she asked. "This must be just awful for you." Arden had her brother's compact, made-for-TV build, as if she'd started off normal, then been condensed to seven-eighths of her original size. The large nose that looked perfect on her brother's face was a little too big for hers, and her ponytail revealed slightly protuberant ears.

"I'm okay." I smoothed my blouse. "I mean, I think I'm still in shock." In shock at Drue's death, in shock at everything I'd learned since finding her body.

"It must have been awful," Arden said again.

I looked at the hot tub, as if its bubbling had suddenly gotten interesting, and weighed the risks and the potential payoff of telling her what Nick had told me. Finally, I decided to go for it. "I'm not sure if you've heard, and, if you haven't, I'm sorry to be the bearer of bad news. But there's a rumor going around about your brother."

Arden didn't look entirely surprised. She tilted her chin up, lips thinned, eyes narrowed. "What rumor is that?"

"People saw him on the beach last night. With another woman."

If I was expecting shock, whispered pleas for my silence or heated denials, I'd have been disappointed. "He was with Corina," Arden said calmly. "They're friends, Daphne. Friends talk."

"Someone saw them doing more than talking."

"Who did you hear this from?" Arden's voice had gotten higher.

I shrugged. She narrowed her eyes.

"But it's secondhand?"

I nodded.

"Well. There you go." She shook her head, flipping her ponytail from one shoulder to the other. "It's just gossip. Nasty gossip. You probably don't know this, but Corina just broke up with someone back in LA. Stuart was probably consoling her. If people saw anything, that's probably what they saw."

"Okay," I said.

Arden looked at me for a long, silent moment. "Shit," she finally said. She pulled out a chair, sat, put her elbows on the table, and cradled her head in her hands. "I told Stuart not to go through with this," she said. "I told him Drue was bad news." She looked up at me, as if she was waiting to be challenged. "Sorry. I know you were her friend."

"We were close, years ago. In high school. But we haven't spent a lot of time together since then."

"Because, let me guess. She did something awful to you." I pressed my lips together, not wanting to speak ill of the dead. Arden had no such compunctions. "I knew what she was the first time I met her. She was so fake with me." Her nose crinkled. "Like she'd googled 'how to make your boyfriend's little sister like you' five minutes before we met." She sighed, smoothing her hair. "She was gorgeous. I'll give her that. And Stuart was just head over heels in love. He thought he could ride the tiger."

That didn't seem like an especially generous way to discuss your brother's newly deceased intended and your almost sister-in-law, I thought, as Arden kept talking.

"I was the one who tried to tell him about her. After they'd been dating for six months, the second time, he came home and asked Mom for Grandma Frances's ring. I told him. I said, she's going to screw you over the same way she did before. The same way she's screwed over everyone, and it's not like you haven't seen her do it. He didn't listen." She shook her head, looking rueful. "Drue must have been amazing in bed. That's the only explanation."

"I wouldn't know. And like I said, I barely knew her as an adult, but I hoped that she'd grown up and changed."

"I guess Stuart hoped so, too. He said, 'You can't judge someone on the way they behaved in high school.'" Arden rolled her eyes. "I told him, a leopard doesn't change its spots."

"So what happened?" I asked, keeping my voice quiet and level, trying to sound like all the therapists I'd ever seen on TV. "I know what she did to me. Tell me what she did to your brother."

Arden reached back with both hands, elbows pointing skyward as she yanked her ponytail tight. "I think that Stuart's a catch," she said. "That's not me being his sister, that's me being objective. He's cute, he's smart, he's creative, and he works hard. He's got a good heart. You'd think that would have been enough for Drue, right?" Arden didn't wait for me to answer before shaking her head. "The first time they were dating, they went to a football game together. And Drue met another guy, a classmate's older brother. Who was smart and good-looking, and also Michael Leavitt's son."

Michael Leavitt, I knew, was a tech billionaire, one of the wealthiest men in the world, which would make his son one of the world's most eligible bachelors.

"And Drue went after him."

"Like a dog after a rabbit." Arden's eyes were fixed on the water. "Stuart said you could hear the wheels turning the first time she saw him. Like, *How am I going to get that?*"

"What happened?"

"She got him. For a little while. They went out for a few months, and then Jeremy ended it. Said he couldn't give her what she deserved. How's that for a line?"

"Maybe she really loved him," I ventured. Arden gave a cynical shrug that made her look a lot older than twenty-four.

"I'm not sure Drue ever loved anyone. I think some people just always want more. There's no such thing as enough." She shrugged again. "Who knows? If she'd married Jeremy, maybe she'd have dumped him to try for Prince Harry."

Something was sticking in my mind, nagging at me like a splinter. I shut my eyes, trying to replay our conversation. "When did this happen? When did Drue dump Stuart so she could go after Jeremy Leavitt?"

"Oh, that was Round One," said Arden. She unfurled herself from her tuck, stretching her arms up over her head. "That's what my parents and I call it, the first time they got together."

"In college, right?"

Arden shook her head, her ponytail swinging. "Nope. When they were in high school. At Croft."

Croft? "Drue went to the Lathrop School," I said. "In New York City. With me."

"Through twelfth grade, sure. I'm talking about after. She met Stuart at Croft. It's a boarding school. In California. Stuart had been there, the whole way through. Drue showed up there after she graduated from Lathrop to do a PG year." At my blank look, Arden gave a cynical smirk. "Yeah, I know she made it look like she was doing a gap year. I saw her Instagram. All of those pictures of Australia, or doing Habitat for Humanity, or whatever. The truth was that she went to Croft, the year after Lathrop, trying to get her grades and her SATs up high enough for Harvard."

"So, those trips . . ." I tried to remember the pictures I'd seen on the Lathrop School's website, tried to square this revelation with what I'd previously believed. "She faked them?"

"No. She did all that stuff, she just did it on vacations. In between all the tutoring she needed to make it across the finish line and into Hah-vahd. There was even some scandal at Croft about her parents paying someone to take her SATs. The school hushed it up. And it worked. She got in. Happily ever after."

I closed my mouth, which had fallen open in disbelief. I'd stayed away from Drue's social-media presence as much as I could, so I wasn't sure how much to trust my own memory. Had she ever explicitly said she was on a gap year, or had she just made it look that way and guessed, correctly, that it was what most people would think?

I shook my head. "Wow. I always figured she got into Harvard the old-fashioned way. Good grades, good test scores, and a big donation from Mom and Dad."

Arden smirked. "Even with her dad handing over the big bucks, she still had to show Harvard that she was going to be able to do the work. I guess she needed an extra year to clear the bar."

Interesting, I thought. Of course, it wasn't surprising that Drue wouldn't advertise how she'd needed extra help or extra time to get into college. Drue was smart—smart enough to be one of our class's top students if she'd applied herself. But she hadn't. She preferred to party, and to shop, and to hook up with guys. *I'll never be this young again*, she'd say. Which meant that she'd slack off for the better part of a semester, then do all of the reading in a single all-night binge, fueled by gallons of coffee and her mother's diet pills. She also had me as her secret weapon, ever available to help write her papers, type them, run spellcheck, and sometimes, when she was feeling especially lazy, take her idea and do the actual writing.

So the idea that she'd needed extra help and extra time wasn't completely surprising. Nor was the idea that she'd gone out west to get it. Many of the top prep schools were in New England, but if Drue had gone to one of them she'd undoubtedly have run into people who knew her, or her family, and her secret would be out.

I decided to put aside the mystery of Drue's post-Lathrop, pre-Harvard year and return to the topic of her love life. "So Drue and Stuart dated at Croft, and then again when they were in college?"

Arden stood up and bounced a few times on the soles of her feet, like she was getting ready to run a fast five miles. "Yup. And the same thing happened there. Drue was happy with Stuart until some guy who'd dropped out after freshman year and invented some app that made a fortune came back to campus to give a talk." Arden stroked her ponytail, sifting the fine brown strands through her fingers. "First Drue told Stuart that she wanted to take the guy out for coffee so she could network with him, get his business advice. Then they're having dinner together to *further their conversation*. Then it's 'Oh sorry, Stuart, but Devon is my soulmate.'"

"Oof."

"Yeah. So when she and Stuart hooked up again . . ." Arden's voice took on a nasty edge. "None of us wanted to hear it. Fool me once, shame on you; fool me twice . . . Well, you know. My mom and dad and I didn't want to see him go through it again with her, but he wouldn't listen. She could always get him back. Whistle, and he'd come running." Her voice tightened on the last few words. Looking down, I could see her hands curling into fists. "We never understood it. And he didn't even try to explain it to us. *Drue is special*, he'd tell us. *We have fun*."

I nodded, feeling complete and total empathy for Stuart Lowe. I couldn't have explained it, either, but I knew what it was like to be the center of Drue Cavanaugh's universe, how her regard could make you feel like the brightest, shiniest, sharpest, most perfect version of yourself, and how she could turn an ordinary day into an adventure. I thought of a line from a Joe Henry song: *And I don't miss you half as much / As who you made me think I was.* That had been Drue's magic, the part I'd never been able to quite explain to Darshi: the way Dru would treat you like you were amazing, and how you'd actually start to think that she was right.

"And what about Corina?"

"Corina was great." Arden sounded wistful. "Maybe not the sharpest crayon in the box, but sweet. Easy to be with. She loved him, and we all loved her. We would've been happy if they'd stayed together."

I have to tell McMichaels, I thought as Arden turned to go. But although the revelation had rocked my world, informing the detective that Drue had secretly attended an extra year of prep school and that she'd dated Stuart twice before was hardly a game-changer. And if I told him what I'd learned about the will, I'd also have to disclose that I'd been eavesdropping on the mourners for my intel.

I'd keep quiet, I decided. At least until I learned more.

"Hey," I said. Arden had her hand on the gate that enclosed the pool. I heard her sigh as she turned. "Do you know anything about Stuart and Drue doing any social media brand outreach around the wedding?"

Her forehead furrowed. "Huh?"

"Like, putting together a pitch deck?" Her blank expression told me she had no idea what that was. "Were they asking businesses if they wanted to partner with them and sponsor the wedding or the honeymoon?"

Arden stared at me. "You mean like selling ads?"

"No, not ads . . . well, sort of. More like a trade. Going to American Airlines and saying *Give us tickets for our honeymoon and we'll do an Instagram post that mentions you.* Or promising to post a shot of yourself on the plane, with the logo visible."

Arden seemed genuinely puzzled. "Why would they need to do that? Didn't Drue have more money than God?"

"As far as I knew."

"That was the only part of Drue and Stuart that made sense to me," Arden said. "My guess is that she promised to use some of the family fortune to help my brother with his start-up."

"Do you think they loved each other?" I asked.

The question seemed to catch her off guard. "He was going to marry her," she said.

Which wasn't exactly an answer. I waited, watching her face, wondering if she'd fidget, or start playing with her ponytail again. Arden said, "Look. Stuart's older than I am, and he'd left for boarding school by the time I was eight. We weren't close. If you want my opinion, I think it was Drue's whole world that he found attractive. That, and the way she made him feel." She shrugged. "And from what I saw, they wanted a lot of the same things. Money and power. People build lives together on a whole lot less than that."

I was trying to think about what else I could ask her when I heard the sound of a car's tires crunching over the shells. A nondescript Toyota stopped in front of the garage. The front door opened, and Darshini Shah emerged. In black dress pants and a matching blazer, with her laptop bag slung across her chest, she was the most beautiful sight I could imagine.

Chapter Thirteen

"Tell me everything you've learned so far." Darshi took a seat on the bench at the bottom of my bed, and I was collapsed against the headboard. I'd opened the glass doors to catch the breeze, and we could hear the waves as they advanced and retreated on the beach below us. Occasionally, some kind of seabird would squawk, and we'd see it, aloft and almost motionless outside the windows, hovering on an air current. Darshi had walked into the room, looked through the windows at the deck (now festooned with crime scene tape) and the ocean beyond it, and given a single "Nice." Not much for aesthetics was my roommate, even under the best of circumstances, but her presence, the sound of her voice, her scent of coconut conditioner and sandalwood perfume, all of it calmed me.

"First of all," I began, "did you know that Drue did a thirteenth year at the Croft School in California before she went to Harvard?"

I was gratified when Darshi's eyes widened. "Whoa," she said.

"I know, right! I mean, did you have any idea that she had problems getting into college?"

Darshi shook her head again. She rolled up the cuffs of her

jacket, then rolled them down again. In addition to coconuts and sandalwood, I could catch a whiff of an unfamiliar perfume, and wondered if Carmen had been at the conference, too, and if Darshi had sent her home to come help me. "I figured her parents just gave the school money," she said.

"I know! Me too!" My voice sounded a little screechy. I made myself take a breath. "And also, I heard Drue's grandmother discussing her will. Drue's will, not the grandmother's. And it turns out Drue left a high school chum some money."

Darshi stared. "You?"

"I don't know." The idea that I could somehow end up with a giant chunk of cash at the end of this left me feeling shivery, hot and then cold, like I was coming down with the flu.

"What about your mystery man?" Darshi asked.

I told Darshi that no one had answered the *Lady Lu*'s phone, that the woman who'd answered had hung up on me as soon as I'd said Drue's name, and that Google was giving me hot yoga instructors, not the guy I'd met the night before. "I wrote down every single thing I could remember about him," I said, showing her my notebook. Darshi's eyebrows lifted incrementally.

"Amazing at sex? Seriously?" She shut the book, looking dubious. "Well, good for you, I guess."

"Yeah. If it turns out Drue was murdered and I end up in jail, at least I'll have some nice memories." I sighed, then looked at her. "If you want to say 'I told you so,' now would be the time."

Darshi shook her head. "I'm sorry," she said. Her voice was quiet, and her tone was hard to read. "I am. I didn't like Drue very much, but I'm sorry for her. For her family. And I'm sorry for you."

I nodded, with tears stinging my eyes. "Thank you for coming."

Darshi nodded and reached for the notebook again. "Your gentleman caller mentioned his aunt and uncle and cousins, but not parents or siblings. Scar on ankle. No tattoos." She shook her head, with a combination of bemusement and exasperation on her face. "Very thorough. Okay, get your purse."

"What?"

"We're going for a ride."

I looked around, as if someone had overheard her. "I'm not supposed to leave!"

"I didn't see a guard at your door."

I grabbed my purse and kept my head down as I skittered out the door, down the stairs, and across the crunchy shell driveway to the car Darshi had rented. It wasn't until she'd pulled onto Route 6 that I was able to relax slightly, convinced that no one was following us, and that I wasn't about to get arrested for leaving the scene of the crime.

"Where are we going?"

"The sailing school. Maybe if we ask whoever you spoke to in person, she'll be more inclined to help."

The Provincetown Yacht Club was just as Nick had described it—a hole-in-the-wall on the west end of Commercial Street, which was Provincetown's main drag. The club was small, occupying what looked like a modest clapboard house, next door to a fancy-looking deli called Relish. An old debossed wood plaque above the doorway read YACHT RACING CLUB; a hand-lettered square of construction paper underneath said "Raffle Tix and T-Shirts for Sale. Please Knock!" Darshi stood behind me as I knocked on the front door. When no one answered, we followed the sounds of voices around back. The house was much longer than it was wide, with its back side open to the water, and two big garage doors rolled up to expose two deep bays. I saw high, shadowy ceilings, a concrete floor, and rows of wooden racks that held the bodies of sailboats and kayaks. Above and between the boats, dozens of colorful life jackets hung drying over clotheslines that stretched from one end of the room to the other. The sails were furled in stacks along the walls.

There was a metal showerhead screwed into the corner of the house. Just past it, a flight of outdoor stairs led to the second floor. Beyond the house, a short, sandy slope led down to a small crescent of beach and a dock. The water glittered in the sunlight, and a dozen sailboats zigged and zagged back and forth between the shore and a sandbar. The kids on the boats laughed and shouted as they made their turns, calling "Boom coming over" or "Coming about!"

"H'lo?"

I looked up. An older woman was standing on the second-floor landing, leaning over the railing, looking at us. I thought that I recognized the gruff female voice from my phone call that morning. She had pale white skin and thick gray hair falling out of a bun and framing her face in wisps. A pair of reading glasses hung from a seed-pearl chain and rested on her capacious bosom.

"Raffle ticket?" she called down.

"Hi!" I called, shading my eyes. "We're, um, visiting the Cape. Can we talk to you for a minute?"

She shrugged, turned, and went back inside. Darshi and I looked at each other, then mounted the wooden steps. On the second story we found a small office with low ceilings, exposed wooden beams, and walls of the same unpainted wood as the first-floor storage area. The air smelled like the inside of the cabins at the summer camp in Maine: must from the off-season, wet wood and mold, bug spray and sunscreen, sunshine and sweaty kids. The essence of summertime.

A large, fluffy white dog lay curled on an oval-shaped blue and green rug, eyes closed and pink tongue protruding. The gray-haired woman sat behind a metal desk that was cluttered with papers and folders and a small electrical fan that whirred as it turned. She was dressed in a loose green T-shirt that read PROVINCETOWN YACHT CLUB in black letters, and a pair of faded tan cotton clamdiggers, and orange Crocs on her big feet. The dog cracked an eye open when we entered, determined we did not constitute a threat, and promptly gave a loud sigh and went back to sleep.

"Oh, what a beautiful dog!" I said, hoping to appeal to her, dog-lover to dog-lover. "Who's this good boy?"

"Lance," she said, in the same sour, begrudging mutter.

"Hi, Lance!" I said to the dog. He didn't open his eye again, but his tail thumped twice on the rug, raising dust. "Can I pet him?"

"I wouldn't," she said.

Darshi cleared her throat and drew herself up straight.

"Thank you for talking with us," I began. "I'm Daphne Berg, and this is Darshi Shah. We're visiting from New York City."

"Dora Fitzsimmons," said the woman, confirming that she was the one I'd spoken to earlier. She didn't offer her hand, but she did nod at the chairs. "Have a seat." Darshi and I settled ourselves. "You two got a kid?" Her down-east accent was so heavy it sounded like she was asking if Darshi and I had gutted a child. I bit my lip as a nervous giggle escaped.

"What? Oh, no! Just a few questions. I, um, called you earlier this morning . . ."

The woman's eyes narrowed, and her lips thinned.

"I'm not a reporter! I promise," I said, holding my hands in the air. "I just met a guy last night, and I need to find him, and he said he'd been a camper here . . ."

"Sailor," she interrupted.

"Pardon me?"

"We call the kids sailors. Or skippers, once they've passed their test."

"Oh. Sorry. Sailor. Anyhow, he's about my age, twenty-five

or -six, and he was here about sixteen years ago. His name—at least, the name he gave me—is Nick Andros."

"Nup." Dora picked up one of the folders on her desk, dismissing us without having to say we'd been dismissed.

"Can I describe him to you? He had curly brown hair and a scar on his ankle."

"Nup," she repeated.

"Did you know Drue Cavanaugh?" Darshi asked.

The woman leaned forward. Her chair creaked. The dog opened one eye again, keeping it trained on me and Darshi as his mistress stared at us.

Swallowing hard, I said, "I was at Drue's house last night when I met the guy. He mentioned knowing her."

"The Lathrop house," the woman corrected. "The Cavanaughs sold their place here. Years ago."

"Right," I said. "Although, actually, I think I was at the Weinbergs' house. That's who Nick told me it belonged to. Drue's family had rented it for the weekend. For Drue's wedding."

Some expression moved across the woman's face, too fast for me to read it. Sorrow, I thought, and scorn, too.

"Drue was one of my sailors, ayuh." I waited for more. More was not forthcoming.

"Was Drue a good sailor?" Darshi asked.

Dora gave a single slow blink. "Good enough."

"Do you remember anything else about her?"

"I shan't speak ill of the dead." After a moment of silence, it was clear that she'd said all she meant to say about Drue.

I looked at Darshi, hoping she'd pick up the interrogation, but she was staring into the dim recesses of the building and appeared to be lost in thought.

I turned back to Dora. "Do you know a fishing boat called the *Lady Lu*?" I asked.

She shrugged. "I know most of the charters, sure."

"This guy, Nick, he told me he worked on a boat called the *Lady Lu*. Do you know anyone connected to the boat? A captain or something?"

"Skipper," Dora said. I heard, or imagined I could, amusement in her voice. Wonderful, I thought. It was nice that the two landlubbers were providing her with a laugh. "His name's Dan Brannigan. But if he's out t'sea, there's no way to reach him."

"No radio?" Darshi asked. Her voice was cool. "Aren't ships required to have radios, so the Coast Guard can reach them?"

"For emergencies, sure." She gave us a look just short of scornful. "You two don't look like an emergency."

"Ms. Fitzsimmons. Drue is dead," I said. "Which you know already. And the police need to talk to this Nick, or whoever he was. He crashed the party, and he gave me a fake name, and the police are trying to find him." I swallowed, telling myself to breathe, attempting to calm down. "We're trying to do him a favor."

She stared at us, her gaze direct. "Are you, now?"

"I am." I put my hand against my heart. "I swear." Another crumb of a memory had just surfaced. "He told me Drue used to lock him in the supply closet. And send him on snipe hunts. And make up marks of sail."

"Points of sail," said Dora. She stared at us for what felt like a long time. "Look. I'd help you if I could. But I can't."

In desperation, I said, "Is there anyone in town who might know this guy? Anyone who could help?"

She shrugged. "I s'pose you could go to the dock. Ask if anyone's seen this fella around the *Lady Lu*. But all of the charters are going to be out t'sea on a day like today. Won't be back 'til sundown." She gave us a long, assessing look and finally said, "Fella at the intersection of Bradford and Commercial Street? Dressed up as a Pilgrim, ringin' a bell? He might be particularly helpful."

Fantastic, I thought. A traffic cop dressed as a Pilgrim. How lucky that we'd arrived on mess-with-the-out-of-towners day. "Thank you," I said, getting to my feet. The dog opened its eye again and released a long and mournful fart before rolling onto its opposite side.

"Tell him Dora sent you," she said.

I whispered to Darshi that we should walk slowly, taking our time making our way back to the car, hoping that Dora would reconsider, that she'd come running after us to tell us the guy's name, along with his address and phone number, but all I heard as Darshi unlocked the doors was the sound of children's voices, high and cheerful, carrying across the water.

"She knows him," Darshi said as we climbed into that car.

"I also got that impression."

"She knows him and she's covering for him. But why?" She frowned, squinting in the sunshine. Darshi was a night owl, not a big swimmer or a fan of beaches. Between that and the overwhelming whiteness of the population, or at least the parts of it we'd seen, my roommate seemed immune to Cape Cod's charms. "Look for a man directing traffic dressed up as a Pilgrim. Puh-leaze."

"You don't think we should check?" I asked.

Darshi pulled back onto Commercial Street, narrowly missing a collision with a man clad in a tiny silver Speedo and nothing else, pedaling an old-fashioned cruiser-style bike that was painted hot pink. "Something about this . . . about Nick, or whatever his name is." She shook her head in frustration. "It's like it's on the tip of my tongue, but I can't remember."

"So you don't think we should go look for a Pilgrim directing traffic?"

Darshi started to drive, then stomped the brakes again. This time, the hold-up was a drag queen in a neon-yellow minidress and towering pink wig who was riding an adult-size tricycle down the center of the street. Signs on both sides of the rear wheels advertised her show that night at a place called the Crown & Anchor. "I don't know," she said. "Maybe that isn't any weirder than the rest of this."

The Pilgrim-costumed traffic cop turned out to be real. In between dongs of the brass bell he held and almost balletic spins he performed in his buckled shoes, he said that he did know that Dan Brannigan had a new mate this summer—"Tim O'Reilly's got the shingles, don't you know," but, alas, he didn't know the name of "the young feller." He estimated the boat would be back by five o'clock; five-thirty at the latest. It was barely noon, not even seven hours since I'd found Drue. It felt like a week had already elapsed, if not an entire month.

"We can come back," said Darshi. The traffic Pilgrim had sent us to the Portuguese Bakery for a snack. "Get the malasadas, if they're fresh," he'd said. They were, and we had, and, in spite of everything, the deep-fried, sugar-coated pastries were delicious, the happy marriage of a fritter and a piece of fried dough. Unfortunately, the guys behind the counter hadn't known the name of Dan Brannigan's mate. Neither did the guys at the bicycle shop next door, although that visit jarred loose the memory of Nick telling me he'd worked at a bicycle shop somewhere else on the Cape, only I couldn't remember the name of the town, if he'd told me. Darshi and I had spent the next twenty minutes sitting on a bench outside Town Hall, watching the drag queens hand out flyers for their shows and calling every nearby bike shop that had a listed phone number. No one remembered a Nick, or a guy who'd matched his description, from the previous summer.

"Maybe we could bring Dora some malasadas," Darshi suggested. "We could try to bribe her. Loosen her up with carbs and fat."

I shook my head. By then, I was getting antsy. When I closed my eyes, I could see Detective McMichaels knocking on my bedroom door, pushing it open, finding me gone, and deciding that I'd been responsible for Drue's demise, because only a guilty person would have fled. I would have given anything to be back in New York, needle-felting the Nativity scene I'd promised a client. I'd already done the sheep, donkeys, and Wise Men, and I'd special-ordered blue wool roving for Mary's gown. I'd make myself a cup of tea and have one of the crumbly sweet cornmeal cookies that I liked, and sit on the couch with Bingo curled up beside me, and know that I was as happy as anyone had a right to be.

"I think we should go," I said.

Darshi and I got back into the car and began the slow and perilous trip back to Route 6. The streets were narrow, and there were pedestrians everywhere, guys in pairs or groups, exhausted-looking couples lugging armloads of towels or beach chairs, pushing strollers or carrying toddlers in slings or on their shoulders.

While Darshi paused to let another crew of barely clad men go by, muttering "Doesn't anyone in this town wear shirts?," I shut my eyes and pictured Nick: his tousled hair, his crooked smile. I remembered his smell, the smoothness of his skin, the way he'd looked in the hot tub when he'd pulled me into his lap. I shook my head, not wanting to play that tape forward, and rewound it instead. The way he'd looked at the party, his tanned, corded forearm on the table. The way he'd looked, sitting on the deck, tilting his head back to take in the big house.

And then I had it.

"What?" Darshi asked as I jolted forward. "What is it? Are you okay?"

"Holy shit," I said. "Darshi, we have to go back."

"Why?"

"I know where he is!"

"Where?" Darshi gaped at me. I leaned across the gearshift and pounded on the horn, earning a dirty look from the last two shirtless fellows carrying boogie boards across the street.

"Back at the house! Come on!"

"What? How do you know?"

"Just, can you please go any faster?"

"Um, not really," Darshi said, gesturing at the red light we'd reached. "Calm down. Tell me what you remembered."

I shook my head, worried that I'd jinx it or that it would sound silly once I'd said it out loud, so I sat in silence as Darshi drove, fingers crossed, praying I was right.

Back at the Weinbergs' house, there weren't any cops waiting for us in the driveway, and the first floor was empty. The salon bedroom was unoccupied, and the bedroom Minerva had been assigned was empty except for a pair of hard-sided silver suitcases.

I pointed at the door between the bedrooms and nodded. Darshi reached into her purse and pulled out a Swiss army knife. I put my finger to my lips and put my hand on the doorknob. Locked. No surprise. I beckoned Darshi forward . . . but before she could start to work on the lock, the door opened. A hand shot out of the darkness and gripped my wrist, hard, yanking me into the darkness.

"Hey!" I squealed as the door slammed shut behind me. I had the impression of a hard chest against my back, warm breath on my neck.

"Shh," said the man who'd called himself Nick Andros, with his lips against my ear. "Shhh! Don't scream. I'm not going to hurt you. I just want to explain."

Darshi, meanwhile, had pulled the door open. "Let her go!" she said, brandishing her knife . . . which, I saw with a sinking feeling, she'd opened to the manicure scissors instead of the blade. Nick released me immediately. Darshi looked him over, still aiming her scissors in his direction. "Is that him?" she asked.

"That's him."

"Shh!" Nick said. "Please. Both of you. Close the door. I'll explain everything."

"You can explain out here," said Darshi. She crossed her arms over her chest and smirked at him. "Luckily, one of us is immune to your hotness."

"Please," Nick repeated. His eyes were locked on my face. "I didn't mean to run out on you. Just give me five minutes. I swear, I'll explain everything."

I looked past Nick, inspecting the small room. There was a refrigerator, piles of cardboard boxes, a pet carrier, a few suitcases, a lamp with no shade. The air was cool and smelled faintly of mildew and dust. A single lightbulb screwed into the ceiling cast a weak glow over the walls filled with tufted pink insulation and the concrete floor. A sleeping bag was spread out on an inflatable mattress; a reading lamp was plugged into an outlet near the baseboard. Nick's phone was plugged in, too, and he'd provisioned himself with a bottle of seltzer. He also had a book, an old paperback of *The Lion, the Witch and the Wardrobe*, which made me feel a little more relaxed. Probably there were some crazed killers who enjoyed spending time in Narnia, but I doubted there were many.

"You made yourself right at home, I see," I said.

His face seemed to contort. With an effort, he smoothed it out. "I used to live in this house," he said. "When I was little."

I felt my eyebrows ascend. "What?"

"When I was a little boy, I lived here with my mom." He swallowed hard. "That's why I crashed the party. I wanted to see it."

"And knocking at the front door and asking permission was too much trouble?" Darshi asked.

Nick, or whoever he was, rocked from his heels to his toes and back again. Head hanging, eyes on the concrete floor, he said, "Honestly, I didn't plan any of it. I was at a party yesterday afternoon, down on Corn Hill Beach. I took a walk, and I saw the caterers and the tent people doing the setup, and I figured I'd find someone to ask and see if there was any way they'd let me take a look inside."

I breathed in the cool, musty air, remembering one of the first things Nick had asked: *Are you staying in the big house?* My cheeks got hot. "So I was your way in," I said. Of course, I thought. Of course I was a means to an end. Of course this cute guy with his wind-burned cheeks wasn't into me. Of course he'd only wanted a way into the house. "Why didn't you just ask me? I would have given you a tour."

Looking shamefaced, Nick said, "I probably should have. And I'm sorry I didn't." He reached for my hand. Darshi gave him a hard look. He let his arm drop. "I swear. I wasn't planning on, um, you know." The tips of his ears looked pink as he cleared his throat and rocked again. "Things just happened. I was walking on the beach, and I saw you and Drue coming down the stairs, and at first I thought she'd recognize me, but she didn't—"

"So you did know Drue," I said.

He nodded. "We went to sailing camp together, like I said." He looked at Darshini. "Are you Daphne's roommate?" I'd told him about Darshi the night before, about how she'd been at Lathrop with Drue and me, and how we shared an apartment.

"Never mind who I am. How about you tell us your name?" Darshi said. "Your real one."

"Nick Carvalho," he said. No hesitation, no glance up and to the left, no tugging at his ears or fidgeting with his shirt or jamming his hands in his pockets. If he was lying, he was good at it. Out of the corner of my eye, I saw Darshi pull out her phone.

"I lived here with my mother until I was four years old," Nick said. "I don't have too many specific memories, but I remember . . ." He pulled in a breath and rubbed his eyes. "My mom used to mark my height against the wall down here," he said, and pointed to the side of the doorway, where I could see a series of lines in faint pencil. "I wanted to see if the marks were still there."

"Aidan," said Darshi. Nick flinched. I turned to see her staring at him, with her phone glowing in her hand.

"You're Aidan Killian, aren't you?" she said. "You're Christina Killian's son."

The names tickled something way at the back of my brain. They didn't mean anything to me yet, but they obviously meant something to Nick. Or Aidan. Or whoever he was. His tanned skin seemed to go a little pale in the lightbulb's glow, and his body seemed to shrink in on itself, with his chest sinking and his chin dipping down. He bent his head and gave a slow, defeated nod. "Yes," he said. "That's right."

"I don't understand," I said. "Why'd you lie? Why didn't you tell me your real name?"

"Because . . ." Nick began, but Darshi interrupted.

"Because it's not his name anymore." She jerked her chin at Nick. "You probably changed it. After. Isn't that right?"

He nodded again. "Nicholas is my middle name. It's what my aunt and uncle started calling me after . . ." He swallowed again. "After I came to live with them. Carvalho is their last name. They changed my name after they adopted me." He rubbed his hands against his shorts and looked up, his eyes finding mine. "After my mother was murdered."

The memory arrived in my brain all at once. I heard myself gasp, felt my skin bristling with goose bumps as I remembered the story. As I stood, frozen, Nick found two white wicker armchairs with pink and green cushions—banished, I supposed, because they hadn't matched Drue's nuptial color scheme—and pulled them toward the center of the room. "Please," he said. Darshi and I exchanged a glance. When I shrugged and sat down, she did, too, and Nick started talking, rubbing his face, and running his hands through his hair.

"My mom grew up in Boston, and she spent her summers here. She was the youngest girl in her family. She was thirty-eight when she had me. She never told anyone who the father was. She just said that it—that I—was going to be her baby. Her family had a couple of houses up here, and she got her father to let her live in the smallest one. This place." He gave me his crooked smile. "I know it's hard to believe, but a few million dollars ago, it was just a four-room cottage."

"So you lived here with your mother," I said.

He nodded. "She was a freelance writer. Before she had me, she lived in New York City and wrote about art and fashion. She did some of that from here, after I came along."

More memories were starting to surface: Drue arriving at school one Monday morning bursting with the news, saying, "You guys won't even believe what happened! They just arrested the man who killed a woman in the same town where I go in the summer." Over lunch, she'd told me and Ainsley and Avery all the juicy details of the formerly cold case: how, ten years ago, a young single mother had been found dead in her kitchen, with her little boy curled up around her. "He'd brought a pillow and a blanket from the bedroom and tucked her in, like she was asleep," Drue had said, leaning so close that I could smell Frosted Flakes on her breath. I remembered how she looked, her face alight with the prurient glee of repeating something shocking. "They don't even know how long her body was there. It could have been *days*."

"I'm so sorry," I said. I could almost hear the sound of Drue's voice, bubbling with excitement as she'd told us that the scene of the crime was on the same dune where her grandparents lived, picturing the story she'd shown us about the trial in the *New York Times*. "I'll bet I've walked right by that house a million times," she'd said with a dramatic shudder. "Maybe I even walked by the killer."

Nick swallowed hard. "It took the cops ten years to finally figure out who did it. And that was only after they interrogated every man my mom had ever dated, or was friends with, or said hello to in the post office." He winced. "Before they found the killer, someone wrote a book about it, and the book got turned into a movie on Lifetime."

I remembered the movie. Drue had invited me and Ainsley and Avery over to watch it. Abigay had made us popcorn, topped with brewer's yeast instead of butter, because Drue was dieting. A soap-opera star had played the murdered woman, a pop singer turned actor was her boyfriend, who'd become the chief suspect, and they'd shot parts of it on the Cape. "That's our house!" Drue had said when her grandparents' mansion made an appearance. "That's the post office! That's the beach!"

Nick's voice was soft. "After all that, it turned out that the man who'd killed my mother had never even met her before. He worked for the company my mom had hired to clean out her gutters. He came here, and he saw her, and . . ." Nick rubbed his face with his hands. "Her death had nothing at all to do with her personal life. She wasn't killed by someone she knew. It was just a random, terrible thing." He shook his head, breathing in slowly. "So. After my mother died, her sister and her brother-in-law adopted me. I took their last name and started going by my middle name." Looking right at my face, he said, "I'm sorry that I lied to you. And, for what it's worth, everything else I told you was true. I do work with kids in Boston during the school year, and I am working on a charter fishing boat for the summer." He grimaced. "At least, I was. I'm not sure I've still got a job after blowing off work today, but I couldn't leave." He sighed. "And I did know Drue. At least for one summer."

"So why give me a fake last name? I wouldn't have known you weren't on the guest list."

He looked down, his expression unhappy. "Because people

here know my aunt and uncle, and they know the story. They might not have recognized me, but they'd recognize my last name. It was more than twenty years ago, but out here, that's like yesterday. The Outer Cape's like a small town. People talk."

"So what about last night?" Darshi prompted. "Why'd you take off?"

Nick raked one hand through his hair. From the way it was standing up, I guessed he'd been tugging at it all morning. "Okay. After we . . ." He looked at me and rubbed his face again. "Um."

"I know you guys hooked up," Darshi said. "Cut to the chase."

He nodded. "After you fell asleep—I wanted to look around, to see if anything was the way I remembered it. I got dressed, and I went upstairs, and I heard a man and a woman in the living room, on the sofa all the way by the far wall, having an argument."

"What about?" Darshi asked.

"The man was saying stuff like, *Just be patient. Stick to the plan*, and the woman said, *I'm done waiting. I've waited long enough.*"

I shuddered and wrapped my arms around my shoulders. "Who were they?"

"I think the man was Drue's father. I didn't get a good look at him during the party, but I heard his voice, and I looked him up later." He nodded toward his phone, plugged into an outlet at the baseboard. "The woman, I'm not sure."

"Not Drue?" I asked. Nick shook his head.

"Not Drue's mom?" asked Darshi.

He shook his head again. "She sounded younger."

I thought it over. Maybe the mystery lady was Mr. Cavanaugh's mistress, some side piece who'd shown up at the wedding to claim her place or make trouble. *I'm done waiting. I've waited long enough.*

"So then what?" I asked.

"I was standing there in the dark, holding my breath, trying to figure out how I could sneak back downstairs, and they heard me."

I tried to picture it—Nick in his Nantucket Reds and white shirt. The shadowy figures, tucked into the deep couch by the windows that looked out over the bay. The man narrowing his eyes, calling, *Who's there?*

"Mr. Cavanaugh stood up. He didn't come toward me, he just stood there, and said, 'Get out.'" Nick gave me a look somewhere between defiant and pleading. "And, you know, I thought, if he caught a random guy in the house . . ."

"Got it. So then what?" I asked.

"So I ran." Nick sounded disgusted at himself. "I went down the stairs, and out the door. I had to circle around to get my shoes, because they were still on your deck. Then I went back down to the beach, and I just started walking." He dragged both hands through his hair and gave a brief chuckle. "Running, actually. I was almost to the top of the hill when I figured, even if I ran for the next three hours, I'd be somewhere on Route 6 when the sun came up. Not anywhere near where I had to be for work, and I didn't have anywhere else to go. So I just figured. Well." He nodded at the inflated bed, and his phone, and the book. "I remembered this room. Sometimes I'd hide here when I was a kid. I figured, if someone had recognized me and was trying to track me down, they wouldn't look for me inside the house. I thought I'd just stay here, wait until the house emptied out, and then try to find you and explain. At least leave a note."

Darshi made a scoffing noise. I rolled my eyes. Nick must have seen me do it, because he bent down and found a scrap of paper that seemed to have been torn from the paperback. He handed it to me. I moved until I was directly under the bare bulb, which gave me enough light to read what he'd written.

Dear Daphne, I had a wonderful time with you last night, and I'm very glad we met. I am sorry for running out on you, and I am even more sorry to say that I misled you. I told you that I was an acquaintance of Drue's from sailing camp, which is true. However, I also let you believe I was a wedding guest, which is not true. I would like to tell you the whole story, and explain myself, if you'd be willing to listen. I know this isn't the most auspicious beginning, but I'd like to see you again. If not, I understand, and I thank you for a memorable evening.

He'd signed his name simply *Nick*, and written down a phone number.

I read it through twice, flushed with pleasure, even in the midst of my fear. *A wonderful time. I'm glad we met. I'd like to see you again.*

"Does your family still have a house here?" It was far from the most essential question, but it was all that occurred to me to ask.

He shook his head. "My grandparents sold this place, and the big house, after my mother died. My aunt and uncle sold their place years ago. They made a kil—a fortune," he said, cutting himself off before he could say *killing*. "I've got an apartment in Wellfleet that I'm sharing with three other guys for the summer."

"How long were you planning this?" asked Darshi. Her voice was crisp, not unpleasant, but not especially friendly, either.

"I didn't plan it at all, I swear. The whole thing was a . . . a whim."

"I don't think I believe you," Darshi said.

Nick shrugged. "It's the truth."

I put my hands on my hips. "So at what point did you realize that you'd left me alone with a corpse in the hot tub?"

Nick sighed. "When I went back to the deck to get my shoes, there wasn't anyone there. After I came down here, I must've fallen asleep. The sirens woke me up. I could hear there was something happening." He looked chagrined as he said, "I could hear you screaming. I figured that would be a bad time to try to slip out, with cops crawling all over the house. Then I heard people saying that Drue was dead." He pulled in a deep breath and let it out slowly. "You have to understand how badly the cops fu— how badly they screwed up investigating my mother's murder," he said. "They brought every boyfriend she'd ever had in for questioning, every man she'd ever dated. Every man she'd ever met. Their names got dragged through the mud. All those guys ended up under suspicion for years, because the cops were stuck on the idea that it had to be some man she'd, you know, been with." This time, after he raked his hands through his hair, he gave the roots a tug before he let go. "Imagine if I popped out of the storage room and said, 'Oh, hey, I'm the son of the woman who was murdered in this house twenty-one years ago, just letting you know that I crashed the party last night and lied about my name and spent the whole night hiding down here, but I absolutely didn't have anything to do with Drue's death.' How do you think that would have gone over?"

"We don't even know how Drue died yet. And you've got an alibi," I said.

"Not for the entire night," he replied. He looked at Darshi, then at me. "If I go up there, they are going to arrest me," he said. "They won't care that I was, um, occupied for most of the night. The cops ended up looking incompetent the last time someone died. For them, it's all about the path of least resistance. If someone looks obvious, that's who they're going to arrest, just so they can arrest someone, and not be accused of screwing the pooch again."

I turned to Darshi, wondering what we were supposed to do now, when I heard the sounds of shouting and feet pounding down the stairs. Darshi cracked the storage room door open. I stood behind her, looking out into the foyer, and Nick stood behind me. Two police cruisers sped down the driveway. Behind us, a phalanx of uniformed cops, with McMichaels at their head, was pounding down the stairs, marching a handcuffed young woman toward the door.

"I didn't do it," the young woman said, her voice low and carrying. She looked like a teenager, with short dark hair, arched brows, and a fine-boned frame. I had a quick glimpse of a pressed white shirt, black pants, and a black apron. "I didn't do anything!" There was something familiar about her, I thought, but the cops had her out the door and into the back seat of one of the police cars before I could figure out what.

"Oh my God," I said. The wedding guests were surging down the stairs, crowding into the foyer or lined up on the staircase, hanging over the railings to watch. I stepped into the foyer, looking for someone who could fill me in. "What happened?"

"They arrested someone," said Arden Lowe. She had none of Drue's beauty, but her face was lit with the same kind of witchy glee that I remember animating my friend's features all those years ago. "Or at least they're bringing someone in for questioning."

"Who?"

"One of the caterers. They found a gun in her glove compartment. And a bunch of pictures of Drue, and printouts of stories about the wedding, and maps to the house."

"A gun?" I said. "Drue wasn't shot." I would have noticed a gunshot wound, if there had been one to notice.

Arden shrugged. "That's what I heard."

The police cruisers, with their lights flashing, were backing out of the driveway. McMichaels had hung back and was standing on the concrete lip of the garage, talking to a man in chef's whites, who was gesticulating, waving his hands at his sides, then lifting them past his head and spreading them wide, palms up; the universal posture of *How was I supposed to know?*

I felt a tap on my shoulder. When I turned around, Nick took my hand and pulled me back into the darkness of the storage closet. "That was her," he said, his voice low, close to my ear. My body gave a pleasurable tremble, even as my brain pointed out that, for all I knew, he might be the killer.

"What?" I asked. "Who?"

"The girl from last night. The one talking with Mr. Cavanaugh. That was her."

Part Three

So Grows the Tree

Chapter Fourteen

Drue Lathrop Cavanaugh had been, as far as I knew, a Christian, but it turned out that someone on her father's side was Jewish—at least, Jewish enough that they'd requested the services of one Rabbi Howard Medloff, as one of three members of the clergy who'd been scheduled to perform the marriage. Rabbi Medloff was now, it emerged, in charge of Drue's funeral.

"I am at the hospital with the family," he'd pronounced, in the plummy tones of a man who made his living speaking in public and enjoyed the sound of his own voice. Darshi and I had been up in my room when the phone rang. I'd taken the call, and Darshi had gone outside to stand in the fresh-smelling breeze, making phone calls as she glared suspiciously at the ocean. Nick was outside, too. He'd taken off his shoes and was pacing barefoot, back and forth along the deck, avoiding the hedge that concealed the hot tub and was now cordoned off with yellow crime scene tape. A man in a suit and a young woman in a police officer's uniform were standing behind the tape, heads bent in quiet conversation.

"I'm sure you're on your way home, but would you have time to make a stop?" the rabbi asked. "I am trying to learn as much as I can about Drue. For the eulogy."

Eulogy. The word tolled in my brain. "Of course. I'll be there as soon as I can," I said. Darshi came inside and sat down beside me.

"Are you sure you're okay?" she asked.

I nodded. "As okay as I can be."

"And you're sure about Nick?" When I didn't answer, Darshi smoothed her curls back over her shoulders. She said, "Look, I don't want to rain on your love parade or whatever. But this guy lied to you about his name, and he lied about being invited to the wedding, and he ditched you with a body in your bathtub . . ."

"Hot tub," I corrected. "And in his defense, there wasn't a body in there when he left."

"Says him," Darshi said. In a gentler tone, she asked, "Do you believe that he was going to come back?"

I grimaced. Darshi had just voiced my fear: that I'd been the victim of a classic case of fuck and run. Maybe Nick had woken beside me, considerably more sober than he'd been when he'd fallen asleep. Maybe he'd looked me over and thought, *I had sex with that?* Maybe his abrupt departure hadn't had anything to do with a desire to see the house where he'd once lived. Maybe he'd just wanted to get away from me, as fast as he could.

I straightened my shoulders and gathered my self-confidence. "You know what? I'm going to choose to believe that he actually wanted to be with me."

Darshi's brows drew down. "I didn't mean—"

"And that he actually did intend to come back." My voice was getting loud.

"I wasn't implying anything about you," said Darshi. "I'm just not sure I trust him."

I shut my eyes and nodded, trying to pull myself together, feeling the stress and the sleeplessness of the previous night starting to drag at me.

Darshi gave me a probing look. "Do you believe that he had nothing to do with this?"

"The police are questioning someone."

"The police, according to this guy, are completely incompetent."

"Oh, so now you trust him?"

Instead of answering, Darshi thumbed her phone's screen into life and handed it to me. "While you were on the phone, I googled everything I could find about Christina Killian's murder. I remembered reading about it—that's why I almost had it, back in Provincetown. Nick wasn't wrong about the cops questioning every man his mother had ever met." She scrolled through the stories, headlines and phrases jumping out at me: *"Local Fisherman Fell for Murdered Woman 'Hook, Line, and Sinker.'" "Neighbors: 'She Was a Flirt.'" "The Single Mom Murder: When a fashion writer left the fast lane to raise her out-of-wedlock baby, was she chasing her own destruction?"* Words like "turbulent" and "dramatic" and "party girl" appeared, as tabloid stories and blog post suppositions constructed the narrative of a bored rich woman on the Cape taking her pleasure with the locals until one of them snapped. The implication was that if Christina Killian hadn't been exactly courting her own death, she bore at least some of the responsibility for her own sad end.

"Slut-shaming city," I murmured.

"I agree," Darshi said. "And I don't doubt that Nick suffered because of it. But don't you think it's weird that he just decided on a whim to come back to this house, for the first time since his mom was killed, the night Drue was getting married, and now Drue's dead, too?"

"Why would he want to hurt Drue?" I asked. "How was she part of this?"

Darshi touched her hair again. "I don't know. Maybe because Drue treated him the way she treated 99.9 percent of the people she met? Maybe she did something awful to him, and he's just been waiting all these years to take his revenge."

"That's crazy." But even as I spoke, I thought of all the nights I'd lain awake, my head filled with fantasies of getting back at Drue.

"And why isn't he online?" she asked. "What's that about?"

I sighed, realizing what she'd been doing out on the deck: taking advantage of the Wi-Fi to google Nick's particulars. "Darshi, you're barely online."

"'Barely' isn't 'not at all.' I'm on LinkedIn, and I've got a Facebook page so my students can ask if whatever I covered in my lecture is going to be on the exam—which, by the way, yes, it is. And I'm on Instagram so I can follow you."

"And Bingo," I muttered. It had not escaped my attention that, between me and my dog, Darshi left most of her comments and likes on Bingo's page.

"Even if I don't post anything, I'm there. And I think it's weird," she said stubbornly. "It's like he's got something to hide."

I thought about telling her that even people with something to hide were online; maybe especially people with something to hide. I considered pointing out that Darshini herself had, in college, posted dozens of pictures of herself at the South Asian Student Association's various events and not a single one from the Gay-Straight Alliance, of which she'd been vice president; or how she'd posted a beautifully composed shot of the roti and dal and coconut chutney, without mentioning that I'd been the one who'd prepared it all ("*Beti*, you cooked!" I'd heard Dr. Shah exclaiming on speakerphone, and Darshi had said "It came out perfectly" before giving me a guilty look and closing her bedroom door.)

I decided to stay focused on Nick. "I completely understand why he wouldn't want to be online. His mother was murdered. Maybe he doesn't want creepers and conspiracy theory nuts bothering him." Except he could have used a fake name, or opened accounts that gave no indication of his connection to the Cape.

There were lots of things Nick could have done to have an online presence, and he hadn't done any of them, as far as the two of us knew.

Darshi's expression was pained. There was a vertical line between her eyebrows, her forehead was furrowed, and the left side of the plum-colored silk shell she had on underneath her jacket was incrementally less tucked in on the right side. For Darshi, that was hurricane-level dishevelment. "Being in a house while your own mother gets murdered . . . being left alone with her corpse for days . . . then reading every crazy person's theories about how being single and sexually active was what killed her . . . Don't you think that could have an impact on a person? Affect them?"

"Absolutely. Hundred percent. I'm just not sure it would turn a person into a homicidal maniac who'd wait twenty-five years and then kill a bride on her wedding day."

"Maybe he didn't want to kill the bride." Darshi's voice was steady. It took me a second to figure out what she meant, and when I finally got it, I shuddered uncontrollably.

"You think he wanted to kill me?" I said. I tried to sound indignant. Instead, my voice was so high that I sounded like one of Bingo's squeaky toys. "Why? Do you think I'm that bad in bed?"

"Hashtag self-esteem," Darshi murmured. "What if it turns out that Drue was poisoned?" she asked. "What if it turns out whoever killed her just put poison in a drink, and left the drink by the hot tub? Who had access to that hot tub, besides Drue? Who was it for?" Darshi barely paused before she answered her own question. "You. Just you."

I cringed, my skin bristling with goose bumps, hearing the echo of Drue's voice as she showed me my room. *I want you to be happy. I'm so grateful that you're here.*

"Okay, but what about a motive? If Nick's the killer, would he want to kill me?" I asked. I made a face, trying to keep my tone light. "I'm nobody."

Darshi wasn't laughing. She reached for my phone, opened up the photo app, and scrolled through the pictures that Nick had taken of me and Drue the night before. "Look," she said, and angled the screen to show me.

Even after all these years, all the internal pep talks, all the articles I'd read and all the pictures I'd posted online, I still found it hard, sometimes, to look at pictures of myself. Now I forced myself to look, and see what Darshi wanted me to see. Nick had placed me, not Drue, in the center of all of the pictures. A few of them showed Drue with her eyes oddly squinched shut or her mouth half-open, but not me. Not once. I was smiling in one shot, laughing in another; backed by a corona of glowing light, as if I'd been dusted in golden pollen. I looked pretty.

"I think he likes you," Darshi said.

I waved her words away, pleased and unsettled. "So which is it? He's into me, or he wants me dead?"

"Maybe he's confused." She got off the bed and tucked her shirt back in. "Maybe sleeping with a woman in the house where his mother was murdered set him off somehow. Maybe he's got some kind of wires crossed, with sex and death."

"Darshi," I said, "Nick isn't a psychopath. No one wants to kill me. And we're not even sure anyone wanted to kill Drue. I'm sure this is all a big . . . misunderstanding." At least, I hoped it was all a big misunderstanding. I couldn't think of anyone who would want to hurt me, unless that guy from the bar had held a grudge for four years and had come after me. "And again, the police have already arrested someone."

"Speaking of which." Darshi held her hand out for her phone. "The woman the cops brought in is Emma Vincent, of Eastham, Massachusetts, which is about fifteen miles from here. She's twenty-six years old, a part-time community-college student. She waitresses, caters, works at the Chatham Bars Inn. No criminal record that I can find and not much of an online presence."

Darshi's audible sniff conveyed her frustration. "People upstairs are saying that Drue's mom is still in the hospital in Hyannis." She lowered her voice. "They're also saying that Drue's dad is MIA."

I lowered my voice and told her what I'd heard from the Lathrop side of the family, and from my own father, about Mr. Cavanaugh's finances and infidelities.

"Maybe that's it," said Darshi. "Maybe Emma's a girlfriend."

I was shocked. "She's Drue's age!"

Darshi gave me a pitying look. "Right. Shocking. Because no wealthy, powerful man has ever hooked up with a woman young enough to be his daughter."

I shook my head, got to my feet, and went back to filling my suitcase with the clothes I'd unpacked just the day before. Darshi gave me one last look, then slipped out the door. I checked the closet to make sure I'd gotten all of my dresses, sat down on the bed, and opened the Instagram app. The picture I'd posted, the one of me and Drue, with all of the wedding hashtags, had gotten thousands of likes and hundreds of comments that I couldn't bring myself to read. Instead, I hit the "edit" feature and started to write. I typed, *By now, some of you might have heard the news . . .* Then I erased it. I typed, *I am sitting here, stunned. I still can't believe that such a beautiful night ended in tragedy.* Then I erased it. I slumped back against the headboard, biting my lip. Anyone who'd spent ten minutes on Instagram could tell you that authenticity was the name of the game, that people wanted honest, unfiltered connection; they wanted to feel like the men and women they saw on their phones were living, breathing people, just like they were; they wanted us to be real. But what could I honestly, authentically say about my friend, and what had happened, and how scared I was that the police would decide that I, or the man I'd slept with, had something to do with her death?

I stared at the screen for a long moment, trying to figure out how to be real. *Rest in peace, beautiful girl*, I finally typed. I'd just hit "Post" when Nick stuck his head into the room. "Can I talk to you?"

"Sure." I got to my feet and followed him upstairs.

On the third floor, the living room and kitchen were both almost empty. A few caterers were straightening stacks of napkins and refilling pitchers of water. They'd set out a spread of two-bite sandwiches, meatball subs, and sliders, along with an assortment of miniature desserts. There were fresh doughnuts and tiny éclairs, and little paper cones of frites, glistening with oil, lined up in a metal rack.

"This was the midnight snack." I tried to remember the line from *Hamlet* about funeral-baked meats furnishing the wedding table. Only this was the other way around, a wedding feast served to mourners. "I helped Drue pick the menu." Drue had nixed things like ceviche and brie en croute in favor of diner food. "Carbs and fat. That's what people are going to want to eat when they're drunk and happy at two in the morning." It hit me again as I stood there, smelling grease and salt and meatballs. Drue would never gorge herself on French fries in the wee small hours. Drue would never be drunk, or happy, ever again.

Nick led me to a couch in the corner, beside windows that looked out over the bay. "So that girl is your roommate?"

I nodded. "Darshini. She's one of my best friends."

"Was she a friend of Drue's, too?"

"Ha!"

Nick stared at me, his face expectant.

I took a deep breath. *Get it together*, I told myself sternly. "I mean, no. Darshi . . ." *Hated her* was on the tip of my tongue. I pulled it back to "Darshi wasn't a fan."

"What was she doing in Boston?"

"A conference. She's getting her PhD in economics, and there was some big supply-side guy speaking at Harvard."

His eyebrows drew down as he looked at me. "You don't think the timing's a little strange?"

"What do you mean?"

"That someone who hated Drue and lives in New York City just happened to be in Boston when she died?"

I looked at him. Then I pictured Darshini, all five feet, two inches of her; Darshi, whose parents were still quietly disappointed that she'd chosen to get a PhD at Columbia and would never be what they considered a "real" doctor. "There is no way she's involved with any of this."

Nick's shoulders were hunched; his voice was tight. "She got here fast. And she was close."

I stared at him. "So you think Darshi came to Boston, drove up here and killed Drue last night, drove back to Boston so people could see her at breakfast this morning, then came back here to comfort me?"

"I've heard of stranger things." Nick looked, for an instant, like he was going to take my hand. Instead, he leaned forward with his elbows on his thighs. "One of my mother's friends was this guy named Lars. He was an artist. A children's book illustrator. I remember that he'd bring me balloons, and he'd blow them up like swords. Or hats. Or animals." He shook his head very slightly. "He was the one they thought did it for a while. Because he'd been at the house the night before. And because he and my mom had dated. People thought that maybe he was my dad."

I made sympathetic noises and wondered if, in the years since his mother's death, he'd ever found out his father's identity. "They never arrested him," Nick said. "They brought him in for questioning, over and over again. For years, he had to live under this cloud of suspicion. Everyone thought he'd killed my mother." The faint lines I'd noticed around Nick's eyes seemed to have deepened overnight, and his tan seemed to have faded. "I want them to get this right. Because, if they don't, it's going to really screw with people's lives."

"I understand," I told him. "But Darshini . . ." I paused, searching for the detail that would convey how impossible it was for me to imagine her killing someone. "Darshi's a vegetarian." Which, of course, didn't mean she was incapable of murder, but it was the most disproving thing I could come up with. And even as I said it, I was remembering the texts she'd sent, and remembered Darshi crowing as she'd told me about the conference, and how lucky it was that it coincided so perfectly with Drue's wedding. "Why are you saying this?" I asked. "Does Darshi look guilty to you?"

"I'm just saying that it's convenient. Convenient that she'd be in Boston for the weekend. And she didn't like Drue. You said so yourself."

"A lot of people didn't like Drue. That doesn't mean all of them are suspects."

"I just want us to be careful."

I nodded. Then I took in what he'd said. "Us?"

"I don't want to leave you alone." The *with her* was left unspoken. And, just as Nick didn't want me alone with Darshi, I was positive that Darshi wouldn't leave me alone with Nick. Which left me as one leg of the world's weirdest triangle.

"I can go with you guys to the hospital," Nick said. "I'll catch a bus from Hyannis back to Wellfleet when we're done."

"You don't have to do that."

"I know. But . . ." He paused, then got to his feet and started pacing again. "I want to make sure you're safe."

"I've known Darshi since high school!"

"You knew Drue, too."

I looked at him, his worried eyes, his wind-burned cheeks, and wondered how much he wanted to protect me, and how much he just wanted to make sure the crime really had been solved, to ensure that Drue got the justice his own mother hadn't. I knew better than to go off alone with a guy I'd just met—even one I'd also just slept with—but was there a world where Darshi really had done something to Drue Cavanaugh?

I shook my head and went back down to my room. Five minutes later, I was towing my suitcase over the shells, thinking it through. Nick suspected Darshi. Darshi had suspicions about Nick. For all I knew, both of them might be secretly thinking that I'd had something to do with Drue's death, that I'd been overcome with envy or sublimated attraction, or something. *This is going to be the most awkward car trip ever*, I thought, and as soon as we'd made it out of the driveway, my suppositions were confirmed.

"Tell me about how you met Drue," Nick said. Darshi was driving, clutching the wheel with her back hunched and her eyes intent on the road. I was sitting next to her—I'd offered Nick the passenger's seat, but he'd politely declined.

"Yes, Daphne," Darshi said, her voice soft in a way that only someone who knew her very well would recognize as dangerous. "Tell him all about it."

"There isn't much to tell." I could still remember standing in front of the class, holding my breath, hoping the kids who were staring would decide that I was okay, that they liked me, that they'd be my friends. "We met in sixth grade, when I started at the Lathrop School. We were friends all through high school. And then we weren't."

"Why not?"

A cold finger pressed against my heart.

"It was stupid," I mumbled. "Teenage-girl drama."

"Tell me," he said.

"Yes, Daphne." Darshi's voice was poisonously sweet. "Tell him."

I sighed, remembering how I'd already told him about starring in a slightly viral video. Time to come clean and tell him the whole sad tale.

"When I was home from college my sophomore year, for spring break, I went out to a bar with Drue," I began. I sketched the contours of the story as briefly as I could—a guy I hadn't realized I'd been set up with, how I'd overheard his objections, our eventual face-off on the dance floor. "Drue was angry. She thought that I should have been grateful."

"Seriously?" Nick's voice was incredulous.

"Seriously," said Darshi, before I could speak. "Believing that other people should be grateful for her largesse was Drue's default mode."

I opened my mouth to object, to say that maybe Drue had been trying to help, in her clumsy, condescending way, but before the words could come, I heard an echo of what she'd shouted at me that night: *We all just felt sorry for you!*

"It was a long time ago," I finally said. My voice was raspy and my head throbbed with pain. "And I thought, by the time Drue showed up in my life again, that we'd both grown up." Trying to smile, I said, "I think Drue could appreciate my many fine qualities. And I could see her for what she was."

Darshi's voice was cool. "Which was what?"

I thought for a minute before I answered. "Someone who wasn't invincible," I said. "Someone who had flaws, and things she wanted. In high school, I couldn't even imagine Drue wanting anything, or being jealous of what I had." I thought of the party, of the way her father had shouted at her, how her mother had been more concerned with appearances than with her daughter, how her fiancé hadn't come to comfort her.

"And now?" Nick asked.

"Now," I repeated. "Now I'm not so sure."

Chapter Fifteen

Rabbi Medloff was waiting for me in a conference room on the third floor of the hospital, just down the hall from Lily Lathrop Cavanaugh's room. "Thank you for making the time," he said, pouring me a plastic cup of water from the plastic pitcher at the center of the table.

"Of course." The rabbi was young, in his thirties, with short, dark hair and a neatly trimmed beard. He had a pale, earnest-looking face and blue-gray eyes behind gold-rimmed glasses. A gold band gleamed on his left hand, and he wore a pressed blue suit with a shiny light-blue silk tie. The suit he'd brought up here, I guessed, to marry Drue and Stuart.

"Thank you for coming. This is such an unbelievable tragedy, for a young woman to lose her life on her wedding day. I want to make sure she is remembered, and celebrated, appropriately." He had a legal pad and a pen, and he flipped to a blank page. "What can you tell me about Drue?"

That she didn't deserve to die, I thought. Whatever she'd done, whomever she'd done it to, whatever she'd deserved, it wasn't this. I felt my throat get tight as the rabbi looked at me, waiting.

"She was funny," I said. "Lively. She had a great sense of adventure. She could turn any day into an occasion. If that makes sense."

The rabbi nodded, and as he wrote, I told him everything I thought he could use. I told him that Drue loved jokes, and didn't say how often my classmates and I had been the target of them. I told him that she liked pranks and fun, and didn't mention her cruel imitations of our math teacher's limp or a classmate's stutter. I said that she'd been popular, with lots of friends and lots of boyfriends, and I didn't mention her habit of starting up with a new guy before she'd entirely ended things with an old one, leaving me to offer explanations and excuses to the wronged party. I said that she loved music, and art, and that she had a great sense of style. I said that she was beautiful, and didn't tell him that she'd had her nose and her breasts both done, or how she'd flirted with bulimia all through high school. I could still remember the time I'd found her in the bathroom after lunch, on one of the rare occasions she'd actually eaten something substantial. She'd been poised above the toilet bowl, holding her hair away from her face, and she hadn't even needed to stick her fingers down her throat. She'd just bent down, opened her mouth, and sent her grilled cheese splashing into the water. *See?* she'd said. *Easy!*

"What else can you tell me?" said the rabbi. When I hesitated, he said, "Don't worry about trying to be entirely complimentary. I want to get a real sense of her. Of course, I'll make some choices about the stories I tell. But I want to know what she was really like, as much as I can."

My throat ached, and my eyes stung. I thought about the quote from *The Great Gatsby*, about how Tom and Daisy Buchanan "smashed up things and creatures and then retreated back into their money or their vast carelessness . . . and let other people clean up the mess." I thought of how awful Drue had been, how carelessly cruel, and, still, how much I'd loved her, how I'd been powerless in the face of her charms; how, as soon as I heard the familiar cadences of her voice, as soon as I felt her attention, her regard, all of that focused on me, I was ready to forgive her, to forgive everything, just to have her in my life again, because life with Drue was a good time, a memorable time. Every moment with her had the potential to turn into an adventure. She'd made me feel clever and beautiful, just by association. She'd made me feel special.

When I felt like I could speak, I cleared my throat. "When she asked me to be in the wedding, I think it was the first time that she asked about me, and what I was doing, and really listened when I answered. It was the first time she didn't see me as . . . oh, I don't know. A sidekick. Someone lesser than she was. Or a cautionary tale. Someone she could look at and say, *At least I'm thinner and prettier than she is. At least I'll never be that.*" My eyes were burning again, and my throat felt tight. "I think that she was sorry that she'd hurt me, and that she wanted to do better." I sniffled and took a sip from the cup of water. "That's what I'm going to believe. Because that's how I want to remember her."

Rabbi Medloff touched my hand. "In the Jewish tradition, when someone dies, we say '*Baruch dayan ha'emet*,' which means 'Blessed is the true judge.'" He looked at me, his eyes intent. "God knows your friend. God knows her heart. Who she was, and who she was trying to become." He squeezed my hand. "There is a true judge, and I believe that judge will see her."

I nodded, and sniffled, and wiped my cheeks.

"Do you have friends here?" His voice was gentle. "Any family? People who can be with you?"

I felt gratitude flood through me, that Darshi was here, and that Nick was, too, and that my parents were standing by, waiting to hear from me, wanting to help. Then I thought about Drue again, the way her eyes had followed her father at her engagement party, how her parents had squabbled over the cost of the wedding, how her fiancé hadn't come to comfort her. I wondered if, at the end, she had known that she was dying, if she'd been in pain or if she'd been afraid, and I thought about how, in spite of all the ways we were different, Drue had spent a lot of her life being lonely . . . just like me.

Chapter Sixteen

The hospital cafeteria smelled like overboiled coffee and industrial cleanser. The floors were pea-soup green; the walls were a dispirited beige. A pink and silver IT'S A GIRL! balloon hung, half-deflated, from a chair where it had been tied with pink ribbon. At a table for four, three women in blue jeans sat in the metal-legged chairs, their heads together as they talked softly. A janitor wearing earbuds pushed a mop behind a cart made of scuffed yellow plastic, bobbing his head in time to music only he could hear. I spotted Darshini and Nick at a table. Nick looked tanned and healthy in his pinkish-red shorts and white shirt. Darshi had discarded her jacket, and her shimmering silk plum shell matched the sheen of her lipstick. I felt something painful and familiar flare up inside of me. She was pretty and he was handsome. They looked like they belonged together, like they matched in a way that Nick and I never would.

I turned away to fill a paper cup with coffee, doctoring it with sugar and cream, when, out of the corner of my eye, I saw a familiar figure dart down the hall. I turned around in time to see a flash of Corina Bailey's silvery hair as she vanished into a room with a sign that said CONFERENCE ROOM on its door.

"The plot, she thickens," I whispered. Abandoning my coffee on the table, I told Darshi and Nick what I'd seen and padded quietly down the hall, hard on the heels of the not-groom and his erstwhile fiancée. When I arrived at the conference room door, I gave them a minute, knocked once on the door, and pushed it open before anyone answered.

Inside, sitting on a couch with padded vinyl cushions, was Stuart, dressed in the standard-issue white-guy uniform of Docksiders, khaki shorts, and a blue-and-white-checked short-sleeved button-down. Corina, in a tight white T-shirt and pale-pink capri pants, was curled against him, her head on his chest, one hand stroking his cheek. They weren't kissing, but the way Corina was touching him was not the way a woman would touch a friend.

I cleared my throat. Neither of them noticed me. "Excuse me," I said. That did the trick. Stuart jolted upright, jerking himself away from Corina and putting twelve inches of vinyl seat cushion between them. Corina moved more slowly, unwinding her limbs slowly, extending her legs and stretching her arms over her head. Her T-shirt rose over the firm, golden-brown convexity of her belly. She moved languidly, like a woman who'd just rolled out of bed.

"Daphne," said Stuart, his resonant voice thin. He cleared his throat. "It . . . it isn't what you think."

Corina rolled her eyes and said, "Actually, Daphne, it's exactly what you think." Her voice was pitched normally. Instead of sounding like a little girl, she sounded like an adult, and I remembered Drue telling me, *She isn't what you think.*

"Corina . . ." Stuart said.

She turned her eye roll on him. "What's the point of hiding now? We don't have to lie anymore! The dog days are over!" The breathy baby-doll voice, the kittenish gestures, the girlish affect, all of it was gone. Maybe this wised-up, hard-edged woman was the real Corina. Maybe there was no real Corina at all, just different versions, different Corinas for different occasions.

Stuart put his hand on her shoulder. Corina shook it off. "No. No, don't shush me. I've had it. I'm done with the lies." She turned to me, a smug expression making her pretty face significantly less pretty. "Stuart and I love each other. We never stopped loving each other. And now we're going to be together. Love wins."

Corina gave me a smile that showed all of her teeth. Stuart, meanwhile, looked like a man trying to pass a kidney stone. I thought of the woman whose voice Nick had heard in the darkness, the woman who'd said *I'm done waiting* and *I've waited long enough.*

"Did Drue know that you and Corina were still together?"

Stuart's shoulders slumped. Corina sat up straighter. "Of course she knew," she said. At some point, she'd taken time to put on a full face of makeup, from foundation to lip liner to fake lashes. Her nipples strained against the fabric of her T-shirt, and she'd scooted so close to Stuart that the side of her thigh was right up against his.

"Look," she said. "I know Drue was your friend, so I'm sorry. But she was a horrible person. She treated Stuart like her servant. Do this, do that. Fly there, stand here. Marry me in June, on Cape Cod, so the whole world can see, and not . . . ow!" I looked. Stuart had taken her by the wrist and was pinching her. Not gently.

"That's enough," he said.

Corina wrenched herself away from him, glaring. On the show, her fingernails had been short and polished pale pink, her fingers bare. Now her nails were painted blood red, so dark that they could have been lacquered with the same stuff that Tinsley, the show's villainess, had worn.

"We don't have to talk to you," she said.

"No," I acknowledged. "But if it turns out that Drue was murdered, and that the girl they arrested didn't do it, you two are going to be at the top of the list. I mean, I'm no Angela Lansbury, but this"—I made a gesture that encompassed the two of them and, I hoped, their activities the night before—"doesn't look good."

"We have alibis." Corina's voice was smug.

"Seriously? You're going to tell the cops that you were together last night?" I asked, letting her hear the skepticism in my voice.

Maybe Corina was oblivious, but Stuart, evidently, could grasp how terrible an idea it was. "Corrie . . ." he said.

She ignored him. "It's the truth. And the truth shall set you free." Turning toward me, silvery hair swinging, she said, "They were never in love. And there wasn't even going to be a wedding. The whole thing was a fake."

I looked at her, then turned to Stuart, who was bent over, with his elbows on his thighs and his head cradled in his hands.

"What," I asked, "was going on?"

"Drue needed money," he said, without looking up. "The family business was in trouble, and she wanted to save it. She couldn't get access to her trust fund until she turned thirty, unless she got married before then."

I nodded, remembering how Drue had explained it to me. "Okay, so she needed to get married. But didn't you just say there wasn't going to be a wedding today?"

Stuart Lowe had the grace to at least look ashamed. He couldn't even meet my eyes, so he addressed his remarks to the floor. "Drue and I got married six months ago, at City Hall. She got her trust fund. And we started planning this whole thing." He nodded toward the door, toward Truro, and the rented mansions, and the beachfront party, the caterers, the DJs, the hand-knotted silk rugs on the sand. "The plan was . . ." He looked up at Corina, his expression miserable. She gave him a tight-lipped nod.

"Go on," she said. "Get it all out."

He sighed. "Okay, so the plan was for me to leave Drue at the altar. Instead of 'I do,' I was going to say 'I can't.' I was going to say that I still loved Corina." At that, Corina gave a smug smile and cuddled up even closer to him. I stared, remembering the pitch deck Detective McMichaels had shown me: *There will be guaranteed glamour, celebrity sightings, and maybe a surprise or two!*

Well, I thought. That certainly would have been surprising. It also explained Drue's indifference to her husband-to-be, the way she'd rolled her eyes and said "Meh" when I'd asked if he'd mind her ditching their engagement party. And, of course, the way he hadn't been around last night. "So that's what you promised the businesses you were pitching. That was the big plot twist."

He gave a small, miserable-looking nod. "We figured if the wedding didn't happen, that would be in the news, and all three of us would get a bunch of new followers on social. We wanted to have deals in place before that happened, so that we could, you know . . ."

"Monetize the scandal?" I said.

"It was my idea," Corina announced proudly. If she was even the tiniest bit sorry about what she and Stuart had been planning, if she felt even the merest scintilla of guilt, I could see no sign of it on her pretty face.

"And what was going to happen after that?" I asked.

Corina smoothed her silvery hair. "Stuart and I would get back together. He'd say that he never stopped loving me. In a year or so they'd get divorced and we'd get married. Like we'd planned. Only by then we'd be even more famous. Real famous, not just reality-TV famous."

"And what about Drue?"

"I know she was talking to the producers about having her own season of *All the Single Ladies*," Stuart said. "I don't know if she'd locked it in."

That part, at least, made sense. I could imagine the *People* magazine covers, the cover shot of Drue gazing into the distance, looking beautiful and forlorn, with a headline reading HEIRESS'S HEARTBREAK. And then, a few months later, Drue beaming, holding an armful of the colorful bow ties that the bachelorettes on "All the Single Ladies" distributed to their male suitors. DRUE BOUNCES BACK!!! I thought of the hashtags—#singleladies and #lookingforlove and #singlegirlproblems and #loveyourselffirst. I thought about all the single and searching women who'd follow her story, on TV and on social media; all the businesses who'd want a bite of the apple. Maybe she'd even have ended up as the face of one of the dating apps, if she didn't land a man on the show.

"And Stuart would have the money to get his business off the ground," said Corina.

At that revelation, Stuart slumped even farther on the couch, as if he was hoping the crevice between the cushions would swallow him up. "Money from the trust fund?" I guessed. At his unhappy nod, I said, "For the brain smoothies?"

"You think it's a joke." There were cords standing out on Corina's neck. Her cheeks were stained a mottled, unlovely pink. "They're going to be huge. Just wait. You'll see."

"So Stuart would launch his business. He'd get rich," I said. "All three of you would get famous. You two could be together, and everyone would get to be on TV. Am I missing anything?"

"Yes. You're missing the point. You're making it sound like Drue was the victim." Corina's lips were curled, her teeth bared. "Like it was this plot we cooked up against her, when it was actually something we came up with together. Drue knew the score." She raised her chin. "And she deserved it. Getting dumped on her wedding day. She was a bitch." Corina's voice was low and furious. "A one-hundred-percent, twenty-four-karat bitch. I guarantee, the only reason she wanted you around was so she could get a bunch of fatties to follow her."

I felt my stomach twisting, my entire body suddenly cold. *That isn't true*, I wanted to say as Corina kept talking. "You want to know what your friend was really like? Want to know how the whole thing started?" Stuart stared at the floor as Corina stood up and came stalking toward me, flaxen hair swinging. Spittle flew from her painted lips, spots of color burned in her cheeks. "She saw Stuart on TV. Right when the show started airing. And she decided that she had to have him back."

I stood still, thinking that this sounded possible, maybe even probable.

"After the first, like, three episodes, after she saw how Stuart was blowing up, she called him. At first it was all sweet talk." Corina pushed her hair behind her ears and raised her voice to a simpering falsetto: "Oh, I made a terrible mistake when I dumped you, you're the only man I want, I love you so so much." Corina rolled her eyes. "Like that. When Stuart didn't fall for it, when he told her that he loved me, that he'd moved on, that's when she offered the money."

I looked at Stuart. "And all you'd have to do was . . . what? Marry her in secret, then pretend to be engaged for a while, and leave her at the altar?"

"Oh, she had a whole list of demands," Corina said. She sat down next to Stuart and crossed her legs. "She wanted a June wedding on the Cape. She wanted it in the paper, and the magazines. She wanted five hundred thousand followers on Instagram, she wanted five major corporate sponsors. She wanted to win. At least for a little while. Everything was a contest to her, and she always had to win."

My head was throbbing, and my face still felt frozen and numb. "And Drue was okay with the whole left-at-the-altar thing?"

Stuart cleared his throat. "My impression was that maybe she had someone else, too," he said. "She wasn't going to be alone."

"So why didn't she just marry that guy? She could have been with someone she loved and gotten the money."

"Win-ning," Corina said. "That wouldn't have been winning. She couldn't just marry any guy, it had to be a guy like Stuart, and taking him away from someone else was, like, icing on the cake." She went back to her spot on the couch, curling against Stuart, who caressed the side of her head, murmuring something I couldn't hear.

"Did you ever love her?" I asked him. "Did you even like her?"

Stuart was silent for a long moment. "Drue was fun. When I met her at Croft, she was, you know, always up for a good time. But in the end . . ." His voice trailed off. "She had a goal, and I was her way to get there."

All three of us turned at the sound of the door opening. Lily Cavanaugh stood in the doorway. Her face was as blank as a wiped-off whiteboard. Her eyes were sunk into deep grayish circles. They widened as she took in the sight of Stuart and Corina on the couch together. Then her body sagged against the doorframe, her eyes rolling up until only a crescent of white showed. Stuart raced across the room, fast enough to grab her by the shoulders, an instant before she would have hit the floor.

Chapter Seventeen

"Get a nurse!" I said as Stuart eased Drue's mom onto the couch. I heard feet pounding away—Corina's, I hoped.

"Can you get her some water?" Stuart asked. I was starting out the door when Mrs. Cavanaugh's eyes fluttered open. She looked at Stuart, then at me, and her lips started to tremble.

"My baby," she whispered. I knelt down beside her and took her hand.

"Mrs. Cavanaugh, I'm so sorry," I said. I could feel her fine bones, frail beneath her skin. "Let's get you back to your room."

When she nodded, Stuart and I helped her to her feet and into the room down the hall. When we settled her on the bed, she looked at Stuart from out of her haunted eyes and pulled herself upright. "I want you out of here," she said, her patrician voice sounding like a whip's crack. "Out of this room, out of this hospital. I never want to see you again."

Stuart's eyes widened, but he didn't respond. He backed out of the room, shutting the door gently behind him. Mrs. Cavanaugh collapsed back against her pillows, looking old and unwell.

I looked around for water. The bedside table and the windowsill that ran along the side of the room were crammed with white flowers: delphinium and roses, snapdragons and lilies. I wondered if any of them had been meant for Drue's wedding bouquet.

I finally located a pitcher amid the greenery and blooms and poured a cupful of water. Mrs. Cavanaugh took a sip, grasping the cup with both hands. I settled myself on the edge of the bed. Up close, I could see her hair, with strands of gold and honey and butterscotch, and the tiny scars at her ears and underneath her chin. I remembered how once, in high school, she'd gone to the hospital for a few days. Drue told me that she was getting her face lifted and her saddlebags sucked, and that she was also having some work done down south. "Face, ass, and cooch," Drue had gleefully announced. *You're lying*, I told her, and she'd smirked and said, "It's called vaginal rejuvenation. Look it up." At the party, Lily Cavanaugh looked chic, hair and skin and teeth all displaying the sheen of good health and the best products and care money could buy, like she could have been anywhere from forty-five to seventy. Now she looked every year of her age and more.

Mrs. Cavanaugh took another gulp of water and set the cup down. The door opened, and Darshini stood there, holding another plastic water pitcher. Nick was behind her.

"The doctor is coming," he said.

"Daphne," Mrs. Cavanaugh whispered, and grabbed for my hand.

"I'm so sorry," I said, feeling helpless. Looking at Darshi, I mouthed, *Mr. Cavanaugh?* Darshi shook her head.

"That Stuart," she whispered, so quietly that I could hardly make out the words. "I knew what he was." She shook her head again. "But Drue wanted . . ." Her hand drifted up from her chest, where it had been resting, and wavered, describing a circle in the air. "A big wedding. Press. All of it. She kept telling me it would all pay off in the end." Her chest rose as she inhaled. "And her father . . ." A tear slid out of the corner of one eye and inched its way down her cheek, magnifying age spots and tiny wrinkles as it rolled toward her chin. "He got mad at me for spending so much, but he was the one who wanted it to look like a million-dollar wedding. Even though he didn't have a million dollars." She gave a dry, coughing sound that it took me a minute to recognize as laughter. "Drue wanted to save him," she said. "So he'd love her."

I said, "I don't understand."

Mrs. Cavanaugh sighed and slumped against her pillow. "All her life, all she wanted was for her father to love her. But he was busy. Distracted. With work. With all of his women." Her lips thinned over her teeth. "That's why we had to leave the place where my family's spent summers for six generations. My favorite place in the world, and he had to ruin it." Her hands tightened on the blanket. "The year Drue was five, he got two different au pairs pregnant. Had to pay for two different abortions." She closed her eyes, sagging back into the pillows. "I should have left him," she said. "Part of me wanted to. But I wanted Drue and Trip to have a father, even a poor excuse for one. And I knew he'd never leave. My money," she replied, to the question I hadn't asked. "Before he lost it all."

"Well, the good news is that the police are talking to someone," Darshi said, her voice bluff and hearty, too loud in the close, stuffy room. "At least we'll know the truth about what happened to Drue."

Mrs. Cavanaugh opened her eyes. In a not terribly curious voice, she asked, "Who?"

"A woman named Emma Vincent," Darshi said. "She was on the catering crew."

I saw Lily Cavanaugh flinch. "Oh, God," she murmured, and croaked out a choked-sounding laugh as she shut her eyes again. "These cops. My goodness. Emma didn't do it."

I blinked. "You know her?"

Lily Cavanaugh gave a brief nod.

"And you don't think she did it?"

Opening her eyes, she gave me the saddest smile. "Emma had no reason to hurt Drue."

"One of the guys at the party heard Emma talking to Mr. Cavanaugh the night Drue was killed. She was talking about how she was done waiting; how she'd waited long enough."

Mrs. Cavanaugh nodded, looking unsurprised. Another tear slid down her cheek, but she didn't speak.

"Did Drue know . . ." How was I going to ask this? "Did Drue know that her father and Emma Vincent were together?"

Lily Cavanaugh gave me a curious look before she shook her head. "Oh," she said. "Oh, honey, no. Emma wasn't Robert's girlfriend." She closed her eyes as a nurse came bustling into the room, frowning as she saw the three of us. "Emma was Robert's daughter."

Chapter Eighteen

According to the Internet, there were two Vincents who lived nearby on the Cape: one an E. Vincent, in an apartment in Hyannis; the other a B. Vincent, in a ranch-style house about a mile away from the ocean in Brewster. Nick had offered to stay with us, and Darshi and I had been happy to have him along, navigating and filling us in on Cape Cod geography and socio-economics. Or at least, I'd been happy about his company, and Darshi had been willing to tolerate it. We had banged on the door of E. Vincent's apartment, gotten no answer, and moved along.

"The E. Vincent was Emma, so the B. has to be her mom." I was googling to confirm that the B. Vincent's house we'd found matched the one that TMZ had described as the place where Emma had grown up with her single mother.

"This must be it," Darshi said. She'd turned onto a side street, where three vans from three different TV stations, each with a satellite dish on its roof, were parked along the curb. A knot of men and women, casually dressed in shorts or jeans or sun-dresses, leaned against the center van's sun-warmed sides, talking or drinking coffee or looking at their phones, while a young woman with wavy blond hair, wearing a snug teal dress with an incongruous pair of running shoes, was using her phone in selfie mode to inspect her makeup. I could feel their stares as we walked up the redbrick path. "Friends of the family?" one of them called. We kept quiet. Darshi knocked on the door. A moment later, a short, gray-haired woman peeked through the window.

I gave what I hoped was a reassuring wave and a friendly smile. "We're not reporters!" I called. The woman stared at us, then cracked the door open. She wore a zipped-up hoodie and jeans. Her hair was short and gray, cut in a no-nonsense feathered style. A pair of terriers with oversized ears jumped and yapped at her small, bare feet. A basset hound stood behind them, stately as an ocean liner, regarding us with dolorous, red-rimmed eyes as its ears trailed along the floor.

"Mrs. Vincent?" I said, talking fast before she could shut the door. "My name is Daphne Berg. I'm a friend of Drue Cavanaugh's, the woman who died in Truro last night. These are my friends Darshini and Nick. We were hoping to speak with you."

Mrs. Vincent did not seem to have heard me. She was looking past me, over my shoulder, her gaze focused on Nick. As I watched, she raised her hands to her face. Her lips began to tremble, and her eyes filled with tears.

"You're Christina's boy, aren't you?" she asked, her voice low.

Beside me, I heard Nick sigh, and remembered what he'd said about going by his middle name. *People here remember what happened. And they talk.*

He gave a curt nod. I decided to try to get the conversation back on track. "We're sorry to bother you. We're just hoping to talk to your daughter."

"Oh," the woman breathed, pressing her hands to her chest. She was still looking at Nick, as if I hadn't even spoken. "Oh, look at you!"

Darshi and I exchanged a glance. When Darshi widened her eyes, as if to ask *What's going on here?*, I gave a small *I have no idea* shrug.

"Come in," she said, and swung the door open. The dogs had gone quiet. All three of them were looking up at Nick just as raptly as their owner. Mrs. Vincent's voice was breathless. "I knew this day would come, but I guess there's no getting ready for a thing like this. Come in," she repeated. The three of us crowded into her small foyer, where a mirror hung on the wall above a vase of dried seagrass. I thought she'd launch right into a defense of her daughter's innocence, that she'd offer an alibi, or excuses, or some rationale: *Emma couldn't possibly have killed her own half sister.* Instead, she seemed oblivious to the matter of her daughter's arrest. She only had eyes for Nick. Her hands fluttered at her chest before she reached up, smoothing Nick's eyebrows with her thumb, first the left one, then the right.

"I'm sorry," Nick said, staring down at the woman. "Have we met?"

She smiled. "A long time ago. You wouldn't remember. But you . . ." The woman swallowed and pressed her hand to her heart. "I don't even know how to say it." She breathed in deeply, then, looking Nick in the eye, said, "You're my Emma's half brother."

"What?"

"Robert Cavanaugh is my daughter's father. And he's your father, too."

Mrs. Vincent—"Call me Barb," she said—led us into a small, sunny living room, where a satin-covered couch and love seat were arranged in front of a fireplace on top of the freshly vacuumed floor. Darshi and I had taken the couch. Nick sat alone on the love seat. His hands dangled, his mouth hung slightly open, and his eyes were wide in his pallid face. He looked, as my nana might have said, like he'd been hit by a bus.

"Have you heard from your daughter?" Darshi asked.

Barbara Vincent nodded. "Emma's still at the police station, but I'm sure she'll be home soon." At Darshi's look, she said, "There's no way Emma could have killed Drue last night. Emma came home at about two in the morning and spent the night in her bedroom down the hall. She got up to go at just past six this morning. She stays here when she's catering in Truro or P-town. Saves her about half an hour of driving time."

"Do you think just your word will be enough?" asked Darshi.

"It's not just me. She filled up her car on her way home last night, so the fellow at the Cumberland Farms saw her, and then she got a cruller at the Hole in One on her way in, so Maisie saw her there."

I looked around at the sunny little room. Birch logs sat in the pristine fireplace. Above them stood a mantel lined with pictures of Barbara and her daughter. In the shot closest to me, I could see that Emma had an oval face, light-brown hair, and dark-brown brows that formed peaks in the center, just like Nick's did. Just like Drue's had.

"How about Mr. Cavanaugh? Have you heard from him?" I asked.

Barbara nodded. "He came here from the hospital, and he's gone to the airport." Straightening in her seat, she said, "He flew in some big-shot lawyer from New York to help Emma."

"How kind of him," Darshini said, her voice a little arch. If Barbara noticed her tone, she didn't react. She only had eyes for Nick. Meanwhile, the subject of her attention was staring off into the distance, looking blank; a GPS system set on "rerouting" after its driver had suddenly veered off course. I wanted to sit next to him, to take his hand. I couldn't imagine how it would feel, to have never known who your father had been, and to learn his identity after the death of one half sister you never knew and the arrest of another.

"Nick?" I said. "Do you want some water? Or some tea or something?"

"Tea!" said Mrs. Vincent, and sprang to her feet. I followed her into her kitchen, a narrow galley with dark wood cabinets and white Formica countertops that smelled of rosemary and dish soap. Copper pots and pans hung in neat rows from hooks on the wall. A large wooden cutting board rested next to the stove, with a bowl of oranges and lemons beside it. *Kitchen needs updating*, a real estate agent would probably have said, but even if it lacked fashionable granite counters or stainless-steel appliances, the kitchen was a pleasant room; sunny, thanks to the big window over the sink, and cozy, with a table for two at one end. Wooden letters spelling EAT hung over the pantry, and a painted plaque reading "Bless us with good food, the gift of gab, and hearty laughter. May the love and joy we share be with us ever after" hung on the wall beside the table.

"Emma made that for me, in art class in sixth grade." Mrs. Vincent filled a teakettle, put it on the stove, and gathered mugs, teabags, a sugar dish, and a cow-shaped pitcher from the cupboards. Her movements were quick and assured as she dropped tea bags into four mugs and poured milk from a plastic quart container into a hole on the ceramic cow's back. "She made these, too." She showed me a pair of mugs with rainbows painted on them in a child's unsteady hand, and one that read I LOVE YOU, MOM, with "love" rendered as a giant heart.

"They're very nice."

This earned me a smile. "Em's a good girl. She's at CCCS—Cape Cod Community College—now. Still figuring out what she wants to be when she grows up." When the kettle whistled, Barbara poured boiling water into the mugs and arranged them on a blue and white tray. "I just can't believe it," she murmured as she carried the tray into the living room. "Christina's boy. After all these years." She took a seat and handed the mugs out, saving Nick's for last.

"You knew my mom?" Nick asked.

Barbara Vincent nodded. "I'll tell you the whole thing. Or at least, the parts that I know." She sat down, smiling faintly, and said, "This was almost twenty-seven years ago. I was working at the Red Inn, in P-town. Robert came in for dinner one night. He'd been set to fly to Boston, then back to New York, but there was a storm. All the planes were grounded, and the chop was so bad the ferries weren't going out, either. So instead of going back home, he came in and sat at the bar, so he'd be close to the airport in case the fog cleared and the planes started flying again." Her face softened as she remembered. "I brought him oysters and beer. We got to talking. And that was that." She lifted her mug to her mouth, wiped her fingertips along one dry, freckled cheek, and shifted in her armchair. I tried to picture her gray hair longer, dark blond or light brown, pulled back in a ponytail. I erased the wrinkles and put some color in her cheeks, and painted her lips pink. Instead of the blocky body underneath the sweatshirt and the high-waisted jeans, I imagined a petite, curvy figure, shown off to advantage in a white cotton blouse with a black apron pulled tight around her waist, tied in a bow in the back. I imagined her laughing, blue eyes sparkling, her head tipped back and her throat flushed.

"I knew he was married," Barbara said. She was looking down, with one thumb tracing the rim of her mug. "I didn't have any excuses. He didn't wear a ring, but that first night, he drove me home, and I saw a booster seat in the back of his car. So I knew. But I was only nineteen, and the farthest I'd ever been off the Cape was a school trip to Washington." She sipped, and set her cup carefully down. "When you're nineteen and an older man, a handsome, powerful, rich man, tells you that you're the prettiest thing he's ever seen, and that his wife doesn't understand him and that they're getting a divorce, you want to believe it." She sighed. "You want to believe that you're special enough to catch the attention of a man like that." Her mouth quirked. "When I got pregnant, he told me it was my choice, and that if I wanted to keep the baby, I could. He swore he'd be divorced by the time she was born, and that we'd be together." She turned to address Nick. "It wasn't until I saw you and your mom in the Stop & Shop that I finally figured out how he was playing with me."

At the words "you and your mom," Nick gulped. Barbara reached across the coffee table, took his hand, and squeezed it.

"People on the Outer Cape knew Christina. Knew her family, I should say. When your mother, God rest her soul, showed up in Truro pregnant, with no husband, no boyfriend, people talked. But I didn't realize that Robert had been . . ." She paused for another sip of tea. ". . . had been her boyfriend, too, until one day, when Emma was a baby, I went to do my marketing. You must've been two or three, and Em was only six months old, but I could see." She stretched toward Nick, extending her arm, and, with one thumb, gently touched his eyebrow again. "Just like Emma's. Your hands are even the same shape!" Barbara's face was soft and sorrowful, lost in memory. "By then, I had a pretty good idea that there wasn't ever going to be a divorce. And then, when I saw you, I knew for sure. I was just another one of his girls."

Nick was looking pale and holding himself very still. "And you're sure Mr. Cavanaugh—you're sure he's my father?"

Barbara nodded. "After I saw Christina in the supermarket, I got her number from a friend of a friend. I called her up, and I said who I was. Turns out, she already knew about me. 'You're the new girl,' she said. Not like she was angry, or even sad. More just . . . resigned. And maybe a little glad to have someone she could talk about it with. Someone who'd understand." Barbara closed her eyes and shook her head. "I was very young when it all happened, but, being a single mom, you grow up fast. I told Robert it was over. He acted brokenhearted, but I'm sure he was relieved, with two babies already on the Cape and a new one at home. He said he'd help me as much as he could, and that he'd always be there for Emma. The next week, I had coffee with Christina. We met in Wellfleet, at the Flying Fish, and we talked for a long time. After that, we'd get together every once in a while." She smiled at Nick, her face brightening. "We'd take you kiddos to Corn Hill Beach, and let you splash around. Christina would bring a cooler, with juice and cut-up fruit and wine." She touched her hair. "I felt so unsophisticated next to your mother. Like a little gray wren next to a peacock." She smiled a little, looking off in the distance. "Christina was so glamorous. She'd lived in New York City—that was where she'd met Robert—and she'd been all over the world. Her hair was almost down to her waist," she said, gesturing with her hands to indicate where Christina's hair had fallen, "and she wore these long, colorful skirts, with fringes, or with bits of mirrors sewn on the hems." Barbara's hands fluttered to the earlobes beneath her own neatly cut gray hair, then down to her neck. "Big, dangling earrings, bracelets and beads, amber and opal and turquoise, all the way from her wrists to her elbows. She looked like that gal from Fleetwood Mac."

"Stevie Nicks," said Nick. His voice was hoarse. "How did she meet . . ." He stumbled over what to say next and finally landed on "Robert Cavanaugh."

"At a coffee shop in New York City. She was waiting in line to pick up her latte. He asked if he could buy her a coffee, and she said she'd already paid, and that she was on her way to an interview. Robert asked for her card, and the next day he had some fancy cappuccino maker sent to her apartment, with a note that said 'So you'll never have to wait in line again.'" She smiled. "He knew how to sweep a girl off her feet, that's for sure."

"I remember that machine. Big brass thing. It took up half

the counter space in the kitchen." Nick still looked dazed, but at least he was talking.

Barbara gave him a smile. "Your mother told me that after she turned thirty-five, she stopped looking for Mister Right and started trying to find a sperm donor, more or less. A man with good genes and some money in the bank." Looking at her lap, she murmured, "I guess Robert fit the bill. He was handsome and successful. He couldn't marry her, but he could at least help support her while she was home with you. And to his credit, he tried to be a father. He'd see the babies when he could." She gave a wry smile and nodded at Nick. "Tuesdays were Emma's night. Wednesdays were yours."

"So he would see me? He spent time with me?" Nick shook his head, sounding almost angry when he said, "I don't remember any of this."

"Well, you were a little guy. But it happened. I promise you, it did."

Barbara told us about how she and Christina would take their children to the beach. How they'd take turns, one of them watching the babies and the other one napping in the sun ("being single moms, working, then up in the night with a baby who was teething, we wanted sleep more than we wanted sex," Barb said, then put her hand over her mouth, blushing). She told us how they'd babysit for each other when Barbara got called in to cover a waitressing shift, or if Christina had to meet a deadline for an article, or some project she'd undertaken. "But I know that's not what you're here to talk about." She rocked forward, clasping her hands at her heart. "His daughter . . . my God, what a mess." Looking at Nick, she said, "I think your mom had the right idea. She never wanted to tell you anything about your dad."

"She didn't exactly live long enough for us to discuss it," Nick said.

"No, but she talked to me. I remember telling her that I wanted

Emmie to know her father, and Christina saying that she thought Robert would lose interest in you in a year or two, and that she'd never tell you his name. 'No good can come of it,' she said. And she was right." Barbara's face sagged, and her blocky body drooped. "Emma grew up knowing exactly who her father was, and that didn't get her anything, except a broken heart." Barbara pressed her lips together. "And Christina was right. When Emma was ten or eleven, he stopped coming around."

"Why?" Darshi asked. Barbara shrugged.

"Got bored, I guess. Or maybe he had another baby by then."

"So how did Emma end up catering Drue's wedding?" I asked.

Barbara Vincent got very interested in the cords of her hoodie, first tugging the left one out to its full length, then tugging at the right. "She works for Angel Foods. She's been part of their summer crew for years. They call her when there're big parties."

"Did she have any idea who the bride was when she got called for this wedding?" I asked.

Barbara gave a nod that looked reluctant.

"Did she talk to you about it? Like, 'Here's my big chance to finally meet my half sister'?"

Barbara's neck flushed pink. She pressed her lips together as one of the terriers by her foot gave a low, warning growl. "She didn't go there to hurt anyone," she said. "As to whether she'd planned on trying to meet Drue, I couldn't say."

"The police found pictures of Drue in Emma's car," Darshi said. "And a gun."

Barbara lifted her chin, settling her eyes on the wall just over Darshi's head. "When Emma was thirteen, after she found out that she had a sister almost exactly her age, she was wild to meet Drue. I told her that wouldn't be happening. I'd given Robert my word. I promised him that we'd never bother him, or embarrass him. But, with the Internet, I couldn't keep Em from finding out about him, and his real family. She knew where Drue went to school, what she did on vacation, the kinds of clothes she wore . . ." Barbara shook her head. "It would have been better if Robert's real family wasn't so public. If there hadn't been so much out there for Emma to learn." She shook her head again, picking up her mug and setting it down. "Robert gave us money. Enough for me to put a down payment on this house and go from full-time to part-time so that I could be home with Emma. But there wasn't going to be any la-di-da Lathrop Academy for her." I jumped, a little startled at the sound of my school's name coming out of this stranger's mouth. "No house in the Hamptons, no debut at the Whatever Club. No Harvard. Just public schools and Cape Cod Community College. Robert told us money was tight ever since the markets crashed in 2008. By then, we hadn't seen him in years." She smiled, very faintly. "Christina and I used to say that he loved the babies more than the moms. He'd keep coming around to see them, even after he stopped being . . . you know . . . interested in us that way. He'd bring Emmie toys, or dolls, or dresses from the fancy places in P-town. For her birthday, he'd take her to high tea at the Chatham Bars Inn. But by the time she got to be ten or eleven, he'd moved on, I guess." She pressed her hands against her thighs, smoothing the denim. "Emma felt like she'd been cheated. Like she should have been the one who lived with him, and worked with him, and got to be in the newspapers and travel the world." Another sigh. "She kept track of Drue. Her social media, her pictures. She bought yearbooks from the schools that Drue went to, from eBay. Magazines she'd been in. Everything."

"So Emma never even met Drue," I said.

"No. Or, not that I know of, I should say. I know she went to New York once—just as a trip, with friends, she told me. They were going to get tickets to see something on Broadway, hold up signs in front of the *Today* show. At least, that's what Emma said." Barbara's shoulders slumped. "Did she try to find Drue? Did she go to Robert's office, or his home? I can't imagine they'd have let her in. And if she'd actually managed to meet Drue, would Drue even have believed Emma when she told her who she was?"

I tried to imagine Drue being confronted by a stranger, a stranger with dark hair and her father's eyes, claiming to be her half sister. I couldn't picture such a meeting ending well.

"Would Emma try to hurt Drue?" Darshi asked.

"I guess that's what the police thought," Barbara said bitterly. "When they found the gun. But I swear, Emma only got it because she used to close up at Blackfish—that's the restaurant where she worked for a while in Truro. She'd lock up and drop money off at the bank, all by herself in the middle of the night. She didn't feel safe, and so her boss told her to get a gun. She took lessons and went to the shooting range, and she had a license to carry it, but I think she just kept it locked in her glove box. I'll bet she didn't give it a thought when she went to work at the wedding. I'll bet she didn't even remember it was there." Barbara twisted her hands in her lap. She paused, then, looking me in the eye, she said, "Emma would have known that Drue was engaged, and that she was getting married on the Cape. It wouldn't have been hard for her to find out the details. It wouldn't have been hard for her to get close." She sighed, shoulders slumping, leaning back into her chair like she wanted to disappear. "For all I know, she did have something planned. Maybe she'd been in touch with Robert. Maybe she was going to confront him. Demand that he acknowledge that she was his daughter, in front of his wife and all those people. I don't know."

I remembered the conversation that Nick had overheard, a young woman's voice saying that she'd waited long enough, that she was tired of waiting. Barbara Vincent looked at me as though she could read my thoughts. She lifted her head, her cheeks flushing pink, and looked first at Darshi, then at me. "I don't know if Emma had anything planned, but I do know my daughter. I know what she wanted. If she was angry, she was angry at her father, but she would never have hurt Drue."

"Why not?"

"Because," said Barbara. "If she wanted anything from Drue, it would have been acknowledgment. Maybe she wanted to be included in Drue's life, but I know that she didn't want to end it." Her cheeks were tinged red, but her eyes were steady. "I know my daughter. I know this for sure."

We adjourned to the kitchen for refills on tea, and for Barbara to check her messages. The dogs followed after us, the terriers scampering and darting, close on their mistress's heels, the basset hound trailing behind at a magisterial pace. "May I use your bathroom?" Darshi asked, and was directed to the first left down the hall. Nick shuffled his feet, cleared his throat. Finally, he asked Barbara if she had any pictures of his mother.

Barbara looked thoughtful. "You know, I think I might. When you were babies, not every phone had a camera, so picture-taking wasn't as common, but let's go have a look." She was leading us back to the living room when my phone vibrated. I looked at the screen and saw a text from Darshi: *Walk down the hall like you're going to the bathroom and check out the bedroom on the right.*

I excused myself and followed Darshi's directions, past the neat pale-blue powder room, and into a small bedroom. A twin-size bed was pushed up against one wall; a bookcase stood against the other; a desk was underneath a window. Instead of posters, the walls were papered with maps—a detailed one of Cape Cod; a larger one of the United States above the bed, a map of the world over the desk, with cities and countries marked with gold stars and red circles—Manhattan, Miami, El Paso, Albuquerque. Perth, Peru, Iceland, Copenhagen.

I'd been holding my breath, thinking that maybe I'd find a

serial-killer wall, featuring dozens of pictures of Drue with red lines and arrows and her face in crosshairs. I was relieved to only see the maps and a bulletin board filled with thumbtacked pictures from photo booths or from parties—Emma holding a bottle of champagne, wearing a giant pair of novelty New Year's Eve sunglasses that read "2016"; Emma in a hoodie with her arms around the neck of a grinning boy with short red hair at a bowling alley; Emma and her friends in their prom-night finery, lined up in pairs on the front lawn of her house. On the desk were neat stacks of college textbooks. *Introduction to Principles of Economics*, *Magruder's American Government*, *World Literature*, a dogeared copy of *Portrait of a Lady*. On the bottom shelf of the bookcase were clues about her interest in Drue: a pile of Lathrop School yearbooks, and one from the Croft School; a glossy Cavanaugh Corporation prospectus ("Building the Future" read the headline on the cover, with a picture of Robert and Drue on the rooftop, smiling). In a frame, in the center of the desk, I found what Darshi must have wanted me to see. It was a framed snapshot of a little girl, her dark hair in pigtails, perched on a bare-chested man's shoulders as he stood in the water, in the instant a wave broke around them. The man had broad, sloping shoulders and curly black hair on his chest. He wore a Red Sox cap, blue swim trunks, and an eat-the-world grin. It took me a moment to add some pounds, subtract some hair, and recognize Drue's father, younger, and tanned, and happy. I lifted the picture, studying it. He and the little girl on his shoulders both looked so vivid, so vital, in the blue-green water with the blue sky stretched out behind them. I could smell the sunscreen Barbara Vincent would have rubbed on her daughter's back and shoulders; I could imagine the shouts and laughter of the kids tossing a Frisbee or building sandcastles for the waves to devour. Emma's eyes were squinting in the sunshine; her mouth was open, laughing, as her little hands gripped her father's head.

Some small sound made me jump and drop the picture on the desk with a clatter. I turned to see Barbara Vincent standing in the doorway, holding a piece of paper in her hand. "My phone number. Will you take it?" Before I could answer, she said, "Emma loved her father. It broke her heart when he stopped coming around. Even if all she ever got were Drue's crumbs, it would have been better than nothing."

I nodded, even as I wondered if maybe Emma was the one who'd gotten the best that Robert Cavanaugh had to offer; if Drue was the one who'd gotten crumbs. Had Drue's father ever taken her to the beach? Did Drue even have one happy memory, one recollection of a good day they'd had together, one mental snapshot of making her father smile?

Barbara Vincent took my arm and squeezed it, and pressed the slip of paper into my hand. "Please," she said. "Please help find who did this. Don't let them put my girl in jail."

I wanted to say that I wasn't a detective, that I was just a babysitter and a not-very-influential influencer, that I had no idea how I could solve this crime. Somehow, what came out of my mouth was "I'll do my best. I promise."

Chapter Nineteen

My father sent my favorite smoked sable and bialys from Russ & Daughters. My mother sent her favorite earrings, clusters of rubies set in twists of gold wire. The Lathrop classmates who'd seen the pictures of Drue and me on the Cape sent condolences, texts and emails and direct messages over Twitter and Facebook and Instagram, offering sympathy and, in some cases, not so discreetly probing for details that hadn't made the papers. And even though I'd insisted that I was fine, Leela Thakoon messengered over a black jersey jumpsuit. *Try it with the wedges you wore with the Amelie dress*, read the note she'd attached. I thought that she, along with my other clients, had to see the silver lining in the tragic turn of events. In the days since Drue's death, the police had announced that she'd been poisoned. Emma Vincent had been released. And I'd added almost thirty thousand new followers across my platforms. Most of them were probably morbid lookie-loos, online vultures scouring my feed for more pictures of or inside information about Drue. But maybe a handful would be inspired to buy yoga mats or doggie treats. *Everybody wins*, I'd thought, and then I had started to cry.

On Tuesday morning I'd gotten up early to attend a ninety-minute yoga class, thinking I would need all the Zen I could get. At home, I'd done my hair and applied my makeup, making myself look at my entire face in the mirror, practicing kindness and positive self-talk. *My eyes are a pretty color. I got a little bit of a tan on the Cape.* At nine-thirty, I slipped on the jumpsuit and the wedges. At nine-forty-five, I called an Uber and rode in air-conditioned style for the thirty-block trip to the Lathrop School, where my friend's life was being celebrated.

"Wedding?" the driver asked as he turned onto East Eighty-Third Street and saw the reporters and photographers on the sidewalk, arrayed on both sides of the marble steps. A pair of police officers kept the press and the gawkers out of the way as mourners proceeded up the staircase and into the school.

"Funeral," I said, and slipped on my sunglasses, ducked my head, and walked as fast as I could toward the school's front door.

"Is that the friend?" I heard a male voice yell. I didn't look, but I imagined I could feel the air pressure change as all of that concentrated attention was suddenly focused on me.

"Daphne, any news?"

"What can you tell us about the fight the night before the wedding?"

"Daphne! Did Emma Vincent confess?"

Ignoring them, I put my hand on the door's curved handle. The brass was heavy against my palm, warm from the morning sun. The feel of it sent me right back to my school days, and I braced for the sight of the blond wood cubbies and the green-and-white-tiled floors, the warm-chicken-soup smell of the hall-way, the squeaky sound that I knew my shoes would make on the floor of the multipurpose room, which had, back in Lathrop's religious days, been a chapel.

"Daphne, is it true that Stuart Lowe and Corina Bailey are back together?" a girl called, holding her phone aloft to film me. I kept my head down, my lips pressed together. None of them had asked me if I knew about the newly freed Emma Vincent's relationship to the Cavanaugh family, so it seemed that the news hadn't hit the Internet yet.

I opened the door and walked down the hall, hearing the familiar squeaks, smelling the familiar scents, feeling all the old ghosts rise; the ancient insecurities circling around my head, taunting me. *You're ugly. You're fat. No one likes you. No one ever will.* I could see Drue's face, contorted in anger, could hear her saying *We all just felt sorry for you.* I walked past the classroom where my father had once taught, past the Senior Lounge, a nook under a staircase with two padded wooden benches. Once, during finals, I'd walked into the nook and found Drue holding her phone to her face. "Shh!" she'd hissed, and nodded at the bench, where Darshi had fallen asleep, leaning against the wall and snoring audibly, with her head slumped on her shoulder, her mouth wide open, and a strand of drool trickling from her chin to her cardigan.

"Drue," I'd said, batting at Drue's hand. Too late. With a giggle and a click, Darshi's snoring and drooling had been posted on the Lathrop Class of 2010's Facebook page, memorialized for eternity. As class prefect, Drue was one of only four students allowed to post to the page. Theoretically, she was supposed to keep us up-to-date on things like exams and homecoming rallies. In reality, Drue posted every embarrassing, cringe-inducing moment she could capture. Kids picking their noses, nip slips and fashion disasters, girls who'd been surprised by their periods or boys who'd been surprised with erections. Drue would post, and as soon as some administrator saw what had been posted, it would get taken down, but by then, all sixty-seven members of our class would have seen . . . if not the original post, then a screenshot.

I breathed in, reminding myself that high school was over, and that we were all grown-ups now, that Darshi was fine and that Drue wouldn't be tormenting anyone, ever again. In the former chapel, a high-ceilinged room with wooden pews and arching stained-glass windows donated by long-dead alums, I was touched to see that the Snitzers had come to pay their respects. I greeted the doctors and bent to whisper hello to Ian and Izzie. "I'm very sorry that your friend died," Ian said.

I squeezed his hand. "Thank you," I said. "I'm very sorry, too."

I found the seat my parents had saved me, three rows from the front. A lectern stood between two waist-high urns full of pungent white lilies, their scent overpowering the classy perfumes of a hundred ladies-who-lunched, all of them dressed in their funereal best. I saw sleek black skirts and sharp black jackets, fitted dresses and sky-high black stilettos, designer sunglasses, even, here and there, a black straw hat. It was part funeral, part fashion show, and I was glad of Leela's gift, which made me stylish enough to fit in but was comfortable, with pockets for my sunglasses and my tissues.

A minute before the service began, Darshi slipped through the door and into the seat beside me, in a fitted black suit, a white blouse, and a pair of black high-heeled shoes. Her curls were pulled back into a sleek bun, her eyes were lined. She nodded at my mom, smiled at my father's "namaste," and returned my "Hello" with a muttered "Hi." Darshi hadn't wanted to come. "I hadn't been Drue's friend in a long, long time," she'd argued. "Why would I come to her funeral?"

"Because I need you," I'd told her. "Please." Finally, she'd agreed to take the morning off from school.

"When are they going to start?" she whispered as ten o'clock came and went. The room was getting warmer; the mourners were getting restless. Just as Rabbi Medloff stepped out from the wings, I heard a familiar voice murmur, "Excuse me." I looked up and saw Nick Carvalho finding a seat in the center of a row just behind us.

"Nick!" I whispered, waving.

"Oh, jeez," Darshi murmured.

"Who is that?" asked my mom. Darshi widened her eyes—*You didn't tell her?* I glared back, hoping my expression communicated that I'd had no desire to give my parents the details of my post-party hookup.

"Nick!" I whisper-shouted. When I'd caught his eye, he gave me a wave and a nod. I wanted to ask what he was doing here, why he'd come, and where he was staying, but the rabbi had reached the podium. The crowd stilled. The rabbi stood behind the lectern, holding it on each side, before bowing his head.

"Friends. Family. We are gathered to celebrate the memory of Drue Lathrop Cavanaugh. Drue was a daughter, a sister. A colleague, and a friend. A beautiful, talented young woman with a brilliant life ahead of her." A sob ripped through the silence. I looked and saw Ainsley Graham, Drue's former wingwoman who hadn't wanted to be in her wedding party, red-faced and crying. I recognized Abigay, the Cavanaughs' cook, a few rows back, with a handkerchief fisted in her hand. Drue's mother was in the front row. Her face was veiled, her body so motionless that I wondered if she was on sedatives. She didn't seem to be crying. Or breathing, for that matter. Drue's father sat beside her, handsome and impassive in a navy-blue suit and blindingly white shirt. I guess he'd concluded his business on the Cape with his secret daughter, and was now prepared to mourn his public one. Drue's brother, Trip, sat on his mother's other side, his shaggy blond hair unkempt, his face slack, his expression blank and shocked.

"We mourn for what could have been," said the rabbi. Which was smart, I thought, insofar as *what had been* was not great. Drue had left mostly wreckage behind her, burnt bridges and broken friendships and hurt feelings. Not to mention the husband she hadn't loved and had more or less bought. Better to focus on what she could have done, who she might have been—the wife

Drue would never get to be, the work she would never get to do, the children she would never get to bear, or raise. Maybe babies would have softened her. Maybe she and Stuart would have fallen in love for real, or maybe she'd have divorced him and spent a happy life with some other man. Maybe Drue could have built incredible skyscrapers, or inventive affordable housing. Maybe she could have been a wonderful mother. Maybe she could have changed the world.

"Drue's brother will share some memories with us first," said the rabbi. Trip walked to the lectern with a sheet of paper in his hand.

"If you knew my sister, you know she was the kind of person who could turn a trip to the bodega into an adventure," he began, his voice a wooden monotone, his eyes on his written speech. "When we were little, she'd make up games. She'd tell me that the living room was the North Pole, and we'd pretend to be explorers trying to make it across the ice floes. Or she'd say that the kitchen was the Gobi Desert, and we'd have to gather supplies. Which usually meant me sneaking past Abigay to get potato chips from the pantry." I saw smiles at that and heard a sprinkling of laughter. In the front row, Lily Cavanaugh sat, unmoving, as if she'd been frozen in place. Her husband patted her back, the motions of his hand as regular as a metronome.

Trip's voice got a little less stiff, a little warmer as he continued. "I'm probably mangling this quote from Oscar Wilde, who said he saved his truest genius for his life—that his life was his real work of art. That was Drue. She had a genius for living."

"Smart," Darshi murmured. I agreed. Announcing that someone had a genius for living excused all kinds of material shortcomings. Never finished that dissertation, or committed to a relationship, or a job? No worries! Your life was your art!

"My sister had a brilliant future ahead of her. It is a tragedy that her days were cut short." He swallowed, his Adam's apple jerking. "Miss you, sis," he whispered. As he sat down, my mother started to cry. The rabbi walked back to the lectern.

"And now, Drue's friend Daphne Berg will speak."

My father squeezed my hand. My mother patted my shoulder. Darshi pressed her lips together in a tight line. I got to my feet, smoothed out my jumpsuit, and walked to the front of the room, with the eyes of the crowd on me. The trip couldn't have been more than ten yards, but it felt like it took me forever. I unfolded the sheet of paper I'd had in my pocket and smoothed it out on the lectern. "Drue and I went to school together, right here at Lathrop," I began. "I met her in the sixth grade. I remember thinking that I couldn't believe someone as beautiful and as glamorous as Drue even noticed me. She always had a kind of star quality, even in sixth grade." That got a few laughs, and I felt myself relax incrementally. "Drue was everything people said. Funny, and sharp, and smart, and beautiful, and occasionally ruthless." That got a little more laughter. "Like her brother said, Drue had a talent for life. When you were with her, you were always your most interesting self. Any party she walked into got more fun. And every day could turn into a vacation, or a party, or an impromptu trip to the Hamptons." I heard a woman sniffle, a man noisily blowing his nose. I unfolded the piece of paper that I'd printed out that morning, a poem I'd read in high school, called "To Keep the Memory of Charlotte Forten Grimké." "This is for Drue," I said, and began to read.

Still are there wonders of the dark and day:
The muted shrilling of shy things at night,
So small beneath the stars and moon;
The peace, dream-frail, but perfect while the light
Lies softly on the leaves at noon.
These are, and these will be
Until eternity;
But she who loved them well has gone away.

Each dawn, while yet the east is veiléd grey,
The birds about her window wake and sing;
And far away, each day, some lark
I know is singing where the grasses swing;
Some robin calls and calls at dark.
These are, and these will be
Until eternity;
But she who loved them well has gone away.

The wild flowers that she loved down green ways stray;
Her roses lift their wistful buds at dawn,
But not for eyes that loved them best;
Only her little pansies are all gone,
Some lying softly on her breast.
And flowers will bud and be
Until eternity;
But she who loved them well has gone away.

Where has she gone? And who is there to say?
But this we know: her gentle spirit moves
And is where beauty never wanes,
Perchance by other streams, mid other groves;
And to us there, ah! she remains
A lovely memory
Until eternity;
She came, she loved, and then she went away.

The night before, I'd been working on my speech, and I'd asked my father for advice. *If you don't have anything good to say*, he'd counseled, *read a poem.* I knew the one I'd chosen wasn't a perfect fit—Drue was many things, but "gentle spirit" was not among them. Still, the poem had the benefit of being more about the world the departed had left—the flowers, the mist, the moon—than about the departed herself. But I loved the line about *the muted shrilling of shy things at night*. And I loved the idea of Drue as "a lovely memory, until eternity." All of that promise, and none of it fulfilled.

I looked out into the audience. My mother was sniffling. Drue's father sat, stone-faced and unmoving. Trip Cavanaugh was crying. As I refolded my page, Lily Cavanaugh started to tremble. First just her neck, her head, then her shoulders, and finally her entire torso, every part shuddering as if she'd been doused in ice. Her husband appeared not to notice, moving his hand up and down and up and down again even as she shook as if she was coming apart underneath his palm. Pat, pat, pat. Then, as I watched, Mrs. Cavanaugh bent forward from her waist, opened her mouth and gave a terrible keening shriek, a noise that reminded me of a sound I'd heard when a neighbor's cat had been hit by a minivan; an agonized, animal howling. It went on and on and on, endlessly, as if Mrs. Cavanaugh no longer required air, until, finally, Trip Cavanaugh took one of her shoulders and Robert Cavanaugh took the other, and the two of them hoisted her upright. I'd meant to take my seat but found that I couldn't move, as Robert Cavanaugh's eyes pinned me in place. For an endless moment, he held his wife and glared at me, before helping his son half-walk, half-carry Lily Cavanaugh out of the room.

I walked down the aisle and collapsed in my seat, hearing Nana's voice in my head. *Shut your mouth, you're drawing flies.* In my pocket, my telephone buzz, buzz, buzzed. Darshi raised an eyebrow. I pulled the phone out to mute it and saw a picture of myself, a shot that must have been taken twenty minutes ago as I was walking into the school. The jumpsuit's fabric flowed over my body, the wide legs making my waist look small, the neckline flattering my chest. In my red lipstick and my dark glasses, I looked as close to glamorous as I'd ever been. I hated myself for the tiny thrill I felt, admiring myself while my friend was dead and my friend's mother was wailing out her grief. *Hang in there*, Leela had written. She'd added a lipstick emoji, a manicured-hand emoji, and two red hearts, one whole, one broken. I put my phone back in my pocket as Rabbi Medloff returned to the podium. "Please rise and join me in the mourners' Kaddish," he said. The room filled with the sounds of movement as everyone got to their feet and the rabbi began to chant, in Hebrew, the prayer for the dead.

When it was over, I led my parents out of the room. Groups of mourners stood talking in the halls, impeding our path to the door or any view I'd hoped to catch of Nick. I pushed and *pardon me*'d my way outside, got my parents in their Uber, and went back inside to collect Darshi. I'd just cut through a throng of older couples planning a post-ceremony lunch at La Goulue when I bumped up against a dark-haired, dark-skinned man in a badly fitting blue suit and sneakers.

"Beg your pardon," he said quietly, in a voice that sounded familiar. I felt the hairs on the back of my neck rise.

"Hey," I said. "Hey!"

The guy's eyes widened behind his glasses as he saw me.

"Wait a second. I need to talk to you!"

He spun on his heel and cut through the crowd, slipping around the knots of people with astonishing speed.

"Hey!" I was trying to catch him, but there were people everywhere, and his sneakers had the advantage over my heels. "Stop!"

He gave me an apologetic look over his shoulder, and pushed through a knot of disgruntled-looking mourners and out through the big double doors. I was preparing to give chase when I felt a hand on my shoulder and heard another familiar voice.

"Daphne? Can I talk to you for a minute?"

Detective McMichaels wore a sober gray suit and a dark-blue tie. He had bags under his eyes, and his formerly close-shaved cheeks and chin had been colonized by silvery stubble.

"Thank God," I said. "That was the guy! The one I saw outside Drue's bedroom! The one with the water!"

He pulled out his phone, pressed a button, murmured into it, and put it back.

"Don't you want to go question him?" I felt wild, wide-eyed, and frantic.

"Right now, I'd rather speak to you." He gave me a hard look before raising his eyebrows. "Want to do it right here, or find somewhere a little more private?"

I led him to a French classroom, where the walls were covered in colorful travel-agent posters for Paris and Quebec. There was a wooden desk at the front of the room and three rows of six molded desk-chair combos, with wire baskets underneath the seats for books. Detective McMichaels leaned against the teacher's desk. I considered the desks, the same kind I'd sat in as a student, and decided to stand.

"What can I do for you?" I asked. "What brings you to New York?"

"We've learned a few things."

I kept my mouth shut, feet planted, waiting.

"Emma Vincent is not a suspect in the murder of Drue Cavanaugh," he said.

I tried to keep my face still as my heart tumbled, over and over. So it was official. Drue had been murdered. And Emma had not done the deed. "Oh?"

"She had an alibi," he told me. When he didn't offer it, I didn't ask.

"Do you have other suspects?" I asked.

"We're casting a wide net. That's why I'm here."

"Here at the memorial, or here in New York?"

"Both." Smoothing his tie, he asked, "Want to know how your friend died?"

My mouth felt very dry. "If you want to tell me."

"Someone put cyanide in something that she ate or drank just before her death." He looked at me and I immediately pictured myself, a glass of ice water in one hand and a pair of shot glasses in the other, trotting up the outdoor staircase and into Drue's bedroom.

"Did it hurt her?" My voice sounded strange in my ears. "Did she . . . you know . . . did she feel anything?"

"It was quick," said the detective. "That's what the coroner tells me. Quick, but unpleasant." He put his hands in his pockets. His shoes squeaked as he turned, making a show of looking around the room. "Fancy place. How much does it cost to go here?"

"When I was a student, about fifty thousand dollars a year. I had a scholarship. And they gave my family a break because my dad's a teacher."

"A scholarship girl." With the first two fingers of his right hand, he stroked his bristly mustache, the picture of a man deep in thought. "You know, when someone dies, the first question they tell you to ask is *Cui bono*." He looked at me. "You know what that means?"

"They make you take Latin here. One of the things fifty thousand bucks a year buys you. So yes. It means 'to whom the good.' Or, more colloquially, 'who benefits.'"

He nodded. "Correct. And that's what I've been wondering, ever since your friend's death. To whom the good?"

My knees wanted to shake. I refused to let them, clenching my leg muscles hard. "So have you come up with an answer?"

Instead of responding, he asked, "Did you know that Drue and Stuart Lowe were already married?"

Again, I tried to school my face, hoping I didn't look surprised that he'd found out. "Stuart mentioned it to me a few days ago." If he knew about the wedding, I wondered if he knew about the whole scheme—Stuart's plan to leave Drue at the alter, Drue's discussion with the *Single Ladies* producers, the way Drue and

Stuart and Corina Bailey had planned to make money from the scheme.

He gave a curt nod. "Do you know that Drue had a trust fund?"

"I—yes, I'd heard about that, too."

"Twenty million dollars," Detective McMichaels said. His tone was dry, almost expressionless. He could have been telling me Drue was set to inherit a piece of furniture, or a vintage fur coat, instead of an eight-figure payday. "This was from her mother's side of the family, the Lathrops. According to the terms of the trust, she got the first ten million upon marriage or turning thirty; the balance after the birth of her first child, or her thirty-fifth birthday, whichever came first." He touched his earlobe, rubbing the dimpled scar where an earring had once been.

"That's a lot of money."

"It is that." Pushing himself away from the desk, he took a slow stroll around the room, stopping to examine a "Visit Paris" poster that featured a stylized drawing of the Eiffel Tower beneath a full moon.

"So who benefits?" he asked, with his back to me. "Her husband looked like an obvious choice. If she died after they were married, without a will, he'd get it all. Except Drue had already transferred two million dollars into his corporate account. Why would he kill the goose that was laying the golden eggs?"

"Good question," I said.

"Her father was another possibility," he continued. "He was shouting at her the night of her death. Multiple witnesses heard him yelling, accusing her and her mom of trying to bankrupt him. Only Drue had moved five million bucks into the family business's coffers the month before. Just enough to cover the interest on their loans for the next month." He left the Eiffel Tower poster and began to examine one that showed the cathedral of Notre Dame. "Dad's out. Husband's out. Who does that leave me with?" he asked.

I kept quiet, wondering if he expected me to raise my hand.

"I mentioned that Stuart Lowe would inherit everything if she didn't have a will. But she did. Turns out, her lawyers insisted. Before she got all that trust-fund money, she had to make arrangements for where it would go, in the unlikely event that something happened to her. Good thing, too. Because, six months later, something did. And here we are."

"Here we are," I echoed.

McMichaels tilted his head. "Any guesses for me?"

"No."

He curved his lips into a joyless, unpleasant smile. "Aw, c'mon! Give me a guess. People tell me that you're a smart girl. And you knew her. Maybe better than anyone." He walked toward me until he was close enough for me to smell his aftershave, all citrus and musk. "Take a guess." I could smell coffee on his breath, could see threads of red in the whites of his eyes. "Tell me what you think the will said. Tell me who benefits."

"Maybe some other boyfriend?"

He shook his head. I tried to remember what I'd overheard back on the Cape.

"Or a charity?"

That didn't even merit a response.

"Her mother? Her brother?"

He shook his head. "She left her jewelry to her mother. The brother's got a trust of his own. So who got money?"

I tried to make myself look surprised. "Me?"

"Ding ding ding!" He pointed. "Give the lady a prize! Better yet, give her half a million dollars."

I felt dizzy. "I didn't know," I said, which was most of a lie. "Drue never told me." That, at least, was true.

"I wonder," McMichaels said in a musing voice. "I do wonder about that. And here's another headline." He pulled out his phone, looked down at the screen, and read, "I, Drummond Cavanaugh

Lowe, do devise and bequeath to any person past the age of majority confirmed as the child of Robert John Cavanaugh by Quest Diagnostics or its equivalent in DNA testing, one-tenth of my estate entire." He pocketed his phone and looked at me. "Did you know that Emma Vincent was Robert Cavanaugh's natural child?"

"I . . . I . . . her mother may have mentioned something about that," I stammered.

"Doesn't matter," he said. "The real question is, did Emma know? Not about her father—she knew about him, for sure—but about the money."

"How could she? Unless Drue told her. And I don't think they ever met." I wasn't thinking about Emma; I was thinking about Nick. According to Barbara Vincent, Nick's mother had never told anyone who the father of her baby was. But how many secrets stayed secret forever? *The Outer Cape's like a small town*, I remembered Nick saying. *People talk.*

"By the way," said the detective, his voice very casual, "did you ever find that fellow you met the night of the party?" He looked at me, pinning me with his gaze.

I felt sure he already knew the answer, but I spoke up anyhow. "His name is Nick, but not Andros. Nick Carvalho." I decided not to complicate things by mentioning that Nick was also Robert Cavanaugh's child. Or that his mother was Christina Killian, who had been murdered in the house where Drue had died. Or that Nick was also in New York, probably just down the hall from our classroom.

The detective gave a single, slow nod. "Christina Killian's boy." When he turned around to look at another poster, I could see the back of his neck flushed a dark, angry red. "I swear, that woman is haunting me from beyond the grave." He paced to the front of the room and back again. "You know, the police back then interviewed all the men she'd been with. They never found out who her baby-daddy was." He turned to me. "I've got a pretty good guess now. Trouble is, I've got another dead girl on my hands. And here I am, paying three hundred dollars a night for a hotel room the size of my closet where the bed's a futon on the floor." He shook his head in disgust.

"Nick didn't do it," I said. "He had no reason to kill Drue."

"If it turns out he's her half brother, he had five hundred thousand reasons," McMichaels said. "And unless you were wide awake, with your eyes on him, every minute of the night, you don't know where he was or what he could have gotten up to."

"He didn't kill Drue!"

Detective McMichaels set his hands on the desk. "You don't know what he did. You don't know what he knew. And if I find out that you had anything to do with this . . ." Moving with slow deliberation, he came around the desk to stand in front of me, so close that his lapels brushed my chest, and when he spoke, his voice was almost a growl. "I promise, you will not like the consequences."

Chapter Twenty

As soon as my legs stopped shaking and I felt more or less certain that I wasn't going to throw up, I went outside into the perfect, sunny, early-summer day. The sky was robin's-egg blue, the sunshine was warm but not oppressive, and a light breeze stirred the air. On the sidewalk outside, mourners were piling into cars, or walking east, toward the subway stop two blocks away. Darshi and Nick were standing at the base of the stairs, waiting for me.

"We need to get out of here," I said, and set off down the street.

"What happened?" asked Darshi as I walked and pawed through my purse, trying to find my sunglasses. "What'd he want?" My hands were shaking so hard that I ended up dropping the bag. Nick picked it up and handed it to me. He was wearing black jeans with a heathery tweed sports coat, a button-down shirt, and a red and gold tie, and he had a black backpack and a laptop case at his feet. I licked my dry lips and tried to get my thoughts in order.

"Drue was poisoned," I began. "That's how she died. Someone put cyanide in her food or drink. That's the first thing."

"What's next?" asked Darshi.

"They let Emma Vincent go," I said. "She had an alibi. So now they're back looking for suspects." I gulped, and went on. "Drue inherited half of her trust fund when she married Stuart. Ten million dollars. She'd already given seven million of it away. Some to Stuart, most of it to her dad."

"So are they suspects now?" Darshi asked.

I shook my head. "McMichaels said they wouldn't want to kill Drue. That she was the goose laying the golden eggs."

"So who would?" asked Nick.

I turned to him, knowing that I looked as miserable as I felt. "She left me half a million dollars. And she left you half a million dollars, too."

"Me?" Nick asked. His voice cracked. "Why? She didn't even know me!"

"She left it to anyone who could take a DNA test and prove that Robert Cavanaugh was their father. Which I'm assuming is you." I licked my lips. "I guess she knew that there were other children, and she wanted to share the wealth." I finally remembered that my sunglasses were in my pocket. I pulled them out and fumbled them onto my face. "And I saw the guy from outside her room, the night she died. The one who ran away. He was there, but he took off when he saw me."

Darshi put a hand on my wrist and held me still. "Daphne. Listen. It's great about the money. I'm happy for you. But maybe we all need to step back from this."

I took a deep breath, trying to steady myself, before shaking my head. "I can't."

"Why not?"

"Drue's dead. And whatever you thought about her, she deserves justice." I breathed slowly. "Also, if the cops can't figure out who actually did it, maybe they'll try to make a circumstantial case. Prove it was someone with motive and opportunity. Like me."

Nick's voice was bleak. "Or me, I guess."

Darshi turned to look at him. "Why are you here?"

"Part of it was I wanted to get a look at my father. But Drue was my . . . my half sister," he said, stammering over the word "sister." "I wanted to be here for the service." He shifted his weight from left to right and back again. "I want Drue to have justice. I want to help. I found an Airbnb." He pulled out his phone and squinted at its screen. "It's in, um, Bushwick? In Brooklyn. I hope that's not too far."

"Oh, boy," Darshi muttered.

"It's not near," I said. "But, on the plus side, it's very trendy."

Nick shrugged. "Hopefully, I won't be there too much. Or for very long."

"Let's go to my parents' place," I said, thinking that I wanted to be around my mom and dad. I needed my father's steadiness, his calm voice and reassuring presence. Even if my mom was flipping out—maybe especially if she was flipping out—she'd be glad to see me. And there would be snacks. "We can set up a war room there."

Darshi checked the time on her phone. "Give me a few hours. I need to finish some stuff on campus. I can meet you there later."

"I'll come with you," Nick said to me.

"Are you okay walking? It's about two miles." I wasn't dressed for walking, but I needed to move, needed to burn off some of the anxiety that came from learning that I was both newly wealthy and a murder suspect.

He slung his laptop bag across his chest and put his backpack over his shoulders. "Lead on."

We dropped Darshi at the subway and kept going, heading up Fifth Avenue. "We can cut across the park by the reservoir at Ninety-Sixth Street," I told him.

"That's fine," he said. "It feels good to walk. It was a long bus ride." After a minute, he said, "You're fast."

"Jeez, don't sound so surprised," I muttered, flashing back to a guy I'd met at a party in college, who'd said, *You're very light on your feet*. Which I thought was code for *You move well for a fat girl*. But maybe that wasn't what Nick had meant. "I'm sorry. That was rude." I gestured at the rest of the pedestrians, hustling across the intersection to beat the red light. "You kind of have to be fast if you live here."

Nick sounded a little doleful as he said, "I guess everyone here's in a hurry."

"Have you been to New York City before?" I asked.

Nick's mouth was tight, like he'd tasted something bad. "Once," he said. "In high school. Class field trip. We saw *Cats*."

"You did not."

"I swear!" He raised his right hand. "Now and forever."

"That's terrible."

"We saw the Statue of Liberty and the Empire State Building. We rode the subway. That was a big deal. But what struck me most was how crowded it was." He looked around, at the verdant park, the well-kept apartment buildings, the benches that stood at regular intervals along the sidewalk. "My mother loved it here. At least, that's what my grandparents told me. But I remember thinking that if I had to take the subway to and from work every day, I'd die."

"The subway can be challenging." I was remembering one December, when my mom and I had gone to the big department stores, to look at their windows and do some holiday shopping. My father was Jewish, and my mom had been raised as a Unitarian. Neither one of them was terribly religious, but my mom loved Christmas. She collected glass ornaments and saved snippets of wrapping paper, wallpaper samples, and discarded calendars all year long to repurpose as colorful garlands and wreaths and cards. Our gifts would be so beautifully wrapped that my father and I almost hated to open them.

After a day of shopping in Manhattan, footsore and weary

and laden with bags, my mom and I had boarded a packed train at Forty-Second Street. The only vacant spot was between two teenage boys, each one sitting with his legs spread wide. My mother slowed down, considering the space. The boys had looked up. One of them stared at my mother's body, his eyes crawling from her thighs to her hips to her bosom, before he looked her full in the face, and said, "Aw, hell nah!" He and his companion had started cackling. I saw my mother's face fall. I could feel how ashamed she was as she led me to the end of the car and stood there, wordlessly clutching the pole until we reached our stop. Like she, and not these boys, had done something wrong.

Nick must have seen something on my face. He touched my arm. "You okay?" he asked. "Want to stop for a minute?"

"Sure." He led me to a bench. We watched the runners on the track that encircled the reservoir, the slower ones trying not to get run down by the sprinters. The wind ruffled the dark surface of the water. I saw a family go by, speaking what sounded like Dutch, followed by a line of preschool-aged kids, holding a rope, with teachers at each end. I sat and, automatically, I reached for my phone.

Nick put his hand on my forearm. "Hey," he said. His touch was gentle, but his voice was sharp. "Could you not?"

I looked at him, startled.

"I'm sorry. I know it's part of your job." Before I could apologize, he blurted, "I just hate when people do that."

"Do what? Look at their phones?"

"*Live* on their phones," he said, and sighed. "I know it's a cliché. You know, that Norman Rockwell Thanksgiving picture, only Mom and Dad and Bobby and Sally are all on their phones or their iPads and not even looking at each other. But it really does bother me. I think about it a lot, especially with the kids. How are they going to learn to have real relationships when most of their interactions are online? How are they going to tolerate distress if they can just distract themselves with their phones?"

"Well, welcome to the twenty-first century," I said. My own voice was a little waspish. "And you're right. This is part of my job. If I don't interact, I don't get seen, and if my posts don't get seen, I can't make money."

"I know." Nick's voice was low, and he was staring at the ground, not meeting my eyes. "It's just not my thing."

"Why not?" When he didn't answer, I asked, "Is it the Internet in general? Or social media specifically? Or just Instagram?"

"All of it." His shoulders were hunched, and his hands were curled into fists. "When I was twelve, I went online and looked at what people said about my mom, after she died. People who didn't even know her, calling her a slut. Saying she slept around and she got what she deserved. All of these people, taking bites out of what was left of her, after she couldn't defend herself. Like a bunch of zombies, eating her corpse."

I thought of a twelve-year-old Nick, going online and seeing all of that spite and vitriol; all that hate, preserved and waiting for him to find it, because the Internet was forever. I remembered something my father had told me, about the comments I'd gotten after my bar-fight video had come out: *When you're a hammer, everything looks like a nail. When you're angry, everything looks like a target. There are a lot of angry people in the world. And these days, they're all online.*

"Those people didn't know your mother," I said. "You know that, right? They weren't going after her. And I'm sure they weren't thinking about her child ever seeing what they said. They were going after the idea of her, or whatever that meant to them. Single mothers, or their ex-wives, or some girl who turned them down when they asked her out."

"I know," he said, still looking glum.

"And it's not all bad." I tried to remember my talking points, the ones I'd used on my own skeptical parents. "Social media means we're listening to different voices. It's not just the same old powerful white men who all went to the same places for college. It means everyone gets a soapbox. And if you've got something important to say, you can get people to listen."

He didn't look at me. "How does it feel," he asked, "when people go after you?"

For a minute, I didn't speak as I wondered how deep of a dive into my social media he might have done over the last few days, how much he'd seen. "Honestly, I try not to look." I gave what I hoped was a casual shrug. "I tell myself that a click is a click is a click, and even the people showing up to be horrible are engaging with my content."

"Tough way to live."

"Sometimes," I said. "But it's not all bad—"

"I know it's not."

"I have a community."

"I understand." He looked sincere, but he sounded the tiniest bit patronizing. "It's just—in my opinion—the Internet is a place where people end up making themselves feel awful, or hurting other people. And everyone pretends." His throat jerked as he swallowed. "Everyone tries to put the best versions of themselves across. To fake it. And when they're not doing that, they're sitting behind their screens, passing judgment and feeling superior to whoever they think's being sexist or racist that day."

I swallowed, wondering about Nick's politics. If he was online, would he be one of those guys with an American flag in his profile and an insistence that there were only two genders underneath it? "You're not entirely wrong. Yes, people pretend, and yes, they dogpile, and they edit the bad parts out of their lives. But that isn't the only thing that happens. Young people—young women—get to tell their stories and find an audience." Even as I spoke, I was thinking about the girl who'd asked, *How can I be brave like you?*, and how, so far, the best answer I'd come up with was telling her to fake it; how I'd told Ian Snitzer that social media was a place where everyone could pretend. I squeezed my hands together, thinking that if Nick and I somehow ended up together, I'd need to find a new line of work.

"I looked at your Instagram, on the bus ride down," he said.

This did not fill my heart with joy. I glanced at him out of the corner of my eye. "You did?"

I braced myself for a discussion of my bar-fight video, or a critique of the posts that were basically ads—my spon-con—but Nick surprised me.

"I liked what you wrote about going out to eat with your dad. What'd you call it? Dinner on Sundays?"

"Sunday suppers!" I said, feeling marginally less miserable. For the past year, every Sunday, I'd posted about a place my father and I had visited together, either in the past or that very day. I'd write about what we'd eaten, or the route we'd taken, or some bit of history or current event from the region that had provided the meal.

"Did you and your dad really go out every Sunday?"

"We did, when I was a kid. Now it's more like once or twice a month." I thought about our meals: the fragrant exhalation of steam from a soft-bodied pork bun; the way my lips had tingled from the bird's-eye chilis in the Thai dishes that had left my father and I both gasping. The sweet crunch of sugar on my favorite brioche, the subtle heat of Jamaican patties with their flaky bright-gold pastry crusts.

"Do you like to cook?"

"I do. Some people in New York don't. They say it's a waste, when you can just order any food you can ever dream of, and it's probably better than what you could make at home, but I like cooking. My father loves to cook. He's got a huge cookbook collection. You'll see."

Nick was easy to talk to. Easy to be with. The attraction that I'd felt on the Cape was still there. Of course, now it was tempered by the knowledge that he despised what I did online, mixed with a hint of terror that he might have killed my friend. I wondered why he was really here, in New York City, how much of it had to do with the father he couldn't remember meeting and the half sister he'd never known at all, and how much had to do with me.

"What are your aunt and uncle like?" I asked him.

"They're fine," he said with his eyes on the ground.

"Fine?" I teased. "That's all I get?"

He tugged at the knot of his tie. "Let's see. My uncle owned an auto-body shop. My aunt was a claims adjustor at an insurance company. They're both retired now. And they are fine. You know. Good people." He was quiet again. Then he asked, "How well do you know him? Robert Cavanaugh," he added, in case I was confused about the "him" in question.

"Hardly at all," I said. "When I was in high school I spent a lot of time at Drue's house. But he was never there. He traveled."

Nick's lips quirked upward in a thin, bitter smile. "I'll bet."

In that moment, I felt a great enfolding sympathy for him, a sorrow so piercing and complete it was hard to breathe. Had I really spent so many years feeling miserable because I was bigger than other girls, when there were people who'd grown up without their parents? Had I pitied myself because I'd failed at Weight Watchers, and because my high school BFF and I had fallen out, when there were people who'd found their own mother's dead body on the floor? Had I fretted because I'd never been in love, and that I'd wasted two years on Wan Ron, when I had a mother and a father who loved me, who would have given me whatever help they could, who wanted nothing but my happiness?

I wanted to hug him; I wanted to cry; I wanted to tell him how terrible it was that his mother had been murdered and that his father was a stranger. Not just a stranger, but a preening, overbearing bully who'd cheated on his wife and slept with lots of other women. And, of course, I wanted to tell him how sorry I was that he was now a murder suspect. Except now I was one, too.

Instead of speaking, I reached for his hand. At first, Nick looked startled. Then, gratefully, he squeezed it back. Even in my sorrow and my anxiety, it felt reassuring to be with him, to feel his shoulder nudging my shoulder, his hand holding mine; the comforting warmth of another body beside mine. "Come on," I said. This time, I was the one who pulled him to his feet. "Time to meet the parents."

I felt my heart lift, the way it always did, when we turned the corner onto my tree-lined block, and I saw the building where I'd grown up, with its brownstone façade and double front doors, its large, rectangular glass windows, with four panes of glass on each side, and the Japanese maple trees. One of those trees had grown right outside my bedroom, tinting the light in my room green, making me feel like I lived in a tree house. On Sundays, I'd wake up to the pealing of the bells from West End Presbyterian Church on 105th and Amsterdam.

"Come on up," I said, and brought Nick inside and upstairs to where my parents were both waiting.

My mother wrapped her arms around me, holding on tight. I hugged her back, extricated myself, and turned to see Nick, looking amused at the scene.

"Nick, these are my parents, Jerry and Judy. Mom, Dad, this is Nick . . ." I got stuck, trying to remember his actual last name.

"Nick Carvalho," he said, and extended his hand.

"Nick was an old friend of Drue's." I'd fill my parents in on the half brother part later.

"We heard they let go of the girl they'd been questioning," said my mother, sniffling as she pulled a bit of tissue from her favorite tunic's front pocket. "Do you know if the police have other suspects?"

I shook my head. "That's why we're here. Nick and Darshi and I are going to try to figure it out."

"Figure out what?" my mom asked.

"Who killed Drue," I said.

Before my mom could ask more questions, we went to the kitchen, where the refrigerator was still covered with my artwork, from my preschool finger-painted smears to the watercolor portrait I'd done of my mom as part of my senior-year project at Lathrop. I was wondering if I'd be able to slip into the living room and move the life-size papier-mâché rendering of Bingo I'd made from its spot on the mantel to a closet or the trash.

My father, I saw, had been shopping. He'd already set out a dish of olives, a bowl of pretzels, a saucer of hummus with a slick of oil, pita chips, walnuts, a wooden board full of charcuterie, grainy mustard and crackers, and a small plate of crumbly almond cookies from his favorite Italian bakery in Brooklyn.

"Beer?" he offered Nick, rearranging the bowls and adding a small pile of linen cocktail napkins to the assembly. "Red wine? White wine? Coffee? Tea? I can make sangria, or I can mix up a pitcher of Manhattans . . ."

"Dad," I said, "it's one o'clock in the afternoon."

"Well, it's five o'clock somewhere," he said, exactly the way I knew he would.

Nick held out my chair for me. I could see my parents notice, and the look of approval they exchanged.

My mother took her customary seat at the foot of the table. My father, in jeans and his oldest SUNY Purchase T-shirt, sat for a few seconds before popping up to his feet again to put out a wedge of Stilton, a dish of glazed apricots, another dish of wasabi peas, and a sleeve of water crackers.

"Coffee would be great," said Nick. I mouthed the words "Thank you." If my father was busy with the French press, he wouldn't be able to keep emptying the contents of the refrigerator and pantry onto the kitchen table. My phone buzzed. "Oh, Darshi's here!" I got up to let her in. She greeted my parents, and the five of us gathered around the table.

"Where should we start?" I asked.

My parents exchanged another look. "Daphne," said my mother, "we aren't sure that you should be involved in all of this."

Darshi nodded emphatically. I ignored her.

"I understand. But here's the thing. I brought Drue a drink the night she died. The police say that she was poisoned. So they'll be looking at anyone who touched anything she had to eat or drink."

My mother made a tiny, moaning sound and pressed her knuckles to her lips. My father put his elbows on the table, steepling his fingers and resting his chin on them as he frowned. "Okay," he said. "Does Drue have enemies? Any vengeful ex-boyfriends? Does the groom have any unbalanced ex-girlfriends? That would be the obvious place to start."

I hadn't yet told my parents about Drue's real marriage and sham engagement. "At the hospital, Stuart told me he thought that she might have had another boyfriend at some point. But I don't know who."

"And there was that guy," Nick said. "The one waiting outside her room at the party. The one at the funeral. Do you think maybe . . ."

"No," I said, remembering the guy's unruly hair, his cheap, badly fitting clothes, his absolute lack of any resemblance to the kind of men I knew that Drue preferred. "He might have been a stalker, but he absolutely wasn't a boyfriend."

"So who would know?"

I sighed, shaking my head. "Even if we find this guy, he might just be another dead end."

"What about Drue's friends?" asked my mom.

The three of us looked at her. My mother fidgeted, but didn't drop her gaze. "I'll bet Drue hurt other people." The phrase "the way she hurt you" was unspoken, but it still hung, audibly, in the air. "And, I don't know, but if she was poisoned . . . well, to me that feels like a woman. Men use guns and knives. Poison feels like a woman's weapon."

Nick looked at me. I shrugged. "I don't know much about Drue's friends, or her life after Lathrop. Just that she did a gap year at a private school in California. Then Harvard. Then back here. And when she came to find me, she made it sound like there weren't a lot of people she was close to." I remembered what she'd said, in the Snitzers' kitchen: *I don't have anyone else*, and *You were the only one who ever just liked me for me.*

I reached for my phone; googling "Drue Lathrop Cavanaugh Harvard roommates" spat out a handful of names. Changing "Harvard" to "Croft" yielded a few more. I read them over, wondering if I could cold-call Madison Silver or Deepti Patel or Lily Crain and start asking questions about their dead roomie. If they were smart, they'd have turned off their phones and recruited friends to screen their social media to avoid the reporters, the same way I had. Out loud, I said, "We need someone who knew her back then. At Croft, or at Harvard. Preferably both."

"Did anyone from Lathrop go to Harvard with her?" asked Nick.

"Tim Agrawal," said Darshi. "They weren't friends."

"Does Tim know anyone she was friends with?" I asked.

Darshi shrugged. "I can ask him, but I wouldn't get your hopes up. I think they were in different circles." Which I knew meant that Drue had probably ignored Tim if their paths had ever crossed up in Cambridge.

"Who else knew her?" asked my mother. "Her mom? Her brother? Who else would have known her friends?"

I drummed my fingers on the table. "Let's start with the roommates. And then, maybe we can go back to Drue's social media accounts," I said. "We can divide them up and start calling her friends."

"She had a lot of friends," said Darshi.

"Well, obviously, we don't try to call the five hundred thousand people who followed her. Maybe we just reach out to the people she followed. How many is that?"

Darshi checked. "Twelve hundred and ninety-six." She brought the phone up closer to her glasses. "But some of them are celebrities. Unless she actually knows Chrissy Teigen?"

I shrugged as my heart sank. "I don't know. Maybe. It's possible."

"What about Abigay?" asked my mom.

When the three of us looked at her, my mom appeared startled, but she didn't drop her gaze. "Daphne, you told me that Drue wasn't very considerate to the people who worked for the family. If she got used to treating them like furniture, maybe Abigay saw something, or heard something, or knows something . . ." Her voice trailed off. My father deposited a kiss on her forehead, and hugged her, murmuring something too quietly for me to hear. Then he turned to me.

"Her number's in the Lathrop directory." Abigay, it turned out, was one of Drue's emergency contacts and was listed in the school phone book.

She picked up after two rings. "Daphne, what a pleasure! I'm sorry I didn't get to say hello to you this morning." Her sunny, musical voice became somber. "Such a terrible thing."

I told her what we needed.

"I don't know that I can help, but I'll surely try." Abigay had to be at work in an hour, but she had a little time to spare. We agreed to meet at Ladurée on Madison, near her current employers on the Upper East Side.

"You two go," Darshi said. "I'll hang here and we can start calling Drue's friends."

I gave her a hug and summoned a car, which took Nick and me to Ladurée, which had celery-green walls accented with gold and a black-and-white-tiled floor, glass cases full of macarons in pink and lavender and raspberry, and cake stands piled with croissants and kouign-amann pastries. This place hadn't been opened when Drue and I had been in high school, but it had the familiar feeling of every coffee shop where we would hang out, drinking lattes, crunching rock-hard biscotti between our teeth while we talked about tests and boys and colleges and what Drue would wear to her debut.

Nick looked at me. "You okay?" he asked.

"I feel like I'm moving backward in time," I said. "First school. Now this place. I feel like, maybe by the end of the night, I'll be back in preschool or something."

"Don't worry," he said, and smiled. "I promise that I'll share my juice box with you."

The café had a handful of tables in the back, with white-lacquered chairs with green cushions. It smelled like sugar and butter and coffee, and was quiet, except for the hiss of the cappuccino machine. We found a table and, without thinking, I pulled out my phone. "Sorry," I said when I realized what I'd done.

Nick held up his hands. "It's fine."

"It's just that I haven't posted anything since—well, since—and I have contracts with these companies, and—"

"Daphne," said Nick, "don't apologize. It's your job. I get it. It's fine." I nodded and bent over my phone, steeling myself before I opened my email. Already, a few of my clients had reached out, mixing condolences with ever-so-gentle reminders that I needed to start posting again. I began scheduling content for the coming day, then the coming week: posts for Alpine Yum-Yums, for Leef, for the Yoga for All yoga mat. I'd grabbed just one sad picture of the mat on Cape Cod, unrolled on my deck, before the deck had turned into a crime scene. And what was I supposed to say? *Great mat; bad weekend?* I finally arrived at, *I hope this beautiful shot of a fabulous yoga mat above a beautiful beach inspires you to get your beautiful self moving today.* I added the appropriate links and tags—#plussizefitness, #plussizeyoga, #everybodyisayogabody—and scheduled the post to go up in four hours, when the company's research indicated that the largest slice of mat-buying browsers was online.

I'd moved on to the pet treats when Abigay sailed through the door, dressed in a gray pleated skirt and a black silk blouse. Her broad face was a little more lined and creased, but her smile, when she saw me, was just as welcoming as I remembered, from that first day I'd gone to Drue's house and asked for peanut butter and apples for a snack.

"A terrible t'ing." Abigay hugged me, pulling me tight against her, then holding me out at arm's length. "It's good to see you again," she said. "You holding up?"

I said that I was and introduced Nick. His mouth quirked up when I said, "Nick is a friend of the family." Abigay sat down after checking the time on the slim gold watch with a rectangular face that was clasped around her wrist. "A going-away present from the Cavanaughs," she said. "See?" She removed it and passed it across the table. The metal still felt warm as I read the engraving on the back. *To our Abigay, who has been part of the family, with love and thanks.*

"It's very pretty." I wondered how Abigay felt about *our Abigay*, and the *part of the family* bit; how many hours she'd spent away from her own family, her own children, in service to the Cavanaugh kids.

"Yes indeed," she said, her expression still neutral.

"What can we get you?" Nick asked. After some coaxing, she asked for a latte, and I asked for Earl Grey tea. Nick went up to the counter. Abigay settled into her chair with a sigh.

"It's nice to see you, but I don't know how much I can help. I left the Cavanaughs three years ago. With both kids mostly out of the house, and with the missus on those juice diets, they barely needed me at all."

Nick came back with our drinks and a plate of pastries. "It all looked so good," he said. When Nick set Abigay's latte in front of her, she took a sip and set her cup back in its sauce with an expression suggesting that she could have done better.

"Did you and Drue keep in touch after you left?" I asked her.

Abigay made a face that was almost a smirk. "What do you think?"

I sighed. "Not to speak ill of the dead."

"Oh, go on," Abigay said. Her voice still had that familiar musical quality, every sentence rising and falling like a song. "Tell the truth and shame the devil; that's what my mama used to say."

I cleared my throat. "From what I saw, she wasn't very nice to you."

Abigay tapped her tongue on the roof of her mouth, considering. "Well. It wasn't a question of nice or not nice. Miss Drue wasn't very anything to me. Or to Flor, who cleaned, or Delia and Helen, who came to do the flowers, or to Ernesto and Carl down in the lobby. She didn't see us." Abigay clasped her hands on the table. "Which was to be expected. As the twig is bent, so is the tree inclined. Drue and her brother saw the way their parents treated the help, and they treated us the same."

"I remember her asking you for ridiculous snacks."

A brief smile flickered across Abigay's face. "That used to be a game. When Drue was little. She'd say, 'Abigay, make me a castle,' and I'd make her one, with pineapple cubes and marshmallows. Or, 'Make me a tree with snow on top,' and I'd give her broccoli with parmesan cheese." She sighed, then nibbled the miniature biscotti that came with her drink. "She was a sweet little girl. A long time ago." She took another sip. "Maybe that's why it didn't fuss me, her asking me for ridiculous foods. I could still see that little girl inside her."

"What happened?"

"She grew up. Grew up and got beautiful and discovered that she was rich. That, and she saw how her folks behaved."

I stirred sugar into my tea and held the cup, letting it warm my hands. "Do you have any idea who could have wanted to hurt her?"

Abigay shook her head. "Probably a long list of people she wronged."

"Could it have had to do with the Cavanaugh Corporation? We've heard stories that the company's in trouble."

She nodded. "I've heard the same. But to kill a young woman on her wedding day? That doesn't feel like business to me. That feels personal."

I said, "We're also hearing that her father may have been unfaithful. And that he might have had other children."

Abigay sighed unhappily. In a low voice, she said, "He brought a few of them home. When the missus was away, at that yoga place in the Berkshires." She smoothed her paper napkin with her fingers. "Now, if someone had killed the mister, I'd be looking at a wronged woman. But why would one of them kill Drue?"

"Did you meet any of Drue's boyfriends?" asked Nick.

Abigay looked at him, widening her eyes. "Ooh! He talks!"

Nick smiled. "He even sings, if he's got enough beer in him."

"Hmm," she said, folding and refolding her napkin. I expected an immediate denial. It didn't come. Instead, Abigay said, "You understand, this is going back a few years. I came in on a Saturday when I wasn't scheduled to work because I needed my good cast-iron pan, and I'd left it at the Cavanaughs'. I wasn't expecting anyone to be there. The mister was traveling, the missus was doing her yoga, Trip was married by then, and Drue should have been at school. So up I go, and there's Miss Drue with a fellow."

"Not Stuart Lowe," I said.

"No, not him," Abigay confirmed. "I never met him. This was a foreign-looking fellow. Dark skin, dark hair. A few years older than Drue. I walked into the kitchen, and there they were. Cooking." She sounded amused at the memory. "Or, at least, he was cooking. And she was helping."

"So he was a boyfriend?" I asked.

"She introduced him to me as her friend. But, from the way they were looking at each other, I would say boyfriend, mm-hmm. Boyfriend, for sure. Don't ask me his name," she said, holding up one smooth palm in warning before I could do just that. "I don't remember. And I've tried." She sipped her latte, then made her *I can do better* face again. "What I remember is that she looked happy with him. She was glowing. All smiles. 'Abigay, this is my friend!'" Abigay shook her head. "She helped me find my pan. Put it in a bag for me and everything."

"How did she seem with him?" I asked.

"Comfortable," Abigay answered after a brief silence. "I remember that I felt like she was finally starting to grow up. Like I could see the outlines of who she was going to be. If everything went right. Sometimes a twig can unbend itself, right? It's never too late."

Until it is, I thought.

Abigay patted her lips with a paper napkin and got to her feet. "I should get on the good foot."

"Thank you for your help."

"Did I help?" She cocked her head and looked at me. "I hope so." I asked her to promise to call if she remembered anything else. She said that she would, and hugged me, whispering, "You be careful now." When I pulled back, she was looking at me. "I should let you know, the police were asking me about you, too."

I felt my stomach sink and my knees start to quiver.

"What did they ask?"

"Did you and Drue fight. Had you ever been angry at her.

How did she treat her classmates at Lathrop." Abigay shook her head. "I told them that Drue wasn't very kind, but that I couldn't imagine any of the girls I'd met ever hurting her that way." She brushed a crumb off her skirt. "I can't imagine it," she said softly. "But someone did."

The door's bell jingled as she left. Nick and I sat, thinking. Or at least, I assume he was thinking. I was trying not to start screaming as I sat there, terrified, imagining myself in jail for a crime I didn't commit.

"Here." Nick pushed my cup toward me. "Drink. Stay hydrated." I nodded glumly and took a bite of a kouign-amann filled with raspberry jam, thinking that they probably didn't have pastry like this in jail.

"We need to find this guy," I said. "The mystery chef."

"Right," said Nick. "Any ideas?"

"No," I said, and got to my feet. "But don't give up on me yet."

Chapter Twenty-One

Back at my parents' place, my mother had gone to work—she taught an afternoon sculpting class three days a week—and my father had made a quick trip to the fish market and was in the kitchen, assembling his famous cioppino. "Fish is brain food!" he called as he zested a lemon, filling the rooms with the citrus tang. In the living room, Darshi had borrowed one of my mom's easels, and had propped a piece of white cardboard up for us to see. On the top, in large purple letters, she'd written OPERATION FIND DRUE'S SECRET BOYFRIEND.

"Nick filled me in," she said. "So how are we going to find this guy? Do we just keep going through Drue's social?"

"The problem is, if this guy is an ex-boyfriend, they might not be friends anymore."

"If she was never really going to stay married to Stuart, she never had to really break up with the Mystery Man," said Nick.

"Except she'd want to cover her tracks. To make it look authentic." I looked around, wondering where my dad had moved the snacks. "I wish there was a way to look at Drue's social media and see who she was friends with five years ago."

"There is," said Nick. He unzipped his laptop case, opened

up his computer, and started to type. "Okay," he said, turning the laptop around and tilting the screen. "God bless the Wayback machine. This is a picture of Drue's Facebook page three years ago."

"How many friends did she have?" I asked, scooching up next to Nick. He smelled nice, and his warmth was a comfort.

Tap tap tap. "Twelve hundred and sixty-seven."

"Okay, but we can eliminate the women," I said. "Hang on." I carried his laptop to the tiny, cluttered office where, for the last twenty years, my father had been trying to write a novel. I printed off the six-page list of Drue's e-friends and grabbed three black markers on my way out. Passing them markers, I handed Darshi and Nick two pages apiece and kept two for myself. "Cross off the women," I said. "And anyone whose last name is Cavanaugh or Lathrop." That left ninety-six men unaccounted for.

"Abigay said he was foreign. Darker skinned," I said. "Cross off anyone who's got a number after his name. Or anyone who's visibly white. And anyone who's over fifty."

We each used our laptops to look up profiles. In the end, we had just four names to research. The first candidate was Stephen Chen, who worked at the Cavanaugh Corporation. When I pulled up his profile on my laptop, we saw a sedentary-looking forty-seven-year-old who lived in a suburb in New Jersey and had a wife and three kids.

"Maybe Drue liked older guys," Darshi said. Her voice was dubious.

I shook my head and drew an X through the guy's name on the easel. "Next," I said.

Next was Cesar Acosta, twenty-nine and handsome, a Lathrop classmate, one of the soccer boys. Nick found him first.

"He looks like a possibility," he said. Then we discovered that, per Facebook, Cesar worked as a currency trader and was living in Singapore. "That doesn't mean he didn't do it," I argued. "Just because he lives in Singapore doesn't mean he didn't visit the States. Or he could've hired someone to poison Drue's drink."

"True," said Nick, "but if he's there now, which it looks like he is, he'll be hard to talk to in person." We agreed to put a pin in Cesar and continue the search.

The third man, Danilo Bayani, was Drue's age, a Harvard classmate. He was almost startlingly good-looking, with a thick shock of glossy black hair and a wide, gleaming smile. But in his profile picture he had his arms around another handsome man, a fellow with close-cropped black curls and full lips. "Three Years Today!" read the text above a second picture of the two men in tuxedoes, holding hands as they stood in front of a minister.

"Maybe he's bi," I said, staring at his pictures on my screen. "And unfaithful."

Darshi looked over my shoulder, sniffed, and said, "He seems pretty happy. Not like a guy with murder on his mind."

Which left the final candidate. "No," said Darshi as soon as his picture appeared on her laptop. Nick took a look.

"I . . . am not seeing it," he said.

Darshi slid her laptop toward me. I glanced at it, then screamed, "Oh my God, that's him!"

"Him who?" Darshi asked.

"The guy! The guy from the funeral! The one outside her room in Cape Cod! That's him! What's his name? Where's he live? Tell me everything!"

We learned that the guy's name was Aditya Acharya. Per the pictures, he had thinning hair, sloping shoulders, and a paunchy middle. His glasses were thick, the frames unfashionable. Instead of a Rolex or a Patek Philippe he wore an inexpensive-looking Timex on a stretchy gold-plated band. One side of his polo shirt's collar curled limply toward his chin. He looked like the kind of guy Drue would have targeted in high school, a guy she would have filmed and photographed and mocked, not one she'd have been secretly in love with.

"Seriously?" Darshi asked.

"Well. Hey, Dad, what's that thing Sherlock Holmes said?" I called into the kitchen, where my father had moved on from his lemons and had started cleaning the squid.

"When you have excluded the impossible, what remains, however improbable, must be the truth," my father called back.

Darshi looked at Aditya's picture for a long moment before shaking her head. "I think we should go back to the gay guy."

Nick snapped a screenshot and resumed tapping at his phone.

"What are you doing?"

"Texting Abigay. I'm asking if this is the guy she met."

"You got her number? When did you get her number?"

"I have my ways," said Nick. An instant later, his phone buzzed. He looked at it and gave me a thumbs-up. "Abigay says she's not positive, but she thinks this could have been him."

"Well, there you go."

Darshi, meanwhile, was staring at Aditya's picture, tilting the phone from side to side with the idea. "I'm trying to imagine more hair," she said. "Or better clothes."

"Maybe he has secret talents," I suggested.

"Or a secret fortune," said Nick.

"Nah," I said. "If he'd had money, she would have married him."

"No." Darshi's voice was flat. "Not if he looked like Hrithik Roshan and was richer than Jeff Bezos." She shook her head. "Drue would never have married a brown guy."

"So what now?" I looked at Nick. "Can you find his phone number?"

Nick nodded. "I've got it already. And his address. He lives in New Haven. But I don't think we should call."

"Why not?"

"New Haven's, what, two hours away? I think we should go there. Same as we did with Emma's mom."

"Beard him in his den," said Darshi.

"Surprise him," said Nick. "So he doesn't have any warning. Or any time to run or come up with a story."

"Makes sense," Darshi said. Nick stretched out his hand to help me up off the floor. Not only did I let him, but I forgot to do my usual trick of taking as much of my weight as I could. "Heave me erect!" I instructed, and Nick actually laughed, and didn't seem to struggle as he pulled me to my feet. I felt good knowing that even in the depths of this misery, even though my friend had died and I was still probably a murder suspect, I could still make someone, briefly, happy.

Chapter Twenty-Two

We took my parents' Camry. Nick drove confidently, not blowing down the highway at ninety miles an hour, but not poking along in the slow lane, either. Darshi and I worked our phones, scouring the Internet for information about the man we hoped to meet. According to his Facebook profile, which Aditya had illustrated with a picture of a friendly looking black Lab, he was a graduate student at Yale's department of statistics and data science. He was the oldest of three children, a native of Edison, New Jersey, who'd gone to Rutgers as an undergraduate, then to Harvard for a master's degree, then on to Yale for his PhD. On Twitter, he retweeted left-leaning political commentators and comments about the Manchester United football team. On Reddit, he followed a subreddit called Dogs Being Derps, where people posted videos of their pets doing silly things, and another one on vegetarian cooking, where he asked politely worded, correctly punctuated questions about chana dal and fondue and whether Impossible Burgers were any good.

"Drue's true love." Darshi's voice was skeptical. "What do you think he'll be like?" All the way up I-95, the three of us traded theories. I was betting that Aditya's grad-student life was a cover, and that he was really a James Bond–style villain, all expensive suits and dark intent, that his social-media presence was just an elaborate front. "I'll bet he's got an accent," I said, pretending to swoon.

"I find it hard to believe, but maybe Drue was secretly into nerds," Darshi said. "People don't always play to type, right? Her father wasn't dating models. Barbara Vincent wasn't a glamourpuss."

Nick's voice was quiet. "My mother was."

"Let's review," I said, before Darshi got snippy and Nick started brooding again. "What do we know about this man? He enjoys videos of dogs falling down stairs," I said, answering my own question.

"And videos of dogs trying to drink from hoses," Darshi added. "Let's not sell Aditya short."

"He loves his family," said Nick.

"Or at least he posts pictures of them," I added, even though I think the pictures looked pretty convincing. I'd seen Aditya beaming at his niece's first birthday party, cradling the birthday girl in his arms with an ease that suggested comfort around babies and toddlers. I'd seen Aditya in a cap and gown and hood at Harvard. He'd used duct tape to spell out LOVE YOU MOM AND DAD on his mortarboard. "I think he really loves them. I wonder if he's our guy."

"I guess we'll see," said Nick.

Aditya lived on the second floor of an old Victorian-style brick house on Bradley Street on the edge of the Yale campus. The exterior paint was peeling. The entryway, inside a heavy, scarred oak door, had an unpleasantly musty smell, and the brown carpet on the staircase was ugly in the places it wasn't worn away. "Starving grad student," Darshi murmured as we made the climb.

I knocked on the door with a brass number 2 hanging crookedly from a single nail. A minute later, the door opened. "Yes?" asked a man as he wiped his hands on a dishcloth tucked into his waistband. The smell of something simmering billowed out behind him, a cloud of ginger and coconut. When he looked at me, his narrow shoulders drooped.

"Oh," he said. "Hello."

I stared, mute and stunned, as I got my first good look at the guy from the party. The guy from the service. The guy who'd run away. He'd grown a few days' worth of scruff since the rehearsal dinner party, and if you added more beard and discounted the skin tone, he could have been my father at age thirty. He had the same thoughtful expression, the same mournful brown eyes behind glasses. His belly pushed against his shirt, swelling the fabric in a gentle curve. He wore a plain blue T-shirt, untucked over loose nylon track pants, and a pair of leather sandals on his feet. *Mandals*, I heard Drue mocking in my head. I breathed in deeply, smelling whatever he was cooking, and tried to reconcile the girl I'd known, headstrong, judgmental Drue, with this quiet, seemingly humble, un-handsome man.

"Mr. Acharya? I'm Darshini Shah," I heard Darshi say. "This is Nick Carvalho, and this is Daphne Berg. We're friends of Drue's."

"Of course." Up close, I could see that his eyes were red-rimmed behind his glasses, and that he was twisting a dish towel in his hands, like he didn't know what else to do with them and he had to hold on to something. His gaze traveled from me to Nick to Darshi, and he seemed to relax a little as he took her in. "Please, come inside."

In his living room, he had a battered-looking leather couch, armchairs that didn't match (one of them, I saw, had been patched with duct tape), a Persian rug of startling beauty, a desk piled high with textbooks, with a blue Medicine Buddha statue on a shelf above it. "Please, please," he said, ushering us inside. I saw, on his wrist, the cheap-looking gold watch that I recognized from the pictures, and a gaudy class ring was on his right hand. He was a fashion disaster, the kind of guy Drue would have laughed at back at Lathrop, and his expression, his slumped shoulders and mournful eyes, said that he knew it; that he was not unfamiliar with being the object of mockery.

"I recognized you from the video," he told me as we settled into a living room that featured a chipped wicker table and a sagging tweed couch.

"The video?"

"From the bar. With the man."

"Ah."

"Drue must have played it for me a dozen times. She showed me all of your Instagram posts. She was so proud of you. She said, 'That's my friend!'"

"Oh," I said, as my heart shuddered and my eyes filled. "I didn't know that."

"She would tell me, 'I could never be that brave.' She admired you a great deal." Clasping his hands in front of him, he said, "I'm sorry that I ran from you. But I wasn't invited. Not to the party, or to the service. It was . . . complicated." He bent his head and said, very quietly, "But I wanted to be there. For Drue."

Nick handed me a Kleenex that he'd gotten somewhere. When Aditya went to make tea, I looked around, at the cheap furniture, the profusion of plants in clay pots in the single south-facing window, a framed picture of Lord Shiva on the wall, and on a side table, a copper statue of Ganesh with his elephant head and a mouse at his feet. The mantel over the bricked-up fireplace held a single framed photograph, a picture of Drue and Aditya at Fenway Park. They were both wearing red Boston Red Sox caps and grinning from seats way up in the bleachers.

"Ah," said Aditya, returning to the room and following my gaze.

"She looks so happy."

"It was a wonderful day." He handed out mugs and put a plate of Parle-G biscuits, the same kind that Darshi's mother sometimes served, on the coffee table. I took a sip as he sat down in a battered armchair, laced his hands across his belly, and sighed. I knew that I was staring, but I couldn't make myself stop. Part of it was how much he looked like my father, and part of it was how I could not picture Drue, glamorous, gorgeous, rich, beautiful Drue, with a guy like this. Had Drue climbed those stairs beneath the ceiling's peeling paint, and breathed that musty, cabbage-y smell? Had she sat on this couch; had she slept on the futon that I bet myself was in Aditya's bedroom, and cooked with him in the galley-style kitchen, and watched movies with him on this tiny old TV?

"You are wondering what she saw in me." Aditya's tone was good-humored, but his eyes were sad. Darshi started to say something, then stopped as Aditya shook his head. "No, don't apologize. I wondered, too. Every day we were together, I felt the same way. Like it couldn't be real."

"How'd you two meet?" asked Darshi.

"Drue was volunteering two nights a week at a high school in Boston. She was helping the kids write their college essays, fill out their applications, prepare for their tests. That sort of thing."

"Wait. What?"

Aditya nodded. It made my heart ache a little, seeing the pride on his face. "She would joke about it. She'd say that if anyone in her high school could have seen her, they would have thought she'd joined a cult. It was important to her, she told me, to give back, and do some good."

Before I could ask what he meant by that, and what Drue was making amends for, he said, "I noticed her right away. Drue was impossible not to notice. She was lovely, and intelligent. One of the women who ran the program told me her last name and who her father was. We were all told to treat her nicely, because the business had a charitable arm, and maybe they'd give us a grant. I would have never approached her. I would have been content to just see her those two nights a week."

"So what happened?"

"Drue asked you out," said Nick.

Aditya nodded, smiling a little at whatever he was remembering. "We both stayed late to clean up one night, to return the desks and chairs to where they'd been, and she asked if I'd go with her to the Isabella Gardner Museum. It was May." His eyes went soft. "A lovely afternoon. In the garden, there were lilacs and honeysuckle. We sat on a bench, beside a statue of a satyr, and we talked. I had no idea it was a date, of course. I thought she wanted advice, or a reference for a graduate school application. It was the only thing I could think of. I couldn't imagine that someone like Drue was interested in someone like me, and when it became clear that she was . . ." He cleared his throat. ". . . interested, I assumed that she had to want something." He smiled, a terribly sad smile. "She told me that she liked me. She liked how I was interested in her mind, not her money or her status. She said that I reminded her of someone she'd known when she was younger."

I swallowed, pressing my lips together hard, feeling sorrow pierce me. I remembered how it felt, to hardly believe that this lovely, beautiful, effortlessly perfect girl was interested in me. And I remembered Drue telling me how great my father was, after our eating excursion. *You're lucky.* I remembered the picture in Emma's bedroom, a little girl perched on her father's shoulders, and I remembered what Lily Cavanaugh had said about Drue and her father—*she wanted him to love her*. My eyes stung with tears as I thought about my father, who had always had time for me, and about Drue, whose father was never around. Drue, who'd had to hold on to a day's worth of memories of my dad, because her own had given her so little. *Lucky*, I thought. God, I was so lucky.

"We were together for a year," he said. "I never would have believed we'd last even that long."

"And then what happened?" I asked.

Aditya slid his sandaled feet back and forth along the beautiful rug. "I used to think, sometimes, that there were two Drues. Two people inside of one. There was the girl who was happy with me, volunteering and going to Red Sox games and sitting in the bleachers, or staying in and cooking. Going for walks or bike rides because I couldn't afford much more, and I wouldn't let her pay for everything. We would visit museums on Wednesdays, when admission is free. We'd buy discounted student tickets for plays. We took the ferry, once, from Boston to Provincetown. We ate oysters for lunch, walked along the beach, and stayed in her parents' beach house that night."

I nodded, wondering if, for Drue, being with Aditya felt like role-playing: Marie Antoinette in her shepherdess costume, petting her perfumed sheep before going back to Versailles.

"Then there was the other Drue. The woman she was raised to be. Her father's good right hand. Her mother's daughter. A woman who would be photographed at charity balls, and for newspapers and magazines. A woman who very much wanted her father to love her, which meant that she had a certain image to maintain."

"And you didn't fit the image," I said.

He smiled sadly, making eye contact with Darshi before shaking his head. "No," he said in the same flatly definitive tone Darshi had used to answer the same question. "Not even if I had all the money in the world."

Aditya's belly shifted as he sighed. "And so I knew there was no future. No happily ever after for us. But I let myself love her. Because I wanted to believe. I wanted it to be true." He pressed his lips together and refolded his hands in his lap. "A year ago, Drue came to my apartment. We went to lunch, and she told me she couldn't see me any longer. That she had reconnected with an old boyfriend and was making plans to marry him. That was how she said it: making plans to marry him. I asked her if she loved him. 'No,' she said. 'No. I love you.'" He twisted the dish towel, clutching it tight in his hands. "She told me that she was sorry, but that she was doing what she had to do. She said that I was the best man she'd ever known, and that she would always love me. She promised that she would come back to me, when she could, and that we would be together. But that she would understand if I chose not to wait."

Nick and Darshi were both looking at me. I could guess what they were thinking—did Aditya have any idea that there'd been an arrangement? Should we tell him? Would it help him to know that Drue hadn't loved Stuart, that the marriage had been for money and the engagement just for show? Or would that just make things worse?

"Did she talk about when?" I finally asked. "When she'd come back?"

He wiped his cheek and shook his head, his expression resolute. "I never asked. It was a fantasy. A dream on top of a dream. She was going to marry someone more appropriate, and that would be that. I couldn't let myself keep hoping for something that would never happen. And then, to go to the house . . . to the party . . ." He shook his head again. "Madness. But I had to see her. And then, after the fight, I saw her run up the stairs, and I thought . . . I thought that maybe . . ." He closed his mouth. I remembered him, in the darkness, in his white shirt and his red shorts and with his glass of ice water, standing in the dark outside of Drue's bedroom, waiting. Waiting for her to need him; waiting for her to say *Take me home.*

"I knew she would never change her mind. Or at least, I knew it was unlikely. I only wanted to see her. Maybe to convince myself that it was really over."

"And the memorial service?"

He sighed. "I wanted to say goodbye."

"Did Drue ever mention that she had a half sister on Cape Cod?" asked Darshi.

Aditya shook his head again, looking surprised but not shocked. "Was that the girl the police were questioning?" he asked. When Nick told him that it was, Aditya said, "Drue knew that her parents had been unhappy. She knew that her father had affairs, that he'd been with women on the Cape. I know she suspected there were other children. She mentioned wanting to do something for them, to give them money. She said it wasn't fair that she'd grown up with such advantages, and they had not."

I listened, thinking that this was a Drue I'd never seen—one who saw her own privilege. One who was trying to do better.

"So who do you think would have wanted to kill her?" I asked.

Aditya gave me a sad smile. "She hurt people. As I believe you know. The Drue I'd known would not. But the girl she'd been—that girl did harm." He smoothed the dish towel over his lap. "She told me what she'd done to you. It was one of the reasons she was so impressed with your video. She said you'd taken what had been a weakness and turned it into strength. She admired that a great deal."

I swallowed hard. Nick put his hand on my shoulder.

"And she felt guilty about what she'd done in her life, the damage she'd caused. She gave money away, to places where it made a difference. And gave her time. That was why she was at the tutoring center. She told me that in high school she'd gotten a girl to take the SATs for her, and when it was discovered, the other girl was the only one to experience any consequences."

I remembered Stuart's sister telling me about a scandal at Croft. This had to be it. "I heard that the school hushed it up."

"Do you know if the girl who took the test was a Croft student?" I asked. "Was she a classmate of Drue's?"

He shook his head. "Drue didn't like to talk about it. She only told me the story once, in the middle of the night, in the dark. I wanted to turn on a light, but she wouldn't let me. She said . . ." He sighed. "She wanted to tell me, but she couldn't stand for me to look at her while she did. She was very ashamed. The other girl had been a scholarship student, and Croft had been her big chance. After what happened, Drue wasn't sure if she'd ever gone to college at all."

Darshi was already googling, but searching for Drue's name plus "Croft School" and "SAT" and "cheating" and "expulsion" yielded no results. Which was no surprise. "Those prep schools know how to clean up their messes," Darshi said.

"Let me see if I can find a list of girls in her graduating class," said Nick. A moment later, he was reading off a short list of names. "Any of them sound familiar?"

I shook my head. So did Darshi and Aditya. We divided up the list, and searched for the next twenty minutes, scrutinizing one social-media profile after another. The Croft girls were graduate students and medical students and law students. A few of them had already been brides, two were already mothers. On Facebook and Instagram, in shot after shot, I saw college graduations and beach vacations and Christmas trees, Tough Mudder races and rugby games, baby showers and christenings and first-birthday parties and happy couples beaming, holding SOLD signs next to new homes. One girl posted Paleo diet recipes; another, nothing but right-wing political screeds. One girl, Kamon Charoenthammawat, had no social-media profile at all. "Aggravating," I heard Darshi murmur.

"Okay. We'll keep looking for the test-taker," I said.

Aditya nodded. "My best guess is that it will turn out to be someone like that. Someone she hurt, inadvertently or not. Someone she knew from Harvard, or someone from your high school, or from the one she attended after. Someone from her travels; someone from her sorority, or her job."

A lot of someones, I thought. My heart sank.

He left us with a list of eight women; names where he had them, descriptions when he didn't. Sorority sisters whose money or term papers or boyfriends Drue had borrowed in college; a classmate whose car she'd crashed. There was a former friend whose brother Drue had slept with; another former friend whose father she'd seduced.

None of the names or the descriptions sounded familiar, or lined up with anyone I remembered meeting at the wedding. A cursory google with words like "Drue Cavanaugh" and "car accident" and "Cambridge" and "2012" didn't help, and of course, looking for "Drue Cavanaugh" and "stolen boyfriend" wouldn't help.

Darshi went to use the bathroom. Nick rocked forward, then back as he worked his phone, with the couch squeaking beneath him. Aditya gave another belly-shifting sigh. "I should have pushed her to make more amends, I suppose, if only because it would have given her some relief."

"She apologized to me," I said. "And she left money to your charity, and to her father's other children. I'm sure she planned on doing more."

Aditya gave me a sad smile and no answer. I bent back over my phone. My temples were throbbing; my stomach was in knots. I was wondering if Detective McMichaels had decided to return his focus to me, or to Nick; if he'd be waiting for us when we got back to the city.

Aditya reached across the coffee table to take my hand. Gently, he said, "She loved you, you know."

I nodded, not trusting myself to speak.

"She told me about a day she spent with you and your father. I wanted to impress her, so I asked what a perfect day for her would look like. I was so sure she'd say hearing her favorite opera in Vienna, or taking a private plane to Paris, but she told me about how you'd eaten dumplings and ridden the subway, and you'd gone to a coffee shop to read. She said it was more time than her father had ever spent alone with her, and how jealous she was that you got that every Sunday. She said it was one of the best days she'd ever had."

I nodded. *Oh, Drue*, I thought, and started to cry.

Chapter Twenty-Three

"What now?" asked Nick. After an hour and a half on I-95, we'd finally hit the West Side Highway. Nick was at the wheel. I was beside him, and Darshi had ridden in the back seat without saying a word. Between her silence and the disgusted expression she'd worn since we'd left New Haven, I hadn't had too much trouble reading her mood.

"I have to go," she said. "I have office hours."

"Daphne, how about you?" Nick asked.

"I'm thinking," I answered. Actually, I was trying not to think. I was keeping my mind blank. "I'm hoping an answer's going to swim up to the surface of my brain, like one of those blind cave fish."

"How's that working out?" asked Darshi.

I cracked one eye open to glare at her. "Do you have a better idea?"

"Yes," she said. "My idea is that we stop this. You didn't do it, and the police are going to find whoever did. And I'm all out of sympathy for Drue. She made her choices."

"And so what? You think that she deserved this?" I asked.

"I think," said Darshi, her words clipped and precise, "that if you use people your entire life, if you manipulate them and take from them, and throw them away when you don't need them anymore, then yes, there are consequences. Bad things happen."

I opened my mouth and then closed it. I couldn't tell Darshi that she was wrong; couldn't tell her that Drue hadn't behaved in exactly the manner she'd described. Drue had used Aditya and thrown him away, just like she'd done to Darshi. Just like she'd done to me. And karma might be a hashtag for Westerners, but Darshi had been raised as a Hindu. She believed that actions had consequences, in this life or the next.

"I'm sorry," I said. "You're right."

Darshi didn't respond. The car hummed with tension. Finally, in a voice so soft I could hardly hear it, Darshi said, "You chased after her when she was alive. Are you going to keep chasing now that she's dead?"

I thought about how to answer and what I could possibly say. "Everyone deserves justice," I finally said.

"You have to let her go," said Darshi.

"I know."

Darshi obviously disagreed. She clicked her teeth, looking frustrated and sad, but she didn't respond. The uncomfortable silence stretched until Nick pulled off the highway onto Ninety-Sixth Street.

"Can you drop me off here?" I asked.

"Where are you going?" asked Nick.

"I'm going to walk for a while. Sometimes I think best when I'm moving." It was just after seven o'clock. "I'll walk, and I'll think, and I'll meet you back at my parents' place in an hour or so, okay?"

"Are you sure? If you wait, I can walk with you."

"No," I said. "Thank you, but no. I think right now I need to be alone."

"It's getting dark," Nick pointed out.

"Broad twilight. *L'heure bleue.* Seriously, I'll be fine. And I have my phone." Not only did I have my phone, but I needed to use it, to respond to some of my followers, to make sure all the links that I'd posted were working. Maybe I'd even finally write back to that poor girl who'd asked me how to be brave. Not like I had any more of an answer now than I'd had the day she'd posted her query, the day I'd met Leela Thakoon.

Nick didn't seem happy to leave me alone, but, in the end, he pulled away, with Darshi in the passenger's seat and with plans to meet me at eight. When the taillights had disappeared, I pulled my hair back into a ponytail, set the pedometer on my phone (a habit from my dieting days that I'd never been able to break), and started to walk. I was still wearing the Leef jumpsuit, but I'd swapped the wedges for a pair of flat black sneakers. I held my head high, swinging my arms purposefully, even though I wanted to drag my feet and let my hands and head hang like sacks of rocks. I could see it: Detective McMichaels, with his gray brush cut and his caterpillar mustache, waiting in the hallway. *Just a few more questions*, he'd say, standing too close to me, staring me down. He'd have printed out Darshi's text messages, pried out of the cloud, and he'd show them to me: Why were you and your friend discussing murdering Ms. Cavanaugh? Why were you texting pictures of knives? *Just confess now*, he'd say. I'm sure the prosecutor will make you a deal. Hey, you must have had your reasons! Get out in front of it. Tell us the truth.

I tried to shut off my mind, tried to think of something else, anything else. My hand went automatically to my phone. I opened up Instagram, opened the comments on the last picture I'd posted, bracing myself for the condolences, the *so sorrys* and the broken-heart emojis and, inevitably, the people who wanted to share their own stories of loss, to tell me about their friend who'd been murdered, or their sister, their daughter, their mom. I'd have to remember to tell Nick that this was another one of social media's uses, the way it gave even the small and anonymous a place to tell their stories and find comfort, to be recognized and seen, even if it was only briefly.

Everyone deserves justice, I thought. Even people who lie. And everyone lies. Especially on social media, where there were lies of commission and lies of omission on everyone's page, woven into everyone's public presence. I pretended to be brave, and Darshi pretended to be straight, and Drue pretended to be rich and glamorous and happy when she was, in actuality, only rich and glamorous. Maybe it was different for men. Aditya seemed to be exactly who he said he was, and Nick wasn't online at all.

Focus, I told myself, and put the phone away. I remembered the question the detective had asked. *Who benefits?* Well, who besides me and Nick and Aditya and Emma, I thought, and sighed as I edged around the homeless fellow sprawled in the middle of the sidewalk. Maybe there were positives to getting arrested in your own city, in your own apartment. This way, at least I'd get to pick out a nice outfit for the perp walk. My sponsors would probably be delighted, I thought grimly. You couldn't pay for that kind of attention.

And then it hit me. I stopped, so fast that the woman with three Whole Foods grocery bags who'd been walking behind me almost slammed into my back. "Jeez, lady!" she huffed. I couldn't even draw enough breath to mutter an apology. Thoughts, remembered sentences and phrases, firefly flickers of half-remembered conversations were zipping through my mind like the patterns of a kaleidoscope, forming and re-forming themselves until they aligned in a conclusion that I probably should have seen long ago.

There's probably about a million girls she'd hurt who would want her dead. Corina.

To kill a young woman on her wedding day? That doesn't feel like business to me. That feels personal. Abigay.

She told me that the girl had been a scholarship student, and that had been her big chance. Drue wasn't sure if she'd ever gone to college at all. Aditya.

And, finally, a familiar voice saying something I should have remembered much sooner: *High school was kind of a shit show. You know, the mean girls. It took me a while to pull it together, but I made it out alive.*

"Oh my God," I said, my voice a squeaky quiver. "Oh my God oh my God oh my God." I grabbed my phone out of the bag, scrolling through my recent calls until I found one with a 508 prefix. I held my breath until Barbara Vincent picked up, saying, "Hello? Hello, Daphne, is that you?"

I told her what I needed, talking her through it, step by step. "Just take a picture, then open it up in the Photos app. On the left-hand side, at the bottom of the frame, there's a little box with an arrow coming out of the top," I said. "Click on that and type my phone number."

Ten seconds later, my phone buzzed. My heart felt like it had stopped beating. My ears were humming, like I was deep underwater. I opened up the text Barbara had sent, clicking on the attachment, which showed a photograph of the Croft School's graduating class from 2011. Barbara had taken the picture from the yearbook that Emma had purchased, to keep tabs on the half sister who hadn't even known that she existed, the rich girl who'd gotten everything Emma thought she'd ever wanted, all the prizes and the plums. At Aditya's apartment, Nick and Darshi and I had gone through the list of names. Now here were the faces: sixteen girls in white dresses, each holding a single white rose; an equal number of boys in blue blazers and khakis. They must have taken the picture before graduation, before they'd learned that Drue had cheated on the SATs, before they'd buried the bad news and kicked out the cheater and sent Drue on to Harvard. My old best friend stood in the very center of the front row. Her hair was long and straight, her smile was bright and confident. She wore the look of a world-beater, a girl who could do anything and be anything she wanted. Beside her was Stuart Lloyd Lowe. His hair was a little longer, and he was a little less muscular than he'd been on TV, but he had that same aura of privilege and a life spent on smoothed paths; the same lucky-penny glow. In the back row, right behind Drue, standing close enough to touch, with bangs that almost covered her eyes, long, dark hair, thick eyebrows, and a shy smile on her round face, was a girl identified as Kamon Charoenthammawat. A girl who, at some point, had changed her name, lost twenty pounds, pierced her nose, dyed her hair in shades of silver and lavender, and transformed herself into the woman I'd known as Leela Thakoon.

I called Darshi. When she didn't pick up, I called Nick. When he didn't answer, I left him a message. I used the editing feature to circle Kamon in red and forwarded the snapshot to both of them with a note: THIS GIRL IS LEELA THAKOON, THE DESIGNER WHO'S BEEN PAYING ME TO WEAR HER CLOTHES. SHE WENT TO CROFT WITH DRUE. I'LL BET SHE'S THE ONE WHO GOT EXPELLED. I THINK SHE'S THE KILLER. There. Now, if I got hit by a bus, or arrested on my way home, there'd be evidence pointing the police in Leela's direction.

I texted McMichaels a version of the same message, adding some context about Drue going to Croft and paying someone to take the SATs for her. My phone was giving its death beeps, so I shoved it into my pocket again and walked, faster and faster, thinking through what I'd learned. Already, I was second-guessing myself, wondering if it was all too tenuous, a handful of dots that only the most wishful thinking could connect. And what if I was wrong? What if someone else had gotten in trouble for taking the SATs for Drue? Or what if Leela had been the test-taker, and she had been expelled from Croft, but the killer was someone else entirely? Should I call 911? Not yet, I decided. Not until I had some actual proof. Not unless I was sure.

I pulled my phone out of my pocket, saw there was only two percent of my battery life remaining, and put it back in. I wanted to silence my brain, to stop thinking about Drue, to stop thinking at all. But the city felt haunted, every inch of every block painted with memories. Here was the Zara where I'd shoplifted a Bump It, at Drue's direction; there was the bakery where I would treat myself to a pillow-soft cinnamon roll if Drue had been especially awful to me that week.

I decided that, instead of going straight to my parents' place, I'd go to my apartment first. I'd charge my phone, walk my dog, then bring Bingo with me. Nick and Darshi, if she was still willing to help, could regroup there and help me figure out what to do next.

As I walked, I found myself imagining Drue at a tutoring center in some public high school in Boston, a place with worn textbooks and scuffed tile floors. I pictured her bending over some kid's book, or demonstrating how to diagram a sentence or solve a quadratic equation. I pictured Drue with Aditya in some hole-in-the-wall restaurant, the kind I'd gone to with my father, eating galbi or tea-leaf salad and pumpkin-pork stew. I saw her peeling ginger root and sweet potatoes or mashing garlic and rinsing rice, shoulder to shoulder with Aditya in his kitchen, with its brown linoleum floor and the chipped Formica counters. I saw them sharing a beer in the cheap seats at Fenway Park or holding hands in the hush of a museum's gallery on a pay-what-you-can Wednesday. The person she could have been, should have been, a smiling young woman, dressed down in a ponytail and a baseball cap, not the glossy, polished corporate creature in the Cavanaugh Corporation's brochure. I'd chased after her, and she'd chased after her father, craving his love and attention, never getting what she needed. All that effort, trying to shore up the business and prove her worth and get her father to love her; never knowing that none of his children held his interest for very long. I wondered if she'd ever been tempted to give up, to stay with Aditya, who clearly adored her. They could have moved to Boston, and reclaimed Cape Cod and gone back there every year in the summertime. They could have been happy together.

I unlocked my front door and jogged up the stairs, my head full of a life that could have been. I was halfway down the hall with my keys in my hand when I heard Bingo's whimper. I looked up to see that someone was, indeed, waiting for me, just as I'd imagined. But it wasn't the police.

"Don't scream," said Leela Thakoon as she drew a neat little gun out of her crossbody bag and pointed it at my heart.

I felt the breath leave my body, felt my knees turn to liquid.

"Open the door. Get inside, and give me your phone." I did what she told me, handing her my phone, and stepped inside. From the bathroom, I could hear water running in the tub. When Bingo came charging toward us, snorting and wriggling with delight, Leela gave her a swift, sharp kick that sent her tumbling head over bottom. Bingo yelped, her expression betrayed. She hid behind my legs, cringing.

"If that animal comes near me again, I'll shoot it. Put it in the closet."

"She won't stay." I was shaking all over, my knees and wrists and even my lips, every strand of hair on my head trembling.

"Do it."

I whispered "Be a good girl" into Bingo's ear, dropped her onto the coat closet floor, and closed the door. Immediately, Bingo started whining and scratching, butting at the door with her head. Leela ignored her.

"Sit," she said, waving the gun toward the living room. I practically fell into the armchair in the corner. "Pleasedon'tkillme," I said, the words coming in a rushed exhalation.

Leela sighed. "I don't want to. Really, I don't." She had the nerve to give me her twinkling, dimpled smile as she wagged a scolding finger. "But you! You couldn't let it rest!"

"I . . ." I said. I stopped. Swallowed. Licked my dry lips with a tongue that felt like a lump of felted wool, and tried to play it cool. "I don't know what you're talking about."

"Oh, c'mon. Let's not lie. It's just us chickens!" She flashed her dimples at me again and, with her free hand, pushed her silvery-lilac hair behind her ears, before lifting one finger. "First of all, you posted something from New Haven, where Aditya Acharya lives. And Aditya was friends with Drue. Friends with benefits. At least, that's according to the people I paid to keep eyes on her." *One of my scheduled posts*, I thought. It must have gone up while we were in Connecticut, and I must have forgotten to turn off my geo-tagging, which let the whole world know where I was, and now my partnership with the yoga mat company was going to get me killed. "I told myself that it could have been a coincidence. Maybe you've got friends in Connecticut, right?" Another finger went up. "However, I also have my website set up to alert me when I get visitors with IP addresses from the Outer Cape. Which I did, about an hour ago. The cops, I assume." She *tsk-tsk*ed, shaking her head. "Unless someone in the Truro Police Department was looking for the perfect cotton-Lycra jumpsuit."

I swallowed hard. "Darshi's going to be home any minute."

"Darshi has office hours," Leela corrected, her voice still cheery. "She's going to be on campus until ten o'clock. I called to make sure."

"Please," I whispered. "Please don't kill me."

"I'm not going to kill you," Leela said. Before hope could take hold, she said, "You're going to kill yourself. See, you're distraught. Overcome with grief about murdering your BFF on her wedding day." She reached into her pocket and pulled out a prescription bottle full of white oval-shaped pills. "I got these for myself, in case things went bad." When she gave the bottle a shake, the pills rattled like bones. "You'll just write out a note, slip into a warm bath, swallow a bunch of these with some vodka, pull a bag over your head, and goodbye, cruel world." I was shaking, shuddering all over, my feet bouncing and jittering on the floor. Leela saw, and looked sad. "I'm sorry. I know Drue hurt you, too. But I am not going to jail for that bitch."

"You . . ." I licked my lips. *Flatter her*, I thought. Keep her talking. "I have to give you credit. It was a brilliant plan. Who gave Drue the poison?"

"Some guy," she said, shrugging. "Some guy who needed twenty thousand dollars and could get himself hired by the catering company. All he had to do was pour a vial into Drue's cocktail. I never met him. I don't know his name. And, of course, he doesn't know mine."

I'd read enough mysteries to know how I was supposed to feel—my palms sweating and my mouth dry, trembling, or frozen with terror. Even though I was still trembling, terror had left me blessedly cool and clear-eyed. I could see everything, from the pile of vintage children's books on my craft table to the flick of black liner Leela had applied at the outer corners of her lashes. I recognized the piece of clothing she was wearing: the Anna dress, with its Empire waist and midi-length skirt, in a shade she called Damson Plum. The perfect outfit for a murder.

"And the poison? Where did you get it?"

"Stop stalling." She jerked the gun toward the hall.

"Just tell me," I said, and made myself feign interest. "Come on. Think about it. You're never going to be able to explain it all to anyone else, right? I'll take your story to the grave."

"You will, won't you?" Leela said, looking pleased at the thought. "I got it from the dark web!" Her voice was smug. "Turns out, there are websites that are basically Amazon for controlled substances. I found the pills, and the poison, and the hit man, all on the same website!" She giggled merrily. "One-stop shopping!"

Keep her talking, I thought again. Maybe Darshi would

come home early. Maybe my across-the-hall neighbor would notice the unlocked door. Maybe my parents would decide to do their first-ever unannounced pop-in. I squeezed my eyes shut, pain piercing me as I realized I'd never see my mom and dad again.

Leela's tone was brisk. "Bath time."

I made myself stand up. "I just want to understand. Before I die. I want to know what she did to you that was so bad that she and I both have to die for it."

Leela rolled her eyes. "You already know what she did."

"She got you kicked out of school?"

"She *stole my life*," Leela said, her voice suddenly loud and wild and raw. Her chest rose and fell as she breathed. "You don't understand what it was like. You can't imagine. My parents came to this country, not speaking the language, with five hundred dollars between them. They paid my father's aunt to take care of me so they could work around the clock in a convenience store. They'd take turns sleeping in the storage closet so they wouldn't have to pay rent." Her voice was shaking. "They told me every single day that it was all for me, so I could have an American life; so I could go to a good prep school and an Ivy League college, and be a big American success." She paused, breathing hard. "You don't know what it's like to be one of the only Asian kids at a place like Croft. To be different. To never fit in."

"I was a scholarship kid—" I interrupted, hoping I could get her to see the similarities between us. "I didn't look like Drue and the rest of her friends."

"You think that means we're the same?" Leela sneered. She gestured toward my midriff, her eyes hard as pebbles, her face twisted with scorn. "You could lose fifty pounds and be just like the rest of them. I never could."

"We're all people," I whispered.

Leela shook her head. "You don't get it. You could never understand. How it felt to work, and work, and study and study, and finally have it all pay off and get into every college you applied at. And then to have everything you worked for just . . ." She stretched out one open palm, then snapped it shut. "Just taken away." She caught her breath and licked her lips.

"I do know," I said. "I promise. Maybe it's not exactly the same, but I know what it's like to be different."

It was like she couldn't hear me, like she couldn't hear anything but the rage inside her head. "I thought Drue was my friend. My beautiful American friend. I'll bet you thought that, too." She smirked. "She told me all about you, you know. How pathetic you were. How you followed her around like—how'd she put it?—a pudgy little puppy dog."

Ouch. Even though Drue was dead, even with Leela pointing a gun at me, it seemed there was a part of me that was still available to feel that slap.

"I thought that what we had was different." Leela's voice was musing. "I thought she was telling me about you because she wanted me to know that she respected me. That I wasn't pathetic, like you were."

"And then she burned you," I said. "The same way she burned everybody else. So you weren't special at all."

Leela made a noise that might have started its life as a laugh, and came out sounding more like a sob. "When I got caught, she denied everything," she said. "She told the headmaster and the Honor Committee that I was crazy. Obsessed with her. In love with her. She said it was my idea to take the test in her name, that she'd never even known about my plan. She said I'd hacked into her computer and found her Social Security number and registered in her name. And they believed her. Or at least, they decided to believe her." Leela paused, her face thundery with rage and remembered shame. "She was someone, and I was no one. She mattered, and I didn't. I was expendable. I'd always known it, deep down, but that was when I really saw it. That was when I saw the way the world really is, and how little I mattered."

"And then what?"

"The day we had to go before the Honor Committee, Drue's parents showed up with lawyers. My parents weren't there. They couldn't get off from work, and even if they could have, they couldn't afford tickets to fly across the country." Her voice was cracking. "I had no one. And they believed her. Croft kicked me out. All the schools that had accepted me rescinded their offers. Harvard, Yale, Princeton. Poof. Gone. My parents . . ." Her voice thickened. "They were so ashamed. They told me not to come home." Her shoulders slumped. "And when I did, they wouldn't even let me through the door. They said I'd disgraced them. Which I had."

She paused, collecting herself, smoothing her hair, then her top, shaking out the skirt of her dress. "So I had nothing," she said. "No home. No college. No family. No place to go. No friends, because Drue made sure that she was the only friend I had. I tried to kill myself, and I couldn't even do that right." She pushed up her left sleeve, lifted her wrist, and turned it, showing me the faint line of a scar. "I ended up in a psych ward. The September after senior year, Drue went to Harvard, and I went to the loony bin. For a long time, I wanted to die. What did I have to live for?" Her gaze was fixed on a point above my head; her eyes were far away. "And every single day, I got to go online and see her leading her perfect, shiny life."

I wanted to tell her that it hadn't been shiny or perfect at all, that Drue had been lonely, had been rejected by a parent; that Drue had walked away from a man who had loved her, that Drue had suffered, but the words froze and crumbled in my mouth. Besides, Leela wouldn't have believed me. How could my words outweigh the evidence of Drue's happiness, her perfection, her wealth and her power, all of it just a click away on Instagram, for Leela and the entire world to see?

Leela smoothed her hair. She smiled. "And then I realized that I did have something to live for. Revenge." She raised her head. "I decided I was going to take everything away from her. And make a fortune while I did it. Easy-peasy one-two-three. Change my hair." She touched her silvery-lavender locks. "Lose some weight, get a few new piercings, and contacts instead of glasses. I wondered if she'd recognize me, but by the end, I barely recognized myself. Then all I had to do was suck up to a few dipshit rich kids, which was something I'd gotten very good at when I was at Croft. Get a few of them to think that you're their friend, and they introduce you to their friends, and the friends of their friends. By the time she announced her engagement, I was ready. All I had to do was buy a bunch of followers and pay someone to design some clothes that I could sell." She looked at me, one businesswoman to another. "Woke rich people will buy any stupid thing, as long as you tell them it's environmentally correct, or upcycled, or that it's made by indigenous people. And then I found you." Her smiled widened. "That was the cherry on top. Knowing that every time someone clicked on a story about her murder, they'd see your picture. They'd see my clothes."

"You know, she'd changed," I said. Even though Leela would never believe me, it seemed there was a part of me that was determined to try to convince her.

Leela made a rude sound and gave a very Drue-like eye roll.

"No, really. I think she was actually trying to do better. She knew how she'd hurt people. She was trying to make up for it. She volunteered to tutor kids. She left money to her father's kids, even though she'd never even met them. She fell in love . . ."

"And then dumped that guy, and stole Stuart Lowe away from Corina."

"But it wasn't real." As Leela had been talking, I'd been looking around, trying to calm my thundering heart. *Name five things you can see.* The floor. The walls. My trembling knees. And there was the X-Acto knife, peeking out from under the wallpaper sample books on my craft table. It would be bringing the proverbial knife to a gun fight, but it was all I could think of: the only weapon in sight. I kept talking. "She only hooked up with Stuart because she needed money. Her father's business was going bankrupt. She needed to get married to get her hands on her trust fund. She was going to try to bail her dad out. And help Stuart with his business."

Leela made a face: *big deal.*

"That was all she wanted. She was trying to get her dad to care about her. You and I, we both had parents who cared." I'd hoped to appeal to Leela's sympathies by pointing out what we'd shared. From the look on her face, reminding her about her parents and how she'd lost them had been a mistake. "And look at you!" I said, changing course. "You're a success! A self-made woman. You didn't need Drue, or Harvard, or any of it, after all. You built an empire, all on your own."

I thought I saw her face soften, just enough for me to feel a tiny flicker of hope. Then Leela shook her head.

"It's not real," she said. Her voice was almost regretful. "The clothes aren't mine. Most of the followers are bots. And just because it looks good doesn't mean it feels that way." She shook her head, sighing. "I should have been a doctor. That was what my parents wanted. That was what I wanted for myself. And now I'll never get the life I should have had. Can't put the toothpaste back in the tube. And honestly," she said, looking at me slyly, "you can't tell me you didn't enjoy it a little when Miss Shiny Perfect actually experienced a consequence?" She giggled, her expression turning malicious. "I wonder if she knew she was dying! That was my only regret: that I couldn't be there to watch it, or tell her that I was the one who'd done it. I thought about asking the guy to tell her, 'Kamon says hello.' But that would have given it away."

I made myself look as appealing and as frightened as I could.

The frightened part, at least, wasn't hard. "Please, Leela. If you do this, you're no better than she is," I said. "You have so much to live for! If you're not happy doing"—I gestured, briefly speechless—"what you're doing, then try something else!" As a last, desperate Hail Mary pass, I said, "I'll bet your parents are proud of you now!"

"They never forgave me." Her voice was very soft. "Every year I send them letters, on their birthdays and mine. I send checks. And every year, the envelopes come back, with 'Return to Sender' written on the front."

It occurred to me, in the faraway part of my brain that was still thinking, how both Drue and Leela had wanted the thing that I'd had and had taken for granted—my parents' love and approval. But before I could try to convince Leela to spare me, to tell her that there might be better days ahead, she waved the gun, gesturing toward the hallway. "C'mon. Let's get going. You'll write your note, and we'll get this over with. I bought you some really great bath oil."

"Fantastic. Just what every suicide wants." I took a halting step, suddenly aware of how much bigger than Leela I was. I probably weighed twice as much as she did; I was taller and, presumably, stronger.

"Let me get some paper." I walked to my craft table, rummaging among the wallpaper samples, looking for the knife. "Think about it," I said, pushing aside a pot of Mod Podge and a box of foam-tipped brushes. "We both had parents who loved us and encouraged us. Drue never had that. Think about how she must have envied us."

"Yeah, yeah, poor little rich girl," Leela sneered.

I was rifling through the scraps of magazine paper, fingers shaking, feeling Leela's breath on my back. *Distract her*, I thought. *Surprise her*. I took a deep breath and then I screamed as loud as I could, sweeping everything off my desk, the wallpaper books and the scrapbooking paper, the bottles of glue and paint, the pens and paintbrushes and rulers and colored pencils and wooden boxes, sending all of it crashing to the floor. Bingo howled from the closet. Just for an instant, Leela turned.

And then there was no more time to look for the knife, no more time to think. I launched myself at her, flinging my body against her with all the force I could muster. I heard every cup and mug and plate in the kitchen rattle, and the furniture thump as we fell; I heard Leela's pained screech and my own grunt. The gun flew out of her hand as we landed, with Leela on her back and me on top of her.

"Help!" I screamed as Bingo started to howl. "Help me!" Leela was thrashing, bucking her hips, trying desperately to shake me loose, but there was too much of me and not enough of her, and I had gravity on my side. I grabbed a handful of her hair, pulling hard, and settled my knee against her midriff as I heard footsteps, pounding in the hall. *Be a neighbor*, I thought, *be a stranger.* Be Detective McMichaels, even. I don't care.

But it was Nick.

"Get the gun!" I screamed. I watched from the floor as he grabbed it and pointed it at Leela.

"Don't move," he told her, but she'd stopped fighting, her body limp, her eyes closed. I stayed there, my hand in her hair as he called 911, telling the operator, in an impressively calm voice, that the police were needed at my address, that a woman with a gun had tried to kill me. Then he reached out his free hand, repeated, "Don't move," to the woman on the ground, and helped me to my feet. I let Bingo out of the closet and hurried to the bedroom, where I found two pairs of tights. I went back to the living room and handed them to Nick, who began deftly knotting them around Leela's wrists.

"What are you . . . how did you . . . ?"

His face was tight. "I got your message, and you weren't answering your phone. I got worried. I thought I'd check here and walk with you."

I was shaking all over, knees knocking, teeth chattering. When Leela was immobile, Nick wrapped his arms around me, pulling me tightly against him, and I buried my face in the sweet-smelling warmth of his shoulder, letting him hold me, letting him soothe me, rubbing my back and saying "You're safe" and "Don't worry, it's over, I promise," until the police arrived.

After I'd called my parents and told them what had happened; after the trip to the police station, where I'd given my account of the events, first to the New York City detectives and then again to Detective McMichaels once he'd shown up; after I'd accepted tearful thanks from Mrs. Cavanaugh and Drue's brother, Trip, and exchanged cool nods with Mr. Cavanaugh, Darshi turned to me. "Want to go home?"

I shuddered, imagining walking up the stairs and seeing Leela and her gun in the hallway, or sitting in the corner with my eyes on the knife.

In the end, Nick and Darshi and Bingo and I went back to my parents' place. My mother hugged me hard, and my father mixed up a pitcher of sidecars and served us his cioppino with chickpea salad and hearts of palm and toasted wedges of baguette.

My mother hovered and fretted and wrung her hands and cried when she thought I wasn't looking. My father slipped Bingo a small summer sausage, which she propped between her paws and devoured with noisy relish. Darshi fielded calls from her parents, her brothers, both sets of grandparents, and her great-grandmother, and, finally, Carmen, with whom she had a murmured conversation in the kitchen that I thought ended with "I love you." Nick called his aunt and uncle to tell them that he was fine. At around midnight, my parents excused themselves and retreated to their bedroom. A few minutes later, Darshi stood up and stretched ostentatiously.

"Well," she said, "guess I'll take the pullout couch." I gave her a pair of my pajamas to wear. In the living room, we made the pullout couch together.

"I owe you an apology," I said, smoothing the comforter over the skimpy mattress.

Darshi looked at me curiously. "For what?"

"You were right. I did chase after Drue, even though she was never a good friend to me. And you were. You always have been."

Darshi waved away the praise, looking uncomfortable. "I owe you an apology, too," she said. "No matter how bad Drue was, everyone deserves justice. And who knows? Maybe she really was trying to change." She tried for a smile. "Maybe someday we could have all hung out together. You and me and Drue and Aditya. And Nick."

"And Carmen?" I asked, eyebrows raised. Darshi's smile faded. Then she sighed. "It won't kill them," she said, half to me, half to herself. I knew she meant her parents.

"No," I said. "It won't. They might be surprised, but in the end, I think they'll be fine. Because they love you."

Darshi sighed again and nodded. "Sleep tight, you two," she called into the kitchen, and took the pajamas and the toothbrush into the bathroom and closed the door behind her.

I took Nick by the hand and led him to my bedroom, where he took the desk chair, and I sat, cross-legged on my bed.

"So what should we do for our second date?" he asked. "I'm thinking dinner and a movie."

I burst into shrieky laughter, which quickly turned into tears. Nick came over to the bed and sat down beside me. "I'm sorry," I said. "It seems I'm a little emotional right now."

"Don't apologize," he said. "You're allowed to be sad." He let me lean against him, holding me until I stopped crying.

"What about you?" I asked when I could speak. *What about us?* I thought.

"I should go home," he said.

Ah. I nodded. I'd expected it, even though hearing him say it left me hollow inside.

"I'll miss you," I said. "It's been . . . well. It's been something."

He pulled me close for a squeeze. "I'll go back to the Cape to officially quit. Assuming I haven't been fired by now. Then I'll go to Boston to resign and say goodbye. Then I'll come here."

"And do what?"

Shrugging, he said, "Get used to riding the subway, I guess." I felt his body shift as he sighed. "On the bus ride down, I had a lot of time to think. My whole life, I've kind of taken the path of least resistance. I went to college in Vermont because I like to ski; I took the job in Boston because one of my buddies ran the program and it came with health benefits. I just did whatever was easy. And I could probably keep doing that—just the next thing, and the next thing, and the next thing—until I'm old. Or dead." He rubbed his thumb against my cheek. "I want to make a choice. This was my mother's place. It's where she worked. It's where she met my father. I know that she loved it on the Cape, but that was where she went to hide. This is where her life was, her real life. I think I want to try living here, too." He shrugged again. "Maybe get one of those Instagram accounts the kids are talking about. I guess it's time."

"It's funny," I told him. "I was thinking that I could maybe ditch all of this and move to Cape Cod. Maybe do less of the influencer thing. Work on my art for a while."

I felt him smiling more than I saw it.

"We can talk it over," he said. "Maybe we'll try it here, then try it there. Or somewhere else completely. But, whatever we decide, I'd like to stick together. I mean, I might have to rescue you again."

"Excuse me, I believe that I rescued myself just fine."

"True." He pulled me upright and brought me close, resting his forehead against mine.

"Hi," he whispered.

"Hi," I said. His fingers were warm against my fingers, his lips gentle against mine, and I thought how lucky I was, how lucky we were, that, in spite of everything, we'd found each other.

When we broke apart, I said, "Listen. You don't have to make me any promises." I smoothed my hair and tried to catch my breath. "We've both had a traumatic experience. This is just biology. Our bodies are telling us to do something life-affirming."

He was giving me a lazy smile. "So is it a bad thing if we listen?"

"My point is that this . . ." I gestured at him, then down at the bed. "It doesn't have to mean anything."

He put one finger under my chin, tilted my face toward his, and brushed his lips against mine. The kiss started off gentle but soon deepened, until his tongue was in my mouth, and both of my hands were in his hair, which felt smooth against my fingers. He smelled like pine and salt, clean and good; and he felt warm against me, solid and present. I could feel his heart beating when he held me.

"What if I want it to mean something?" he asked. His forehead was against my forehead, his hands were on my arms.

"I think that maybe I could be okay with that."

He whispered "Sweetheart" into my ear. When Bingo tried to climb onto the bed at an inopportune moment, he set her gently on the floor. And, after more kissing and less clothing, after I'd made sure he had a condom and that the door was locked, a moment arrived when I was nothing but sensation, nothing but lips and hips and the glorious feeling of Nick moving inside me, with the force of the tide's pull against the ocean floor, when my brain finally shut off, and I stopped thinking about Leela, and Drue, and anything at all.

At four in the morning, Nick was asleep, lying on his side, making adorable whistling snores with every exhalation. Bingo was curled up underneath the crook of his legs, her chin resting on his calf, adding her own snores to the choir. I eased myself out of his embrace and tiptoed across the floor, climbed through the window and out onto the fire escape, the place where I'd sat and cried, plotting my revenge, thinking, *I'm going to change my life, and when I do, everything will be different. I'll be thin, and I'll be pretty, and I'll make Drue Cavanaugh pay.*

I turned on my phone. Ignoring the dozens of messages and friend requests and reporters asking for interviews, I went first to Instagram, where I flicked through pictures of Drue Lathrop Cavanaugh. Drue at a Women's Economic Summit, in a pink silk blouse with a bow at the collar, looking smart and exceedingly competent; Drue in a pair of tight jeans and a black turtleneck sweater, perched lightly on Stuart's lap, looking sexy; Drue with her arm around me in the Snitzers' kitchen, Drue next to me in the water on the Cape. *Me and my best friend.*

She looked good in every shot, and not one of them had told the truth about the two of us, or about her, about who she was, or what she wanted, or who she'd been in love with. Not any more than my Instagram account told all of my truth, or Darshi's account, or Leela's.

I clicked the link for Leela's page, thinking that it might already have been taken down, but there it was, replete with pictures that told a familiar tale of ease and joy and beauty. *Here I am with my famous friends, here I am at this great party, here I am on this beautiful beach. I'm happy, I'm happy, I'm happy.* Every repetition a lie.

I looked at the pictures for a long time. Finally, I went to my Instagram draft file, and the question that had been waiting. *I am a teenage girl, and I want to know how can I be brave like you.*

I wrote, *I'm not brave all the time. No one is. We've all been disappointed; we've all had our hearts broken, and we're all just doing our best. Make sure you have people who love you, the real you, not the Instagram you. If you can't be brave, pretend to be brave, and if you can't do that yet, know that you aren't alone. Everyone you see is struggling. Nobody has it all figured out.*

I posted it, closed the app, and looked out into the darkness. I thought about what it would be like to quit social media for good, to give up my influencer dreams. I'd imagined someday being as big as Drue, or Leela, but now that dream felt hollow, like running a race for a medal, only to learn that the gold I'd sought was just colored foil wrapped around empty air. Nick and I could live on a beach somewhere, in a house on the edge of a dune, with ocean views and no Internet connection. I had money, or I would, and Nick would, too, assuming Drue's will held up in court. I could give some to my parents and some to charity and keep the rest to begin whatever life I chose. I could be as public or as private as I liked, sharing only as much of myself as I wanted.

Through the window, I watched as Nick rolled over, sighing in his sleep. I could see the sky just starting to change colors, the black giving way to pearly gray. I looked at my phone, at the shots that Nick had taken of Drue and me in the water, on the last night of her life. Both of us were laughing, heads thrown back, the skirts of our dresses gathered in our hands. She'd been splashing me. Drops of water hung, sparkling, suspended in the air, and the sky stretched, vast and brilliant, behind us. She looked—we both looked—young and beautiful. Only one of us would stay that way forever.

I thought about all the things Drue hadn't known, in that picture—that she had a brother and a sister. That all of her scheming would come to nothing, that she'd never save her father's business, or launch her husband's; she'd never get to be on TV, never divorce the man she didn't love and marry the one she did. I stared, as hard as I could, but it was impossible to square the lovely, laughing girl in the picture with her current and absolute absence from my life, and from the world. *A lovely memory / Until eternity; / She came, she loved, and then she went away.*

Sitting under the brightening sky, the metal bars cool and familiar against my back, I felt my throat tighten and my eyes prickle with tears. *She envied you*, Aditya had said. A week ago, even a day ago, it would have sounded unbelievable, because what did I have that Drue could have ever wanted? But now I knew. It was all around me. A mother and father who loved each other and loved me. A man who might love me, too. A job I liked, a loyal dog, a true friend. Enough confidence to at least try to get the world to take me on my own terms. A body that had saved me.

I smiled down at my thighs and gave them an approving pat. "Thank you, thighs," I whispered. I looked out at the city, the gorgeous end-of-night sky, and thought about a young woman who could have had any guy in the world and who had loved one just like my father. I could hear her, in the doorway of her bedroom, whispering, *Thank you for being my friend.* And I could see her, after the Sunday we'd spent together, with a plastic bag full of olives and almonds and baba ghanoush swinging from her arm, young and pretty and heading into her brilliant future, smiling and saying, *This was the best day of my life.*

Acknowledgments

I am grateful to be published by the wonderful people at Simon & Schuster and at Atria. My thanks to Carolyn Reidy and her assistant, Janet Cameron, to Jon Karp and to Libby McGuire and her assistant, Kitt Reckord-Mabicka. Thanks to my agent, Joanna Pulcini.

Lindsay Sagnette was a thoughtful, patient, and perceptive editor who helped coax this story to its fullest potential. My thanks to her and to her assistant, Fiora Elbers-Tibbitts.

At Atria, I am lucky to be supported by an amazing team of women and men who help my stories make their way into the world. Thanks to Suzanne Donahue, who is always great company; to Kristin Fassler; to the brilliant and creative Dana Trocker; to subrights wizard Nicole Bond; to my wonderful publicist Ariele Fredman and her daughter Millie, who gives me perspective and reminds us all that the purest love in the world is the love of a little girl for a big garbage truck.

Thanks to James Iacobelli and Olga Grlic, who are responsible for *Big Summer*'s stunning, summery cover, and to Andrea Cipriani Mecchi for making my author photo shoots a party instead of an ordeal. In the audio department, I am grateful to

Chris Lynch, Sarah Lieberman, and Elisa Shokoff. In the production department, thanks to Katie Rizzo, Dana Sloan, Vanessa Silverio, Paige Lytle, Jessie McNiel, and Iris Chen.

Dhonielle Clayton and Preeti Chhibber were smart, discerning readers who pushed me to write a world inhabited by fully realized characters of all races and ethnicities. My thanks to both of them.

Thanks to Michelle Weiner (no relation—at least, none that we've discovered!) and to my brothers, Jake and Joe Weiner, who help me out in Hollywood.

For details about life online or in New York City, I am grateful to Amber McCulloch and Katie Murray. Any mistakes are my own.

Thanks to my friends of the writing and nonwriting variety. My husband, Bill Syken, is an insightful editor in addition to being the most dangerous player in the game. Adam Bonin continues to be kind and supportive and the best co-parent I could wish for.

Thanks to my daughters, Lucy and Phoebe, and my small dog, Moochie, who patiently and graciously (for the most part) share me with invented people while I'm living in a made-up world. Thanks to my sister, Molly Weiner, and to my mother, Frances Frumin Weiner, who took me to Cape Cod when I was a little girl and taught me to love the ocean.

My deepest gratitude to all of my readers, who come to my events, follow and interact with me on social media, and "like" my selfies, my tweets, my *New York Times* op-eds, my pictures of my dog, and my occasionally upside-down videos. Whether this is the first of my books you've read, or you've been a reader since *Good in Bed* and have grown up alongside me, I'm very happy that you're here.

This book is dedicated to my fabulous, supportive, funny, and endlessly cheerful assistant, Meghan Burnett. "Assistant" doesn't begin to cover what Meghan has been to me in the fifteen years we've worked together: she is a friend, an advocate, a keen and observant reader, kind enough not to laugh at me when I tell her, for example, that we need to order eight hundred boxes of Girl Scout cookies and patient enough to do it. She is also the person who everyone in my life, including my mother, prefers to deal with instead of me ("Is Meghan there? Put Meghan on the phone!"). Thanks, Meghan, for everything.

Turn the page for a Target exclusive extra chapter

The Golden Girl

One

The first thing he noticed about her was that she was beautiful. Almost immediately after her beauty registered, he saw that she was scared.

She edged into the noisy cafeteria a few minutes before the program was scheduled to begin. Aditya had a vague impression of cream and gold—gold hair, white skin, a gold cuff bracelet. An ivory-colored blouse tucked into jeans, a pair of pale-gold knee-high boots, folded over at the tops like a pirate's. She was perched on her tiptoes, elbows tucked against her sides, eyes a little too wide; poised to run, a gazelle at a water hole, sniffing the air for a lion.

DeVonte, who ran the program, saw where Aditya was looking. He let out a low whistle, meant for Aditya's ears alone, then turned a stern look on the three dozen kids currently sitting or standing around the long, rectangular tables, in a room that still smelled of hot lunch and floor cleaner. The kids had filled the room with their voices, the sound of their overlapping conversations, the songs and the videos they were playing for one another from their phones. DeVonte clapped his hands sharply, two long claps, then three fast ones, before raising two fingers in the air. The room went instantly silent as the kids lifted their own fingers.

"Finish filling out those forms," he said in his booming voice.

"Name! Parent or guardian! Home address! School! And in that space on the bottom, write down what you hope to get out of this program!"

"Mister Washington, I need a pen!" a girl with waist-length blue and purple braids said.

"I lost my forms!" said a boy in a Red Sox cap.

DeVonte reached for the cup on the table, handing the girl a pen and the boy a fresh set of forms to fill out. He nodded at the girl by the wall and said to Aditya, "Go over there, find out if Princess Buttercup's lost."

Aditya approached her slowly, the way he would a skittish animal or a shrine. Details revealed themselves as he got closer—the bronze glints in her gleaming hair, the diamonds sparkling in her ears. Her shoulders were hunched, her head was bent, her teeth were hooked into her lower lip.

"Can I help you?"

She raised her head. Her eyes were extraordinary, a pale, misty gray fringed with dark lashes. "I'm here to volunteer."

"Oh?" He made his voice friendly and hearty, the way DeVonte did when greeting newbies. "That's great. Welcome. As you can see, we need all the help we can get. Right this way!"

It was an after-school drop-in program, where adults were paired with kids from sixth grade up who needed help with their homework, or with college essays and applications. This being Boston, a lot of their volunteers were college students—sorority girls or frat brothers who'd show up, with varying degrees of enthusiasm and, sometimes, sobriety, to fulfill their chapter's charitable commitment. But those kids usually came in packs. This young woman was alone.

"I'm Aditya Acharya," he said.

"Drue Cavanaugh." When he took her hand, he felt a shock, from his palm all the way up to the roots of his hair and down to the soles of his feet. He imagined he could feel her pulse through her skin, her heart beating in time with his. *Coup de foudre*, he thought, faintly. The thunderbolt. He'd read the term in his lit classes but he'd never believed in it. His parents had been married for twenty-nine years. Their marriage had been arranged. They had met for the first time just a week before their wedding, and had learned to like and then, eventually, to love each other. That, to Aditya, seemed like a sensible way to do it, yielding better results than what he saw of his friends' parents', all of whom had married for love. He always imagined that someday he'd meet a woman at school for whom he felt the necessary fondness and with whom he shared the necessary common goals. If that didn't happen, he would ask his parents to find him someone. He was sure they had a list. Already, whenever he went home, for weddings or cousins' birthday parties, there'd be an introduction or two. So far, he'd met a pediatrician, a radiologist, an architect. Pretty, pleasant girls, with dark eyes and hennaed hands. Girls who'd grown up in a household like his, smiling in their saris. He had assumed he would get his degree and choose a girl like that, and build the kind of intentional, deliberate, solid life his own parents had constructed.

But this. But her.

His feet moved. So did his mouth. He heard himself asking her questions. In the time it took them to cross the room, he learned that Drue was a Harvard undergraduate, from New York City. Part of his mind was listening, and another part was wishing he'd worn something more dashing than jeans and an ancient Rutgers sweatshirt, wishing he'd traded his glasses for contact lenses and gotten his thick, unruly hair cut. "What's your major?" he asked her. *Are you seeing anyone?* he wanted to ask. *When did you have your first kiss?* and *Have you ever been in love?* and *What are your favorite things to eat?* and *Where's your favorite place to go?*

When they arrived at his table, DeVonte looked her over, then bent to flip through his folder of completed applications. "I sent everything in last week," Drue was saying. "You guys are pretty thorough!"

She was referring to the background check, the one all the volunteers had to undergo that included mandatory fingerprinting.

"They're kids," DeVonte said. A stranger probably wouldn't have heard the edge in his voice, but Aditya did. "So we're careful." *As careful as you'd be with your own kids*, Aditya heard. With white kids.

A shadow crossed Drue's lovely face. Then she smiled, and the sadness vanished. "It's good that you're careful."

Aditya thought he heard something wistful in her voice, something sad. Had someone been careless with her? He couldn't imagine it. She was a treasure, a girl meant to spend her life in bubble wrap. Untouched, like the Star Wars action figures he'd once collected and kept in their plastic on bookshelves in his bedroom. Mint.

"Hey, Kesha!" DeVonte called. Kesha was a bubbly, friendly, sweet-natured twelve-year-old, a girl who could make conversation with a gym mat. Kesha was also at the top of her class and didn't need tutoring at all. She came with her brother, Kevin, who had learning disabilities, and whose parents and teachers were trying mightily to get him the grades and test scores that would let him succeed at the schools to which his basketball skills would get him admitted.

"Keesh! Over here!"

Kesha came bouncing over. She looked at Drue. "You're pretty," she said.

Drue smiled. "You're pretty, too."

"And I'm smart," said Kesha. "Smart's more important, right?"

"Looks fade," Drue said solemnly. "But intelligence is forever." She offered Kesha her hand, and Kesha took it, already chattering about the three books she was reading and how her ambition was to be an author. Drue looked over her shoulder at Aditya. Her hair was like cascading sheets of gold. Her mist-gray eyes pierced him. She left the smell of flowers in her wake, and Aditya felt his heart rise up to sit, pulsing and tender, at the base of his throat. *Lost*, he thought. *Oh, I am so lost.*

2

Normally, after they made love, Drue would lie on his bed, her body limp, eyes rolling behind fluttering lids as she dreamed. Aditya would watch her. He'd never needed a lot of sleep, and now he was getting by on four hours a night, five hours, tops. He would stay awake and look at her in the candlelight. Her shapely limbs dusted in fine golden hair. Her lashes, feathery black crescents against her cheeks. Her polished red toenails, the pale, thin-skinned curves at the backs of her knees. He felt like he could never get enough of her; like he could listen to her forever and still long for her voice; touch her forever and still crave the feel of her skin. He wanted to know everything she was thinking and everything she'd ever thought. He wanted to soak her up, as if she were liquid and he was a sponge; he wanted to swallow her whole and keep her safe inside him.

Because all that was impossible, he would lie awake and listen to her breathe, the steady inhalations, the flutter of an exhale, wanting to record every moment permanently, wanting to stain the sheets with the imprint of her body, imbue his bedroom with her scent, tattoo her image on the insides of his eyelids so that he'd always be able to see her, so that he would always have her there.

"No bacon?" she asked the first time he'd made breakfast, poking around in his refrigerator, distracting him as she bent over, dressed in nothing but her underpants and his T-shirt.

"I'm a vegetarian," he said.

"Oh!"

"I can make you . . ." He rummaged around. His normal breakfast was leftovers, chickpeas or lentils and rice, but she'd think that was weird, and he had eggs, but no bread for toast. But there was yogurt and a mango ripening on the counter next to the bowl full of ginger and onions and garlic, the rows of spices in glass jars that his mother toasted and ground for him. *Lassi*, he thought. "A smoothie!" he said.

She watched as he peeled and sliced the mango, using his blender to pulverize it into the yogurt. Her first sip left a mustache above her upper lip. He drew her close and kissed it away.

She stayed the weekend and then, the next Tuesday night, it seemed like the most natural thing in the world for him to offer to walk her back to campus when they were done tutoring, and then for him to invite her up to his apartment.

She would walk around his room, trailing her fingers along his desk, his books, studying the pictures of his parents and his brother and sister. Asking questions. Are you a vegetarian for religious reasons? Is everyone in your family? Have you ever tasted meat? Yes and yes and yes, once, a slice of pepperoni pizza, gobbled on a dare. "I don't even remember tasting it," he'd confessed. He told her that his parents were observant; that for his first birthday, his parents had flown back to India with him and made a pilgrimage, carrying him five miles to Venkateswara Temple in Tirupati, and that his mother had insisted on a puja when he and his sister had moved out of the house to start college. "She buried a coconut out behind my dorm," he said, remembering how ashamed he'd been, how he'd paced back and forth, snapping at her to hurry up before someone saw.

"That's sweet," Drue told him.

"How about you?" he asked.

"Well, nobody buried a coconut for me." Her voice was teasing but, again, he saw a shadow move across her face, dimming her misty gray eyes.

"Who took you to college?"

"My mom." He waited for her to say more and, when she didn't, he didn't push.

They fell into a pattern—Tuesday and Thursday nights together, then Saturday nights. She was scrupulous about leaving on Sunday by noon, even though he invited her to stay. Finally, she told him that Sundays were when her parents called.

"I don't have to be here," he said. "I can leave. I'll go pick up dinner, and you can talk to them for as long as you want."

"No," she'd said. "Stay."

And so he did. By two or three on Sunday afternoon, he'd see her start to tense, like an elastic band stretched too far. She would drum her pen against her textbook, nibble the ends of her hair, then guiltily pull them out of her mouth when she saw him looking. When the phone finally rang she would give him a tight smile, lift the phone to her cheek, then turn so that her back was toward him. He would listen as Drue spoke to her mother, the two of them having the sort of conversation that Aditya would have with strangers, like aunties he saw once or twice a year. How was your week? How is school? *Did her mother even know Drue?* he wondered. *Did she realize how rare and wonderful a girl Drue was? Did she see it? Did she care?*

Her father was never on the calls. "He's busy," Drue said. "He travels a lot."

"What is he like?" By then, Aditya had done some research, reading the profiles of Robert Cavanaugh that had run in *Forbes* and the *Wall Street Journal.*

"Oh, he's great!" Drue had flipped on her back. "He wasn't home all the time. But every Sunday he was, we'd go on these food trips. He'd let me pick out a place to eat—any kind of food I wanted, sushi or barbecue or dim sum. Even though Dad has a driver, we'd take the subway or the bus on Sundays, and I'd have to plan our route. We'd spend the whole day together."

"Sounds wonderful," Aditya said, impressed that the details had never appeared in print, that this was a special, private ritual, not for the public.

"He isn't the most demonstrative guy," Drue said, "but I know he loves me." The words were convincing. Her tone suggested anything but certainty. Aditya wanted to tell her that if her father really loved her, she would never have had to say so. She would never have had reason to question his love or feel like she had to earn it. It should have just been there, always, as eternal and unquestioned as air or water or sunshine.

Sometimes, late at night, he would wake up to find her crying, curled on her side, his pillowcase damp with her tears. "I'm not a good person," she would whisper, trembling as he held her. "I've done bad things."

He would rub her back, stroke her hair, listening as she told him—about the girls she'd lied to, stolen from, betrayed. A girl in eighth grade with whom Drue had smoked pot, on school grounds. "The teachers caught us, and she got expelled. All they did to me was tell my parents, and all my parents did was tell me to be more careful next time."

"I guess the rules are different," Aditya said, speaking carefully, "for people like you."

"People like me," Drue repeated. Her tone was bleak, her beautiful face wounded.

She told him about her best friend in high school, Daphne Berg. "She was great, and she loved me, and I just embarrassed her all the time. I was mean to her, and I don't even know why." She told him about another friend from the school she'd attended for a year between high school and college. "I get nervous about tests," Drue said. "No matter how hard I've studied, how well I prepare, I just freeze. So this girl—she had no money, she was on a full scholarship, and I figured, you know, it would be a mutually advantageous situation. She'd take the test for me. I'd give her money." Only the girl, like the pot-smoking girl, had gotten caught and expelled. Once again, Drue hadn't been punished at all.

"You know how they talk about people standing on the shoulders of giants?" she'd asked him once late at night. "I am standing on a pile of broken girls." Her eyes were red and swollen, her lips were trembling. "Broken girls and a big heap of my parents' money."

He began to understand what had brought her to the tutoring program. Why she got up at five o'clock every morning to run for six miles or perform some brutal boot-camp-style workout in the gym, why she never let herself eat sweets or, really, much besides salads. How, once, after a dinner that he wouldn't let her pay for, she'd dashed back into the restaurant, claiming that she'd left her scarf behind, and how a waitress had followed her out onto the sidewalk, almost in tears as she'd reached for Drue's hand. *Thank you, miss. Thank you!* How, a few months after Drue had shown up at the tutoring program, Kesha had come running through the doors, talking so fast that they almost couldn't understand her. Someone had sent her mom money! Five thousand dollars! Drue had listened, smiling faintly, and Aditya's eyes had been on her, taking pleasure in her happiness. Then he'd turned and seen DeVonte staring at Drue, his mouth tight.

"I don't know what she's trying to do," he'd told Aditya later. "But these kids are not her pets. She's not their fairy godmother. And we're not her personal charity project."

"We are a charity," Aditya had pointed out.

"So she can send a check to the organization. Get a tax write-off and everything. But she can't just hand out money to the kids."

Aditya knew what was going on. Maybe not the specifics of what Drue was atoning for, but he recognized the act, of trying to repair the damage you'd done, trying to make amends, trying to make it right.

He tried to soothe her. After she showed him a video of Daphne telling off a guy at a bar, he'd said tentatively, "It looks like she's done all right for herself."

"Yes," Drue had said, her face unreadable. "She's an influencer."

"So maybe—I mean, I'm not saying that the ends justify the means, but maybe—"

"Maybe I hurt her and that helped her get stronger?" Now he could read Drue's face just fine, that expression of sorrow and anger and intractable pain. "It doesn't make it right."

"Maybe you could apologize," he'd suggested, but Drue had shaken her head.

"She'll never speak to me again."

They'd fallen asleep, and then, at two in the morning, she'd shaken him awake. He'd thought she was going to confess, to tell him that she'd been the one who'd sent money to Kesha's mother. Instead, she'd confessed to something else.

"That story I told you, about going out to eat on Sundays," she'd whispered. "That wasn't me. It was Daphne and her father. I went with them once, I was so jealous. I wanted it to be me."

"Your father wouldn't do something like that with you?"

"My father." Drue pulled in a shuddering breath. "My father hardly knows who I am. He's barely spent more than an elevator ride alone with me." Her voice was very small. "Daphne. She was so lucky. And I hated her."

Aditya kissed her cheek. He smoothed her hair. He thought of his own parents. When he was eight, he'd announced his intentions to play Little League the next spring, and his father, who'd never played anything but cricket, had gone out and purchased a whiffle ball, a plastic bat, and a mitt to fit Aditya's little hand. His father would leave for work before the sun came up and get home, his cheeks dark with whiskers and his shoulders stooped with weariness, but he'd still go out to the backyard and help Aditya hit grounders. They hadn't been rich, but there'd been money for whatever he and his sister, Nishali, had needed—tutors, vacations to Florida, the Air Max sneakers Aditya swore he'd die if he didn't acquire in eighth grade. What must it have been like, to have parents who had money for everything and who were still indifferent or cruel? Parents who could give you any material thing, but who couldn't love you? Aditya couldn't imagine. All he knew was that he wanted to love Drue enough to make her forget all the pain of her history, to make her believe that she was as lovely and as worthy as he knew her to be.

3

He had known the end was coming; had known it from the beginning; the day Drue had taken his hand, as they sat on a marble bench in the Isabella Stewart Gardner Museum and she'd said *I like you, Aditya. I like you a lot*. It had felt like a fantasy; like a dream that would evaporate in the time it took him to pull back the covers and put his feet on the floor. When she told him that she was getting married part of him had been reeling in shock, while another part of him thought, *Yes. Of course.* Of course she's getting married, and not to you.

"I love you," she'd whispered, her head buried in the space between his shoulder and his jaw. "But I have to do this now. I won't ask you to wait for me."

Ask, he thought, and almost said. *Ask me. I will wait for you forever.* Instead, he'd patted her back, and said, "All I want is for you to be happy." When she'd raised her face to him, her eyes were dry.

"You're a wonderful man," she said. "You deserve someone better than me." By the time he gathered his breath to say *There is no one better than you*, she was gone, in a flash of gold hair.

Because he had always known that the end was coming, he thought he would be able to accept it, to move on. And yet somehow, the day before her wedding, he'd found himself in the Vineyard Vines store in Farmington, forty miles away, ignoring the clerks' side eye, paying ninety-eight dollars for a pair of ridiculous reddish-pink shorts. The next morning, he'd been in the Avis office, renting a car. He had driven up Route 6, hands tight on the wheel as the road narrowed from two lanes to one, past vacationers with bikes and kayaks strapped to the tops of their cars. He followed the car's guidance system through a maze of back roads and into a development marked PRIVATE RESIDENTS ONLY, finally arriving at an enormous modern house, all glass and hard edges and silvery cedar that stood perched on the edge of a dune. He parked a mile away and sat on the beach, waiting for night to fall. When it did, he walked back to the house. The front door swung open at his knock. "Hello?" he called. No one answered.

He walked through the empty living room, through the sliding glass doors, out onto the deck that looked over the water and the beach, where the party was going on. He could smell smoke from the bonfires on the beach and hear Beyoncé playing above the noise of the crowd.

I just want to see her, he thought. I won't say anything. I won't even let her see me. I just want to see her one more time.

He stood on the deck, in the darkness, as the party noises drifted up from the beach. Then he heard raised voices. A man shouting, a woman's voice—Drue's voice—raised in protestation. A minute later, the thunder of footsteps, racing up the wooden stairs. Drue's father flashed by him, so quickly that he was gone the instant after Aditya recognized him. A minute later, Drue ran past. Her face was a pale, blurred oval. He thought she was crying as she ran fleetly across the deck and into the house. A light inside went on, illuminating a rectangle of curtained glass. He wondered if that was her bedroom, if there were only a few yards of space, a few inches of glass, separating him from his beloved.

He stood up. Sat down. Every muscle in his body was demanding forward motion; every nerve ending in his brain firing off commands. *Go to her. Now.*

But do what?

He'd just gotten to his feet when someone else stepped onto the deck and peered around in the darkness.

"Hey, man." The guy was narrow-faced and dressed in a white shirt and black pants, his pale face glimmering in the dark. He held a tray of drinks. "Signature cocktail?" Blindly, Aditya reached for a glass and took a gulp of something citrus-y and sweet. "Do you have any ice water?"

"Hang on, man. I got you." Aditya sat in the shadows until the guy came back. He accepted the ice water with a murmured "Thank you," and sank back into the darkness. He watched as a girl he recognized as Daphne Berg, Drue's high school friend, crossed the deck and went into the house. He heard or imagined he heard, the rise and fall of female voices; the sound of Drue crying, and Daphne comforting her. When Daphne came outside again, Aditya got to his feet.

"Is she all right?" he blurted, before he had a chance to plan anything.

Daphne shrieked and spun around, squinting into the darkness. "Who's there?"

He stepped forward. "I'm sorry. I didn't mean to startle you." From the look on her face, the way she'd pressed her hand against her heart, he could see that he had, and he was sorry about that, but not so sorry that he wasn't going to learn everything she could tell him. "Is Drue all right?"

"She's fine," Daphne said, her voice a little curt. He imagined he could feel her gaze moving over him, taking in the newly purchased shorts and the white polo-style shirt, which were all right, dropping down to his socks and Tevas, which probably were not. "Are—are you a friend?"

Aditya mumbled some lie about working with Drue's father, and how he'd seen what happened. He showed Daphne the glass of water he'd requested. "Is her fiancé with her?"

"He wasn't when I left."

He could sense her gaze sharpening, the questions forming behind her friendliness. "You're her friend from high school, right?"

This seemed to appease her. "Right. Well. I guess I'll see you at the wedding tomorrow!"

"Yes. See you there."

He waited until she'd gone through a door in a wall of hedges that ran along one side of the deck. Then he crossed to where

Daphne had emerged and tapped on the pane of glass. A moment later, it slid aside. And there was his darling, her eyes swollen from crying, the ends of her hair damp from where she'd been chewing.

"Aditya?" Her voice was husky. It pierced his heart like a blade.

Come away with me, he thought of saying. *I will keep you safe. I will love you forever.* He didn't speak, but his face must have told her what he was thinking. Drue's gray eyes filled with tears. She stepped into his arms.

"I can't," she said, in response to a question he hadn't asked. Her voice was barely a whisper, the words more felt than spoken. He held her, and she closed her eyes, squeezing them shut. "I can't. I have to do this. I have to go through with it. Please don't ask me not to."

His voice was steady. "I would never ask you to do anything you didn't want to."

Numbly, he handed her the glass. She took it, set it down, then threw her arms around his neck and pulled him close. He felt her lips on his. He touched her hair, touched her neck, felt her pulse beating like a trapped bird against his hand.

"I'll be here if you need me," he said. Always, he thought. Always.

She hugged him hard, her wiry arms wound around his neck pulling him against her. Then she let him go and pushed him, gently but firmly, out onto the deck. She stepped back into her room and, without raising her eyes again, she slid the glass door shut.

Driving home, Aditya thought about his parents, and the story he'd been told about his first birthday. How the flight, with stops and layovers, had taken the better part of a day, and how the five-mile hike had taken more than four hours. How the path up the mountain was crowded with thousands of pilgrims, so narrow that his father had to carry Aditya on his shoulders. How his mother and both sets of grandparents had made the climb, to pray at Vishnu's shrine. How he'd cried as his head had been shaved and his ears pierced, as a sacrifice to Lord Venkateswara. When he turned six, he had asked his mother why they hadn't just stayed home and gotten him a cake to smash, the way his friend Logan's family had when Logan's little brother had turned one. She'd looked at him as if he'd lost his mind. "We made prayers for your happiness and protection," she'd said.

"But wasn't it a lot of trouble?"

"It was no trouble," she'd said. "You and your sister, you are our treasures."

"But I don't even remember it!" he'd said. He'd been agitating for an upgraded game system, and in his six-year-old brain, the money spent on flying back to India for a trip he couldn't remember, to put holes in his ears that had closed up, and to cut hair that had grown back, could have gotten him the newest Sega.

"That doesn't matter," his mother had said, and she'd cupped his head. "The gods' protection is upon you, whether you remember it or not. Whether you feel it or not. It is there, keeping you safe."

"You are my treasure," he whispered, into the silence of the car as the road hummed by. "May the gods' protection be upon you. May it keep you safe."